David Morrell was b......
Professor of American Literature at the University of
Iowa. He is a multiple bestselling author, with fifteen
million copies of his books in print, translated into twenty
languages. His novels include FIRST BLOOD,
TESTAMENT, THE TOTEM and BLOOD OATH and
his most recent bestsellers have been THE FIFTH
PROFESSION, THE COVENANT OF THE FLAME,
ASSUMED IDENTITY and DESPERATE MEASURES.
Morrell is a graduate of the National Outdoor Leadership
wilderness survival school. He is also an honorary
lifetime member of the Special Operations Association
and an honorary member of the Association of Former
Intelligence Officers. With his wife, he lives in Santa
Fe, New Mexico.

Also by David Morrell

*Limited edition with illustrations. Donald M Grant, Publisher,
Hampton Falls, New Hampshire

Extreme Denial

David Morrell

First published in Great Britain in1996
by HEADLINE BOOK PUBLISHING

First published in paperback in Great Britain in1996
by HEADLINE BOOK PUBLISHING

A HEADLINE FEATURE paperback

10 9 8 7 6 5 4 3 2 1

ISBN 0 7472 5348 X

Typeset by Avon Dataset Ltd, Bidford-on-Avon, Warks

Printed and bound in Great Britain by
Cox & Wyman Ltd, Reading, Berks

HEADLINE BOOK PUBLISHING
A division of Hodder Headline PLC
338 Euston Road
London NW1 3BH

This book is for Richard Schoegler and Elizabeth Gutierrez, who introduced my wife and me to the City Different.

How do I love thee? Let me count the ways.
>
> Elizabeth Barrett Browning

Denial is not a river in Egypt.
>
> Bumper Sticker

ONE

1

Decker told the Italian immigration official that he had come on business.

'What type?'

'Corporate real estate.'

'The length of your visit?'

'Two weeks.'

The official stamped Decker's passport.

'*Grazie*,' Decker said.

He carried his suitcase from Leonardo da Vinci Airport, and although it would have been simple to make arrangements for someone to meet him, he preferred to travel the twenty-six kilometers into Rome by bus. When the bus became mired in predictably dense mid-city traffic, he asked the driver to let him off, then waited for the bus to proceed, satisfying himself that no one had gotten off after him. He went into the underground, chose a train at random, rode to the next stop, returned to the streets, and hailed a taxi. Ten minutes later, he left the taxi and went back to the underground, took a train to the next stop, and hailed another taxi, this time telling the driver to take him to the Pantheon. His actual destination was a hotel five blocks from there. The precautions were possibly needless, but Decker was convinced that he had stayed alive as long as he had by virtue of being indirect.

The trouble was that the effort was wearing him down.

Staying alive wasn't the same as living, he had decided. Tomorrow, Saturday, would be his fortieth birthday, and of late, he had become uncomfortably aware of the passing time. Wife, children, a home – he had none of these. He traveled a lot, but he always felt apart from wherever he was. He had few friends and seldom saw them. What his life came down to was his profession. That wasn't good enough anymore.

As soon as he checked into his hotel, which had pillars and plush carpets, he fought jet lag by showering and putting on fresh clothes. Sneakers, jeans, a denim shirt, and a blue blazer were appropriate for a mild June day in Rome. They were also what a lot of other American male tourists his age were wearing, and would keep him from attracting attention. He left the hotel, blended with pedestrians, and walked along busy streets for half an hour, doing his best to make certain that he wasn't being followed. He reached the most congested area of Rome, the Piazza Venezia, where the main streets of the city came together. The din of a traffic jam provided background noise as he used a public telephone.

'Hello,' a male voice answered.

'Is this Anatole?' Decker asked in Italian.

'Never heard of him.'

'But he told me he'd be at this number.' Decker gave a number that was different from the one he had used.

'The last two digits are wrong. This is five seven.' The connection was broken.

Decker replaced the phone, checked that no one was watching him, and melded with the crowd. So far no problem. By mentioning specific numbers, the voice was telling Decker to come ahead. But if the voice had told him, 'You're wrong,' the message would have been to stay away because *everything* was wrong.

4

2

The apartment, near Via Salaria, was three flights up, not too fancy, not too plain.

'How was the flight?' the occupant asked. His voice, with a slight New England accent, sounded the same as the one on the phone.

Decker shrugged and glanced around at the modest furniture. 'You know the old joke. The best kind is the kind you walk away from.' He completed the recognition code. 'I slept through most of it.'

'So you don't feel jet lag.'

Decker shook his head.

'You don't need a nap.'

Decker inwardly came to attention. Why is this guy making an issue of jet lag? A nap? Is there a reason he doesn't want me with him for the rest of the day?

The man he was speaking to was someone with whom he had not worked before: Brian McKittrick, thirty years old, six feet one inches tall, heavy set. He had short blond hair, beefy shoulders, and the kind of square jaw that Decker associated with college football players. Indeed, there was a lot about McKittrick that reminded Decker of college football players – the sense of pent-up energy, of eagerness to get into action.

'No nap,' Decker said. 'What I want is to catch up on a few things.' He glanced at the lamps and the wall plugs, deciding not to take anything for granted. 'How do you like staying here? Some of these old apartments have trouble with roaches.'

'Not here. I check every day for bugs. I checked just before you came over.'

'Good.' Satisfied that the room was free of electronic surveillance, Decker continued, 'Your reports indicate that you've made progress.'

5

'Oh, I found the bastards, all right.'

'You mean your contacts did.'

'That's right. That's what I meant.'

'How?' Decker asked. 'The rest of our people have been searching everywhere.'

'It's in my reports.'

'Remind me.'

'Semtex.' McKittrick referred to a sophisticated plastic explosive. 'My contacts spread word in the kind of hangouts these bastards like to use that Semtex was available to anyone willing to pay enough.'

'And how did you find your contacts?'

'A similar way. I spread the word that I'd be generous to anyone who supplied the information I needed.'

'Italians.'

'Hell, yes. Isn't that the point? Cutouts. Plausible deniability. An American like me has to start the ball rolling, but after a while, the team has to be nationals of the country where we're working. The operation can't be traced back to us.'

'That's what it says in the text books.'

'But what do *you* say?'

'The nationals have to be dependable.'

'You're suggesting my contacts might not be?' McKittrick sounded testy.

'Let's just say the money might make them eager to please.'

'For God sake, we're hunting terrorists,' McKittrick said. 'Do you expect me to get informants to cooperate by appealing to their civic duty?'

Decker allowed himself to smile. 'No, I believe in the old-fashioned way – appealing to their weaknesses.'

'Then there you are.'

'But I'd like to meet them,' Decker said.

McKittrick looked uncomfortable.

'Just to get a sense of what we're dealing with,' Decker added.

'But it's all in my reports.'

'Which make for fascinating reading. The thing is, I've always been a hands-on kind of guy. How soon can you arrange a meeting?'

McKittrick hesitated. 'Eleven tonight.'

'Where?'

'I'll have to let you know.'

Decker handed McKittrick a piece of paper. 'Memorize this phone number. Got it? Fine.' Decker took the specially treated paper into the kitchen, poured water on it, and watched it disintegrate, dissolving down the drain. 'To confirm the meeting, call that number at eight tonight, or every half hour after that, up to ten. But after ten, don't bother. I'll assume you couldn't get your contacts together. In which case, try for tomorrow night, or the night after that. Each night, the same schedule for calling. Ask for Baldwin. My response will be Edward.'

'The phone's at your hotel?'

Decker assessed him. 'You're beginning to worry me. No, the phone isn't at my hotel. And when you call that number, make sure you don't do it from here.'

'I know the drill.'

'Call from a payphone you've never used before.'

'I said I know the drill.'

'All the same, it never hurts to be reminded.'

'Look, I know what you're thinking,' McKittrick said.

'Really?'

'This is the first time I'm running an operation. You want to make sure I'm up to the job.'

'You're right, you do know what I'm thinking,' Decker said.

'Well, you don't need to worry.'

'Oh?' Decker asked skeptically.

'I can handle myself.'

3

Decker left the apartment building, crossed the busy street, noticed a passing taxi, and motioned for the driver to meet him around the next corner. There, out of sight from where McKittrick might be watching from his apartment, Decker apologized to the taxi driver, saying that he had changed his mind and wanted to walk a little more. As the driver muttered and pulled away, Decker went back to the corner but didn't show himself. The cafe on the corner had windows that faced the main street and the side street. From the side street, staying out of view as much as possible, Decker could look through the side window and then the front window, providing himself with a view of McKittrick's apartment building. Sunlight reflecting off the front window would help to make Decker unobtrusive.

Sooner than Decker expected, McKittrick emerged from the apartment building. The stocky man drew a hand through his short blond hair, looked nervously both ways along the street, saw an empty taxi, eagerly hailed it, and got in.

While waiting, Decker had needed something to do so he wouldn't appear to be loitering. From a lamp post, he had unchained a motorbike that he had rented. He had unlocked the storage compartment, folded his navy blazer into it, taken out a brown leather jacket and a helmet with a dark concealing visor, and put them on. With his appearance sufficiently changed that McKittrick would not recognize him if he checked for surveillance, Decker started the motorbike and followed.

He wasn't encouraged by the meeting. The problems that he had sensed in McKittrick's reports now seemed more manifest and troubling. It wasn't merely that this was the first time McKittrick had been given a position of authority. After all, if the man was going to have a career, there *had* to be a first time, just as there had been a first time for Decker. Instead, the source of Decker's unease was that McKittrick was too damned sure of himself, obviously not fully skilled at tradecraft and yet not humble enough to know his limitations. Before flying to Rome, Decker had already recommended to his superiors that McKittrick be assigned to another, less sensitive operation, but the son of a legend in the profession (OSS, charter member of the CIA, former Deputy Director of Operations) evidently couldn't be shuffled around without the legend demanding to know why his son wasn't being given opportunities for advancement.

So Decker had been sent to have a look, to make sure that everything was as it should be. To be a nursemaid, Decker thought. He followed the taxi through congested traffic, eventually stopping as McKittrick got out near the Spanish Steps. Decker quickly chained the motorbike to a lamp post and went after him. There were so many tourists that McKittrick should have been able to blend with them, but his blond hair, which ought to have been dyed a dark, non-dramatic color, made him conspicuous. Another lapse in tradecraft, Decker thought.

Squinting from the bright afternoon sun, he followed McKittrick past the Church of the Trinita dei Monti, down the Spanish Steps to Spanish Square. Once famous for its flower sellers, the area was now occupied by street merchants with their jewelry, ceramics, and paintings spread out before them. Ignoring the distractions, Decker kept after McKittrick, turning right past Bernini's Boat Fountain, shifting through the crowd, passing the house where Keats had died in 1821, finally seeing his quarry enter a cafe.

Yet another mistake in tradecraft, Decker thought. It was foolish to seek refuge in a place with so many people outside; someone watching would be difficult to notice. Choosing a spot that was partially sheltered, Decker prepared himself for a wait, but again McKittrick came out sooner than expected. He had a woman with him. She was Italian, in her early twenties, tall and slim, sensuous, with an oval face framed by short dark hair and sunglasses tilted on top of her head. She wore cowboy boots, tight jeans, and a red T-shirt that emphasized her breasts. Even from thirty yards away, Decker could tell she wasn't wearing a bra. McKittrick had his arm around her shoulders. She in turn had an arm around his hips, her thumb hooked into a back pocket of his slacks. They proceeded down Via dei Condotti, took a shadowy side street on the right, paused on the steps of a building, kissed hungrily, then entered the building.

4

The phone call came through at nine p.m. Decker had told McKittrick that the number didn't connect with Decker's hotel. The number did connect, however, with a payphone in a hotel down the street, in the lobby of which Decker could wait, reading a newspaper, without attracting attention.

Every half-hour, starting at eight, he had strolled to the phone, waited five minutes, then returned to his comfortable chair. At nine, when the phone rang, he had been in place to pick it up. 'Hello?'

'Baldwin?' McKittrick's vague New England accent was recognizable.

'Edward?'

'It's on for tonight at eleven.'

'Where?'

McKittrick told him.

The location made Decker frown. 'See you.' Uneasy, he hung up the phone and left the hotel. Despite what he had told McKittrick, he did have jet lag and would have preferred not to work that night, especially since he had been busy for the remainder of the afternoon, going to the international real-estate consulting agency for which he ostensibly worked, reporting in, establishing his cover. His contact at the agency had been keeping a package, about the size of a hardback novel, that had arrived for Decker. After returning to his hotel room, Decker had opened the package and made sure that the pistol he removed, a Walther .380 semi-automatic pistol, was functional. He could have chosen a more powerful weapon, but he preferred the Walther's compactness. Only slightly larger than the size of his hand, it came with a holster that clipped inside the waist of his jeans, at his spine. The weapon didn't make a bulge against his unbuttoned blazer. All the same, it didn't reassure him.

5

There were five of them – the tall attractive woman whom Decker had seen with McKittrick, and four men, all Italian, from early to late twenties, thin, with slicked-back hair. Their appearance suggested that they thought of themselves as a club – cowboy boots, jeans, Old West belt buckles, denim jackets. They even smoked the same brand of cigarettes – Marlboros. But a stronger factor linked them. The facial resemblance was obvious. They were four brothers and a sister.

The group sat in a private room above a cafe near the Piazza Colonna, one of Rome's busiest shopping areas, and the site for the meeting troubled Decker. Not only was it in far too public an area, but with short notice, McKittrick shouldn't have been able to reserve a room in what was obviously a popular night spot. The numerous empty wine and beer bottles on the table made clear that the group had been in the room for quite some time before Decker arrived.

While McKittrick watched from a corner of the room, Decker established rapport, then got to the point. 'The people we're after are extremely dangerous,' he said in Italian. 'I don't want you to do anything that puts you at risk. If you have even the slightest suspicion that you've attracted their attention, ease off. Report to my friend.' He gestured toward McKittrick. 'Then disappear.'

'Would we still get the bonus we were promised?' one of the brothers asked.

'Of course.'

'Can't ask for anything fairer than that.' The young man finished a glass of beer.

Decker's throat was beginning to feel scratchy from the dense cigarette smoke in the room. It didn't help the headache that his jet lag had begun to give him. 'What makes you confident you've found the people we want?'

One of the brothers snickered.

'Did I say something amusing?' Decker asked.

'Not you. Them. The group we were asked to look for. We knew immediately who it was. We went to university with them. They were always talking crazy.'

'Italy for Italians,' their sister said.

Decker looked at her. Until now, she hadn't said much. Since the afternoon, she'd changed her T-shirt. Now it was blue. Even with a denim jacket partially covering it, she obviously still wasn't wearing a bra.

'That's all they talked about. Italy for Italians.' The sister had been introduced as Renata. Her sunglasses remained tilted up onto her dark, boyishly short hair. 'They couldn't stop complaining about the European Community. They kept insisting that lowering national barriers was just a way for Italy to be contaminated by outsiders. They blamed the United States for backing the unified-Europe movement, for trying to create

12

a vast new market for American goods. If the rest of Europe wanted to be corrupted, that was fine, but Italy had to fight to keep the United States from dominating it economically and culturally. So when American diplomats began being killed in explosions, the first people we thought of were this group, especially when they made those phone calls to the police, calling themselves the Children of Mussolini. Mussolini was one of their heroes.'

'If you suspected them, why didn't you go to the police?' Decker asked.

Renata exhaled smoke from a cigarette and shrugged. 'Why? These people used to be our friends. They weren't hurting *us*. But they *would* hurt us after they were released from jail because of insufficient evidence against them.'

'Maybe the authorities could have found sufficient evidence.'

Renata scoffed. The movement of her slim, sensuous body made her breasts move under the T-shirt. 'I assure you these people are not fools. They wouldn't leave proof of what they had done.'

'Then I'll ask you again. Without proof, what makes you sure you've found the people we want?'

'Because after Brian started paying us –' she gestured toward McKittrick, alarming Decker that McKittrick had given her his real name – 'we kept a close watch on our friends. We followed them one night. They were in a car a half block behind the limousine when the explosion killed your ambassador as he was being driven back to the embassy after attending the opera. They must have used a remote detonator.'

Decker concealed the tense emotion that made him briefly silent. The assassination of Ambassador Robbins had been the outrage that caused extremely powerful figures in Washington to lose their customary caution and demand that something be done to stop these monsters – one way or another. The covert pressure on Decker's superiors was the reason McKittrick had attracted so much favorable attention among them. If McKittrick's contacts could positively identify the terrorists responsible for the assassination, half the problem would be solved. The other half would be what to do with the information.

'Maybe they just happened to be in the area,' Decker said.

'They drove away laughing.'

Decker's throat felt constricted. 'Do you know where they live?'

'Renata gave me that information,' McKittrick interrupted. 'But obviously they won't stay at the addresses forever.' He gestured for emphasis. 'They have to be dealt with soon.'

Yet another lapse in tradecraft, Decker noted with concern. Contacts should never know what a handler is thinking. And what did McKittrick mean by 'dealt with'?

'Renata tells me they have a club they like to go to,' McKittrick said. 'If we can get them all together . . .'

6

'What the hell were you doing in there?' Decker asked as he walked angrily with McKittrick after the meeting was over.

'I don't know what you're talking about.'

Decker glanced tensely around. Squinting from the glare of numerous passing headlights, he noticed an alley and gripped McKittrick's left arm to guide him away from the area's clamorous nightlife.

'You compromised the assignment,' Decker whispered hoarsely as soon as he was away from pedestrians. 'You gave them your *real name*.'

McKittrick looked awkward and didn't respond.

'You're sleeping with that woman,' Decker said. 'Didn't your trainers explain to you that you never, never, never become personally involved with your contacts?'

'What makes you think I'm sleeping with—'

'Your imitation of stand-up mouth-to-mouth resuscitation this afternoon.'

'You *followed* me?'

'It wasn't very damned hard. You're breaking so many rules I can't keep up with . . . From the smell of alcohol on you, I have to assume you were partying with them before I arrived.'

'I was trying to get them to feel comfortable with me.'

'*Money*,' Decker said. 'That's what makes them comfortable. Not your winning personality. This is business, not a social club. And what did you mean by "dealt with"?'

' "Dealt with"? I don't remember saying—'

'It sounded to me as if you were actually suggesting, in front of outsiders, that the people we're after are going to be . . .' In spite of his low tone and the relative secrecy of the alley, Decker couldn't bring himself to say the incriminating words.

'Extreme denial,' McKittrick said.

'What?'

'Isn't that the new euphemism? It used to be "terminate with extreme prejudice". Now it's "extreme denial".'

'Where the hell did you hear—'

'Isn't that what this operation's about? Those bastards will keep killing until somebody stops them permanently.'

Decker pivoted, staring from the darkness of the alley toward the pedestrians on the brightly lit street, afraid that someone might have overheard. 'Have you gone insane? Have you told anyone else what you just told me?'

McKittrick hesitated.

'The woman?' Decker demanded. 'You told the woman?'

'Well, I had to introduce the idea to her. How else was I going to get them to do it?'

15

'Jesus,' Decker muttered.

'Plausible deniability. I've invented a rival network. *They* take out the first group, then phone the police, and call themselves the Enemies of Mussolini.'

'Keep your voice down, damn it.'

'No one can prove we're involved.'

'The *woman* can,' Decker said.

'Not when I disappear and she doesn't have physical evidence.'

'She knows your *name*.'

'My *first* name only,' McKittrick said. 'She loves me. She'll do anything for me.'

'You—' Decker leaned close in the darkness, wanting to make certain that only McKittrick heard his fierce whisper. 'Listen to me carefully. The United States government is not in the business of assassination. It does not track down and kill terrorists. It accumulates evidence and lets the courts decide the appropriate punishment.'

'Yeah, sure, right. Just like the Israelis didn't send a hit team after the terrorists who killed eleven Jewish athletes at the 1972 Munich Olympics.'

'What the Israelis did has nothing to do with *us*. *That* operation was canceled because one of the men they killed was innocent. That's why *we're* not in the assassination business.'

'Fine. Now *you* listen to me,' McKittrick said. 'If we let those bastards get away because we don't have the guts to do what's right, both of us will be out of a job.'

'Noon tomorrow.'

'What?'

'Go to your apartment and stay there,' Decker said. 'Don't do anything. Don't contact the woman. Don't go out for a newspaper. Don't do *anything*. I will knock on your door at noon sharp. I will tell you what our superiors have decided to do about you. If I were you, I'd have my bags packed.'

7

Happy fortieth birthday, Decker told himself. In his bathroom mirror, the haggard expression on his face confirmed how poorly he had slept because of his preoccupation with McKittrick. His headache from jet lag and the choking haze of cigarette smoke he had been forced to breathe persisted. A late-night room-service meal of fetuccini and Chicken Marsala sat heavily in his stomach. He seemed to have gained a few more lines of character in his rugged features, the start of crows' feet around his watchful aquamarine eyes. As if all of that wasn't enough, he found a strand of gray in his slightly long, wavy, sandy hair. Muttering, he jerked it out.

Saturday morning. The start of the weekend for most people, Decker thought, but not in *my* line of work. He couldn't remember the last time he had felt the sense of leisure that he associated with a true weekend. For no reason that he immediately understood, he remembered following McKittrick down the Spanish Steps and past the house where Keats had died. He imagined Keats coughing his life away, the TB filling him up, choking him. So young, but already having achieved greatness.

I need some time off.

Decker put on jogging clothes, tried to ignore the hazy automobile exhaust and the crowded sidewalks, and ran to the international real-estate consulting firm that he had reported to the day before, satisfied that his erratic route would keep anyone from following him. After showing his identification, he was admitted to an office that had a scrambler attached to its phone. Five minutes later, he was talking to his supervisor at a similar international real-estate consulting firm in Alexandria, Virginia. The supervisor had a scrambler calibrated to the same frequency as Decker's.

The conversation lasted fifteen minutes and made Decker

even more frustrated. He learned that McKittrick's father had been informed of Decker's intentions, probably by means of a phone call that McKittrick had made to his father late the night before (Decker could only hope that McKittrick had used a payphone and spoken with discretion). The father, not just a legend in the intelligence community but a former chairman of the National Security Council who still retained considerable political influence, had questioned Decker's own profession-alism and accused Decker of attempting to have McKittrick transferred so that Decker could take the credit for McKittrick's achievement in finding the terrorists. While Decker's superior claimed that he privately sided with Decker over McKittrick, the fact was that prudence and his pension forced him to ignore Decker's warnings and to keep McKittrick in place. 'Babysit him,' the superior said. 'Prevent him from making mistakes. Verify the rest of the information in his reports. We'll pass the information to the Italian authorities and pull both of you out. I promise you'll never have to work with him again.'

'It's right now I'm worried about.'

Decker's run back to his hotel did nothing to ease his frustration. He placed towels on the floor of his room and did 150 push-ups, then the same amount of sit-ups, sweat dripping from his strong shoulders, narrow hips, and sinewy legs. He practiced several martial arts moves, then showered and put on fresh jeans as well as a clean blue Oxford-cloth shirt. His brown leather jacket covered his pistol. His stomach continued to bother him.

8

It was noon exactly when, as scheduled, Decker knocked on McKittrick's door.

No one answered.

Decker knocked again, waited, frowned, knocked a third time, waited, frowned harder, glanced to each side along the corridor, then used the lock-pick tools concealed in the collar of his jacket. Ten seconds later, he was in the apartment, securing it behind him, his weapon already drawn. Had McKittrick stood him up, or had something happened to him? With painstaking caution, Decker started searching.

The living room was deserted. So were the bathroom, the kitchen, and the bedroom, including the closets. Decker hated closets – he never knew what might be crouching in them. His chest tight, he completed the search, sat on a padded chair in the living room, and analyzed the possibilities. Nothing in the apartment seemed out of place, but that proved nothing. McKittrick could be in trouble somewhere else. Or it could be, Decker thought for the second time, that the son of a bitch stood me up.

Decker waited, in the process conducting another search of McKittrick's apartment, this time in detail. In, under, and behind every drawer. Under the mattress and the bed. Under the chairs and sofa. In the light fixtures. In and behind the toilet tank.

What he found appalled him. Not only had McKittrick failed to destroy his notes after sending in his report, but as well, he had hidden the notes in a place not hard to predict – beneath shelfpaper in the kitchen. Next to the names of the members of the group Decker had met the previous night, he found addresses, one of which was for the apartment building into which McKittrick had gone with Renata. Decker also found the address of something called the Tiber Club.

Decker memorized the information. He put the notes on a saucer, burned them, crumbled the ashes into powder, peered out the kitchen's small window, saw the brick wall of an alley, and let a breeze scatter the ashes. Hunger fought with the discomfort in his stomach. He cut a slice from a loaf of bread, returned to the living room, and slowly ate, all the while frowning at the front door.

By then, it was three in the afternoon. Decker's misgivings strengthened. But what should he do about them? he wondered. He could go back to the international real-estate consulting firm and make an emergency telephone call to warn his supervisor that McKittrick had failed to be present at an appointment. But what would *that* accomplish, aside from creating the impression that Decker was determined to find fault with McKittrick? The guy's tradecraft was sloppy – Decker had already made an issue of that. So wasn't it likely that McKittrick had either forgotten or deliberately ignored the appointment? Maybe he was in bed with Renata right now.

If that's the case, he might be smarter than *I* am, Decker thought. When was the last time *I* was in bed with anybody? He couldn't remember. Because he traveled so much, he had few close female friends, all of them in his line of work. Casual pickups were out of the question – even before the spread of AIDS, Decker had avoided one-night stands on the theory that intimacy equaled vulnerability, that it didn't make sense to let down his guard with someone he knew nothing about.

This damned job, Decker thought. It not only makes you paranoid; it makes you a monk.

He glanced around the depressing living room. His nostrils felt irritated by the smell of must. His stomach continued to bother him.

Happy fortieth birthday, he told himself.

9

Decker had finished all the bread in the apartment by the time a key scraped in the lock. It was almost nine p.m. McKittrick rushed in, breathless, and froze when he saw Decker.

'Shut the door,' Decker said.

'What are you—'

'We had an appointment, remember. Shut the door.'

McKittrick obeyed. 'Weren't you told? Didn't my father—'

'He relayed a message to me, all right. But that didn't seem a reason to cancel our chat.' Decker stood. 'Where the hell have you been?'

'You don't *know*?'

'What are you talking about?'

'You haven't been *watching*?'

'Make sense.'

McKittrick hurried to the television set and turned it on. 'Three different television crews were there. Surely one of the channels is still broadcasting from—' His hand shook as he kept switching stations. '*There*.'

At first, Decker didn't understand what he was seeing. Abruptly the loud confusing images sent a wave of apprehension through him. Thick black smoke choked the sky. Flames burst from windows. Amid a section of wall that had toppled, firemen struggled with hoses, spewing water toward a large, blazing building. Fire trucks wailed to a stop among the chaos of other emergency vehicles, police cars, ambulances, more fire trucks. Appalled, Decker realized that some of the wailing came not from sirens but from burn victims being lifted onto stretchers, their faces charred, twisted with pain, not recognizably human. Unmoving bodies lay under blankets as policemen forced a crowd back.

'What is it? What in God's name happened?'

Before McKittrick could answer, a television reporter was talking about terrorists, about the Children of Mussolini, about the worst incident yet of anti-American violence, about twenty-three American tourists killed and another forty-three injured in a massive explosion, members of a Salt Lake City tour group that had been enjoying a banquet at the Tiber Club in honor of their final night in Rome.

'*The Tiber Club?*' Decker remembered the name from the list he had memorized.

'That's where Renata told me the terrorists like to go.' McKittrick's skin was ashen. 'She told me the plan was foolproof. Nothing could screw it up. It wasn't supposed to happen like this! Renata swore to me that—'

'Quit babbling.' Decker gripped McKittrick's shoulders. 'Talk to me. *What did you do?*'

'Last night.' McKittrick stopped to take several quick breaths. 'After the meeting, after we argued.' McKittrick's chest heaved. 'I knew I didn't have much time before you took the operation away from me and stole the credit for it.'

'You actually believe that bullshit you told your father? You think I'm *jealous* of you?'

'I had to do something. I couldn't be sure that my phone call to my father would solve the problem. There was a plan that Renata and I had been talking about. A perfect plan. After I left you, I went back to the cafe. Renata and the others were still in the upstairs room. We decided to put the plan into motion.'

'Without authorization.' Decker was appalled.

'Who was I going to get it from? *You?* You'd have told me not to. You'd have done your best to have me reassigned. You'd have used the same plan yourself.'

'I am trying very hard to keep my patience,' Decker said. On the television, flames shot from doorways, forcing firemen to stumble back as another section of wall fell. The wail of sirens intensified. Smoke-shrouded attendants loaded bodies into ambulances. 'This plan. Tell me about this perfect plan.'

'It was simple to the point of brilliance.'

'Oh, I'm sure it was.'

'Renata and her group would wait until the terrorists came together in one place – an apartment maybe, or the Tiber Club. Then someone from Renata's group would hide a satchel filled with plastic explosive near where the terrorists would have to pass when they came out. As soon as they appeared, Renata would press a remote control that detonated the explosive. It would look as if the terrorists had been carrying the explosive with them and the bomb went off by mistake.'

Decker listened with absolute astonishment. The room seemed to tilt. His face became numb. He questioned his sanity. This couldn't be happening, he told himself. He couldn't possibly be hearing this.

'Simple? Brilliant?' Decker rubbed his aching forehead. 'Didn't it occur to you that you might blow up the wrong people?'

'I'm absolutely positive that Renata's group has found the terrorists.'

'Didn't it also occur to you that you might blow up a lot of innocent people with them?'

'I warned Renata not to take chances. If there was the slightest doubt that someone else would be in the blast area, she was to wait.'

'*She?*' Decker wanted to shake McKittrick. 'Where's your common sense? Most people wouldn't be capable of detonating the explosion. Why would *she*?'

'Because I asked her.'

'What?'

'She loves me.'

'I must be asleep. This must be a nightmare,' Decker said. 'In a little while, I'll wake up. None of this will have happened.'

'She'd do *anything* for me.'

'Including murder?'

'It isn't murder to kill terrorists.'

'What the hell do *you* call it?'

'An execution.'

'You're amazing,' Decker said. 'Last night you called it "extreme denial". Call it whatever you want. It's still killing, and when someone agrees to do it, you've got to ask yourself what makes them capable of doing it. And in this case, I don't think it's love.'

'I can't believe she's doing this only for the money.'

'Where was the plastic explosive supposed to come from?'

'Me.'

Decker felt as if he'd been slapped. '*You* supplied it?'

'I'd been given Semtex at the start of the operation – so Renata's group could try to infiltrate the terrorist group by offering them Semtex as a sign of good faith.'

'*You* supplied the . . . ?' With greater horror, Decker stared toward the sirens wailing on the television, toward the smoke, flames, and wreckage, toward the bodies. '*You're* responsible for—'

'No! It was a mistake! Somehow the satchel went off at the wrong time! Somehow the club was filled with Americans! Somehow the— I . . . Renata must have . . . mistake.' McKittrick ran out of words, his broad mouth open, his lips moving, no sounds coming out.

'You weren't given enough Semtex to cause that much damage,' Decker said flatly.

McKittrick blinked at him, uncomprehending.

'You had only a sample,' Decker said. 'Enough to tempt the terrorists and make them think they'd get more. Renata had to have access to a lot more of it in order to destroy that entire building.'

'What are you saying?'

'Use your common sense! You didn't recruit a group of students to help you find the terrorists! You idiot, you recruited the *terrorists themselves*!'

McKittrick's eyes went blank with shock. He shook his head fiercely. 'No. That's impossible.'

'They've been staring you in the face! It's a wonder they kept themselves from *laughing* in your face. Classic entrapment. All the time you've been screwing Renata, she's been asking you questions, and you've been telling her our plans, everything we've been doing to try to catch them.'

McKittrick's face became more ashen.

'I'm right, aren't I?' Decker asked. 'You've been telling her *everything*.'

'Jesus.'

'Last night, when you warned them you might be reassigned, they decided the game was over. It was time for them to go back to work. Did *you* suggest implementing the plan and moving against the terrorists, or did Renata?'

'She . . .' McKittrick swallowed. '*She* did.'

'To help you in your career.'

'Yes.'

'Because she loved you.'

'Yes.'

'Was the plan *her* idea in the first place?'

'Yes.'

'And now she's used the sample of Semtex you gave her. I'll bet they've got photographs and tape recordings that document your participation. She put the sample with some of her own, and she blew up a tour group of Americans. You wanted to promote your career? Well, buddy, your career is over.'

10

'What a mess.' In the international real-estate consulting firm, Decker listened to his superior's weary voice on the scrambler-protected telephone. 'All those people killed. Terrible. Sickening. Thank God it's not my responsibility anymore.'

Decker took a moment before the implication struck him. He sat straighter, clutching the phone harder. 'Not your responsibility? Whose is it? *Mine?* You're dumping this on *me*?'

'Let me explain.'

'I had nothing to do with it. You sent me in at the last minute. I reported back that I thought the operation was in trouble. You ignored my advice, and—'

'*I'm* not the one who ignored your advice,' Decker's superior said. 'McKittrick's father took over. *He's* in charge now.'

'*What?*'

'The operation is *his* responsibility. As soon as he got his son's phone call, he started badgering everyone who owed him favors. Right now he's on his way to Rome. He ought to be arriving at . . .'

11

The Astra Galaxy eight-seat corporate jet, ostensibly privately owned, set down at Leonardo da Vinci Airport just after midnight. Decker waited beyond customs and immigration while a tall, white-haired, patrician-looking man dealt with the officials. As near as Decker could tell, there were no other passengers on the jet. The man was seventy-two but in amazing shape, broad-shouldered, tan, with craggy handsome features. He wore a three-piece, blended-wool, gray suit that showed no effects of the long, hastily scheduled flight any more than did Jason McKittrick himself.

Decker had met the legend three times before and received a curt nod of recognition as McKittrick approached him.

'Did you have a good flight? Let me take your suitcase,' Decker said.

But McKittrick kept a grip on the suitcase and walked past Decker, proceeding toward the airport's exit. Decker caught up to him, their footsteps echoing in the cavernous facility. Few people were present at so late an hour.

Decker had rented a car, a Fiat. In the parking area, McKittrick watched him scan the vehicle to make sure that no eavesdropping devices had been planted while Decker was in the airport. Only after McKittrick was inside the Fiat and Decker was driving through a gloomy drizzle toward the city did the great man finally speak.

'Where's my son?'

'At a hotel,' Decker said. 'He used the passport for his alternate identity. After what happened . . . I assume you were told en route?'

'About the explosion?' McKittrick nodded somberly.

Decker stared ahead past the flapping windshield wipers. 'After the explosion, I didn't think it was safe for your son to stay at his apartment. The terrorists know where he lives.'

'You suspect they might attack him?'

'No.' Decker glanced at numerous headlights in his rearview mirror. In the dark and the rain, it was difficult to determine if he was being followed. 'But I have to assume they'll release information and evidence about him to the police. I take for granted that was the point – to connect an American intelligence operative to a terrorist attack against Americans.'

McKittrick's expression hardened.

'As soon as I've assured myself that we're not being followed, I'll drive you to him,' Decker said.

'You seem to have thought of everything.'

'I'm doing my best.'

'So have you thought about who's going to be blamed for this?' McKittrick asked.

'Excuse me?'

Rain pattered on the car's roof.

'You, for instance?' McKittrick asked.

'There is no way I am going to take the blame for—'

'Then think of someone else. Because if there is one thing you can be confident of, it is that my son is *not* going to take the blame.'

12

The modest hotel was on a modest street – nothing about it attracted attention. After nodding to the night porter and showing one of the hotel's keys to prove he belonged there, Decker escorted McKittrick across the small lobby, past the elevator, up carpeted stairs. The son's room was only a few floors above them, and whenever possible, Decker avoided the potential trap of elevators.

McKittrick seemed to take the precaution for granted. Even carrying his suitcase, the tall, elderly man displayed no sign of exertion.

They came to room 312. Decker knocked four times, a code to let McKittrick's son know who was coming in, then used his key to unlock the door. The room's darkness made him frown. He flicked a light switch and frowned more severely when he saw that the bed had not been slept in. 'Shit.'

'Where is he?' McKittrick demanded.

Knowing that the effort was futile, Decker peered into the bathroom and the sitting room. 'Your son has a bad habit of not following orders. This is twice today that he didn't stay put when I told him to.'

'He must have had an excellent reason.'

'That would be a change. He left his suitcase. Presumably that means he's planning to come back.' Decker noticed an envelope on the bedside table. 'Here. This is addressed to you.'

McKittrick looked uneasy. 'You told him I was coming?'

'Of course. Why? What's the matter?'

'Perhaps that wasn't the wisest thing.'

'What's wrong with telling him that his father was coming?'

But McKittrick had already opened the note. His aged eyes narrowed. Otherwise, he showed no reaction to what he was reading.

At last, he lowered the note and exhaled.

'So?' Decker asked.

McKittrick didn't answer.

'What is it?'

McKittrick still didn't answer.

'Tell me.'

'I'm not certain.' McKittrick sounded hoarse. 'Perhaps it's a suicide note.'

'Suicide? What the—' Decker took the note from him. It was handwritten, its salutation giving Decker an image of an Ivy-Leaguer who had never grown up.

Pops –

I guess I screwed up again. Sorry. I seem to say that a lot, don't I? Sorry. I want you to know that this time I really tried. Honestly, I thought I had it all figured out. The bases covered. The game in the bag. Talk about being wrong, huh? I don't know which is worse – embarrassing you, or not becoming you. But I swear to you, this time I won't run away from my mistake. The responsibility is mine. And the punishment. When I've done what needs to be done, you won't be ashamed of me any longer.

Bry

McKittrick cleared his throat as if he was having difficulty

29

speaking. 'That was my nickname for Brian. Bry.'

Decker reread the note. ' "*The responsibility is mine. And the punishment.*" What's he saying?'

'I'm very much afraid that he intends to kill himself,' McKittrick said.

'And that's going to stop you from being ashamed of him? You think that's what his last sentence means?' Decker shook his head. 'Suicide might wipe out *his* shame, but it wouldn't stop *yours*. Your son isn't talking about killing himself. That wouldn't be dramatic enough.'

'I don't know what you're—'

'He's a grandstander. "I won't run away from my mistake. The responsibility is mine. And the punishment." He's not talking about suicide. He's talking about getting even. He's going after them.'

13

As Decker swerved the rented Fiat onto the side street off Via dei Condotti, his headlights pierced the persistent rain, revealing two police cars, their roof lights flashing. Two policemen in rain slickers stood in the illuminated entrance to an apartment building, talking to several distressed-looking people in the vestibule, all of whom wore pajamas or night robes. Lights were on in many windows.

'Damn it, I hoped I'd be wrong.'

'What *is* this place?' McKittrick asked.

'I followed your son and a woman here on Friday,' Decker said. 'Her first name's Renata. I wasn't given her last. Probably an alias. She's the leader of the group your son recruited, which means she's the leader of the group that blew up the Tiber Club. In other words, the terrorists.'

'That's an assumption. You can't be certain that the two groups are the same,' McKittrick said.

'Your son keeps using a phrase that I'd say you're in – extreme denial.'

Decker slowed, easing past the police cars on the narrow street. As tires splashed through puddles, the policemen looked toward the Fiat, then resumed talking to the people in the vestibule.

'And you can't be certain that those policemen have anything to do with Brian,' McKittrick said.

'You know as well as I do – we can't accept coincidence. If I were Brian, this is the logical place that *I'd* go first. To try to get even with the woman who betrayed him. There's one way to find out. You want me to stop so you can go back and talk to the police?'

'Lord, no. Keep driving. Because I'm an American, they'd want to know why I was interested. They'd ask so many questions, I'd be forced to show my credentials.'

'Right. And if Brian can be linked to whatever happened at that apartment building, you'd be linked to *him* and to what happened at the Tiber Club, assuming the terrorists sent the police evidence about his involvement in the explosion. Wouldn't that be a pretty mess?'

'Do you suppose Brian found the woman?' McKittrick's voice deepened with concern.

'I doubt it. There wasn't an ambulance.' Decker sped onto another street.

'You're worried that he was furious enough to have killed her?'

'No. What worries me is the reverse.'

'I don't understand.'

'*Her* killing *him*,' Decker said. 'Your son's out of his depth. What's worse, he isn't humble enough to know it. These people

31

are expert killers. They don't just do their work well. They love it. It gave them a kick to toy with Brian, but if they ever thought he was a serious threat, he'd be dead in an instant. There might not be enough of him left to send home for a funeral.'

McKittrick sat tensely straighter. 'How can we stop him?'

Decker squinted toward the rain past the flapping windshield wipers. 'Your son likes to leave documents around his apartment – a list of his contacts and their addresses, for example.'

'Dear God, are you telling me his tradecraft is that faulty?'

'I get the feeling you haven't been listening to me. Twenty-three people are dead, forty-three injured. That's how faulty his tradecraft is.'

'The list,' McKittrick said, agitated. 'Why did you mention the list?'

'Before I burned it, I memorized it,' Decker said. 'Renata's name and address were at the top. It's logical for him to have gone there first. I think it's also logical that he'll go to every other address until he finds her.'

'But if they're really the terrorists, they won't be at those addresses.'

'Exactly.' Decker swerved around another corner. 'They're professionals. They wouldn't have given Brian their real addresses. Renata probably used that apartment back there as an accommodation, part of the scam. But it doesn't look like Brian figured that out. He's too furious. He wants to get even. The people he terrorizes at those addresses won't have the vaguest idea what's going on. Maybe Renata counted on him to do this. Maybe it's her final joke.'

McKittrick's tone was urgent. 'Where's the closest address on the list?'

'Across the river. But I don't see any point in going there. He's got too big a head start.' Decker increased speed, his tires hissing on the wet pavement. 'He might be at the third or fourth' address by now. I'm going to skip to the farthest, then the second farthest, go at them in reverse order, and hope our paths cross.'

14

The rain increased. The only thing in our favor, Decker thought, is that it's the middle of the night. There aren't any traffic jams to slow us down.

All the same, he had to concentrate to drive swiftly and yet safely on the slick pavement. His troubled sleep the previous night had not been sufficient to overcome his jet lag. Now his sense of sleep deprivation intensified, his eyes feeling scratchy, his forehead aching. He felt pressure behind his ears.

Amazingly, especially given his age, McKittrick showed no signs of jet lag at all, his tall frame erect. He pointed. 'What are those large buildings ahead?'

'City University.' After pausing to check a map, Decker took a side street, then another, each more gloomy and narrow, trying to see the numbers on buildings squeezed together. He stopped before a doorway. 'This is the address.'

McKittrick stared through the windows. 'Everything's quiet. No lights on. No police.'

'Looks like he hasn't been here.' A noise in the car made Decker whirl.

McKittrick had his hand on the door latch. He was getting out, standing on the curb, only partially visible in the night and the rain.

'What are you—'

'It's been quite a few years,' McKittrick said with dignity. 'But I still remember how to conduct surveillance. Leave me here. Go to the next address.'

'But—'

'Perhaps my son is already here, or perhaps he's on his way. Perhaps we'll pass him without knowing it if we go to the next address. But this way, if I remain, at least *this* address is secure.'

'I don't think splitting up is a good idea,' Decker said.

'If I were a man your age, would you argue about what I'm doing?'

' . . . No.'

'Then there you have it.' McKittrick started to close the door.

'Wait,' Decker said.

'I won't let you talk me out of this.'

'That's not what I wanted. Here. You'd better take this. When I heard you were flying in, I had a package delivered to the office. I've been waiting to see if it was necessary to give it to you.'

'A pistol?' McKittrick reacted with astonishment. 'Do you honestly think I need a *pistol* to confront my son?'

'I have a very bad feeling about what's happening tonight.'

'I refuse to—'

'Take it, or I'm not leaving you here.'

McKittrick studied him. His dark eyes intense, he accepted the weapon.

'I'll be back as soon as I can,' Decker said. 'How will I find you?'

'Drive slowly through this area. *I'll* find *you*.' McKittrick shut the door, shoved the pistol beneath his suit coat, and walked away into the darkness. Only when the elderly man's rain-haloed figure was no longer visible in the Fiat's headlights did Decker drive onward.

15

It took Decker eight minutes to reach the next-to-last address on the list. Along the way, he debated what to do if there was no indication that Brian had been there. Stay, or go on to another address?

What happened next settled the matter. Even from blocks away, Decker heard sirens wailing in the darkness. He saw a crimson glow above rain-obscured buildings. His stomach hard with apprehension, he steered the Fiat onto the street he wanted and braked immediately before the glaring lights of rumbling fire trucks and other emergency vehicles. Flames licked from the windows of an apartment building. Smoke billowed. As firemen aimed hoses toward the blaze, ambulance attendants ministered to survivors, draping blankets around them, giving them oxygen.

Appalled, Decker got out of the Fiat, came close enough to determine that the fiery building was in fact the one he had come to check, then hurried through a gathering crowd back to the car, reversed direction, and sped away into the rain.

His heart pounded. What the hell is happening? he thought. Was Brian trying to get even by setting fire to the buildings, hoping to trap the terrorists inside? Surely even someone so out of control as Brian would have realized that other people besides the terrorists would be injured – if the terrorists were injured at all, if they had been foolish enough to remain at the addresses they had given Brian.

He has only one more address to go, Decker thought. Where I left his father. Driving urgently through the rain-filled night, Decker skidded and regained control of the Fiat. Near the university, he again took a side street, then another, feeling trapped in the narrow confines. The address where he had left McKittrick's father was only a half block farther when Decker stomped his brake pedal, swerving, nearly hitting a tall burly figure who suddenly appeared in the glare of his headlights. The figure was drenched, his face raised to the storm clouds; he was shaking his fists, screaming.

The figure was Brian. Decker's windows were closed. Only when he scrambled out of the Fiat, racing through puddles to restrain Brian did he hear what Brian screamed.

'*Liars! Bastards!*'

Decker had left his headlights on, their illumination reflecting off the rain streaming down Brian's face.

'*Cowards!*'

Lights came on in windows.

'We have to get you off the street,' Decker said.

'*Fight me!*' Brian screamed inexplicably toward the darkness.

More lights came on.

'FIGHT ME!'

Cold rain soaked Decker's hair and chilled his neck. 'The police will be looking for you. You can't stay here. I have to get you out of here.' He tugged Brian toward the car.

Brian resisted. More windows became illuminated.

'For God's sake, come on,' Decker said. 'Have you seen your father? I left him here.'

'*Bastards!*'

'Brian, listen to me. Have you seen your father?'

Brian wrenched himself free of Decker's grasp and once more shook his fists toward the sky. '*You're afraid!*'

'What's going on down there?' a man yelled in Italian from an upper apartment.

Decker grabbed Brian. 'With the commotion you're making, your father couldn't help but know you're here. He should have joined us by now. Pay attention. I need to know if you've seen him.'

At once a premonition chilled Decker. 'Oh, Jesus, no. Brian. Your father. Has something happened to him?'

When Brian didn't respond, Decker slapped him, twisting his head, sending rain drops flying from Brian's face.

Brian looked shocked. The Fiat's headlights reflected off his wild eyes.

'Tell me where your father is!'

Brian stumbled away.

Apprehensive, Decker followed, seeing where Brian led him – to the address that Brian's father had intended to watch. Even in the rainy gloom, Decker could see that the door was open.

Trying to restrain his too-quick breathing, Decker withdrew his pistol from beneath his leather jacket. As Brian entered, Decker pushed him to a crouch and stooped to hurry after him, his eyes adjusting enough to the darkness to make him aware he was in a courtyard. He saw a wooden crate to his right and shoved Brian toward it. Kneeling on wet cobblestones, Decker aimed over the crate, scanning indistinguishable objects, peering up toward the barely detectable railings of balconies to the right and left and straight ahead.

'Brian, show me,' Decker whispered.

For a moment, he wasn't certain that Brian had heard. Then Brian shifted position, and Decker realized that Brian was pointing. As Decker's vision adjusted even more to the darkness, he saw a disturbing patch of white in the far-right corner.

'Stay here,' he told Brian, and darted toward another crate. Aiming, he checked nervously around him, then hurried forward again, this time to what might have been an ancient well. His wet clothes clung to him, constricting his muscles. He was close enough to determine that the patch of white he had seen was hair – Jason McKittrick's hair. The elderly man lay with his back propped against a wall, his arms at his sides, his chin on his chest.

Decker glanced once more around him, then ran through the rain, reaching McKittrick, crouching beside him, feeling for a pulse. Despite the gloom, it was obvious that an area on the right breast of his gray suit coat was darker than the rain would have caused. Blood. Decker kept checking for a pulse, feeling McKittrick's wrist, his neck, his chest.

Inhaling with triumph, he found one.

He whirled to aim at a sudden approaching figure.

It was Brian, scrambling across the courtyard and collapsing next to his father, pressing his face against his father's head. 'Didn't mean to.'

'Help me,' Decker said. 'We have to get him to the car.'

'Didn't know who he was.'

'What are you talking about?'

'Didn't realize.'

'*What?*'

'Thought he was one of *them*.' Brian sobbed.

'*You* did this?' Decker grabbed Brian, finding that he had a revolver in his jacket pocket.

'I couldn't help myself. He came out of the darkness.'

'Jesus.'

'I had to shoot.'

'God help—'

'I didn't mean to kill him.'

'You didn't.'

'I'm telling you I—'

'He isn't dead!'

In the darkness, Brian's stunned look was barely discernible.

'We have to get him to the car. We have to take him to the hospital. Grab his feet.'

As Decker reached for McKittrick's shoulder, a bumble bee seemed to buzz down past Decker's head. A projectile whacked against the wall behind him.

Flinching, Decker scurried toward the protection of a crate. The shot – from a sound-suppressed weapon – had come from above him. He aimed fiercely upward, blinking from the rain, unable to see a target in the darkness.

'They won't let you,' Brian said.

'*They?*'

'They're here.'

Decker's heart felt squeezed as he realized why Brian had been yelling in the street. Not at the sky or God or the Furies.

He'd been screaming at the terrorists.

Brian remained in the open, beside his father.

'Get over here,' Decker told him.

'I'm safe.'

'For God's sake, get over here behind this crate.'

'They won't shoot me.'

'Don't talk crazy.'

'Before you got here, Renata showed herself to me. She told me the best way to hurt me is to let me live.'

'What?'

'So I can suffer for the rest of my life, knowing I killed my father.'

'But your shot didn't kill him! He isn't dead!'

'*He might as well be.* Renata will never let us take him out of here. She hates me too much.' Brian pulled his revolver from his pocket. In the gloom, it seemed that he pointed it at himself.

'Brian! No!'

But instead of shooting himself, Brian surged to his feet, cursed, and disappeared into the darkness at the back of the courtyard.

Amid the pelting rain, Decker – shocked – heard Brian's footsteps charging up an exterior wooden staircase.

'Brian, I warned you!' a woman shouted from above. The husky voice was Renata's. 'Don't come after me!'

Brian's footsteps charged higher.

Lights came on in balcony windows.

'I gave you a chance!' Renata shouted. 'Stay away, or I'll do what I did at the other apartment buildings!'

'You're going to pay for making a fool of me!'

Renata laughed. 'You did it to yourself!'

'You're going to pay for my father!'

'You did *that* yourself!'

Brian's footsteps pounded higher.

'Don't be an idiot!' Renata shouted. 'The explosives have been set! I'll press the detonator!'

Brian's urgent footsteps kept pounding on the stairs.

Their rumble was overwhelmed by thunder, not from the storm but from an explosion whose blinding flash erupted out of an apartment on the fourth balcony at the back. The ear-stunning roar knocked Decker backward. As wreckage cascaded, the ferocity of the flames illuminated the courtyard.

A movement to Decker's left made him turn. A thin, dark-haired man in his early twenties, one of the brothers whom Decker had met at the cafe the night before, rose from behind garbage cans.

Decker stiffened. They must be all around me, but in the dark, I didn't know it!

The young man hadn't been prepared for Renata to detonate the bomb. Although he had a pistol, his attention was totally distracted by a scream on the other side of the courtyard. With wide-eyed dismay, the young man saw one of his brothers swatting at flames on his clothes and in his hair that had been ignited by the falling, burning wreckage. The rain didn't seem to affect the flames. The second brother kept screaming.

Decker shot twice at the first brother, hitting his chest and head. As the gunman toppled, Decker pivoted and shot twice at the man in flames, dropping him, also. The gunshots were almost obscured by the crackle and roar of the fire as it spread from the fourth balcony.

More wreckage fell. Crouching behind the crate, Decker scanned the area in search of more targets. Brian. *Where was Brian?* Decker's peripheral vision detected motion in the far-left corner of the courtyard, near the door that he and Brian had come through.

But the movement wasn't Brian. The tall, slim, sensuous figure that emerged from the shadows of another stairway was Renata. Holding a pistol equipped with a sound-suppressor, she shot repeatedly toward the courtyard, all the while running toward the open doorway. The muffled shots, normally no louder than a fist against a pillow, were totally silent because of the roaring chaos of the blaze.

Behind the crate, Decker sprawled on the wet cobblestones and squirmed forward on his elbows and knees. He reached the side of the crate, caught a glimpse of Renata nearing the exit, aimed through the rain, and shot twice more. His first bullet struck the wall behind her. His second hit her in the throat. She clutched her windpipe, blood spewing. Her throat would squeeze shut. Death from asphyxiation would occur in less than three minutes.

Despite the din of the flames, Decker heard a scream of anguish. One of Renata's brothers showed himself, racing from the open stairway, shooting toward the courtyard, grabbing Renata where she had fallen, dragging her closer to the open doorway. At once he shot again – not at Decker, but instead toward the stairwell at the back of the courtyard, as if protecting himself from bullets that came from that direction. As Decker aimed, the last brother appeared, shot repeatedly in Decker's direction, and helped to get his sister out of view into the street. Decker emptied his pistol, hastily ejected its magazine, and inserted a full one. By then, the terrorists were gone.

Sweat mixed with rain on his face. He shuddered, spun in case there were other targets, and saw Brian jump down the last few steps of the open stairway at the back of the courtyard.

Brian clutched his revolver, his hand shaking.

'We have to get out of here!' Decker yelled.

No more than a minute had passed since the explosion. People wearing pajamas and sometimes less were charging onto the balconies and down outdoor stairways to get away from the fire.

Decker avoided a chunk of flaming wreckage and rushed to Brian, who had an arm around his father, lifting him.

'I can feel him breathe!' Brian said.

'Give me his legs.'

Decker heard people rushing in panic down the stairs as he and Brian carried McKittrick across the courtyard toward the open doorway.

'Wait,' Decker said. He set down McKittrick's legs and aimed cautiously out toward the street. He saw a car speed away from the curb, its red taillights becoming rapidly smaller, the vehicle skidding through puddles, around a corner, disappearing.

Decker was far enough from the roaring flames to hear the pulsing wail of approaching sirens. One of the terrorists might have stayed, hiding behind a car, hoping to create an ambush. But Decker was betting that the sirens were as worrisome to the terrorists as to himself.

He decided to take the chance. 'Let's go!' he told Brian.

As people crowded behind them, he and Brian hurried to carry McKittrick toward the Fiat and set him in the back seat. Brian stayed in back with his father while Decker slid behind the steering wheel and sped away, narrowly missing people in the street. At the same time, numerous sirens wailed louder behind the Fiat. Pressing his foot on the accelerator, Decker glanced nervously at the rearview mirror and saw the flashing lights of emergency vehicles appear on the rainy street behind him.

But what about up ahead? he wondered, his hands tense on the steering wheel. The street was so narrow that if fire trucks or police cars sped around a corner, heading in Decker's direction, there'd be no way around them. The Fiat would be trapped.

A rain-slick corner loomed. Decker swerved, finding himself

on a street that was wider. No approaching lights flashed in the darkness ahead. The sirens were farther behind him.

'I think we got away,' Decker said. 'How's your father?'

'He's still alive. That's the best I can say.'

Decker tried to breathe less quickly. 'What did Renata mean about threatening to do what she did at the other apartment buildings?'

'She told me she rigged explosives at some of them. After I showed up, looking for her and the others . . .' Brian had trouble speaking.

'As soon as you were out of the area, she set off the charges?'

'Yes.'

'You'd made such a commotion, barging into the apartments, that the other people in the building would have come out to learn what was going on? They'd associate you with the explosions?'

'Yes.'

'Renata wanted an American to be blamed?'

'Yes.'

'Damn it, you let her use you again,' Decker said.

'But I got even.'

'Even?'

'You saw what I did. I shot her.'

'*You* . . . ?' Decker couldn't believe what he was hearing. He felt as if the road wavered. '*You* didn't shoot her.'

'In the throat,' Brian said.

'No.'

'You're trying to claim *you* did?' Brian demanded.

My God, he truly is crazy, Decker thought. 'There's nothing to brag about here, Brian. If you had shot her, it wouldn't make me think less of myself or more of you. If anything, I'd feel sorry for you. It's a terrible thing, living with the memory of—'

'*Sorry for me?* What the hell are you talking about? You think

43

you're better than I am? What gives you the right to feel so superior?'

'Forget it, Brian.'

'Sorry for me? Are you trying to claim *you* did what *I* did?'

'Just calm down,' Decker said.

'You hate me so much, the next thing you'll be claiming *I* was the one who shot my father.'

Decker's sense of reality was so threatened that he felt momentarily dizzy. 'Whatever you say, Brian. All I want to do is get him to a hospital.'

'Damned right.'

Decker heard a pulsing siren. The flashing lights of a police car raced toward him. His palms sweated on the steering wheel. At once the police car rushed past, heading in the direction from which Decker had come.

'Give me your revolver, Brian.'

'Get serious.'

'I mean it. Hand me your revolver.'

'You've got to be—'

'Just once, for Christ's sake, listen to me. There'll be other police cars. Someone will tell the police a Fiat sped away. There's a chance we'll be stopped. It's bad enough we have a wounded man in the car. But if the police find our handguns—'

'What are you going to do with my revolver? You think you can use ballistics from it to prove I shot my father? You're afraid I'll try to get rid of it?'

'No, *I'm* going to get rid of it.'

Brian cocked his head in surprise.

'As much as I don't want to.' Decker stopped at the side of the murky street and turned to stare at Brian. 'Give . . . me . . . your . . . revolver.'

Squinting, Brian studied him. Slowly, he reached in his

jacket pocket and pulled out the weapon.

Decker pulled out his own weapon.

Only when Brian offered the revolver, butt first, did Decker allow himself to relax a little. In the courtyard, before he had helped to lift McKittrick's father, he had picked up the elderly man's pistol. Now he took that pistol, his own, and Brian's. He got out of the Fiat into the chilling rain, scanned the darkness to see if anyone was watching, went around to the curb, knelt as if to check the pressure on one of his tires, and inconspicuously dropped the three handguns down a sewer drain.

Immediately he got back into the Fiat and drove away.

'So that takes care of that, huh?' Brian said.

'Yes,' Decker answered bitterly. 'That takes care of that.'

16

'He has lost a great deal of blood,' the emergency-room doctor said in Italian. 'His pulse is weak and erratic. His blood pressure is low. I do not wish to be pessimistic, but I am afraid that you must prepare yourself for any eventuality.'

'I understand,' Decker said. 'This man's son and I appreciate anything you can do for him.'

The doctor nodded gravely and went back into the emergency room.

Decker turned to two weary-looking hospital officials, who stood respectfully in a corner of the waiting room. 'I'm grateful for your cooperation in this matter,' Decker told them. 'My superiors will be even more grateful. Of course, a suitable gesture of gratitude will be made to everyone involved.'

'Your superiors have always been most generous.' One of the officials took off his spectacles. 'We will do our best to make certain that the authorities are not informed about the true cause of the patient's injury.'

'I have total confidence in your discretion.' Decker shook hands with them. The money he slipped into their palms disappeared into their pockets. '*Grazie.*'

As soon as the officials left, Decker sat beside Brian. 'Good. You kept your mouth shut.'

'We have an understanding with this hospital?'

Decker nodded.

'Is this place first rate?' Brian asked. 'It seems awfully small.'

'It's the best.'

'We'll see.'

'Prayer wouldn't hurt.'

Brian frowned. 'You mean you're religious?'

'I like to keep my options open.' Decker peered down at his wet clothes, which were clinging to him. 'What they're doing for your father is going to take a while. I think we'd better go back to your hotel and put on dry clothes.'

'But what if something happens while we're gone?'

'You mean, if he dies?' Decker asked.

'Yes.'

'It won't make any difference whether we're in this room or not.'

'This is all your fault.'

'What?' Decker felt sudden pressure behind his ears. '*My* fault?'

'You got us into this mess. If it wasn't for you, none of this would have happened.'

'How the hell do you figure that?'

'If you hadn't shown up on Friday and rushed me, I could have handled Renata and her group just fine.'

'Why don't we talk about this on the way to your hotel?'

17

'He claims that as soon as you got him out of the hospital, you shoved him into an alley and beat him up,' Decker's superior said.

'He can claim anything he wants.' It was Monday. Again, Decker was in an office at the international real-estate consulting firm, but this time, he was speaking to his superior in person rather than on a scrambler-protected telephone.

The gray-haired superior, whose sagging cheeks were florid from tension, leaned forward across the table. 'You deny the accusation?'

'Brian was injured in the incident at the apartment building. I have no idea where this fantasy about my beating him comes from.'

'He says you're jealous of him.'

'Right.'

'That you're angry because he found the terrorists.'

'Sure.'

'That you're trying to get even with him by claiming that he accidentally shot his father.'

'Imagine.'

'And that you're trying to take credit for shooting the terrorists whom *he* in fact shot.'

'Look,' Decker said, 'I know you need to protect your pension. I know there's a lot of political pressure, and you need to cover your ass. But why are you dignifying that jerk's ridiculous accusations by repeating them to me?'

'What makes you think they're ridiculous?'

'Ask Brian's father. He's awfully weak. It's a miracle he pulled through. But he'll be able to—'

'I already *have* asked him.'

Decker didn't like his superior's solemn tone. 'And?'

'Jason McKittrick verifies everything Brian claims,' the superior said. 'Terrorists shot him, but not before he saw his son shoot three of the terrorists. Of course, ballistic tests might have corroborated what Jason McKittrick says, but *you* saw fit to dispose of all the weapons that were used that night.'

Decker's gaze was as steady as his superior's. 'So that's how it's going to be.'

'What do you mean?'

'Jason McKittrick warned me from the start – his son wasn't going to take the blame. I liked the old man enough that I stopped treating the warning seriously. I should have been more careful. The enemy wasn't out there. He was next to me.'

'Jason McKittrick's character isn't in question here.'

'Of course not. Because nobody wants Jason McKittrick as an enemy. And nobody wants to accept the responsibility for allowing his incompetent son to ruin a major operation. But *somebody's* got to be at fault, right?'

The superior didn't answer.

'How did you manage to hide Brian's involvement in this?' Decker asked. 'Didn't the terrorists send incriminating evidence about him to the police?'

'When you phoned to warn me about that possibility, I alerted our contacts in the police department. A package did arrive. Our contacts diverted it.'

'What about the media? No package was sent to them?'

'A television station, the same station the terrorists had earlier been sending messages to. We intercepted that package, also. The crisis is over.'

'Except for twenty-three dead Americans,' Decker said.

'Do you wish to make any change in your report?'

'Yes. I did beat the hell out of that jerk. I wish I'd beaten him more.'

'Any other change?'

'Something I should have added,' Decker said.

'Oh? What's that?'

'Saturday was my fortieth birthday.'

The superior shook his head. 'I'm afraid I don't see the relevance of that remark.'

'If you'll wait a moment, I'll type up my resignation.'

'Your— But we're not asking you to go *that* far. What on earth do you think resigning will get you?'

'A life.'

TWO

1

Decker lay on the bed in his New York hotel room. Using his right hand, he sipped from a glass of Jack Daniels. Using his left hand, he aimed the television's remote control and restlessly switched channels. Where do you go when you've been everywhere? he asked himself.

New York had always been good for him, a place to which he'd automatically headed when he had a rare free weekend. Broadway, the Metropolitan Opera, the Museum of Modern Art – these had always beckoned like old friends. Days, he had used to enjoy a soothing ritual of jogging through Central Park, of lunching at the Carnegie deli, of browsing through the Strand book store, of watching the sidewalk artists in Washington Square. Nights, he had liked to check out who was singing at the Algonquin Room. Radio City Music Hall. Madison Square Garden. There had always been plenty to do.

But this trip, to his surprise, he wanted to do none of it. Mel Torme was at Michael's Pub. Normally Decker would have been the first in line to get a seat. Not this time. Maynard Ferguson, Decker's favorite trumpeter, was at the Blue Note, but Decker didn't have the energy to clean himself up and go out. All he did have energy for was to pour more bourbon into his glass and keep pressing the channel changer on the TV's remote control.

After flying back from Rome, he hadn't considered returning to his small apartment in Alexandria, Virginia. He had no attachment to the small bedroom, living room, kitchenette, and bath. They weren't his home. They were merely a place for storing his clothes and sleeping between assignments. The dust that greeted him whenever he returned made his nose itch and gave him a headache. There was no way he could allow himself to break security and hire a cleaning lady to spruce the place up for his arrival. The thought of a stranger going through his things made his skin prickle – not that he would ever have left anything revealing in his apartment.

He hadn't let his superior – correction: his *former* superior – know where he was going after he submitted his resignation. New York would have been on the list of predictables, of course, and it would have been a routine matter for someone following him to confirm the destination of the flight Decker had boarded. He had used evasion procedures when he arrived in New York. He had stayed in a hotel, the St Regis, that was new to him. Nonetheless, ten minutes after he had checked in and been shown to his room, the telephone had rung, and of course, it had been his superior – correction again: damn it, *former* superior – asking Decker to reconsider.

'Really, Steve,' the weary-sounding man had said, 'I appreciate grand gestures as much as the next person, but now that you've done it, now that it's out of your system, let's let bygones be bygones. Climb back aboard. I agree, this Rome business is a mess from every angle, an out-and-out disaster, but resigning isn't going to change things. You're not making anything better. Surely you understand the futility of what you've done.'

'You're afraid I'm angry enough to tell the wrong people about what happened, is that it?' Decker had asked.

'Of course not. Everybody knows you're rock solid. You wouldn't do anything unprofessional. You wouldn't let us down.'

'Then you don't have anything to worry about.'

'You're too good a man to lose, Steve.'

'With guys like Brian McKittrick, you'll never know I'm gone.' Decker had set the phone on its receptacle.

A minute later, the phone had rung again, and this time, it had been his former superior's superior. 'If it's an increase in salary you want—'

'I never had a chance to spend what you paid me,' Decker said.

'Perhaps more time off.'

'To do what?'

'Travel.'

'Right. See the world. Rome, for instance. I fly so much I think there's something wrong with a bed if it isn't shaped like an airline seat.'

'Look, Steve, everybody gets burned out. It's part of the job. That's why we keep a team of experts who know how to relieve the symptoms of stress. Honestly, I think it would do you a world of good if you took a shuttle down to Washington right now and had a talk with them.'

'Didn't you listen? I told you I'm sick of flying.'

'Then use the train.'

Again Decker set the phone on its receptacle. He had no doubt that if he tried to go outside, he would be intercepted by two men waiting for him in the lobby. They would identify themselves, explain that his friends were worried about his reaction to what had happened in Rome, and suggest driving him to a quiet bar, where they could discuss what was bothering him.

To hell with that, Decker thought. I can have a drink in my room. By myself. Besides, the ride they gave me wouldn't be to a bar. That was when Decker picked up the phone, ordered a bottle of Jack Daniels and plenty of ice from room service, unplugged the phone, turned on the television, and began

55

switching channels. Two hours later, as darkness thickened beyond his closed drapes, he was a third of the way through the bottle and still switching channels. The staccato images on the screen were the test pattern of his mind.

Where to go? What to do? he asked himself. Money wasn't an immediate problem. For the ten years he had worked as an operative, a considerable portion of his salary had gone into mutual funds. Added to that sum was the sizeable amount of accumulated parachute pay, scuba pay, demolitions pay, combat pay, and specialty pay that he had previously earned as a member of a classified military counterterrorist unit. Like many of the military's highest trained soldiers, he had been recruited into intelligence work after he had reached an age when his body could no longer function as efficiently as his special-operations duties required – in Decker's case, when he was thirty, after a broken leg, three broken ribs, and two bullet wounds suffered in various classified missions. Of course, even though Decker was no longer physically superior enough to belong to his counterterrorist unit, he was still in better condition than most civilians.

His investments had increased to the point that his net worth was three hundred thousand dollars. In addition, he planned to withdraw the fifty thousand dollars that he had contributed to his civilian government pension. But despite his relative financial freedom, he felt trapped in other ways. With the whole world to choose from, he had narrowed his choices to this hotel room. If his parents had still been alive (and briefly he fantasized that they were), he would have paid them a long-postponed visit. As things were, his mother had died in a car accident three years earlier and his father from a heart attack a few months afterward, both while he was on assignment. The last time he had seen his father alive was at his mother's funeral.

Decker had no brothers or sisters. He had never married,

partly because he had refused to inflict his spartan way of life on someone he loved, partly because that way of life prevented him from finding anyone with whom he felt free to fall in love. His only friends were fellow operatives, and now that he had resigned from intelligence work, the controversial circumstances behind that resignation would prompt those friends to feel inhibited around him, not certain about which topics would be safe to discuss.

Maybe I made a mistake, Decker thought, sipping more bourbon. Maybe I shouldn't have resigned, he brooded, switching channels. Being an operative gave me a direction. It gave me an anchor.

It was killing you, Decker reminded himself, and it ruined for you every country where you ever had an assignment. The Greek islands, the Swiss Alps, the French Riviera, the Spanish Mediterranean – these were but a few of the glamorous areas where Decker had worked. But they were tainted by Decker's experiences there, and he had no wish to go back and be reminded. In fact, now that he thought about it, he was struck by the irony that, just as most people thought of those places as glamorous, so Decker's former profession was often portrayed in fiction as being heroic, whereas Decker thought of it as no more than a wearying, stultifying, dangerous job. Hunting drug lords and terrorists might be noble, but the slime of the quarry rubbed off on the hunter. It certainly rubbed off on me, Decker thought. And as I found out, some of the bureaucrats I worked for weren't all that slime-free, either.

What to do? Decker repeated to himself. Made sleepy by the bourbon, he peered through drooping eyelids at the television set and found himself frowning at something that he had just seen. Not understanding what it had been, oddly curious to find out, he roused himself and reversed channels, going back to one that he had just flicked past. As soon as he found the image that had intrigued him, he didn't understand *why* it had intrigued him. All he knew was that something in it had subconsciously spoken to him.

He was looking at a documentary about a team of construction workers renovating an old house. The house was unusual, reminiscent of earthen, pueblo-style dwellings he had come across in Mexico. But as he turned up the sound on the television, he learned that the house, astonishingly elegant regardless of its simple design, was in the United States, in *New* Mexico. It was made from adobe, the construction foreman explained, adding that 'adobe' referred to large bricks made of straw and mud. These bricks, which resulted in an exceptionally solid, sound-proofed wall, were covered with a clay-colored stucco. The foreman went on to explain that an adobe house was flat-roofed, the roof slanted slightly so that water could drain off through spouts called *canales*. An adobe house had no sharp edges; every corner was rounded. Its entrance often had a column-supported overhang called a *portal*. The windows were recessed into thick walls.

Leaving the distinctive dwelling whose sandy texture and clay color blended wonderfully with the orange, red, and yellow of its high-desert surroundings, the announcer made some concluding comments about craft and heritage while the camera panned across the neighborhood. Amid mountain foothills, surrounded by junipers and piñon trees, there were adobe houses in every direction, each with an eccentric variation so that the impression was one of amazing variety. But as the announcer explained, in a sense adobe houses *were* unusual in New Mexico, because they were present in force in only one city.

Decker found that he was leaning forward to hear the name of that city. He was told that it was one of the oldest settlements in the United States, dating back to the fifteen hundreds and the Spanish conquest, still retaining its Spanish character: the city whose name meant holy faith, these days nicknamed the City Different, Santa Fe.

2

Decker was right to be suspicious – two men were waiting for him in the lobby. The time was just after eight a.m. He turned from the checkout counter, saw them, and knew that there wasn't any point in trying to avoid them. They smiled as he crossed the busy lobby toward them. At least, the right men had been chosen for the assignment, Decker thought. Their controllers obviously hoped that he would let his guard down since he knew both of them, having served with them in military special operations.

'Steve, long time. How you been?' one of the men asked. He and his partner were close to Decker's height and weight – six feet tall, a hundred and ninety pounds. They were also around Decker's age – forty. Because they had gone through the same physical training, they had a similar body type – narrow hips and a torso that broadened toward solid shoulders designed to provide the upper-body strength essential in special operations. But there, the resemblance with Decker ended. While Decker's hair was sandy and slightly wavy, the man who had spoken had red hair cut close to his scalp. The other man had brown hair combed straight back. Both men had hard features and wary eyes that didn't go with their smiles and their business suits.

'I'm fine, Ben,' Decker told the red-haired man. 'And you?'
'Can't complain.'
'How about *you*, Hal?' Decker asked the other man.
'Can't complain, either.'
No one offered to shake hands.
'I hope the two of you didn't have to keep watch all night.'

'Only came on at seven. Easy duty,' Hal said. 'Checking out?' He pointed toward Decker's suitcase.

'Yeah, a last-minute change of plan.'

'Where you headed?'

'La Guardia,' Decker said.

'Why don't we drive you?'

Decker tensed. 'I wouldn't want you to go to any trouble. I'll catch a taxi.'

'No trouble at all,' Hal said. 'What kind of buddies would we be if after all these years of not seeing you, we didn't put ourselves out for you. This won't be a minute.' Hal reached into his suit coat, pulled out a thin cellular phone, and pressed numbers. 'You'll never guess who we just bumped into,' he said into the telephone. 'Yeah, we're talking to him right now in the lobby. Good, we'll be waiting.'

Hal broke the transmission and put the phone away. 'Need help with your suitcase?'

'I can manage.'

'Then why don't we go outside and wait for the car?'

Outside, traffic was already dense, car horns blaring.

'See,' Ben said. 'You might not have been able to get a taxi.' He noticed a uniformed doorman coming toward them. 'Everything's under control,' he told the man, motioning him away. He glanced toward the overcast sky. 'Feels like it might rain.'

'It was forecast,' Hal said.

'The twinge in my left elbow is all the forecast I need. Here's the car,' Ben said.

A gray Pontiac, whose driver wasn't familiar to Decker, pulled up in front of the hotel. The car's back seat had tinted windows that made it difficult to see in.

'What did I tell you?' Ben said. 'Only a minute.' He opened the passenger door and gestured for Decker to get in.

Heart pounding, Decker glanced from Ben to Hal and didn't move.

'Is there a problem?' Hal asked. 'Don't you think you'd better get in? You've got a plane to catch.'

'I was just wondering what to do about my suitcase.'

'We'll put it in the trunk. Press the button that opens the trunk, will you?' Ben told the driver. A moment later, the back latch made a thunking sound. Ben took Decker's suitcase, lifted the back lid, set the suitcase inside the trunk, and closed the lid. 'There, that takes care of that. Ready?'

Decker hesitated another moment. His pulse racing faster, he nodded and got in the back of the Pontiac. His stomach felt cold.

Ben got in beside him while Hal took the passenger seat in front, turning to look back at Decker.

'Buckle up,' the thick-necked driver said.

'Yeah, safety first,' Ben said.

Metal clinked against metal as Decker secured his seatbelt, the others doing the same.

The driver pressed a button that caused another thunking sound and locked all the doors. The Pontiac's engine rumbling, he steered into traffic.

3

'A mutual acquaintance told me you said on the phone last night you were tired of flying,' Ben said.

'That's right.' Decker glanced out the tinted windows toward pedestrians carrying briefcases, purses, rolled-up umbrellas, whatever, walking briskly to work. They seemed very far away.

'So why are you catching a plane?' Hal asked.

'A spur of the moment decision.'

'Like your resignation.'

'That wasn't spur of the moment.'

'Our mutual acquaintance said it sure seemed like it.'

'He doesn't know me very well.'

'He's beginning to wonder if *anybody* does.'

Decker shrugged. 'What else is he wondering?'

'Why you unplugged your phone.'

'I didn't want to be disturbed.'

'And why you didn't answer your door when one of the guys on the team knocked on it last night.'

'But I *did* answer the door. I just didn't open it. I asked who it was. On the other side of the door, a man said "Housekeeping". He told me he was there to turn down my bed. I told him I had turned down the bed myself. He told me he had fresh towels. I told him I didn't need fresh towels. He told me he had mints for the bedside table. I told him to shove the mints up his ass.'

'That wasn't very sociable.'

'I needed time alone to think.'

Ben took over the questioning. 'To think about what?'

As the Pontiac stopped at a light, Decker glanced to the left toward the red-haired man. 'Life.'

'Big subject. Did you figure it out?'

'I decided that it's the essence of life for things to change.'

'*That's* what this is all about? You're going through a change of life?' Hal asked.

Decker glanced ahead toward the brown-haired man in the front passenger seat. The Pontiac had resumed motion, proceeding through the intersection.

'That's right,' Decker said. 'A change of life.'

'And that's why you're taking this trip?'

'Right again.'

'To where exactly?'

'Santa Fe, New Mexico.'

'Never been there. What's it like?'

'I'm not sure. It looks nice, though.'

'*Looks* nice?'

'Last night, I watched a TV show about some construction workers fixing up an adobe house there.'

The Pontiac headed through another intersection.

'And that made you decide to go there?' Ben interrupted.

Decker turned to him in the back seat. 'Yep.'

'Just like that?'

'Just like that. In fact, I'm thinking about settling there.'

'Just like that. You know, that's what has our mutual acquaintance concerned, these sudden changes. How do you suppose he's going to react when we tell him that on the spur of the moment you decided to move to Santa Fe, New Mexico, because you saw an old house there being fixed up on television?'

'An adobe house.'

'Right. How do you suppose that'll make him think about the maturity with which you made other snap decisions?'

Decker's muscles hardened. 'I told you, my resignation wasn't a snap decision. I've been thinking about it for quite a while.'

'You never mentioned it to anybody.'

'I didn't figure it was anybody's business.'

'It was a lot of people's business. So what made the difference? What pushed you into making the decision? This incident in Rome?'

Decker didn't answer.

Raindrops beaded the windshield.

'See, I told you it was going to rain,' Ben said.

The rain fell heavier, causing a hollow, pelting sound on the Pontiac's roof. Pedestrians put up umbrellas or ran for doorways. The tinted back-seat windows made the darkening streets seem even darker.

'Talk to us about Rome,' Ben said.

'I don't intend to talk to *anybody* about Rome.' Decker strained to keep his breathing steady. 'I assume that's the point of this conversation. You can go back and assure our mutual acquaintance that I'm not indignant enough to share my indignation with anybody – I'm just damned tired. I'm not interested in exposés and causing a commotion. The opposite – all I want is peace and quiet.'

'In Santa Fe, a place you've never been.'

Again Decker didn't answer.

'You know,' Hal said, 'when you mentioned Santa Fe, the first thought that popped into my mind was, there are a lot of top-secret installations in the area – the Sandia weapons testing lab in Albuquerque, the nuclear lab at Los Alamos. The second thought that popped into my head was Edward Lee Howard.'

Decker felt a weight in his chest. Howard had been a CIA operative who sold top-level details about the agency's Moscow operation to the Soviets. After a failed lie-detector test aroused the agency's suspicions, he had been fired. While the FBI investigated him, he had moved to New Mexico, had eluded his surveillance teams, and had managed to escape to the Soviet Union. The city where he had been living was Santa Fe.

'You're suggesting a parallel?' Decker sat straighter. 'You're suggesting I'd do something to hurt my country?' This time, Decker didn't bother trying to control his breathing. 'You tell our mutual acquaintance to reread my file and try to find anything that suggests I suddenly forgot the meaning of honor.'

'People go through changes, as you've been pointing out.'

'And these days most people go through at least three careers.'

'I'm having trouble following you again, Decker.'

'I had my military career. I had my government career. Now it's time for my third.'

'And what's it going to be?'

'I don't know yet. I wouldn't want to make any spur of the moment decisions. Where are you taking me?'

Hal didn't answer.

'I asked you a question,' Decker said.

Hal still didn't answer.

'It better not be the agency's rehabilitation clinic in Virginia,' Decker said.

'Who said anything about Virginia?' Hal seemed to make a choice. 'We're taking you where you *wanted* us to take you – La Guardia.'

4

Decker bought a one-way ticket. During the six-hour flight, which included a stopover in Chicago, he had plenty of time to think about what he was doing. His behavior was bizarre enough that he could understand why his former superiors were troubled. Hell, he himself was troubled by his behavior. His entire professional life had been based on control, but now he had surrendered to whimsy.

Santa Fe's airport was too small for large passenger jets. The nearest major airport was in Albuquerque, and as the American Airlines MD-80 circled for a landing, Decker was appalled by the bleak sunbaked yellow landscape below him, sand and rocks stretching off toward barren mountains. What else did you expect? he told himself. New Mexico's a *desert*.

At least, Albuquerque's compact four-level terminal had charm, its interior decorated with colorful Native American designs. The airport was also remarkably efficient. In a quick ten minutes, Decker had his suitcase and was standing at the Avis counter, renting a Dodge Intrepid. The car's name appealed to him.

'What's the best way to get to Santa Fe?' he asked the young woman behind the counter.

She was Hispanic and had a bright smile that enhanced the expressiveness of her dark eyes. 'That depends on whether you want the quick route or the scenic route.'

'Is the scenic route worth it?'

'Absolutely. If you've got the time.'

'I've got nothing *but* time.'

'Then you've got the right attitude for a New Mexican vacation. Follow this map,' she said. 'Go north a couple of miles on Route 25. Turn east on Interstate 40. After about twenty miles, turn north on the Turquoise Trail.' The clerk used a felt-tip pen to highlight the map. 'Do you like margaritas?'

'Love them.'

'Stop in a town called Madrid.' She emphasized the first syllable as if distinguishing it from the way the capital of Spain was pronounced. 'Thirty years ago, it was almost a ghost town. Now it's an artists' colony. There's a beat-up old place called the Mineshaft Tavern that brags it has the best margaritas in the world.'

'And are they?'

The woman merely flashed her engaging smile and handed him the car keys.

As Decker drove past a metal silhouette of two racehorses outside the airport and followed the clerk's directions, he noticed that Albuquerque's buildings seemed no different from those in any other part of the country. Now and then, he saw a flat-roofed stuccoed structure that looked something like the adobe he had seen on television, but mostly he saw peaked roofs and brick or wood siding. It worried him that the television program might have exaggerated, that Santa Fe would turn out to be like everywhere else.

Interstate 40 led him past a hulking jagged line of mountains.

Then he turned north onto the Turquoise Trail, and things began to change. Isolated log cabins and A-frames now seemed the architectural norm. In a while, there weren't any buildings at all. There was more vegetation – junipers and piñon trees, various types of low-growing cacti, and a sagebrush-like shrub that grew as high as six feet. The narrow road wound around the back side of the mountains that he had seen from Albuquerque. It angled upward, and Decker recalled that a flight attendant on the MD-80 had made a comment to him about Albuquerque's being a mile-high city, five thousand feet above sea level, the same as Denver was, but that Santa Fe was even higher, seven thousand feet, so it was a climb to get there. For the first few days, visitors might feel slow and out of breath, the flight attendant had told him. She had joked that a passenger once asked her if Santa Fe was seven thousand feet above sea level all year round.

Decker didn't notice any physical reaction to the altitude, but that was to be expected. After all, he had been trained to think nothing of high-altitude low-opening parachute jumps that began at twenty thousand feet. What he did notice was how remarkably clear the air had become, how blue the sky, how bright the sun, and he understood why a poster at the airport had called New Mexico the land of the dancing sun. He reached a plateau, and his breath was taken away as he peered to the left and saw a rolling desert vista that seemed to go on for hundreds of miles to the north and south, the western view bordered by far-away mountains that looked higher and broader than those near Albuquerque. The road's gradual climb took him to further sharp curves, at many of which the vistas were even more spectacular. Decker felt as if he was on top of the world.

Madrid, which Decker had to keep reminding himself was pronounced with an accent on the first syllable, was a village of shacks and frame houses, most of which were occupied by what appeared to be survivors of the counterculture in the sixties. The community stretched along a narrow wooded hollow bordered on the right by a slope covered with coal, the reason the town had been founded at the turn of the century. The Mineshaft Tavern, a rickety two-story wooden structure in need of paint, was about the largest building in town and easy to find, directly to the right at the bottom of the curving slope into town.

Decker parked and locked the Intrepid. He studied a group of leather-jacketed motorcyclists going by. They stopped at a house down the road, unstrapped folded-down easels and half-completed paintings on canvases, and carried them into the house. With a grin, Decker climbed the steps to the tavern's enclosed porch. His footsteps caused a hollow rumbling sound beneath him as he opened a squeaky screen door that led him into a miniature version of a turn-of-the-century saloon complete with a stage. Currency from all over the world was tacked to the wall behind the bar.

The shadowy place was half-full and noisy with spirited conversation. Sitting at an empty table, Decker gathered the impression of cowboy hats, tattoos, and beaded necklaces. In contrast with the efficiency of the Albuquerque airport, it took a long time before a ponytailed man wearing an apron and holding a tray ambled over. Don't be impatient, Decker told himself. Think of this as a kind of decompression chamber.

The knees of the waiter's jeans were ripped out.

'Someone told me you've got the best margaritas in the world,' Decker said. 'Surely that isn't true.'

'There's a way to find out.'

'Bring me one.'

'Anything to eat?'

'What do you recommend?'

'At noon, the chicken fajitas. But in the middle of the afternoon? Try the nachos.'

'Done.'

The nachos had Monterey Jack cheese, green salsa, pinto beans, lettuce, tomatoes, and jalapeño peppers. The peppers made Decker's eyes water. He felt in heaven and realized that if he'd eaten this same food two days earlier, his stomach would have been in agony.

The margarita truly was the best he had ever tasted.

'What's the secret?' he asked the waiter.

'An ounce and a quarter of the best tequila, which is one hundred percent blue agave. Three quarters of an ounce of Cointreau. One and a half ounces of freshly squeezed lemon juice. A fresh wedge of lime.'

The drink made Decker's mouth pucker with joy. Salt from the rim of the glass stuck to his lips. He licked it off and ordered another. When he finished that, he would have ordered yet another, except that he didn't know how the alcohol would hit him at this altitude. Driving, he didn't want to injure anyone. Plus, he wanted to be able to find Santa Fe.

After giving the waiter a twenty-five percent tip, Decker went outside, feeling as mellow as he had felt in years. He squinted at the lowering sun, glanced at his diver's watch – almost four-thirty – put on his Ray-Bans, and got into the Intrepid. If anything the air seemed even clearer, the sky bluer, the sun more brilliant. As he drove from town, following the narrow winding road past more juniper and piñon trees and that sagebrush-like plant that he meant to learn the name of, he noticed that the color of the land had changed so that red, orange, and brown joined what had been a predominance of yellow. The vegetation became greener. He reached a high curve that angled down to the left, giving him a view for miles ahead. Before him, distant, at a higher elevation, looking like miniatures in a child's play village, were tiny buildings nestled among foothills behind which rose stunningly beautiful mountains that Decker's map called the Sangre de Cristo range, the Blood of Christ. The sun made the buildings seem golden, as if enchanted; Decker remembered noticing that the motto on New Mexico's license plates was 'the land of enchantment'. The vista, encircled by the green of piñon trees, beckoned, and Decker had no doubt that was where he was headed.

5

Within the city limits (SANTA FE. POPULATION 62,424), he followed a sign that said HISTORIC PLAZA. The busy downtown streets seemed to become more narrow, their pattern like a maze, as if the four-hundred-year-old city had developed haphazardly. Adobe buildings were everywhere, none the same, as if each of them had also been added to haphazardly. While most of the buildings were low, a few were three stories high, their pueblo design reminding him of cliff dwellings – he discovered they were hotels. Even the city's downtown parking garage had a pueblo design. He locked the Intrepid, then strolled up a street that had a long portal above it. At the far end, he saw a cathedral that reminded him of churches in Spain. But before he reached it, the Plaza appeared on the left – rectangular, the size of a small city block, with a lawn, white metal benches, tall sheltering trees, and a Civil War memorial at its center. He noticed a diner called the Plaza Cafe and a restaurant called the Ore House, bunches of dried red peppers dangling from its balcony. In front of a long low ancient-looking adobe building called the Palace of the Governors, native Americans sat against a wall beneath a portal, blankets spread before them on the sidewalk, silver and turquoise jewelry arranged for sale on the blankets.

As Decker slumped on a bench in the Plaza, the mellowing

effect of the margaritas began to wear off. He felt a pang of misgiving and wondered how big a mistake he had made. For the past twenty years, in the military and then working as an intelligence operative, he had been taken care of, his life structured by others. Now, insecurely, he was on his own.

You wanted a new beginning, a part of him said.

But what am I going to do?

A good first step would be to get a room.

And after that?

Try reinventing yourself.

To his annoyance, his professional training insisted – he couldn't help checking for surveillance as he crossed the Plaza toward a hotel called La Fonda. Its decades-old Hispanic-influenced lobby had warm dark soothing tones, but his instincts distracted him, nagging at him to ignore his surroundings and concentrate on the people around him. After getting a room, he again checked for surveillance as he walked back to the city's parking garage.

This has got to stop, he told himself. I don't have to live this way anymore.

A man with a salt-and-pepper beard, wearing khakis and a blue summer sweater oversized enough to conceal a handgun, followed him into the parking ramp. Decker paused next to the Intrepid, took out his car keys, and prepared to use them as a weapon, exhaling as the man got in a Range Rover and drove away.

This has got to stop, Decker repeated to himself.

He purposefully didn't check behind him as he drove to the La Fonda's parking garage and carried his suitcase up to his room. He deliberately ate dinner with his back to the dining-room entrance. He resolutely took a random night-time stroll through the downtown area, choosing rather than avoiding poorly lit areas.

71

In a wooded minipark next to a deep concrete channel through which a stream flowed, a figure emerged from shadows. 'Give me your wallet.'

Decker was dumbfounded.

'I've got a gun. I said, give me your fucking wallet.'

Decker stared at the street kid, who was barely visible. Then he couldn't help himself. He started laughing.

'What's so fucking funny?'

'You're holding me up? You've got to be kidding me. After all I've been through, after I force myself to be careless.'

'You won't think it's so fucking funny when I put a fucking bullet through you.'

'Okay, okay, I deserve this.' Decker pulled out his wallet and reached inside it. 'Here's all the money I've got.'

'I said I wanted your fucking wallet, not just your money.'

'Don't push your luck. I can spare the money, but I need my driver's license and my credit card.'

'Tough fucking shit. *Give it to me.*'

Decker broke both his arms, pocketed the gun, and threw the kid over the channel's rim. Hearing branches snap as if the kid had landed in bushes next to the stream, Decker leaned over the edge and heard him groan in the darkness below. 'You swear too much.'

He made a mental note of the nearest street names, found a payphone, told the 911 dispatcher where to send an ambulance, dropped the pistol into a sewer, and walked back to the La Fonda. At the hotel's bar, he sipped cognac as a countermeasure to adrenaline. A sign on the wall caught his attention.

'Is that a joke?' he asked the bartender. 'It's against the law to wear firearms in here?'

'A bar is about the only place where firearms *can't* be worn in New Mexico,' the bartender answered. 'You can walk down the street with one, as long as it's in plain sight.'

'Well, I'll be damned.'

72

'Of course, a lot of people don't follow the law. I just assume they're carrying a concealed weapon.'

'I'll be double damned,' Decker said.

'And everybody I know keeps one in their car.'

Decker stared at him as dumbfounded as when the kid in the minipark had tried to hold him up. 'Looks like there's something to be said for taking precautions.'

6

'The Frontiersman is a Christian gun shop,' the clerk said.

The statement caught Decker by surprise. 'Really,' was all he managed to say.

'We believe that Jesus expects us to be responsible for our own safety.'

'I think Jesus is right.' Decker glanced around at the racks of shotguns and rifles. His gaze settled on pistols in a locked glass counter. The store smelled sweetly of gun oil. 'I had in mind a Walther .380.'

'Can't do it. All out of stock.'

'Then how about a Sig-Sauer .928?'

'An excellent firearm,' the clerk said. He wore sneakers, jeans, a red plaid work shirt, and a Colt .45 semiautomatic on his belt. Stocky, in his mid-thirties, he had a sunburn. 'When the US military adopted the Beretta 9mm as its standard sidearm, the brass decided a smaller sidearm would be useful as a concealed weapon for intelligence personnel.'

'Really,' Decker said again.

The clerk unlocked the glass case, opened the lid, and took out a pistol the size of Decker's hand. 'It takes the same ammunition the Beretta does, 9mm. Holds a little less, thirteen in the magazine, one in the chamber. Double action, so you don't have to cock it to shoot it – all you have to do is pull the trigger. But if the hammer *is* cocked and you decide not to fire, you can lower the hammer safely with this decocking lever on the side. Extremely well made. A first-rate weapon.'

The clerk removed the magazine and pulled back the slide on top, demonstrating that the pistol was empty. Only then did he hand it to Decker, who put the empty magazine back into the grip and pretended to aim at a poster of Saddam Hussein.

'You've certainly sold me,' Decker said.

'List price is nine hundred and fifty. I'll let you have it for eight hundred.'

Decker put his credit card on the counter.

'I'm sorry about this,' the clerk said, 'but Big Brother is watching. You can't have the pistol until you fill out this form and the police check you out to make sure you're not a terrorist or public enemy number one. More paperwork, thanks to the federal government. Costs you ten dollars.'

Decker looked at the form, which asked him if he was an illegal alien, a drug addict, and/or a felon. Did whoever designed the form actually believe that anyone would answer 'yes' to those questions? he wondered.

'How soon can I pick up the pistol?'

'The law says five days. Here's a reprint of a George Will article about the right to bear arms.'

Stapled to the article was a quotation from scripture, and that's when Decker realized how truly different the City Different was.

Outside, he basked in the morning sunlight, admiring the Sangre de Cristo mountains that rose dramatically just outside the eastern side of town. He still had trouble believing that he had come to Santa Fe. In his entire life, he had never been this impetuous.

As he drove away, he reviewed his active morning and the various arrangements he had made: opening a bank account, transferring money from the institution he had used in Virginia, contacting the local branch of the national stock-brokerage firm he used, phoning his landlord in Alexandria and agreeing to pay a penalty for breaking his lease in exchange for the landlord's agreeing to pack up and forward Decker's modest belongings. His numerous decisions had exhausted him and made the reality of his presence in Santa Fe increasingly vivid. The more arrangements he made, the more he committed himself to staying. And there were so many other decisions to make. He needed to turn in his rental car and buy a vehicle. He needed to find a place to live. He needed to figure out a way to employ himself.

On the car radio, he heard a report on public broadcasting's 'Morning Edition' about a trend among middle-aged mid-level corporate executives to abandon their high-pressure jobs (before their corporations downsized and eliminated their positions) and move to the western mountain states, where they started their own businesses and survived by their wits, finding that the adventure of working for themselves was exciting and fulfilling. The announcer called them 'lone eagles'.

At the moment, Decker felt alone, all right. The next thing I'd better do is find an alternative to a hotel room, he told himself. Rent an apartment? Buy a condo? How committed *am* I? What's a good deal? Do I simply check the listings in the newspaper? In confusion, he noticed a realtor's sign in front of one of the adobe houses on the wooded street he was driving along, and he suddenly knew he had an answer to more than just the question of where to set up housekeeping.

7

'A fixer-upper,' the woman said. She was in her late fifties, with short gray hair, a narrow sunwrinkled face, and plentiful turquoise jewelry. Her name was Edna Freed, and she was the owner of the agency whose sign Decker had noticed. This was the fourth property she had shown him. 'It's been on the market for over a year. An estate sale. Nobody lives here. The taxes, insurance, and maintenance fees are a nuisance to the estate. I'm authorized to say they're willing to accept less than their asking price.'

'What *is* the asking price?' Decker asked.

'Six hundred and thirty-five thousand.'

Decker raised his eyebrows. 'You weren't kidding when you told me this was a pricy market.'

'And getting pricier each year.' Edna explained that what was happening to Santa Fe had happened to Aspen, Colorado, twenty years earlier. Well-to-do tourists had gone to Aspen, fallen in love with that picturesque mountain community, and decided to buy property there, driving up values, squeezing out locals who had to move to housing they could afford only in other towns. Santa Fe was becoming equally expensive, mostly because of affluent newcomers from New York, Texas, and California.

'A house I sold last year for three hundred thousand came on the market again nine months later and went for three hundred and sixty,' Edna said. She wore a Stetson and wraparound sunglasses. 'As Santa Fe houses go, it was ordinary. It wasn't even adobe construction. All the contractor did was fix up a frame house and apply new stucco.'

'And this *is* adobe?'

'You bet.' Edna led him from her BMW, following a gravel lane to a high metal gate between equally high stuccoed walls. The gate had silhouettes of Indian petroglyphs. Beyond it were a courtyard and a portal. 'The place is incredibly solid. Knock on this wall next to the front door.'

Decker did. The impact of his knuckles made him feel as if

he tapped stone. He studied the house's exterior. 'I see some dry rot in the columns that support this portal.'

'You've got a good eye.'

'The courtyard's overgrown. Its inside wall needs restuccoing. But those repairs don't seem to justify your calling this a fixer-upper,' Decker said. 'What's the real problem? The place is on two acres in what you tell me is a desirable area, the museum district. It has views in every direction. It's attractive. Why hasn't it sold?'

Edna hesitated. 'Because it isn't one big house. It's two small houses joined by a common wall.'

'What?'

'To get from one structure to the other, you have to go outside and in through another door.'

'Who the hell would want that inconvenience?'

Edna didn't have an answer.

'Let's see the rest of it.'

'Despite the layout, you mean you might still be interested?'

'I have to check something out first. Show me the laundry room.'

Puzzled, Edna took him inside. The laundry room was off the garage. A hatch led to a crawlspace under the house. When Decker emerged from below, he swatted dust from his clothes, feeling satisfied. 'The electrical system looks about ten years old, the copper pipes a little more recent, both in good shape.'

'You *do* have a good eye,' Edna said. 'And you know where to look first.'

'There's no point in redesigning the place if the infrastructure needs work, too.'

'Redesigning?' Now Edna was even more baffled.

'The way the property is laid out, the garage is between the adjoining houses. But it's possible to convert the garage into a room, put a corridor in the back of that room, and knock out part of the common wall, so the corridor leads into the other house, unifying both halves.'

'Well, I'll be . . .' Edna glanced at the garage. 'I never noticed.'

Decker debated with himself. He hadn't planned on a house this expensive. He thought about his three hundred thousand dollars in savings, about the down payment and the mortgage payments and whether he wanted to be house poor. At the same time, the investment possibilities intrigued him. 'I'll offer six hundred thousand.'

'Less than the asking price? For this valuable property?'

'For what I believe you called a fixer-upper. Or did my suggestion suddenly make the house more appealing?'

'To the right kind of buyer.' Edna took a good look at him. 'Why do I get the idea you've done a lot of negotiating for property?'

'I used to be an international real-estate investment consultant.' Decker gave her a business card that the CIA had supplied him. 'The Rawley-Hackman Agency, based in Alexandria, Virginia. They're not Sotheby's International, but they handle a lot of special properties. My expertise was finding properties that had more value than they appeared to have.'

'Such as *this* one,' Edna said.

Decker shrugged. 'My problem is, six hundred thousand is absolutely as much as I can afford.'

'I'll make that point to my client.'

'Emphasize it, please. The standard twenty percent down payment is a hundred and twenty thousand. At the current rate of eight percent, a thirty-year mortgage on the remainder is . . .'

'I'll have to get my rate book from the car.'

'No need. I can do the math.' Decker scribbled on a notepad. 'About thirty-five hundred a month. A little more than forty-two thousand a year.'

'I've never seen anybody that quick with numbers.'

Decker shrugged again. 'One other problem – I can't afford the house if I don't have a job.'

'Such as selling real estate?' Edna burst out laughing. 'You've been trying to sell *me*.'

'Maybe a little.'

'I like your style.' Edna grinned. 'If you can sell me, you can sell anybody. You want a job, you've got one. The thing is, how are you going to afford the renovation?'

'That's easy. Cheap labor.'

'Where on earth do you hope to find that?'

Decker held out his hands. 'Right here.'

8

While serving in military special operations and later as a civilian intelligence operative, Decker had experienced fear on numerous occasions – missions that had gone wrong, threats that could not have been anticipated – but nothing matched the terror with which he woke in the middle of the ensuing night. His heart pounded sickeningly. Sweat stuck his T-shirt and boxer shorts to him. For a moment, he was disoriented, the darkness smothering. This wasn't his room in the La Fonda. Immediately he reminded himself that he had moved to a rental unit that Edna was managing. It was even smaller than the apartment he had given up in Alexandria, but at least it was cheaper than the La Fonda, and economizing was an urgent priority.

His mouth was dry. He couldn't find a light switch. He bumped his hip against a table as he groped his way to the sink in the tiny bathroom. He needed several glasses of water to satisfy his demanding thirst. He felt his way toward the single room's window and opened the twig shutters. Instead of a majestic view, he saw moonlight gleaming on cars in a parking lot.

What the hell have I done? he asked himself, beginning to sweat again. I've never owned anything big in my life. And I just signed papers committing myself to buying a six-hundred-thousand-dollar house that's going to cost me a hundred and twenty thousand down and forty-two thousand a year in mortgage payments. *Have I gone crazy?* What's the agency going to think when they hear I'm investing in serious real estate? They're going to wonder what makes me believe I can afford it. The truth is, I *can't* afford it, but *they* won't know that.

Decker couldn't help thinking of a recent scandal that involved an operative named Aldrich Ames who had passed secrets about the agency's Moscow network to the Russians in exchange for two and a half million dollars. The results had been disastrous – operations destroyed, agents executed. It had taken years before the agency's counterintelligence unit suspected a double agent and finally focused its attention on Ames. To the agency's horror, the counterintelligence team discovered that, as a part of a standard review, Ames had nearly failed two lie detector tests but that the results had been described as ambiguous and a judgment made in his favor. Further, the team learned that Ames had made extraordinary investments in real estate – several vacation homes and a ten-thousand-acre ranch in South America – and that he had hundreds of thousands of dollars in various bank accounts. Where on earth had the money come from? Not long afterward, Ames and his wife had been arrested for espionage. The agency, which had become lax about keeping an eye on the personal lives of its operatives, adopted new stringent security measures.

And I'm going to be the target of some of those measures, Decker warned himself. I'm already being watched because of my attitude when I quit. The papers I signed today are going to set off alarms. I have to call Langley first thing in the morning. I have to explain what I'm doing.

That'll be a trick. Just what *am* I doing? Decker touched a chair behind him and sank into it. The darkness pressed harder against him. The purchase agreement I signed has an escape clause, he reminded himself. When the house is inspected tomorrow, I'll use a flaw the inspector comes up with as an excuse to back out.

Right. I was too ambitious. Caution – that's the ticket. Slow and careful. Avoid doing anything out of the ordinary. Put the brakes on. Have numerous back-up plans. Don't be dramatic. I mustn't let my emotions get control of me.

For God's sake, he told himself, that's the way I've been living for the past ten years. I just described my life as an operative. He slammed his hand against the side of the chair. I dealt with fear before. What have I got to lose?

The chance to live.

Three weeks later, he took possession of the house.

9

Santa Fe was Julian's, El Nido, the Zia Diner, Pasqual's, Tomasita's, and countless other wonderful restaurants. It was margaritas, nachos, and red and green salsa. It was spectacular mornings, brilliant afternoons, and gorgeous evenings. It was ever-changing sunlight and constantly shifting high-desert colors. It was mountains in every direction. It was air so clean that there were views for hundreds of miles. It was landscapes that looked like Georgia O'Keefe paintings. It was the Plaza. It was the art galleries on Canyon Road. It was Spanish Market and Indian Market. It was Fiesta. It was watching the aspen turn autumn yellow in the ski basin. It was snow that made the city look like a Christmas card. It was candles stuck in sand in paper bags, lining the Plaza to illuminate it on Christmas Eve. It was glorious wild flowers in the spring. It was more hummingbirds than he had ever seen. It was the gentle rain that fell late every afternoon in July. It was the feel of the sun on his back, of sweat and the healthy ache of his muscles as he worked on his house.

It was peace.

THREE

1

'Steve, you're on floor duty today, right?' Edna asked.

In his office, Decker looked up from a buyer's offer that he was preparing for one of his clients. 'Until noon.' All the brokers in the agency were normally so busy showing properties that they seldom came into the office, but Edna insisted that someone always be available for walk-in clients and telephone inquiries, so each broker was required to spend a half-day every two weeks on 'floor duty'.

'Well, someone's in the lobby, looking for an agent,' Edna said. 'I'd handle it, but I have to get over to Santa Fe Abstract for a closing in fifteen minutes.'

'No problem. I'll take care of it.' Decker put the buyer's offer into a folder, stood, and headed toward the lobby. It was July, thirteen months after he had come to Santa Fe, and any doubts that he'd had about his ability to support himself had quickly vanished. Although some of Santa Fe's realtors failed and dropped out each year, he himself had done well. Techniques of elicitation that he had used to gain the confidence of operatives he was debriefing turned out to have application to making clients feel at ease. He was now up to four million dollars in sales, which provided a six percent commission of two hundred and forty thousand dollars. Of course, he had to split half of that with Edna, who provided office facilities, advertisements, and the nuisance details of running a business, not to mention an organization for Decker to disappear into. Even so, one hundred and twenty thousand was more than he had ever earned in one year in his life.

He came around a corner, approached the front desk, and saw a woman standing next to it, looking at a color brochure of available homes. With her head bowed, Decker couldn't see her features, but as he approached, he took in her lush auburn hair, tanned skin, and slim figure. She was taller than most women, about five foot seven, in excellent shape. Her outfit was distinctly East Coast: a nicely fitted, dark-navy Calvin Klein suit; smartly cut, low-heeled Joan & David shoes; pearl earrings; and a woven, Italian-leather black bag.

'May I help you?' Decker asked. 'You'd like to speak to an agent?'

The woman glanced up from the brochure. 'Yes.'

She smiled, and Decker felt something shift inside him. He didn't have time to analyze the sensation, except to compare it to the sudden change in heart rhythm, almost a lurch, that came during moments of fear. In this case, though, the sensation was definitely the opposite of fear.

The woman – in her early thirties – was gorgeous. Her skin glowed with health. Her blue-gray eyes glinted with intelligence and something else that was hard to identify, something appealingly enigmatic. She had a symmetrical face that was a perfect combination of a sculpted jaw, high cheekbones, and a model's forehead. Her smile was radiant.

Although Decker's lungs didn't want to work, he managed to introduce himself. 'Steve Decker. I'm an associate broker with the firm.'

The woman shook hands with him. 'Beth Dwyer.'

Her fingers felt so wonderfully smooth that Decker didn't want to release her hand. 'My office is just around the corner.'

As he led the way, he had a chance to try to adjust to the

pleasant tightness in his chest. There are certainly worse ways to earn a living, he thought.

The offices in the agency were spacious cubicles, their six-foot-high partitions constructed to look like adobe walls. Beth cast a curious gaze toward the tops of the partitions, which were decorated with gleaming black pottery and intricately patterned baskets from the local Indian pueblos.

'Those window seats that look like plaster benches – what are they called? *Bancos?*' Her voice was deep and resonant.

'That's right. *Bancos*,' Decker said. 'Most of the architectural terms here are Spanish. Can I get you anything? Coffee? Mineral water?'

'No, thanks.'

Beth peered around with interest at a Native American rug and other Southwestern decorations. She paid particular attention to some New Mexican landscape prints, walking over, leaning close to them. 'Beautiful.'

'The one that shows the white-water rapids in the Rio Grande gorge is my favorite,' Decker said. 'But just about any outdoor scene around here is beautiful.'

'I like the one *you* like.' Behind her attempt at good humor lurked a puzzling hint of melancholy. 'Even in a print, the delicacy of the brush strokes is obvious.'

'Oh? Then you know about painting?'

'I've spent most of my life trying to learn, but I'm not sure I ever will.'

'Well, if you're an artist, Santa Fe is a good place to be.'

'I could tell there was something about the light the moment I got here.' Beth shook her head in self-deprecation. 'But I don't think of myself as an artist. "Working painter" would be a more accurate description.'

'When did you get here?'

'Yesterday.'

'Since you want to buy property, I assume you've been here before, though.'

'Never.'

Decker felt as if a spark had struck him. He tried not to show a reaction, but reminded of his own experience in coming here, he found himself sitting straighter. 'And after a day, you've decided you like the area enough that you're interested in buying property here?'

'More than interested. Crazy, huh?'

'I wouldn't call it that.' Decker glanced down at his hands. 'I've known a few other people who decided to live here on the spur of the moment.' He looked at her again and smiled. 'Santa Fe makes people do unusual things.'

'That's why I want to live here.'

'Believe me, I understand. Even so, I wouldn't feel I was doing my job if I didn't caution you to take things slowly. Look at some properties, but give yourself a breathing space before you sign any documents.'

Beth crinkled her eyes, curious. 'I never expected to hear a real estate broker tell me *not* to buy something.'

'I'd be glad to sell you a house,' Decker said, 'but since this is your first time here, it might be better if you rented something first, to make certain Santa Fe is really the place for you. Some people move here from Los Angeles, and they can't stand the leisurely pace. They want to change the town so it matches their nervous energy.'

'Well, I'm not from Los Angeles,' Beth said, 'and the way my life has been going lately, a leisurely pace sounds mighty tempting.'

Decker assessed what she had just revealed about herself. He decided to wait before trying to learn anything else.

'A soft-sell realtor,' Beth said. 'I like that.'

'I call myself a facilitator. I'm not trying to sell property as much as I'm trying to make my client happy. A year down the road, I want you to have no regrets about whatever you decide to do, whether it's buying or not buying.'

'Then I'm in good hands.' Her blue-gray eyes – Decker had never seen eyes that color – brightened. 'I'd like to start looking as soon as possible.'

'I have appointments until two. Is that soon enough?'

'No instant gratification?' She laughed a little. The sound reminded Decker of wind chimes, although he sensed a pensiveness behind it. 'I guess two o'clock it will have to be.'

'In the meantime, if you can give me an idea of your price range— How do you like to be called? Mrs Dwyer? Or Beth? Or . . . ?' Decker glanced at her left hand. He didn't see a wedding ring. But that didn't always mean anything.

'I'm not married.'

Decker nodded.

'Call me by my first name.'

Decker nodded again. 'Fine, Beth.' His throat felt tight.

'And my price range is between six and eight hundred thousand.'

Decker inwardly came to attention, not having expected so high a figure. Normally, when potential clients came in to discuss houses in the upper six figures, they brought an attitude with them, as if they were doing Decker a big favor. In contrast, Beth was refreshingly natural, unassuming.

'Several first-rate properties are available in that price range,' Decker said. 'Between now and two, why don't you study these listings? There are prices and descriptions.' He decided to fish for more information about her. 'You'll probably want to discuss them with anyone who came to town with you. If you like, when we go out looking, bring a friend along.'

'No. It'll be just the two of us.'

Decker nodded. 'Either way is fine.'

Beth hesitated. 'I'm by myself.'

'Well, Santa Fe is a good town to be alone in without being lonely.'

Beth seemed to look at something far away. 'That's what I'm counting on.'

2

After Decker escorted Beth to the exit from the building, he remained at the open door and watched her stroll along the portal-roofed sidewalk. She had a grace that reminded him of the way female athletes moved when they weren't exerting themselves. Before she reached the corner, he made sure to step back inside the building in case she looked his way as she shifted direction. After all, he didn't want her to know that he was staring at her. In response to a question, he had told her that a good place to eat lunch was La Casa Sena, a restaurant that had outdoor tables beneath majestic shade trees in the gardened courtyard of a two-story Hispanic estate that dated back to the 1860s. She would enjoy the birds, the flowers, and the fountain, he had said, and now he wished that he was going there with her instead of heading off to deliver the buyer's offer that he had been working on when Beth arrived.

Normally, the chance to make another sale would have totally occupied Decker's thoughts, giving him a high. But today, business didn't seem that important. After presenting the offer and being told, as expected, that the seller needed the time allowed in the offer to consider it, Decker had a further appointment – lunch with a member of Santa Fe's Historic Design Review Board. Barely tasting his chicken fajitas, he managed to keep up his end of the conversation, but really, he was thinking of Beth Dwyer, their appointment at two, and how slowly the time was going.

Why, I'm missing her, he thought in surprise.

At last, after paying for lunch, he returned to the agency, only to feel his emotions drop when he found that Beth wasn't waiting for him.

'The woman who came in to see me this morning,' he told the receptionist. 'Thick auburn hair. Slightly tall. Attractive. Has she been back?'

'Sorry, Steve.'

Disappointed, he went down the corridor. Maybe she came in when the receptionist wasn't looking, he thought. Maybe she's waiting for me in my office.

But she wasn't. His emotions dropping farther as he sank into the chair behind his desk, he asked himself, What's the matter with me? Why am I letting myself feel this way?

Movement attracted his attention. Beth was standing at the entrance to his office. 'Hi.' Her smile made him feel that she had missed *him*.

Decker's heart seemed to shrink. So much like fear, he thought again, yet so much the opposite.

'I hope I'm not late,' she said.

'Right on time.' Decker hoped that he sounded natural. 'Did you have a good lunch?'

'It was even better than you led me to expect. The courtyard made me think I was in another country.'

'That's what Santa Fe does to people.'

'Northern Spain or a lush part of Mexico,' Beth said. 'But different from either.'

Decker nodded. 'When I first came here, I met someone who worked in the reservation department at one of the hotels. He said he often had people from the East Coast telephone him to ask what the customs restrictions were, the limit on duty-free goods that they could take back home, that sort of thing. He said he had a hard time convincing them that if they were Americans, there weren't any customs regulations here, that New Mexico was part of the United States.'

This time, Beth's laughter made him think of champagne. 'You're serious? They literally believed that this was a foreign country?'

'Cross my heart. It's a good argument for the need to teach geography in high school. So did you have a chance to study the listings I gave you?'

'When I wasn't devouring the best enchiladas I've ever tasted. I can't tell which I like better – the green or the red salsa. Finally I combined them.'

'The locals call that combination "Christmas".' Decker put on his leather jacket and crossed the room toward her. He loved the subtle fragrance of the sandalwood soap she used. 'Shall we go? My car is in the back.'

It was a Jeep Cherokee, its four-wheel-drive essential in winter or when exploring the mountains. Decker's color preference had been white, but when he'd bought the car a year earlier, his long experience as an intelligence operative had taken control of him, reminding him that a dark color was inconspicuous, compelling him to choose forest green. A part of him had wanted to be contrary and choose white anyhow, but old habits had been difficult to put away.

As he and Beth drove north along Bishop's Lodge Road, he pointed to the right past low shrubs and sunbathed adobe houses toward the looming Sangre de Cristo mountains. 'The first thing you have to know is, real estate values here are based in large part on the quality of the mountain views. Some of the most expensive houses tend to be in this area, the east, near the Sangres. This section also gives you a good view of the Jemez mountains to the west. At night, you can see the lights of Los Alamos.'

Beth gazed toward the foothills. 'I bet the views from there are wonderful.'

'This will make me sound like a New Ager, I'm afraid, but I don't think houses belong up there,' Decker said. 'They interfere with the beauty of the mountains. The people who live up there get a good view at the expense of everyone else's view.'

Intrigued, Beth switched her gaze toward Decker. 'You mean you actually discourage clients from buying houses on ridges?'

Decker shrugged.

'Even if it costs you a sale?'

Decker shrugged again.

' . . . I'm beginning to like you better and better.'

Decker drove her to houses she had found appealing in the listings he had shown her: one near Bishop's Lodge, two on the road to the ski basin, two along Acequia Madre. 'The name means Mother Ditch,' he explained. 'It refers to this stream that runs along the side of the road. It's part of an irrigation system that was dug several hundred years ago.'

'That's why the trees are so tall.' Beth looked around, enthused. 'The area's beautiful. What's the catch, though? Nothing's perfect. What's the downside of living around here?'

'Small lots and historic regulations. Plenty of traffic.'

'Oh.' Her enthusiasm faded. 'In that case, I guess we'd better keep looking.'

'It's almost five. Are you sure you're not tired? Do you want to call it a day?'

'I'm not tired if you're not.'

Hell, Decker thought, I'll drive around with you until midnight if you want me to.

He took her to a different area. 'This one's out near where I live. On the eastern edge of town, near that line of foothills. The nearest big hills are called Sun and Moon. You ought to hear the coyotes howl on them at night.'

'I'd like that.'

'This is *my* street.'

Beth pointed toward a sign on the corner. 'Camino Lindo. What's the translation?'

' "Beautiful road".'

'It certainly is. The houses blend with the landscape. Big lots.'

'That's my place coming up on the right.'

Beth leaned forward, turning her head as they passed it.

'I'm impressed.'

'Thanks.'

'And envious. Too bad *your* house isn't for sale.'

'Well, I put a lot of work into it. Mind you, the house just beyond mine *is* for sale.'

3

They walked along a gravel driveway past the chest-high sagebrush-like plants that Decker had been intrigued by when he first came to Santa Fe, and that he had learned were called chamisa. The attractive house was similar to Decker's – a sprawling, one-story adobe with a wall-enclosed courtyard.

'How much is it?' Beth asked.

'Near your upper limit. Seven hundred thousand.' Decker didn't get a reaction. 'It's had a lot of improvements. Sub-floor radiant heating. Solar-gain windows in back.'

Beth nodded absently as if the price didn't need to be justified. 'How big is the lot?'

'The same as mine. Two acres.'

She glanced to one side and then the other. 'I can't even see the neighbors.'

'Which in this case would be me.'

She looked at him strangely.

'What's the matter?' Decker asked.

'I think I'd enjoy living next to you.'

Decker felt his face turn red.

'Do you think the owner would mind being interrupted at this hour?'

'Not at all. The old gentleman who lived here had a heart attack. He moved back to Boston where he has relatives. He wants a quick sale.'

Decker showed her the front courtyard, its desert flowers and shrubs looking stressed from the July heat. He unlocked the carved front door, entered a cool vestibule, and gestured toward a hallway that led straight ahead toward spacious rooms. 'The house is still furnished. Tile floors. Vigas and latillas in all the ceilings.'

'Vigas and . . . ?'

'Large beams and small intersecting ones. It's the preferred type of ceiling in Santa Fe. Plenty of *bancos* and kiva fireplaces. Colorful Mexican wall tiles in the three bathrooms. A spacious kitchen. Food-prep island with a sink. Convection oven. Skylights and—' Decker stopped when he realized that Beth wasn't listening. She seemed spellbound by the mountain view from the living-room windows. 'Why don't I spare you the list? Take your time and look around.'

Beth walked slowly forward, glancing this way and that, assessing each room, nodding. As Decker followed, he felt selfconscious again – not awkward, not uneasy about himself, but literally conscious of himself, of the feel of his jeans and leather jacket, of the air against his hands and cheeks. He was conscious that he occupied space, that Beth was near him, that they were alone.

At once he realized that Beth was talking to him. 'What? I'm sorry. I didn't catch that,' Decker said. 'My mind drifted for a moment.'

'Does the purchase price include the furniture?'

'Yes.'
'I'll take it.'

4

Decker clicked glasses with her.

'It's such a wonderful house. I can't believe the owner accepted my offer so fast.' Beth took a celebratory swallow from her margarita. When she lowered the globe-shaped glass, some foam and salt remained on her upper lip. She licked them away. 'It's as if I'm dreaming.'

They were at a window table in a second-floor Hispanic restaurant called Garduño's. The place was decorated to look like a Spanish hacienda. In the background, a mariachi band strolled the floor, serenading enthusiastic customers. Beth didn't seem to know where to look first, out the window toward one of Santa Fe's scenic streets, at the band, at her drink, or at Decker. She took another sip. 'Dreaming.'

In the background, customers applauded for the guitarists and trumpeters. Beth smiled and glanced out the window. When she looked back at Decker, she wasn't smiling any longer. Her expression was somber. 'Thank you.'

'I didn't do much. All I did was take you around and—'

'You made me feel comfortable. You made it easy.' Beth surprised him by reaching across the table and touching his hand. 'You have no idea how much courage it took to do this.'

He loved the smoothness of her hand. 'Courage?'

'You must have wondered where I got seven hundred thousand dollars to pay for the house.'

'I don't pry. As long as I'm confident that the client can afford it . . .' He let his sentence dangle.

'I told you I was an artist, and I do make a living at it.

But— I also told you I wasn't married.'

Decker tensed.

'I used to be.'

Decker listened in confusion.

'I'm buying the house with . . .'

Money from a divorce settlement? he wondered.

' . . . a life insurance policy,' Beth said. 'My husband died six and a half months ago.'

Decker set down his glass and studied her, his feelings of attraction replaced by those of pity. 'I'm sorry.'

'That's about the only response that means anything.'

'What happened?'

'Cancer.' Beth seemed to have trouble making her voice work. She took another sip from her drink and stared at the glass. 'Ray had a mole on the back of his neck.'

Decker waited.

'Last summer, it changed shape and color, but he wouldn't go to the doctor. Then it started to bleed. Turned out to be the worst kind of skin cancer. Melanoma.'

Decker kept waiting.

Beth's voice became strained. 'Even though Ray had the mole cut out, he didn't do it soon enough to stop the cancer from spreading . . . Radiation and chemotherapy didn't work . . . He died in January.'

The mariachi band approached Decker's table, the music so loud that he could barely hear what Beth said. Urgent, he waved them away. When they saw the fierce expression in his eyes, they complied.

'So,' Beth said, 'I was lost. Still am. We had a house outside New York, in Westchester County. I couldn't stand living there any longer. Everything around me reminded me of Ray, of what I'd lost. People I thought were my friends felt awkward dealing with my grief and stayed away. I didn't think I could get more lonely.' She glanced down at her hands. 'A few days ago, I was at my psychiatrist's office when I came across a travel magazine in the waiting room. I think it was *Condé Nast Traveler*. It said that Santa Fe was one of the most popular tourist destinations in the world. I liked the photographs and the description of the city. On the spur of the moment . . .' Her voice trailed off.

A colorfully dressed waitress stopped at their table. 'Are you ready to order now?'

'No,' Beth said. 'I'm afraid I've lost my appetite.'

'We need more time,' Decker said.

He waited until the waitress was out of earshot. 'I've made some spur of the moment decisions myself. As a matter of fact, coming to Santa Fe was one of them.'

'And did it work out?'

'Even better than I hoped.'

'God, I hope I'll be able to say the same for me.' Beth traced a finger along the base of her glass.

'What did your psychiatrist say about your sudden decision?'

'I never told him. I never kept the appointment. I just set down the travel magazine and went home to pack. I bought a one-way ticket to Santa Fe.'

Decker tried not to stare, struck by how parallel their experiences were.

'No regrets,' Beth said firmly. 'The future can't possibly be any worse than the last year.'

5

Decker parked his Jeep Cherokee in a carport at the rear of his house. He got out, almost turned on a light so he could see to unlock his back door, but decided instead to lean against the metal railing and look up at the stars. The streets in this part of town didn't have lights. Most people in the area went to sleep early. With almost no light pollution, he was able to gaze up past the piñon trees toward unbelievably brilliant constellations. A three-quarter moon had begun to rise. The air was sweet and cool. What a beautiful night, he thought.

In the foothills, coyotes howled, reminding him that he had earlier mentioned them to Beth, making him wish that she were next to him listening to them. He could still feel her hand on his. During their dinner, they had managed to avoid further depressing topics. Beth had made a deliberate attempt to be festive as he walked her the short distance to the Inn of the Anasazi. At the entrance, they had shaken hands.

Now, as Decker continued to gaze up at the stars, he imagined what it would have been like to drive her from the restaurant, past the darkened art galleries on Canyon Road, past the garden walls of the homes along Camino del Monte Sol, finally arriving at Camino Lindo and the house next to his.

His chest felt hollow. You certainly are messed up, he told himself.

Well, I haven't fallen in love for a very long time. He searched his memory and was amazed to realize that the last time he had felt this way had been in his late teens before he entered the military. As he'd often told himself, military special operations and his subsequent career as an intelligence operative hadn't encouraged serious romantic involvement. Since coming to Santa Fe, he had met several women whom he had dated – nothing serious, just casual enjoyable evenings. With one of the women, he had had sexual relations. Nothing permanent had come out of it, however. As much as he liked the woman, he realized that he didn't want to spend the rest of his life with her. The feeling had evidently been mutual. The woman, a realtor for another agency, was now seeing someone else.

But Decker's present emotions were so different from what

he had felt toward that other woman that they unsettled him. He recalled having read that ancient philosophers considered love to be an illness, an unbalancing of mind and emotions. It sure is, he thought. But how on earth can it happen so fast? I always believed that love at first sight was a myth. He recalled having read about a subtle sexual chemical signal that animals and humans gave off, called pheromones. You couldn't smell them. They were detected biologically rather than consciously. The right person could give off pheromones that drove a person wild. In this case, Decker thought, the right person is absolutely beautiful, and she definitely has my kind of pheromones.

So what are you going to do? he asked himself. Obviously, there are problems. She's recently widowed. If you start behaving romantically toward her, she'll find you threatening. She'll resent you for trying to make her disloyal to the memory of her dead husband. Then it won't matter if she lives next door – she'll treat you as if she's living in the next state. Take it one day at a time, he told himself. You can't go wrong if you act truly as her friend.

6

'Steve, there's someone to see you,' the office receptionist said on the intercom.

'I'll be right out.'

'No need,' another voice said on the intercom, surprising him – a woman's voice whose sensuous resonance Decker instantly identified. 'I know the way.'

Heart beating faster, Decker stood. A few seconds later, Beth entered the office. In contrast with the dark suit she had worn yesterday, she now wore linen slacks and a matching tan jacket that brought out the color of her auburn hair. She looked even more gorgeous.

'How are you?' Decker asked.

'Excited. It's moving day.'

Decker didn't know what she meant.

'Last night, I decided I couldn't wait to move in,' Beth said. 'The house is already furnished. It seems a shame to leave it empty. So I telephoned the owner and asked if I could rent the house until the paperwork was done and I could buy it.'

'And he agreed?'

'He couldn't have been nicer. He said I could get the key from you.'

'You most certainly can. In fact, I'll drive you there.'

On the busy street outside his office, Decker opened his Cherokee's passenger door for her.

'I tossed and turned all night, wondering if I was doing the right thing,' Beth said.

'Sounds like me when *I* first came to town.'

'And how did you get over it?'

'I asked myself what my alternative was.'

'And?'

'I didn't have one,' Decker said. 'At least one that didn't mean the same as surrendering to what was wearing me down.'

Beth searched his eyes. 'I know what you mean.'

As Decker got in the car, he glanced across the street and felt something tighten inside him. A stationary man among a crowd of strolling tourists made Decker's protective instincts come to attention. What aroused his suspicion was that the man, who had been staring at Decker, turned immediately away as Decker noticed him. The man now stood with his back to the street, pretending to be interested in a window display of Southwestern jewelry, but his gaze was forward rather than downturned, indicating that what he was really doing was studying the reflection in the window. Decker checked his rearview mirror and saw the man turn to look in Decker's direction as Decker drove away. Common-length hair, average height and weight, mid-thirties, undistinguished features, unremarkable clothes, muted colors. In Decker's experience, that kind of anonymity didn't happen by accident. The man's only distinguishing characteristic was the bulk of his shoulders, which his loose-fitting shirt didn't manage to conceal. He wasn't a tourist.

Decker frowned. So is it review time? he asked himself. Have they decided to watch me to see how I'm behaving, whether I've been naughty or nice, whether I'm any threat?

Beth was saying something about the opera.

Decker tried to catch up. 'Yes?'

'I like it very much.'

'I'm a jazz fanatic myself.'

'Then you don't want to go? I hear the Santa Fe Opera is one of the best.'

Decker finally realized what she was talking about. 'You're asking me to go to the opera with you?'

Beth chuckled. 'You weren't this slow yesterday.'

'What opera is it?'

'*Tosca.*'

'Well, in that case,' Decker said. 'Since it's Puccini. If it was Wagner, I wouldn't go.'

'Smart guy.'

Decker made himself look amused while he turned a corner and checked his rearview mirror to see if he was being followed. He didn't notice anything out of the ordinary. Maybe I'm wrong about that man watching me.

Like hell.

7

The opera house was a five-minute drive north of town, to the left, off the highway to Taos. Decker followed a string of cars along an upward winding road, their lights on as sunset began to fade.

'What a beautiful setting.' Beth glanced at the low shadowy piñon-covered hills on both sides of the car. She was even more impressed after they reached the top of a bluff, parked the car in twilight, and strolled to the amphitheater built down into the far side of the bluff. She was intrigued by the appearance of the people around her. 'I can't tell if I'm underdressed or overdressed.' She herself wore a lace shawl over a thin-strapped black dress that was highlighted by a pearl necklace. 'Some of these people are wearing tuxedos and evening gowns. But some of them look like they're on a camping expedition. They've got hiking boots, jeans, wool shirts. That woman over there is carrying a knapsack and a parka. I'm having a reality problem. Are we all going to the same place?'

Decker, who wore a sports coat and slacks, chuckled. 'The amphitheater has open sides as well as an open roof. Once the sun is down, the desert gets cool, sometimes as low as forty-five. If a wind picks up, that lady in the evening dress is going to wish she had the parka you mentioned. During intermission, there'll be a lot of people buying blankets from the concession booth. That's why I brought this lap-robe I've got tucked under my arm. We might need it.'

They surrendered their tickets, crossed a welcoming open courtyard, and followed the ticket-taker's directions, mingling with a crowd that went up stairs to a row of wide wooden doors that led to various sections of the upper tier of seats.

'This door is ours,' Decker said. He gestured for Beth to go ahead of him, and as she did, he took advantage of that natural-seeming moment to glance back over his shoulder, scanning the courtyard below to discover if he was still under surveillance. It was a reversion to old habits, he realized with some bitterness.

Why did he allow himself to care? The surveillance was pointless. What possible compromising activity would his former employer think he was up to at the opera? His precaution told him nothing; there was no evidence of anyone below who showed more interest in him than in getting into the opera house.

Careful not to reveal his preoccupation, Decker sat with Beth to the right on an upper tier. They didn't have the best seats in the house, he noted, but they certainly couldn't complain. For one thing, their section of the amphitheater wasn't open to the sky, so while they had a partial view of the stars through the open space above the middle seats, their seats in the back didn't expose them as much to the cool night air.

'That opening in the middle of the roof,' Beth said. 'What happens when it rains? Does the performance stop?'

'No. The singers are protected.'

'But what about the audience in the middle seats?'

'They get wet.'

'Stranger and stranger.'

'There's more. Next year, you'll have to go to the opening of the opera season in early July. The audience has a tailgate party in the parking lot.'

'Tailgate party? You mean like at football games?'

'Except in this case, they drink champagne and wear tuxedos.'

Beth burst out laughing. Her amusement was contagious. Decker was pleased to discover that the surveillance on him was forgotten, that he was laughing with her.

The lights dimmed. *Tosca* began. It was a good performance. The first act – about a political prisoner hiding in a church – was appropriately threatening and moody, and if no one could equal Maria Callas's legendary performances of the title role, the evening's soprano gave it an excellent try. When the first act ended, Decker applauded enthusiastically.

But as he glanced toward the lower level, toward a

refreshment area to the left of the middle seats, he suddenly froze.

'What's the matter?' Beth asked.

Decker didn't respond. He kept peering toward the refreshment area.

'Steve?'

Feeling pressure behind his ears, Decker finally answered. 'What makes you think something's the matter?'

'The look on your face. It's like you saw a ghost.'

'Not a ghost. A business associate who broke an agreement.' Decker had seen the man who had been watching him earlier in the day. The man, wearing a nondescript sports coat, stood near the refreshment area down there, ignoring the activity around him, staring up in Decker's direction. He wants to see if I remain up here or go back through those doors and outside, Decker thought. If I leave, he's probably got a lapel mike that allows him to tell a partner with an earphone that I'm headed in the other man's direction. 'Forget him. I won't let him spoil our evening,' Decker said. 'Come on, would you like some hot chocolate?'

They went back to the doors through which they had entered, walked along a balcony, and descended stairs to the crowded courtyard. Surrounded by people, Decker couldn't determine who else might be watching him as he guided her around the left side of the opera house toward the refreshment area where he had seen the man.

But the man wasn't there any longer.

8

Throughout the intermission, Decker managed to make small talk, finally escorting Beth back to their seats. She gave no indication that she suspected his tension. When *Tosca*'s second act began, the burden of not spoiling Beth's evening was temporarily removed from him, and he could concentrate his full attention on what the hell was happening.

From one point of view, the situation made sense, he thought – the agency was still concerned about his outraged reaction to the disastrous Rome operation, and they wanted to make sure he hadn't vented his emotions by finding a way to betray them, selling information about secret operations. One indication of whether he was being paid for information would be how hard he worked as a real-estate broker and whether he spent more money than was commensurate with his income level.

Fine, Decker thought. I expected a review. But surely they would have done it sooner, and surely they could have done it from a distance simply by monitoring my real-estate transactions, my stock and bond accounts, and what I've got in the bank. Why, after more than a year, are they watching me so closely? At the opera, for God's sake.

In the dark, Decker squinted toward the intricately decorated 1800 Italian set, so absorbed in his thoughts that he barely heard Puccini's brooding music. Unable to resist the impulse, Decker turned his head and focused on the shadowy refreshment area to the left of the middle seats, where he had last seen the man who was watching him.

His back muscles became rigid. The man was down in that area again, and there wasn't any way to misinterpret the man's intentions, not when he ignored the opera and peered up in Decker's direction. Evidently the man assumed that he had not been spotted and that the shadows he stood among were sufficient protection for him to continue to keep from being seen. The man didn't realize that the lights from the stage spilled in his direction.

What Decker next reacted to sent a shock of alarm through

his nervous system. Not a ghost, but it might as well have been, so startling was another man's appearance, so unexpected, so impossible. The second man had emerged from shadows and stopped next to the first man, discussing something with him. Decker told himself that he had to be mistaken, that it was merely an illusion created by the distance. Just because the man seemed to be in his early thirties, had short blond hair, and was somewhat overweight with beefy shoulders and rugged square features didn't mean anything. Lots of men looked like that. Decker had met any number of former college football players who—

The blond man gestured forcefully with his right hand to emphasize something he said to the other man, and Decker's stomach contracted as he became absolutely convinced that his suspicion was correct. The blond man down there was the same man who had been responsible for the deaths of twenty-three Americans in Rome, who had been the reason Decker resigned from the agency. The operative in charge of putting Decker under surveillance was Brian McKittrick.

'Excuse me,' Decker told Beth. 'I need to use the rest room.' He edged past a man and woman sitting next to him. Then he was out of the row, up the stairs, through the doors in back.

On the deserted balcony, he immediately broke into a run. At the same time, he studied the moonlit area below him, but if a member of the surveillance team was in the courtyard, Decker didn't see him. There wasn't time to be thorough. Decker was too busy scrambling down the stairs and charging toward the dimly lit left side of the opera house, the direction in which he had seen McKittrick disappear.

The anger he had felt in Rome again flooded through him. He wanted to get his hands on McKittrick, to slam him against a wall and demand to know what was going on. As he raced along the side of the opera house, anguished music throbbed into the high desert night. Decker hoped that it obscured the scrape of his hurried footsteps on concrete steps. At once caution controlled him. Wary, he slowed, staying close to the wall, stalking past the rest rooms, studying the shadows near the refreshment stand, the last place he had seen McKittrick.

No one was there. How could I have missed them? he thought. If they came along the side of the opera house, we would have bumped into each other. Unless they had seats in the amphitheater, Decker told himself. Or unless they heard me coming and hid. Where? In a rest room? Behind the refreshment stand? Behind the wall that separates this area from the desert?

Despite the music swelling from the amphitheater, he heard the sound of movement behind night-obscured piñon trees on the opposite side of the wall. Are McKittrick and the other man watching me from out there? For the first time, Decker felt vulnerable. He crouched so that the low wall gave him cover.

He thought about vaulting the wall to pursue the noises. As quickly, he told himself that in the greater darkness behind the wall, he'd be putting himself at a tactical disadvantage, the noise of his own footsteps warning McKittrick that he was coming. The only other course of action was to race back along the sidewalk next to the amphitheater and wait in front for McKittrick and his partner to come out from the desert. Or maybe they'll just go to the parking lot and drive to town. Or maybe those noises you heard were just a wild dog's paws on the ground. And maybe, damn it, I ought to quit asking myself questions and demand that somebody give me some answers.

9

'Decker, have you any idea what time it is?' his former superior complained. The man's voice was thick from having been wakened. 'Couldn't this have waited until the morning instead of—'

'Answer me,' Decker insisted. He was using a payphone in a shadowy corner of the deserted courtyard in front of the opera house. 'Why am I under surveillance?'

'I don't know what you're talking about.'

'*Why are your people watching me?*' Decker clutched the phone so hard that his knuckles ached. Intense music swelled from the theater and echoed toward him.

'Whatever's going on, it has nothing to do with me.' His former superior's name was Edward. Decker remembered the sixty-three-year-old man's sagging cheeks that always turned red when he was under tension. 'Where are you?'

'You know exactly where I am.'

'Still in Santa Fe? Well, if you are in fact being watched—'

'Do you think I could possibly make a mistake about something like that?' Despite the emotion in his words, Decker strained to keep his voice from projecting across the courtyard, hoping that a crescendo of angry singing concealed his own anger.

'You're overreacting,' Edward said wearily over the phone. 'It's probably only a routine follow-up.'

'Routine?' Decker studied the deserted courtyard to make sure no one was coming toward him. 'You think it's routine that the jerk I worked with thirteen months ago is in charge of the surveillance team?'

'Thirteen months ago? You're talking about—'

'Are you going to make me be specific over the phone?' Decker asked. 'I told you then, and I'm telling you now – I will not leak information.'

'The man you worked with before you resigned – *he's* the one watching you?'

'You actually sound surprised.'

'Listen to me.' Edward's aging, raspy voice became louder, as if he was speaking closer to the phone. 'You have to understand something. I don't work there anymore.'

'What?' Now it was Decker's turn to sound surprised.

'I took early retirement six months ago.'

Decker's forehead throbbed.

'My heart condition got worse. I'm out of the loop,' Edward said.

Decker straightened as he saw movement on the theater's balcony. His chest tight, he watched someone walk along it and stop at the steps down to the courtyard.

'I'm being absolutely candid with you,' Edward said on the phone. 'If the man you worked with last year is watching you, I don't know who ordered him to do it or why.'

'Tell them I want it stopped,' Decker said. On the balcony, the person – it was Beth – frowned in his direction. Hugging her shawl, she descended the stairs. The music intensified.

'I don't have any influence with them anymore,' Edward said.

Beth reached the bottom of the courtyard and began to cross toward him.

'*Just make sure you tell them to stop.*'

Decker broke the connection as Beth reached him.

'I got worried about you.' A cool breeze tugged at Beth's hair and made her shiver. She tightened her shawl around her. 'When you didn't come back—'

'I'm sorry. It was business. The last thing I wanted was to leave you alone up there.'

Beth studied him, puzzled.

From the theater, the singing reached a peak of anguish and desperation. Beth turned toward it. 'I think that's where Scarpia promises Tosca that if she sleeps with him, her lover won't be executed.'

Decker's mouth felt dry, as if he had tasted ashes, because he had lied. 'Or maybe it's where Tosca stabs Scarpia to death.'

'So do you want to stay and hear the rest, or go home?' Beth sounded sad.

'Go home? God, no. I came to enjoy myself with you.'

'Good,' Beth said. 'I'm glad.'

As they started back toward the theater, the music reached an absolute peak. Abrupt silence was broken by applause. Doors opened. The audience started coming out for another intermission.

'Would you like more hot chocolate?' Decker asked.

'Actually, right now I could use some wine.'

'I'll join you.'

10

Decker escorted Beth through her shadowy gate, into the flower-filled courtyard, pausing beneath the portal and the light that Beth had left on above her front door. She continued to hug her shawl tightly around her. Decker couldn't tell if that was from nervousness.

'You weren't kidding about how cool it can get at night, even in July.' Beth inhaled deeply, savoring something. 'What's that scent in the air? It smells almost like sage.'

'It's probably from the chamisa bushes that line your driveway. They're related to sagebrush.'

Beth nodded, and Decker was certain now that she was indeed nervous. 'Well.' She held out her hand. 'Thank you for a wonderful evening.'

'My pleasure.' Decker shook hands with her. 'And again, I apologize for leaving you alone.'

Beth shrugged. 'I wasn't offended. Actually, I'm used to it. It's the sort of thing my husband did. He was always interrupting social evenings to take business calls or make them.'

'I'm sorry if I brought back painful memories.'

'It's not your fault. Don't worry about it.' Beth glanced down, then up. 'This was a big step for me. Last night and tonight are the first times since Ray died—' She hesitated. ' . . . that I've gone out with another man.'

'I understand.'

'I often wondered if I'd be able to make myself go through with it,' Beth said. 'Not just the awkwardness of dating again after having been married for ten years, but even more—' She hesitated again. 'The fear that I'd be disloyal to Ray.'

'Even though he's gone,' Decker said.

Beth nodded.

'Emotional ghosts,' Decker said.

'Exactly.'

'And?' Decker asked. 'How do you feel now?'

'You mean, aside from having flashbacks to being a nervous teenager on the doorstep saying good night to her first date?' Beth chuckled. 'I think—' She sobered. 'It's complicated.'

'I'm sure it is.'

'I'm glad I did it.' Beth took a long breath. 'No regrets. I meant what I said. Thank you for a wonderful evening.' She looked pleased with herself. 'Hey, I was even adult enough to do the asking, to invite *you* to go out with *me*.'

Decker laughed. 'I enjoyed being asked. If you'd let me, I'd like to return the favor.'

'Yes,' Beth said. 'Soon.'

'Soon,' Decker echoed, knowing that she meant she needed a little distance.

Beth pulled a key from a small purse and put it into the lock. In the foothills, coyotes howled. 'Good night.'

'Good night.'

11

Wary, Decker checked for surveillance as he went home. Nothing seemed out of the ordinary. In the days to come, he remained vigilant in his search for anyone watching him, but his efforts achieved no results. McKittrick and his team were no longer in evidence. Perhaps Edward had relayed Decker's message. The surveillance had been called off.

FOUR

1

It seemed to happen slowly, but in retrospect, there was an inevitability about it that made Decker think time was hurrying them. He saw Beth often in the days to come, giving her advice about the mundane matters of where the best grocery stores were and how to find the nearest post office and whether there were real-life reasonably priced stores away from the touristy expensive boutiques near the Plaza.

Decker took Beth hiking up the arroyo next to St John's College, past the Wilderness Gate subdivision, to the top of Atalaya Mountain. It was a measure of how good her physical condition was that she was able to complete the three-hour hike, even though her body had not yet fully adjusted to the high altitude. Decker took her to the massive flea market that occurred on weekends on a field below the opera house. They went to the Indian cliff-dwelling ruins at Bandelier National Monument. They played tennis at the Sangre de Cristo Racquet Club. When they got tired of New Mexican food, they ate turkey meatloaf and gravy at Harry's Roadhouse. Often they just barbecued chicken at Beth's place or Decker's. They went to foreign movies at the Jean Cocteau Cinema and Coffee House. They went to Indian Market and the related auction at the Wheelwright Museum, only a short walk from Camino Lindo. They went to the horse races and the Pojoaque Pueblo casino. Then on Thursday, September 1, at eleven in the morning, Beth

117

met Decker at the Santa Fe Abstract and Title Company, signed documents, handed over a check, and gained ownership of her house.

2

'Let's celebrate,' Beth said.

'You're going to hate me for saying I've got several appointments I absolutely have to keep.'

'I didn't mean right now.' Beth nudged him. 'I might be stealing all your time, but I do admit, once in a while you have to make a living. I meant tonight. I'm sick of eating fat-free white meat all the time. Let's be sinful and barbecue two juicy T-bones. I'll bake some potatoes and make a salad.'

'That's your idea of a celebration – not going out?'

'Hey, this will be my first night as a Santa Fe property owner. I want to stay home and admire what I bought.'

'I'll bring the red wine.'

'And champagne,' Beth added. 'I feel as if I should crack a bottle of champagne against the front gate, sort of like launching a ship.'

'Would Dom Perignon be good enough?'

3

When Decker arrived at six as they had agreed, he was surprised to see an unfamiliar car in Beth's driveway. Assuming that a maintenance person would have used a truck or a car with a business name on it, wondering who would be visiting at this hour, he parked beside the unmarked car, got out, and noted that the blue Chevrolet Cavalier had an Avis rental-car folder on its front passenger seat. As he walked along the gravel driveway toward the front gate, the carved door beyond it came open and Beth appeared beneath the portal with a man whom Decker had never seen before.

The man was slender and wore a business suit. Of medium height, with soft features, he had thinning, partially gray hair and looked to be in his early fifties. His suit was blue, decently cut, but not expensive. His shirt was white and emphasized the pallor of his skin. Not that the man looked sick. It was just that his suit and his lack of a tan were a good indication that he wasn't from Santa Fe. In the year and a quarter that Decker had been living in the area, he hadn't seen more than a dozen men wearing suits, and half of them had been on business from out of town.

The man stopped talking in the middle of a sentence, ' . . . would cost too much for—' and turned toward Decker, raising his narrow eyebrows in curiosity as Decker opened the front gate and approached them beneath the portal.

'Steve.' Buoyant, Beth kissed him on the cheek. 'This is Dale Hawkins. He works for the gallery that sells my paintings in New York. Dale, this is the good friend I told you about – Steve Decker.'

Hawkins smiled. 'To hear Beth tell it, she couldn't have survived here without you. Hi.' He held out his hand. 'How are you?'

'If Beth's been saying good things about me, I'm definitely in an excellent mood.'

Hawkins chuckled, and Decker shook hands with him.

'Dale was supposed to be here yesterday, but some business in New York held him up,' Beth said. 'In all the excitement about closing the deal on the house, I forgot to tell you he was coming.'

'I've never been here before,' Hawkins said. 'But already I

119

realize that the visit is long overdue. The play of sunlight is amazing. The mountains must have changed color a half-dozen times while I was driving up from Albuquerque.'

Beth looked terribly pleased. 'Dale came with good news. He managed to sell three of my paintings.'

'To the same buyer,' Hawkins said. 'The client is very enthusiastic about Beth's work. He wants to have a first look at anything new she does.'

'And he paid five thousand dollars for the first-look privilege,' Beth said excitedly, 'not to mention a hundred thousand for the group of three paintings.'

'A hundred . . . thousand?' Decker grinned. 'But that's fantastic.' Impulsively, he hugged her.

Beth's eyes glistened. 'First the house, now this.' She returned Decker's hug. 'I have plenty to celebrate.'

Hawkins looked as if he felt out of place. 'Well.' He cleared his throat. 'I ought to be going. Beth, I'll see you tomorrow morning at nine.'

'Yes, at Pasqual's for breakfast. You remember my instructions how to get there?'

'If I forget, I'll ask someone at the hotel.'

'Then I'll show you around the galleries,' Beth said. 'I hope you like walking. There are over two hundred of them.'

Decker felt obligated to make the offer. 'Would you like to stay and have dinner with us?'

Hawkins raised his hands in amusement. 'Lord, no. I can tell when I'm in the way.'

'If you're sure.'

'Positive.'

'I'll go out with you to your car,' Beth said.

Decker waited under the portal while Beth went and spoke briefly to Hawkins in the driveway. Hawkins got in his car, waved, and drove away.

Beth made a little skipping motion, beaming as she returned to Decker. She pointed toward the paper bag he was holding. 'Is that what I think it is?'

'The red wine and the Dom Perignon. The champagne's been chilling all afternoon.'

'I can't wait to open it.'

4

Beth twitched her nose as champagne bubbles tickled it. 'Would you like to see a surprise?'

'*Another* one?' The Dom Perignon trickled brightly over Decker's tongue. 'This is turning into quite a day.'

'I'm a little nervous about showing you, though.'

Decker wasn't sure what she meant. 'Nervous?'

'It's very private.'

Now Decker *really* didn't know what she meant. 'If you want to show me.'

Beth seemed to make a decision, nodding firmly. 'I do. Follow me.'

They left the handsomely tiled kitchen, crossed a colorful cotton dhurry rug in the living room, and went down a skylit corridor at the front of the house. It led past a door to the laundry room and took them to another door. *That* door was closed. Whenever Decker had visited Beth, she had kept what was in there a secret.

Now she hesitated, looked deeply into Decker's aquamarine eyes, and let out a long deep breath. 'Here goes.'

When she opened the door, Decker's first impression was of color. Splotches of red and green, blue and yellow. A brilliant rainbow seemed to have burst, its myriad parts spread before him. His second impression was of shape, of images and textures that blended together as if they shared a common life force.

Decker was silent a moment, so impressed that he couldn't move.

Beth studied him more intensely. 'What do you think?'

' "Think" isn't the word. It's what I *feel*. I'm overwhelmed.'

'Really?'

'They're beautiful.' Decker stepped forward, glancing all around the room at paintings on easels, paintings leaning against the walls, other paintings hanging above them. 'Stunning.'

'I'm so relieved.'

'But there must be . . .' Decker did a quick count. ' . . . over a dozen. And they're all about New Mexico. When did you—'

'Every day since the day I moved in, whenever I wasn't with you.'

'But you didn't tell me a word about them.'

'I was too nervous. What if you hadn't liked them? What if you had said they were like every other local artist's work?'

'But they're not. They're very definitely not.' Decker walked slowly from one to another, taking in their images, admiring them.

One, in particular, attracted his attention. It showed a dry creek bed with a juniper tree and red wild flowers on the rim. It appeared simple and unpretentious. But Decker couldn't help feeling that there was something beneath the surface.

'What's your opinion?' Beth asked.

'I'm afraid I'm more comfortable looking at paintings than talking about them.'

'It's not so hard. What do you notice first? What dominates?'

'The red wild flowers.'

'Yes,' Beth said. 'I got interested in them the moment I found out what they were called: "Indian paintbrush".'

'You know, they do look like artist's brushes,' Decker said. 'Straight and slender with red bristles on top.' He thought a moment. 'A painting about flowers called paintbrushes.'

'You're getting it,' Beth said. 'Art critics describe this sort of thing as "self-referential", a painting about painting.'

'Then that might explain something else I'm noticing,' Decker said. 'Your swirling brushstrokes. The way everything blends together. What's the technique called? Impressionism? It reminds me of Cezanne and Monet.'

'Not to mention Renoir, Degas, and *especially* Van Gogh,' Beth said. 'Van Gogh was a genius at depicting sunlight, so I figured I could make the painting more self-referential if I used Van Gogh's techniques to depict the uniqueness of New Mexico.'

' "The Land of the Dancing Sun".'

'You're very quick. I'm trying to catch the peculiar quality of Santa Fe's light. But if you look closely, you can also see symbols hidden in the landscape.'

' . . . well, I'll be damned.'

'Circles, ripples, sunburst patterns. The symbols the Navajo and other Southwestern Indians use to represent nature.'

'References within references,' Decker said.

'All intended to make the viewer sense that even an apparently simple creek bed rimmed by a juniper tree and red wild flowers can be complicated.'

'Beautiful.'

'I was so nervous that you wouldn't like them.'

'What did your art dealer say about them?' Decker asked.

'Dale? He was certain he could sell them all.'

'Then what does *my* opinion matter?'

'It matters, believe me.'

Decker turned to stare at her. Pulse racing, he couldn't stop himself. '*You're* beautiful.'

She blinked, startled. 'What?'

The words rushed out of him. 'I think about you all the time. I can't get you out of my mind.'

Beth's tan turned pale.

'I'm sure this is the biggest mistake I ever made,' Decker said. 'You need to feel free. You need space and— You'll probably avoid me from now on. But I have to say it. I love you.'

5

Beth studied him for what seemed the longest while.

I've really messed this up, Decker thought. Why couldn't I have kept my mouth shut?

Beth's gaze was intense.

'Bad timing, I guess,' Decker said.

Beth didn't answer.

'Can we go back?' Decker asked. 'Can we pretend this never happened?'

'You can never go back.'

'That's what I was afraid of.'

'And it *did* happen.'

'It certainly did.'

'You'll regret it,' Beth said.

'Do you want me to leave?'

'Hell, no. I want you to kiss me.'

The next thing Decker realized, he had his arms around her. The back of his neck tingled from the touch of her hands. When they kissed, he felt as if his breath had been taken away. At first, her lips were closed, their pressure against his tentative. Then her lips parted. Her tongue met his, and he had never felt so powerfully intimate a touch. The kiss lengthened and deepened. Decker began to tremble. He couldn't control the reaction. He had risked his life countless times as a member of military special operations and as an intelligence operative. He had encountered fear in its most powerful forms. What he was feeling now had all the symptoms of fear, but the emotion was quite the opposite. It was ecstasy. His fingertips became numb. His heart pounded with chest-swelling speed. When he lowered his hands to cup her hips, he trembled harder. He pressed his lips against her neck, aroused by the lingering scent of delicate soap and of the deeper primal smell of salt and musk, earth and heat and sky. It filled his nostrils. It made him feel that he was suffocating. He unbuttoned her blouse and slid his hands beneath her brassiere, touching her breasts, her nipples growing, hardening to his touch. His legs would no longer support him. He sank to his knees, kissing the silken skin of her stomach. With a shudder, she sank lower, drawing him to the floor. They embraced and rolled, kissing more deeply. He seemed to float, feeling as if he had been taken out of his body. Simultaneously he was conscious *only* of his body, of *Beth's* body. He wanted to go on kissing and touching her forever, to touch more and more of her. Hurrying, needing, they undressed each other. When he entered her, he felt transported. He couldn't get far enough within her. He wanted to be totally one with her. When they came, he felt suspended in a moment between frenzied heartbeats that lengthened and swelled and erupted.

6

Decker opened his eyes, peering up at the vigas and latillas that beamed the flat ceiling. The evening sun cast a crimson glow through a window. Silent, Beth lay next to him. In fact, she had not spoken for several minutes, since the moment she had climaxed. But as the silence persisted, Decker became uneasy, worried that she was in the throes of regret, second thoughts, guilt that she had been unfaithful to her dead husband. Slowly, she moved, turning to him, touching his cheek.

So it was going to be all right, he thought.

Naked, Beth rose to a sitting position. Her breasts were firm, the size of Decker's cupped palms. He recalled the exquisite hardness of her nipples.

She glanced down at the brick floor she sat upon. They were still in the room where she kept her paintings, the glorious color of which surrounded them. 'Passion is wonderful. But sometimes there's a price to pay.' She chuckled again. 'These bricks. I bet I've got bruises on my spine.'

'My knees and elbows have the top layer of skin scraped off,' Decker said.

'Let me see. Ouch,' Beth said. 'If we'd got any wilder, we'd have to go to the emergency ward.'

Decker started laughing. He couldn't stop himself. It kept coming and coming. Tears welled from his eyes.

Beth laughed, as well: a soul-releasing expression of joy. She leaned toward him and kissed him again, but this time the kiss communicated tenderness and affection. She touched his strong chin. 'What you said before we— Did you mean it?'

'Completely and totally. The words seem inadequate. I love you,' Decker said. 'So much so that I feel as if I didn't know anything about myself until this moment, that I've never been truly alive until now.'

'You didn't say you're a poet as well as an art critic.'

'There's a lot you don't know about me,' Decker said.

'I can't wait to learn it all.' Beth kissed him again and stood.

Decker felt a tightness in his throat as he admired her nakedness. It pleased him that she was comfortable with his admiration. She stood before him, her hands next to her hips, her nude body angled slightly sideways, one foot before the other and positioned at a right angle, suggestive of a dancer's pose, natural, without any trace of embarrassment. Her navel formed a tiny hollow in her flat stomach. Her dark pubic hair was soft and tufted. Her body had the contoured, supple tone of an athlete. Decker was reminded of the sensuous way in which ancient Greek sculptors portrayed nude women.

'What's that on your left side?' Beth asked.

'My side?'

'That scar.'

Decker looked down at it. The jagged indentation was the size of the tip of a finger. 'Oh, that's just—'

'You have another one on your right thigh.' Frowning, Beth knelt to examine them. 'If I didn't know better, I'd say—'

Decker couldn't think of a way to avoid the subject. 'They're from bullet wounds.'

'Bullet wounds? How on earth did—'

'I didn't know enough to duck.'

'What are you talking about?'

'I was with the US Rangers that invaded Grenada back in '83.' Again it grieved Decker to have to lie to her. 'When the shooting broke out, I didn't hit the ground fast enough.'

'Did they give you a medal?'

'For stupidity?' Decker chuckled. 'I did get a Purple Heart.'

'They look painful.'

'Not at all.'

'Can I touch them?'

'Be my guest.'

Gently, she placed a finger into the dimple on his side and then into the one on his thigh. 'You're sure they don't hurt?'

'Sometimes on damp winter nights.'

'When that happens, tell me. I know how to make them feel better.' Beth leaned down to kiss one, then the other. Decker felt her breasts slide along his abdomen toward his thigh. 'How does that work for you?' she asked.

'Everything's working just fine. Too bad they didn't have nurses like you when I was taken to a military hospital.'

'You wouldn't have gotten any sleep.' Beth snuggled next to him.

'Sleep isn't everything,' Decker said.

It was enough to lie close to her, enjoying her warmth. Neither of them moved or spoke for several minutes. Through the window, the crimson of the sunset deepened.

'I think it's time for a shower,' Beth said. 'You can use the one off the guest room, or . . .'

'Yes?'

'We can share mine.'

The gleaming white shower was spacious, doubling as a steam area. It had a built-in tiled bench and jets on each side. After lathering and sponging each other as the spray of hot water streamed over them, after kissing and touching, stroking, caressing, and exploring as steam billowed around them, their slippery bodies sliding against each other, they sank to the bench and made trembling, heart-pounding love again.

7

The evening was the most special of Decker's life. He had never felt such emotional commitment to physical passion, such regard – and indeed awe – for the person with whom he was sharing that passion. After he and Beth had made love for the second time, after they had finished showering and dressed, he became aware of other unfamiliar feelings, his sense of completeness, of belonging. It was as if their two physical unions had produced another kind of union, intangible, mystical. As long as he was near Beth, he felt that she was within him and he within her. He didn't have to be close enough to touch her. It was enough merely to see her. He felt whole.

As he sipped Dos Equis beer while he barbecued the T-bones Beth had requested, he glanced toward stars beginning to appear in the sky, its evening color remarkably like that of Beth's eyes. He gazed down the wooded slope behind Beth's house toward the lights of Santa Fe spread out below him. Feeling a contentment he had never before known, he peered through the screen door into the glow of the kitchen and watched Beth preparing a salad. She was humming to herself.

She noticed him. 'What are you looking at?'

'You.'

She smiled with pleasure.

'I love you,' Decker said again.

Beth came toward him, opened the door, leaned out, and kissed him. A spark seemed to jump from her to him. 'You're the most important person in the world to me.'

At that moment, it occurred to Decker that the hollowness he had suffered for many years had finally been filled. He thought back a year and a quarter to Rome and his fortieth birthday, the ennui he had endured, the personal vacuum. He had wanted a wife, a family, a home, and now he would have all of them.

8

'I'm afraid I'm going to have to leave town for a couple of days,' Beth said.

'Oh?' Driving along the narrow piñon-rimmed curves of Tano Road, north of town, Decker looked over at her, confused. It was Friday, September 9, the end of the tourist season, the first evening of Fiesta. He and Beth had been lovers for eight days. 'Is it something sudden? You didn't mention it before.'

'Sudden? Yes and no,' Beth said, gazing over sunset-bathed low hills toward the Jemez mountains to the west. 'Finding out that I had to take the trip the day after tomorrow is sudden. But I knew I'd have to do it eventually. I need to go back to Westchester County. Meetings with lawyers – that sort of thing. It's about my late husband's estate.'

The reference to Beth's late husband made Decker uncomfortable. Whenever possible, he had avoided the subject, concerned that Beth's memories of the man would make her ambivalent about her relationship with Decker. Are you jealous of a dead man? he wondered.

'A couple of days? When do you expect to be back?' Decker asked.

'Actually, maybe longer. Possibly a week. It's crass and petty, but it *is* important. My husband had partners, and they're being difficult about how much his share of the business is worth.'

'I see,' Decker said, wanting to ask all sorts of questions but trying not to pry. If Beth wanted to share her past with him, she would. He was determined not to make her feel crowded. Besides, this was supposed to be a joyous evening. They were on their way to a Fiesta party at the home of a film producer for whom Decker had acted as realtor. Beth obviously didn't want to talk about her legal problems, so why make her do it? 'I'll miss you.'

'Same here,' Beth said. 'It'll be a long week.'

9

' . . . died young.'

Decker heard the fragment of conversation from a group of women behind him as he sipped a margarita and listened to a jazz trio positioned in a corner of the spacious living room. The tuxedoed pianist was doing a nice job on a Henry Mancini medley, emphasizing *Moon River*.

'From tuberculosis,' Decker heard behind him. 'Only twenty-five. Didn't start writing until he was twenty-one. It's amazing how much he accomplished in so little time.'

Decker turned from listening to the piano player and studied the two hundred guests that his client, the film producer, had invited to the Fiesta party. While uniformed caterers brought cocktails and hors d'oeuvres, the partygoers went from room to room, admiring the luxurious home. Famous local residents mixed freely. But the only person in the room who occupied Decker's attention was Beth.

When Decker had first met her, she had worn only East Coast clothing. But gradually that had changed. Tonight, she wore a festive Hispanic-influenced Southwestern outfit. Her skirt and top were velvet, their midnight blue complementing her blue-gray eyes and auburn hair. She had tucked back her hair in a ponytail, securing it with a silver barrette whose glint matched that of her silver squash-blossom necklace. She was sitting with a group of women around a coffee table made from black-smithed iron that supported a two-hundred-year-old door. She looked comfortable, at ease, as if she had been living in Santa Fe for twenty years.

'I haven't read him since I was at UCLA,' one of the women was saying.

'Whatever made you get interested in poetry?' another woman asked, as if the thought appalled her.

'And why Keats?' a third woman asked.

Decker mentally came to attention. Until that moment, he hadn't known which writer the group was discussing. The reference, through a complex chain of association, sparked his memory, taking him back to Rome. He repressed a frown as he vividly recalled following Brian McKittrick down the Spanish

Steps and past the house where Keats had died.

'For fun, I'm taking a course at St John's College,' a fourth woman said. 'It's called "The Great Romantic Poets".'

'Ah,' the second woman said. 'I can guess which word in the title appealed to you.'

'It's not what you're thinking,' the fourth woman said. 'It's not like those romances you like to read, and I confess I do, too. This is different. Keats did write about men and women and passion, but that's not what he's about.'

The repetition of Keats's name made Decker think not only of McKittrick but of twenty-three dead Americans. It troubled him that a poet synonymous with truth and beauty could be irrevocably associated in his mind with a restaurant full of charred corpses.

'He wrote about emotion,' the fourth woman said. 'About beauty that *feels* like passion. About . . . It's hard to explain.'

Darkling I listen; and, for many a time / I have been half in love with easeful death. Keats's dirge-like lines occurred spontaneously to Decker. Before he realized what he was doing, he joined the conversation. 'About beautiful things that seem even more heartachingly beautiful when seen through the eyes of someone very young and about to die.'

The group looked up at him in surprise, except for Beth who had been watching him with covert affection throughout the conversation.

'Steve, I didn't realize you knew anything about poetry,' the fourth woman said. 'Don't tell me when you're not helping people find beautiful houses like this, *you* take courses at St John's, also.'

'No. Keats is just a memory from college,' Decker lied.

'Now you've got me interested,' one of the women said. 'Was Keats really in his early twenties and dying from TB when he wrote those great poems?'

Decker nodded, thinking of shots being fired in the dark in a rainy courtyard.

'When he was twenty-five,' the fourth woman repeated. 'He's buried in Venice.'

'No, in Rome,' Decker said.

'Are you sure?'

'The house where he died is near Bernini's Boat Fountain, to the right as you go down the Spanish Steps.'

'You sound as if you've been there.'

Decker shrugged.

'Sometimes I think you've been everywhere,' an attractive woman said. 'One of these days, I'm going to get you to tell me the fascinating story of your life before you came to Santa Fe.'

'I sold real estate other places. It wasn't very interesting, I'm afraid.'

As if sensing that Decker wanted to move on, Beth mercifully stood and took his arm. 'If anybody's going to hear the story of Steve's life, it's going to be me.'

Grateful to be relieved from talking about his mood, Decker strolled with Beth outside onto an extensive brick patio. In the cool night air, they peered toward the star-filled sky.

Beth put an arm around his waist. Smelling her perfume, Decker kissed her cheek. His throat felt pleasantly tight.

Leading her off the patio, away from the lights and the crowd, concealed by shadowy piñon trees, Decker kissed her with passion. When Beth reached up, linking her fingers around his neck, returning the kiss, he felt as if the ground rippled. Her lips were soft yet firm, exciting. Through her blouse, her nipples pressed against him. He was breathless.

'So go ahead – tell me the fascinating story of your life.'

'Some time.' Decker kissed her neck, inhaling her fragrance. 'Right now, there are better things to do.'

But he couldn't stop thinking of Rome, of McKittrick, of

what had happened in the courtyard. The dark nightmare haunted him. He had hoped to put everything that McKittrick represented behind him. Now, as he had two months ago, he couldn't help wondering why in God's name McKittrick had shown up in Santa Fe to watch him.

10

'It arrived?'

'This afternoon,' Decker said. 'I didn't have a chance to show you.' After the party, they were driving back along shadowy Camino Lindo.

'Show me now.'

'You're sure you're not tired?'

'Hey, if I get tired, I can always stay at your place and use it,' Beth said.

The 'it' they referred to was a bed that Decker had commissioned from a local artist, John Massey, whose specialty was working with metal. Using a forge, a hammer, and an anvil, Massey had shaped the iron bedposts into intricate designs that resembled carved wood.

'It's wonderful,' Beth said after Decker parked the Cherokee in the carport and they went inside. 'Even more striking than you described.' She touched the metal's smooth black finish. 'And those figures cut out of the headboard – or headmetal – or whatever you call it when it's made out of iron. These figures look like they're based on a Navajo design, but they also look like Egyptian hieroglyphs, their feet out one way, their hands out another. Actually, they look like they're drunk.'

'John has a sense of humor. They're not based on anything. He makes them up.'

'Well, I sure like them,' Beth said. 'They make me smile.'

134

Decker and Beth admired it from various angles.

'Certainly looks solid,' Decker said.

Beth pressed a hand on the mattress. She raised her eyebrows, mischievous. 'Want to try it out?'

'You bet,' Decker said. 'If we break it, I'll make John give me my money back.'

He turned off the light. Slowly, amid lingering kisses, they undressed each other. The bedroom door was open. Moonlight streamed through the high, wide, solar-gain windows in the corridor outside the bedroom. The glow on her breasts made Decker think of ivory. Kneeling, worshipping, he brought his lips down.

11

They must have come over the back wall. That was at seven minutes after three in the morning. Decker was able to be specific about the time because he had an old-fashioned alarm clock with hands, and when he checked it later, he discovered that was when the hands had stopped moving.

Unable to sleep, he lay on his side, admiring Beth's face in the moonlight, imagining that she had already returned from her business trip, that their separation was over. In the distance, he heard the muted pop-pop-pop of firecrackers being set off at private parties that continued the Fiesta celebrations. There were going to be a lot of hangovers tomorrow morning, he thought. And sleepy neighbors kept up by parties next to them. The police will be busy, responding to complaints. How late is it? he wondered, and turned toward the clock.

He couldn't see its illumination. Suspecting that he had put some of Beth's clothing in front of it, he reached to remove the obstacle but instead touched the clock itself. Puzzlement made him frown. Why would the clock's light be off? The pop-pop-pop of distant firecrackers persisted. But the noise wasn't intrusive enough to prevent him from hearing something else – the faint scrape of metal against metal.

Troubled, Decker sat up. The noise came from beyond the foot of his bed, from the solar-gain corridor outside his bedroom, from the door on the right at the end of the corridor. That door led outside to a small flower garden and patio. Faintly, metal continued to scrape against metal.

In a rush, he put a hand over Beth's mouth. The moonlight revealed the shock with which her eyes opened. As she struggled against his hand on her mouth, he pressed his head against her left ear, his voice a tense whisper. 'Don't try to say anything. Listen to me. Someone's trying to break into the house.'

The metal scraped.

'Get out of bed. Into the closet. Hurry.'

Naked, Beth scrambled out of bed and dashed into the closet on the right side of the room. The closet was large, a walk-in, ten by twelve feet. It had no windows. Its darkness was greater than that of the bedroom.

Decker yanked open the bottom drawer on his bedside table and removed the Sig-Sauer .928 pistol that he had bought when he first arrived in Santa Fe. He crouched next to the bed, using it for cover while he grabbed the bedside telephone, but as he put the phone to his ear, he knew that there wasn't any point in pressing 911 – he didn't hear a dial tone.

Abrupt silence aggravated Decker's tension. The sound of metal scraping against metal had stopped. Decker lunged into the walk-in closet, couldn't see Beth, and took cover next to a small dresser. As he aimed toward the corridor beyond his open bedroom door, he shivered from stress, his nude body feeling cold although he was sweating. The back door on the right, which he had been intending to oil, squeaked open.

Who the hell would be breaking in? he asked himself. A burglar? Possibly. But suspicions from his former life took possession of him. He couldn't put away the icy thought that unfinished business had caught up to him.

Immediately the intrusion detector made a rhythmic beeping sound: the brief alert the system provided before the full ear-torturing blare of the alarm. Not that the alarm would do any good – because the telephone line had been cut, the alarm's signal couldn't be transmitted to the security company. If the intrusion detector hadn't been rigged to a battery in case of a power failure, the warning beep wouldn't even be sounding now.

At once the beeps became a constant wail. Shadows rushed into the bedroom. Rapid flashes pierced the darkness, the staccato roar of automatic weapons assaulting Decker's eardrums. The flashes illuminated the impact of countless bullets against the bed sheets, pillow feathers flying, mattress stuffing erupting.

Before the gunmen had a chance to realize their mistake, Decker fired, squeezing the trigger repeatedly. Two of the gunmen lurched and fell. A third man scrambled from the bedroom. Decker shot at him and missed, the bullet shattering a solar-gain window as the man disappeared into the corridor.

Decker's palms were moist, making him grateful that his pistol had a checkered non-slick grip. His bare skin exuded more sweat. Traumatized by the roar of the shots, his eardrums rang painfully. He could barely hear the security system's wail. He wouldn't be able to detect any sound the gunman made trying to sneak up on him. For that matter, Decker didn't know if the three gunmen were the only intruders in the house, and he couldn't tell how seriously he had injured the two men he had shot. Would they still be capable of firing at him if he tried to leave the closet?

He waited anxiously for his night vision to return after the glare of the muzzle flashes. It worried him that he didn't know where Beth was. Somewhere in the spacious closet, yes. But had she found cover, perhaps behind the cedar chest? He couldn't risk glancing behind him in hopes of detecting her murky shadow in the darkness. He had to keep his attention directed toward the bedroom, prepared to react if someone attacked across it. At the same time, he felt a cold spot on his spine, terribly aware that the closet had another entrance, a door behind him that led into the laundry room. If the gunman snuck around and attacked from that direction . . .

I can't guard two directions at once, Decker thought. Maybe whoever else is out there ran away.

Would *you* have run away?

Maybe.

Like hell.

Apprehension made him rigid. The middle of the night, the phone and the electricity cut off, no way to call for help, no way for the alarm to be transmitted to the police – all the gunman had to worry about was a neighbor being wakened by the shots or by the alarm. But could those noises be heard from outside the thick adobe house? The nearest house was several hundred yards away. The noise would be muted by the distance. The gunshots might sound like the distant firecrackers Decker had heard. The intruder might think he had a little more time.

The attack didn't come from the laundry room. Instead an automatic weapon roared from the entrance to the bedroom, the muzzle flashes brilliant, bullets tearing up each side of the closet's doorjamb, strafing the open space between them, hitting the wall beyond, shredding clothes on hangers, bursting shoe boxes and garment bags, sending chunks of fabric, wood, and cardboard flying, fragments striking Decker's bare back. The acrid stench of cordite filled the area.

As suddenly as it began, the din of the automatic weapon

stopped, the only sound the blare of the security system. Decker didn't dare shoot at where the muzzle flashes had been. The gunman would likely have shifted position and be waiting to aim at the flash from Decker's pistol if he returned fire.

Immediately Decker became aware of movement in the closet. Beth's naked figure darted from a shadowy corner. She knew the house. She knew about the door to the laundry room. As she twisted the knob and pushed at the door, the submachine gun roared, its bullets chasing her. Decker thought he heard her moan. There was so much noise he couldn't tell, but as she vanished into the darkness of the laundry room, she clutched her right shoulder. Decker's urge was to rush to her, but he didn't dare give in to that suicidal impulse. The gunman was counting on him to lose control, to show himself. Instead Decker pressed himself closer to the small dresser, ready with his pistol, hoping that the gunman himself would lose patience.

Please, Decker thought. Dear God, *please*. Don't let Beth be hurt.

He strained to watch the entrance to the bedroom. He wished that he could hear if the gunman was moving around out there, but his ears rang even more painfully. That could work the other way around, he realized. Since *his* hearing was compromised, whoever was trying to kill him probably wouldn't be hearing well, either. There might be a way to turn their mutual affliction to his advantage. Next to the dresser that shielded him was a waist-high metal stepladder that he used for reaching items on the top shelf. It was about the width of a man's shoulders. Grabbing a shirt that he had left on the dresser, Decker draped it over the low stepladder. In the darkness, the silhouette looked like someone crouching. He pushed the stepladder ahead of him, praying that the gunman's hearing was indeed compromised, that the wail of the security system would keep him from hearing the scraping sounds the stepladder made on the floor. With force, he shoved the stepladder from the closet, sending it skittering upright across the bedroom toward where he had last seen the gunman.

An explosion of gunfire tore the shirt apart, knocking the ladder over. Simultaneously Decker fired several times at the muzzle flashes in the hallway. The flashes jerked toward the tile floor, illuminating a man who was bent over in pain, his submachine gun blasting holes in the tile floor. As the man fell, the roaring flashes stopped.

Afraid that his own flashes would have made him a target, Decker rolled. He came to a crouch on the opposite side of the closet's entrance, fired again toward the man he had just hit, then toward each of the men he had previously shot, and quickly retreated into the darkness of the laundry room.

Beth. He had to find Beth. He had to make sure Beth wasn't injured. He had to keep her from running again and revealing herself until he knew for certain there was no one else in the house. In the laundry room, the sweet smell of detergent emphasized the bitterness of cordite. Sensing movement between the hot-water tank and the water softener, he inched toward it and found Beth, only to be startled by a fiery blast from a shotgun as the closed door to the laundry room blew inward, stunning him with its concussion. He and Beth dropped to the floor.

His night vision already impaired by the close flash from the shotgun, Decker was further blinded by a second flash, another shotgun blast. The bulky shadow of a man charged inside, firing a third time, as Decker aimed high, shooting upward from where he lay on his stomach.

Hot liquid streamed over Decker. *Blood?* But the liquid wasn't just hot; it was almost scalding. And it didn't just stream; it cascaded. The water tank must have been hit, Decker thought in desperation, straining to ignore his pain from the high temperature of the liquid sloshing over him while he concentrated on the darkness across from him where seconds earlier muzzle flashes had revealed the man with the shotgun. He felt Beth's panicked breathing next to him. He smelled blood, its coppery odor unmistakable. A *strong* odor. But not just from the direction of the man with the shotgun. It also seemed to come from next to him. The terrible thought kept insisting, *Had Beth been hit?*

As his night vision improved after the assault of the muzzle flashes, he detected the murky outline of a body on the floor at the entrance to the laundry room. Beth trembled beside him. Feeling the spasms of her terror, Decker calculated how many times he had fired and struggled against a terror of his own when he realized that he had only one round left.

Drenched by the painfully hot water, he pressed a finger to Beth's lips, silently urging her to be quiet. Then he squirmed across the laundry room's wet floor toward the entrance. Moonlight through the hallway's skylight helped him to see the shotgun that had fallen beside the corpse.

Or at least Decker hoped it was a corpse. Prepared to fire his last bullet, he checked for a pulse. Finding none, he relaxed only slightly as he searched beneath the corpse's windbreaker, his left hand touching a revolver. Immediately he shoved the shotgun into the laundry room, returned to Beth in the darkness, felt for and raised the trapdoor to the crawlspace that led under the house, and guided Beth toward it. Most homes in Santa Fe were built on concrete slabs and didn't have basements; a few, like Decker's, had a four-foot-high service tunnel under the floor.

Rigid, Beth resisted descending the wooden stairs. An odor of dust rose from the gloom. Then she seemed to accept the crawlspace as a sanctuary, trembling, hurriedly descending, hot water pouring down with her. Decker squeezed her right arm in what he hoped she accepted as a gesture of reassurance, then closed the hatch.

The blare from the security system continued to unnerve him as he crept toward the darkness of the far corner, positioning himself beside the furnace. From there, he had a line of fire toward each entrance to the laundry room. He had the gunman's revolver in his left hand, his own pistol in his right, and as a last resort the gunman's shotgun, which he had pulled next to him, hoping that the gunman had not used all its ammunition.

But something else unnerved him, giving him a terrible sense of urgency. He knew that patience was the key to survival. If he tried to investigate the house, he might show himself to anyone who was hiding out there. The prudent thing to do was to stay in place and let *someone else* show himself. But Decker couldn't restrain his need to hurry things. He imagined Beth's growing sense of claustrophobia as she hunkered naked in the musty darkness of the crawlspace. He imagined her increasing pain. When he had touched her right arm to try to give her reassurance, his fingers had come away smeared with a liquid that was thicker than water. The liquid was warm and smelled of blood. Beth had been hit.

I need to get her to a doctor, Decker thought. I can't wait any longer. He crept from behind the furnace, approached the entrance to the hallway, prepared to rush out, to aim one way and then the other, but instead froze as a flashlight beam settled on the corpse before him.

He pressed himself against the inside wall. Sweat mixed with the water that slicked him as he concentrated on that exit from the laundry room, then glanced nervously across to the door that led into the closet. Why would they use a flashlight? It didn't make sense to reveal themselves. The flashlight must be a trick, he thought, an attempt to distract me while someone comes from the opposite direction, from the darkness of the closet.

Surprising him, the flashlight moved away, heading back toward the front door. That didn't make sense, either. Unless . . . Did he dare trust what he was thinking? A neighbor might have decided that the muffled staccato blasts he was hearing definitely didn't come from firecrackers. The neighbor might have called 911. The flashlight might belong to a policeman. That was how a lone policeman would behave – as soon as he saw the body, not knowing what he was involved in, possibly a gunfight, he would retreat and radio for help.

Decker's already sickeningly rapid heartbeat pounded even faster. Under other circumstances, he wouldn't have dared to take the risk of revealing his position. But Beth had been shot. God alone knew how serious the wound was. If he hesitated any longer, she might bleed to death in the crawlspace. He had to do *something*.

'Wait!' Decker shouted. 'I'm in the laundry room! I need help!'

The flashlight beam stopped going away, glared back along the hallway, and focused on the entrance to the laundry room. Decker immediately realized the further risk he had taken. His ears were ringing so painfully that he couldn't tell if anyone shouted back to him. If he didn't answer or if what he shouted didn't logically connect with what the policeman shouted (assuming this in fact *was* a policeman), he would make the policeman suspicious.

'I live here!' Decker shouted. 'Some men broke in! I don't know who you are! I'm afraid to come out!'

The flashlight beam shifted position, as if whoever held it was finding cover in a doorway.

'I can't hear you! There was shooting! My eardrums are messed up!' Decker shouted. 'If you're a policeman, slide your badge down the hall so I can see it from this doorway!'

Decker waited, glancing nervously from the doorway toward

the opposite door that led into the closet, apprehensive that he was leaving himself open to an attack. He had to take the chance. Beth, he kept thinking. I have to help Beth.

'Please!' Decker shouted. 'If you're a policeman, slide your badge down!'

Because he couldn't hear it skittering, he was surprised by the sudden appearance of the badge on the brick floor of the corridor. The badge was stopped by the body of the gunman.

'Okay!' Decker's throat was sore. He swallowed with difficulty. 'I'm sure you're trying to figure out what happened! You're as nervous as *I* am! When I come out, I'll have my hands up! I'll show them first!'

He set the handguns onto a laundry counter to his right where he could scramble back and grab them if he had misjudged the situation. 'I'm coming out now! Slowly! I'll show my hands first!' The moment he stepped free of the doorway, his hands high over his head, the flashlight beam shifted swiftly toward his eyes, nearly blinding him, making him feel more helpless.

It seemed as if time was suspended. The flashlight beam kept glaring at him. The policeman, if that was who this was (and despite the badge on the floor, Decker was suddenly having powerful doubts), didn't move, just kept studying him.

Or was it a gunman aiming at him?

Decker's eyes felt stabbed by the flashlight beam fixed on them, and he wanted to lower a hand to shield his vision, but he didn't dare move, didn't dare unnerve whoever was studying him. The flashlight beam dropped down to his nakedness, then returned to his eyes.

At once time began again.

The flashlight beam moved, approaching. Decker's mouth was terribly dry, his vision so impaired that he couldn't see the dark looming figure, couldn't see how the man was dressed, couldn't identify him.

Then the flashlight and the figure were close, but Decker still couldn't tell who confronted him. His raised hands felt numb. He had the sense that the figure was talking to him, but he couldn't hear.

Unexpectedly the figure leaned close, and Decker was able to make out dimly what the figure shouted.

'*You can't hear?*'

The peripheral glow of the flashlight showed that the figure, a stocky Hispanic man, wore a uniform.

'I'm almost deaf!' The din of the alarm and the ringing in his ears were excruciating.

'. . . *are you?*'

'*What?*' Decker's voice seemed to come from far outside himself.

'*Who are you?*'

'Stephen Decker! I own this house! Can I put my hands down?'

'*Yes. Where are your clothes?*'

'I was sleeping when they broke in! I don't have time to explain! My friend's in the crawlspace!'

'*What?*' The policeman's tone expressed less confusion than astonishment.

'The crawlspace! I have to get her out of there!' Decker swung toward the laundry room, the flashlight beam swinging with him. His hands trembled as he grabbed the metal ring recessed into the trapdoor. He pulled the hatch fiercely upward and groped down the wooden steps into the darkness, smelling earth and dampness and the disconcerting odor of blood.

'Beth!'

He couldn't see her.

'Beth!'

From above him, the flashlight beam filled the pit, and he saw Beth huddled naked, trembling, in a corner. He rushed to her, almost out of the flashlight's range but not so far that he didn't notice how pale her face was. Her right shoulder and breast were smeared with blood.

'*Beth!*'

He knelt, holding her, ignoring the dirt and cobwebs that clung to him. He felt her sobbing.

'It's all right. You're safe.'

If she responded, he didn't know. He couldn't hear, and he was too busy guiding her toward the steps from the crawlspace and up toward the flashlight, the policeman helping her up, startled by her nakedness. Decker covered her with a dirty shirt from a hamper in the laundry room. She stumbled weakly, and he had to hold her up as they made their way along the corridor toward the front door.

Decker had the sense that the policeman was shouting to him, but he still couldn't hear. 'The alarm pad's near the front door! Let me turn it off!'

He reached the pad on the wall at the exit from the corridor and briefly wondered why it was illuminated when the electricity was off, then remembered that the alarm system had a battery that supplied back-up power. He pressed numbers and felt his shoulders sag in relief when the alarm stopped.

'Thank God,' he murmured, having to contend now only with the ringing in his ears. He was still holding Beth up. In dismay, he felt her vomit. 'She needs an ambulance.'

'*Where's a phone?*' the policeman shouted.

'They aren't working! The power's off! The phone's are down!' Decker's ears felt less tortured. He was hearing slightly better.

'*What happened here?*'

Dismayingly, Beth slumped.

Decker held her, lowering her to the brick floor in the vestibule. He felt a cool breeze from the open front door. 'Get help! I'll stay with her!'

'I'll use the radio in my patrol car!' The policeman rushed from the house.

Glancing in that direction, Decker saw two stationary headlights gleaming beyond the courtyard gate. The policeman disappeared behind them. Then all Decker paid attention to was Beth.

He knelt beside her, stroking her forehead. 'Hang on. You'll be all right. We're getting an ambulance.'

The next thing he knew, the policeman had returned and was stooping beside him, saying something that Decker couldn't hear.

'The ambulance will come in no time,' Decker told Beth. Her forehead felt clammy, chilled. 'You're going to be fine.' I need to cover her, Decker was thinking. I need to get her warm. He yanked open a closet behind him, grabbed an overcoat, and spread it over her.

The policeman leaned closer to him, speaking louder. Now Decker could hear. 'The front door was open when I arrived! *What happened? You said someone broke in?*'

'Yes.' Decker kept stroking Beth's hair, wishing the policeman would leave him alone. 'They must have broken in the front as well as the back.'

'*They?*'

'The man in the hallway. Others.'

'*Others?*'

'In my bedroom.'

'*What?*'

'Three. Maybe four. I shot them all.'

'Jesus,' the policeman said.

FIVE

1

A chaos of crisscrossing headlights gleamed in the spacious pebbled driveway outside Decker's house. Engines rumbled. Radios crackled. The eerily illuminated silhouettes of vehicles seemed everywhere, patrol cars, vans, a huge utility truck from Public Service of New Mexico, an ambulance speeding away.

Naked beneath an overcoat that didn't cover his bare knees, Decker leaned, shivering, against the stucco wall next to the open courtyard gate, staring frantically toward the receding lights of the ambulance speeding into the night. He ignored the policemen searching the area around the house, their flashlights wavering, while a forensics crew carried their equipment past him.

'I'm sorry,' one of the policemen said, the stocky Hispanic who had been the first to arrive and who had eventually introduced himself as Officer Sanchez. 'I know how much you want to go with your friend to the hospital, but we need you here to answer more questions.'

Decker didn't reply, just kept staring toward the lights of the ambulance, which kept getting smaller in the darkness.

'The ambulance attendants said they thought she'd be okay,' Sanchez continued. 'The bullet went through her right arm. It didn't seem to hit bone. They've stopped the bleeding.'

'Shock,' Decker said. 'My friend's in shock.'

The policeman looked uncomfortable, not sure what to say. 'That's right. Shock.'

'And shock can kill.'

The ambulance lights disappeared. As Decker turned, he noticed confused movement between the headlights of a van and the hulking Public Service of New Mexico utility truck. He tensed, seeing two harried civilians caught between policemen, the indistinct group coming swiftly in his direction. Had the police captured someone associated with the attack? Angry, Decker stepped closer to the open gate, ignoring Sanchez, focusing his attention on the figures being brought toward him.

A man and a woman, Decker saw as the nearest headlights starkly revealed their faces, and immediately his anger lessened.

The two policemen flanking them had a look of determination as they reached the gate. 'We found them on the road. They claim they're neighbors.'

'Yes. They live across the street.' The harsh ringing persisted in Decker's ears, although not as severely. 'These are Mr and Mrs Hanson.'

'We heard shots,' Hanson, a short, bearded man, said.

'And your alarm,' Hanson's gray-haired wife said. She and her husband wore rumpled casual clothes and looked as if they had dressed quickly. 'At first, we thought we had to be wrong. There couldn't be shots at your house. We couldn't believe it.'

'But we couldn't stop worrying,' Hanson said. 'We phoned the police.'

'A damned good thing you did,' Decker said. 'Thank you.'

'Are you all right?'

'I think so.' Decker's body ached from tension. 'I'm not sure.'

'What *happened*?'

'That's exactly the question *I* want to ask,' a voice intruded.

Bewildered, Decker looked beyond the gate toward where a man had appeared, approaching between headlights. He was tall, sinewy, wearing a leather cowboy hat, a denim shirt, faded blue jeans, and dusty cowboy boots. As Officer Sanchez shone his flashlight toward the man, Decker was able to tell that the man was Hispanic. He had a narrow handsome face, brooding eyes, and dark hair that hung to his shoulders. He seemed to be in his middle thirties.

'Luis.' The man nodded in greeting to Officer Sanchez.

'Frederico.' Sanchez nodded back.

The newcomer directed his attention toward Decker. 'I'm Detective Sergeant Esperanza.' His Hispanic accent gave a rolling sound to the 'r's.

For a fleeting moment, Decker was reminded that 'Esperanza' was the Spanish word for 'hope'.

'I know this has been a terrible ordeal, Mr . . . ?'

'Decker. Stephen Decker.'

'You must be frightened. You're confused. You're worried about your friend. Her name is . . . ?'

'Beth Dwyer.'

'Does she live here with you?'

'No,' Decker said. 'She's my next-door neighbor.'

Esperanza thought about it, seeming to make the logical conclusion. 'Well, the sooner I can sort out what happened, the sooner you can visit your friend in the hospital. So if you bear with me while I ask you some questions . . .'

Abruptly the light above the front door, a motion detector, came on. Simultaneously the light in the vestibule came on, casting a glow through the open front door.

Decker heard expressions of approval from the policemen checking the outside of the house.

'Finally,' Esperanza said. 'It looks like Public Service of New Mexico managed to find the problem with your electricity. Would you tell Officer Sanchez where the switches are for the outside lights?'

Decker's throat felt scratchy, as if he'd been inhaling dust. 'Just inside the front door.'

Sanchez put on a pair of latex gloves and entered the house. In a moment, lights gleamed along the courtyard wall and under the portal that led up to the front door. The next thing, Sanchez had turned on the lights in the living room, their welcome glow streaming through windows, illuminating the courtyard.

'Excellent,' Esperanza said. The lights revealed that he had a 9mm Beretta holstered on his belt. He looked even thinner than he had seemed in the limited illumination from the headlights and flashlights. He had the weathered face of an outdoorsman, his skin swarthy, with a grain like leather. He seemed about to ask a question when a policeman came over and gestured toward a man beyond the open gate, a workman who had *Public Service of New Mexico* stenciled on his coveralls. 'Yes, I want to talk to him. Excuse me,' he told Decker, then headed toward the workman.

The Hansons looked overwhelmed by all the activity.

'Would you follow me, please?' an officer asked them. 'I need to ask you some questions.'

'Anything we can do to help.'

'Thank you,' Decker said again. 'I owe you.'

Esperanza passed them as he returned. 'You'll be more comfortable if we talk about this inside,' he told Decker. 'Your feet must be cold.'

'What? My feet?'

'You're not wearing any shoes.'

Decker peered down at his bare feet on the courtyard's bricks. 'So much has been going on, I forgot.'

'And you'll want to put on some clothes instead of that overcoat.'

'There was shooting in the bedroom.'

Esperanza looked puzzled by the apparent change of topic.

'And in the walk-in closet,' Decker said.

'Yes?' Esperanza studied him.

'Those are the only places where I keep clothes.'

Now Esperanza understood. 'That's right. Until the lab crew finishes in the bedroom, I'm afraid you can't touch anything in there.' Studying Decker harder, Esperanza gestured for them to go into the house.

2

'They cut off the electricity at the pole next to your house,' Esperanza said.

He and Decker were sitting at the kitchen table while policemen, a forensics crew, and the medical examiner checked the bedroom and laundry room areas. There were flashes, police photographers taking pictures. Decker's eardrums were still in pain, but the ringing had diminished. He was able to hear the harsh scrape of equipment being unpacked, a babble of voices, a man saying something about 'a war zone'.

'The pole's thirty yards off the gravel road behind some trees,' Esperanza said. 'No street lights. Widely separated houses. In the middle of the night, nobody would have seen a man climb the pole and cut the line. The same thing with the phone line. They cut it at the box at the side of the house.'

Despite the overcoat Decker wore, the aftermath of adrenaline continued to make him shiver. He stared toward the living room, where investigators came in and out. Beth, he kept thinking. What was happening at the hospital? Was Beth all right?

The men who broke in had ID in their wallets,' Esperanza said. 'We'll check their background. Maybe that'll tell us what this is all about. But . . . Mr Decker, what do *you* think this is about?'

Yes, that's the question, isn't it? Decker thought. What in God's name is this about? Throughout the attack, he had been so busy controlling his surprise and protecting Beth that he hadn't had time to analyze the implications. Who the hell were these men? Why had they broken in? Despite his bewilderment, he was certain about two things – the attack had something to do with his former life, and for reasons of national security, there was no way he could tell Esperanza *anything* about that former life.

Decker made himself look mystified. 'I assumed they were burglars.'

'House burglars usually work alone or in pairs,' Esperanza said. 'Sometimes in threes. But never in my experience, four of them. Not unless they intend to steal something big, furniture, for example, but in that case they use a van and we haven't found one. In fact, we haven't found *any* vehicle that seems out of place in the neighborhood. What's more, they chose the wrong time to break into your house. Last evening was the start of Fiesta. Most people go out for the celebration. The smart thing would have been for them to watch to see if you left the house and *then* to break in as soon as it got dark. These guys were smart enough to cut the phone and power lines. I don't see why they weren't also smart enough to get their timing right.'

Decker's face felt haggard. Tense and exhausted, he rubbed his forehead. 'Maybe they weren't thinking clearly. Maybe they were on drugs. Who the hell knows the way burglars think?'

'Burglars with a sawed-off shotgun, two Uzis, and a MAC-10. What did those men expect they were going to have to deal with in here, a SWAT team?'

'Sergeant, I used to work in Alexandria, Virginia. I traveled into Washington a lot. From what I heard on TV and read in the newspaper, it seemed every drug dealer and carjacker had a MAC-10 or an Uzi. For them, submachine guns were a status symbol.'

'Back east. But this is New Mexico. How long have you lived here?'

'About a year and a quarter.'

'So you're still learning. Or maybe you've already realized, they don't call this the City Different for nothing. Out here, in a lot of ways, this is still the wild west. We do things the old-fashioned way. If we want to shoot somebody, we use a handgun or maybe a hunting rifle. In my fifteen years of being a policeman, I've never come across a crime involving this many assault weapons. Incidentally, Mr Decker—'

'Yes?'

'Were you ever in law enforcement?'

'Law enforcement? No. I sell real estate. What makes you think—'

'When Officer Sanchez found you, he said you acted as if you understood police procedure and how an officer feels in a potentially dangerous situation. He said you emphasized that you'd have your hands up when you left the laundry room, that you'd show your hands first before you stepped into view. That's very unusual behavior.'

Decker rubbed his aching forehead. 'It just seemed logical. I was afraid the officer might think I was a threat.'

'And when I told you to put some clothes on, you took for granted you couldn't go into the bedroom to get them, not until the forensics crew was finished in there.'

'That seemed logical, too. I guess I've seen a lot of crime shows on TV.'

'And where did you learn to shoot so well?'

'In the military.'

'Ah,' Esperanza said.

'Look, I need to know about my friend.'

Esperanza nodded.

'I'm so worried about her I can hardly concentrate.'

157

Esperanza nodded again. 'I tell you what, why don't we stop by the hospital on our way to the police station?'

'Police station?' Decker said.

'So you can make your statement.'

'Isn't that what I'm doing now?'

'The one at the station is official.'

A phone, Decker thought. He needed to get to a payphone and call his former employers. He had to tell them what had happened. He had to find out how they wanted to handle this.

A policeman came into the kitchen. 'Sergeant, the medical examiner says it's all right now for Mr Decker to go into the bedroom to get some clothes.'

Decker stood.

'While we're in there, let's do a walk-through,' Esperanza said. 'It would be helpful if you showed us exactly how it happened. Also . . .'

'Yes?'

'I know it'll be difficult, but this is hardly an ordinary situation. It would save a lot of time if we knew right away rather than waited until tomorrow.'

'I don't understand what you mean,' Decker said. 'What do you want me to do?'

'Look at the faces.'

'What?'

'Of the bodies. Here, instead of in the morgue. Maybe you can identify them. Before, in the dark, you couldn't have seen what they looked like. Now that the lights are back on . . .'

Decker *wanted* to look at the bodies in case he recognized them, but he had to pretend to be reluctant. 'I don't think my stomach would— I'd throw up.'

'You're not obligated. There are alternatives. The forensics crew is taking photographs. You can examine those. Or look at the bodies later in the morgue. But photographs don't always provide a good likeness, and rigor mortis might distort the features of the corpses so they don't seem familiar to you even if you've crossed paths with them before. Right now, though, not long after the attack, there's always a possibility that . . .'

Decker couldn't stop thinking about Beth. He had to get to the hospital. Continuing to feign reluctance, he said, 'God help me. Yes, I'll look at them.'

3

Wearing jeans and a gray cotton sweater, Decker sat in a rigid chair in the almost deserted emergency-ward waiting room at St Vincent's Hospital. A clock on the wall showed that it was almost six-thirty. The fluorescent lights in the ceiling hurt his eyes. To the left, outside the door to the waiting room, Esperanza was talking to a policeman who stood next to a teenage boy with a bruised face who was strapped to a gurney. Esperanza's battered boots, faded jeans, shoulder-long hair, and leather cowboy hat made him look like anything except a police detective.

As a hospital attendant wheeled the gurney through electronically controlled swinging doors that led into the emergency ward, Esperanza entered the brightly lit waiting area. His long legs and lanky frame gave him a graceful stride that reminded Decker of a panther. The detective pointed toward the gurney. 'An accident victim. Drunk driving. Fiesta weekend. Typical. Any news about your friend?'

'No. The receptionist said a doctor would come out to see me.' Decker slumped lower in his chair. His head felt as if someone had tied a strap around it. He rubbed his face, feeling scratchy beard stubble, smelling gunpowder on his hands. He kept thinking about Beth.

'Sometimes, under stress, memory can take a while,' Esperanza said. 'You're sure the bodies you looked at didn't seem familiar?'

'To the best of my knowledge, I've never seen them before.' The cloying coppery smell of blood still lingered in Decker's nostrils. The dead men had all appeared to be in their twenties. They were husky, wore dark outdoor clothes, and had Mediterranean features. Possibly Greek. Maybe French. Or were they— The previous evening, at the Fiesta party, Decker had brooded about his last assignment for the agency. Rome. Could the olive-skinned gunmen have been Italian? Did the attack on his house have something to do with what had happened in Rome a year and a quarter ago? If only Esperanza would leave him alone long enough so he could make a phone call.

'Mr Decker, the reason I asked you if you'd ever been in law enforcement is, I can't get over what you managed to do. Four men break in with assault weapons. They blow the hell out of your house. And you manage to kill all four of them with a handgun. Doesn't that seem strange to you?'

'*Everything* about this is strange. I still can't believe—'

'Most people would have been so overwhelmed with fear, they'd have hidden when they heard someone breaking in.'

'That's why Beth and I ran to the walk-in closet.'

'But not before you grabbed the pistol you keep in your bedside drawer. You're a realtor, you mentioned.'

'Yes.'

'Why would you feel the need to keep a pistol by your bed?'

'Home protection.'

'Well, it's been my experience that pistols for home protection don't do much good,' Esperanza said. 'Because the owners themselves aren't any good with them. Family members end up getting shot. Innocent bystanders get hit. Oh, we have plenty of gun clubs in the area. And there are plenty of hunters.

But I don't care how often you've practiced with a pistol at the firing range or how frequently you've gone hunting – when four men come at you with heavy artillery, you're lucky if you have time to piss your pants from fright before they kill you.'

'I was scared, all right.'

'But it didn't impair your abilities. If you'd been in law enforcement, if you'd been tested under fire, I could understand.'

'I told you I was in the military.'

'Yes.' The weathered creases around Esperanza's eyes deepened. 'You did tell me that. What was your outfit?'

'The Rangers. Look, I don't know what you're getting at,' Decker said impatiently. 'The Army taught me to handle a pistol, and when the time came, I was lucky enough to remember how to use it. You're making me feel as if I did something *wrong*. Is it a crime to defend myself and my friend against a gang that breaks into my house and starts shooting? Everything's turned upside down. The crooks are the good guys, and decent citizens are—'

'Mr Decker, I'm not saying you did anything wrong. There'll have to be an inquest and you'll have to testify. That's the law. All shootings, even justified ones, have to be investigated to the fullest. But the truth is, I admire your resourcefulness and your presence of mind. Not many ordinary citizens would have survived what you went through. For that matter, I'm not sure *I'd* have been able to handle myself any better in your circumstance.'

'Then I don't get it. If you're not saying I did anything wrong, what *are* you saying?'

'I'm just making observations.'

'Well, this is *my* observation. The only reason I'm alive is I got angry. *Furious.* Those bastards broke into my *home*. The sons of bitches. They shot my friend. They . . . I got so angry I

161

stopped being afraid. All I wanted was to protect Beth, and by God, I managed that. I'm *proud* of that. I don't know if I should admit that to you, but I *am* proud. And this might not be the sort of thing to tell a police officer, either, but I will anyhow. If I had to, I'd do the same damned thing over again and be proud of it. Because I stopped the bastards from killing Beth.'

'You're a remarkable man, Mr Decker.'

'Hey, I'm no hero.'

'I didn't say that.'

'All I am is awfully lucky.'

'Right.'

A doctor appeared at the entrance to the waiting room. He was short and slight, in his thirties, wearing hospital greens and a stethoscope around his neck. He had small round spectacles. 'Is one of you Stephen Decker?'

Decker quickly stood. 'Can you tell me how my friend is doing?'

'She sustained a flesh wound just below her shoulder. The bleeding has been stopped. The wound has been sterilized and sutured. She's responding to treatment. Barring unforeseen complications, she ought to recover satisfactorily.'

Decker closed his eyes and murmured, 'Thank God.'

'Yes, there's a lot to give thanks for,' the doctor said. 'When your friend arrived at the hospital, she was in shock. Her blood pressure was low. Her pulse was erratic. Fortunately her life signs are back to normal.'

Back to normal? Decker thought. He worried that things would never be back to normal. 'When will she be able to go home?'

'I don't know yet. We'll see how well she continues to improve.'

'Can I see her?'

'She needs rest. I can't let you stay long.'

Esperanza stepped forward. 'Is she alert enough to make a statement to the police?'

The doctor shook his head. 'If I didn't think it was therapeutic for her to see Mr Decker, I wouldn't allow even him to visit.'

4

Beth looked pasty. Her dark hair, normally lush-looking, was tangled, without a sheen. Her eyes were sunken.

Under the circumstances, Decker thought, she had never seemed more beautiful.

After the doctor left, Decker shut the door, muting noises from the corridor. He studied Beth a moment longer, felt a tightness in his throat, came over to the bed, held the hand that wasn't in a sling, then leaned down and kissed her.

'How are you feeling?' He took care not to brush against the intravenous tube leading into her left arm.

Beth shrugged listlessly, obviously affected by sedation.

'The doctor says you're coming along fine,' Decker said.

Beth tried to speak, but Decker couldn't make out what she said.

Beth tried once more, licked her dry lips, then pointed toward a plastic cup filled with water. It had a curved straw, which Decker placed between her lips. She sipped.

'How are *you?*' she whispered hoarsely.

'Shook up.'

'Yeah,' Beth said with effort.

'How's the shoulder?'

'Sore.' Her eyelids looked heavy.

'I bet.'

'I hate to imagine what it'll feel like—' Beth winced.

' . . . when the painkillers wear off.' For a moment, she managed to tighten her fingers around his hand. Then her grip weakened. She was having trouble keeping her eyes open. 'Thank you.'

'I would never let anything happen to you.'

'I know,' Beth said.

'I love you.'

Decker could barely hear what she said next.

'Who . . . ?'

Decker completed the question he took for granted she was trying to ask. 'Who were they? I don't know.' He felt as if ashes were in his mouth. All he could think of was that the woman he had devoted his life to wouldn't be in the hospital if not for him. 'But believe me, I damned well intend to find out.'

Not that Beth heard him. Her dark-rimmed eyes drooped shut. She had drifted off to sleep.

5

Lack of sleep made Decker's own eyes feel pained by the glare of the morning sun as Esperanza drove him along Camino Lindo. The time was almost nine-thirty. They had spent the last two hours at the police station. Now Esperanza was taking him home.

'I'm sorry about all the inconvenience,' the sinewy detective said, 'but the judge at the inquest will want to make sure I eliminated all kinds of absolutely ridiculous possibilities.'

Decker concentrated to conceal his apprehension. It was alarmingly obvious to him that the threat against him had not been canceled merely because he'd killed the four men who had attacked him. He had to find out why they'd been sent and who had sent them. For all he knew, another hit team was already keeping him under surveillance. As a TV-news van passed the police car, presumably having taken footage of Decker's house, Decker decided that it would seem natural for him to turn and watch the van recede along the road. That tactic was a good way to check to be certain he wasn't being followed, without at the same time making Esperanza any more inquisitive.

'One ridiculous possibility would be you're a drug dealer who's had a falling out with your friends,' Esperanza said. 'You haven't kept your promises to them. You haven't delivered money you owe them. So they decide to make an example of you and send four guys to blow you away. But you're a resourceful guy. You get them first. Then you arrange things to look as if you're an innocent man who barely managed to save his life.'

'Including getting my friend shot.'

'Well, this is merely a hypothetical possibility.' Esperanza gestured offhandedly. 'It's one of a variety of theories the judge will want to make sure I've considered and eliminated.' The detective stopped the police car on the road outside Decker's house, unable to park in the driveway because a van and two other police cars blocked it. 'Looks like the forensics team isn't finished. That shower you said you wanted will have to be postponed a little longer.'

'For a couple of reasons. I just remembered – one of the men who broke in shot the water heater apart. You'd better drive me down to the next house.'

Esperanza looked puzzled for a moment, the creases in his forehead adding to the leathery grain of his narrow handsome face. Then he nodded with understanding. 'That's right – you mentioned your friend lived next to you.'

'I have a key,' Decker said.

As they drove past several curious bystanders who had

gathered at the side of the road and showed obvious interest in the police car, Decker couldn't help wondering, his muscles rigid, if any of them was a threat to him.

'When you were living in Alexandria, Virginia, what was the name of the real-estate company you worked for?' Esperanza asked.

'The Rawley-Hackman Agency.'

'Do you remember their telephone number?'

'I haven't used it in more than a year, but I think so.' Decker pretended to jog his memory, then dictated the number while Esperanza wrote it down. 'But I don't see why it's necessary to involve them.'

'Just a standard background check.'

'Sergeant, you're beginning to make me feel like a criminal.'

'Am I?' Esperanza tapped his fingers on the steering wheel. 'If you think of anything you've forgotten to tell me, I'll be at your house.'

6

Exhausted, Decker locked Beth's front door behind him and leaned against it. Tense, he listened to the adobe-smothered stillness of the house. At once he went into the living room and picked up the telephone. Under normal circumstances, he would have waited until he had a chance to get to a payphone, but he didn't have the luxury of waiting, and as he kept reminding himself, nothing was normal any longer. In an attempt at security, he reversed the charges, preventing a record of the call from showing up on Beth's telephone bill.

'Rawley-Hackman Agency,' a smooth male voice said.

'I have a collect call from Martin Kowalsky,' the operator said. 'Will you accept the charges?'

Martin Kowalsky, the name Decker had given the operator, was a code for an emergency.

'Yes,' the voice said immediately. 'I'll accept.'

'Go ahead, Mr Kowalsky.'

Decker could not be sure that the operator didn't continue to listen. 'Does your console show the number I'm using?' he asked the voice on the other end.

'Of course.'

'Call me right back.'

Ten seconds later, the phone rang. 'Hello.'

'Martin Kowalsky?'

'My identification number is eight, seven, four, four, five.'

Decker heard what sounded like fingers tapping numbers on a computer keyboard.

'Stephen Decker?'

'Yes.'

'Our records show that you severed your employment with us a year ago in June. Why are you re-establishing contact?'

'Because four men tried to kill me last night.'

The voice didn't respond for a moment. 'Repeat that.'

Decker did.

'I'm transferring you.'

The next male voice had a sharp edge of authority. 'Tell me everything.'

With practiced economy, Decker finished in five minutes, the details precise and vivid, his urgent tone reinforcing their effect.

'You believe the attack was related to your former employment with us?' the official asked.

'It's the most obvious explanation. Look, there's a chance the shooters were Italian. My last assignment was in Italy. In Rome. It was a disaster. Check the file.'

'It's on my monitor as we speak. Your connection between

last night's attack and what happened in Rome is awfully tenuous.'

'It's the only connection I can make at the moment. I want you to look into this. I don't have the resources to—'

'But you're not our responsibility any longer,' the voice said firmly.

'Hey, you sure thought I was when I quit. You were all over me. I figured your security checks would never stop. Damn it, two months ago, you were still keeping me under surveillance. So drop the bullshit and listen carefully. There's a detective in charge of investigating the attack on me. His name is Esperanza, and it's obvious he thinks something isn't right about my story. So far I've managed to distract him, but if something happens to me, if another hit team manages to finish the job the first bunch started, he'll be that much more determined. He might find out a hell of a lot more than you think is possible.'

'We'll see that he backs off.'

'You'd better,' Decker said, adding with force, 'I've always been loyal. I expect the same from you. Get me some backup. Find out who sent those men after me.'

The voice didn't answer for a moment. 'I have the number you're calling from on my monitor. Is your location secure enough for me to call you there?'

'No. I'll have to call *you* back.'

'Six hours.' The man hung up.

Decker immediately set down the phone and was surprised when it rang. Frowning, he answered it. 'Yes?'

'I gather you haven't had a chance to take your shower.' The caller's cadenced voice, almost musical, was instantly recognizable – Esperanza.

'That's right. How did you know?'

'Your line's been busy. I've been trying to get in touch with you.'

'I had to contact some clients to cancel some showings.'

'And are you finished? I hope so – because I want you to meet me at your house. I have some information that will interest you.'

7

'The IDs of the men you shot indicate they came from Denver,' Esperanza said.

He and Decker were in the living room. In the background, the investigating team was leaving, carrying equipment out to the van and the two police cars.

'But Denver's five hundred miles from here,' Esperanza continued. 'That's an awful long way for them to have come just to break into a house and steal. They could have done that in Colorado.'

'Maybe they were passing through Santa Fe, and they ran out of money,' Decker said.

'That still doesn't explain the automatic weapons or why they opened fire so quickly.'

'It could be they were startled when they realized someone was in the house.'

'And it could be Denver's a false trail,' Esperanza said. 'The Denver police department did some checking for me. No one using any of the names on those IDs is a resident at those addresses. In fact, three of the addresses *don't exist*. The fourth is a mortuary.'

'Somebody had a grim sense of humor.'

'And access to authentic-looking bogus credit cards and drivers' licenses. So we have to dig deeper,' Esperanza said. 'I've sent their fingerprints to the FBI. It'll take a day or two before we know if the Feds can match the prints with any they have on file. Meanwhile, I've alerted the Bureau of Alcohol, Tobacco, and Firearms. The serial numbers on the two Uzis and the MAC-10 had been burned off with acid, but ATF has ways to try to bring back the numbers. If they can, maybe the numbers will point us in a direction. Where the guns were bought, for example. Or more likely, stolen. But that's not why I wanted to talk to you.'

Decker waited, apprehensive.

'Let's take a walk. I want to show you something in back of your house.'

Show me what? Decker thought. Uneasy, he went with Esperanza along the corridor past the entrance to the master bedroom. The bodies had been removed. The stench of cordite still hung in the air. Sunlight blazed through the corridor's solar-gain windows, one of which had been shattered by a bullet. The sunlight made vivid the considerable amount of blood that had congealed, turning black, on the corridor's tiles. Decker glanced toward the bedroom and saw the bullet-gutted mattress and pillows. Black graphite fingerprint powder seemed everywhere. It rubbed off on Esperanza's hand as he turned the knob on the door at the end of the hallway.

'You heard them pick this lock.' Esperanza stepped out into a small garden of yuccas, roses, and low evergreens. 'That was after they climbed over the wall to this courtyard.'

Esperanza gestured for Decker to peer over the chest-high courtyard wall. 'See where the scrubgrass on the other side has been crushed? There are numerous footprints in the sand beyond the grass. Those footprints match the outline of the shoes the intruders wore.'

Esperanza moved farther along the wall and climbed over where he wouldn't disturb the tracks he had pointed out. He waited for Decker to follow.

Squinting from the brilliant sunlight, Decker jumped down

near two lines of yellow police-crime-scene tape that had been strung among piñon trees to isolate the footprints.

'You have a good-sized lot.' Esperanza's boots made a crunching sound on the pebbly ground as he walked parallel to the tracks, leading Decker down a steep slope. They passed among yuccas, piñons, and a dense swathe of waist-high chamisa bushes, their seeds having turned a mustard color typical of them in September.

All the while, Esperanza kept pointing toward the tracks. He and Decker climbed down past junipers on the increasingly steep slope. At the bottom, they followed the tracks along a ditch and onto a poplar-lined road that Decker recognized as Fort Connor Lane. The footprints were no longer in evidence, but wheelgrooves were dug into the gravel, as if a vehicle had sped away.

'That walk took us longer than I expected,' Esperanza said. 'A couple of times, we almost lost our footing.'

Decker nodded, waiting for him to make his point.

'In daylight. Imagine how long and difficult it would have been at night. Why did they go to all the trouble? Take a look along this road. The houses are expensive. Widely separated. Easy targets. So why would those four men drive here, get out of their vehicle, refuse to make life easy for themselves, and instead decide to hike all over God's creation? From down here, we can't even see if there are any houses above us.'

'I don't get your point,' Decker said.

'Your house wasn't chosen at random. It was exactly the one they wanted. You were the intended target.'

'What? But that's crazy. Why would anybody want to kill me?'

'Exactly.' Esperanza's dark gaze intensified. 'You're holding something back.'

'Nothing,' Decker insisted. 'I've told you everything I can think of.'

'Then think about this. Someone drove their vehicle away. Suppose he comes back with another group of men to finish the job?'

'Are you trying to scare me, Sergeant?'

'I'm putting a policeman on guard at your house.'

8

Decker had never felt so naked as when he took off his clothes and stepped into his shower. Not wanting to be outside his house any more than was absolutely necessary, he had abandoned the idea of returning to Beth's place so he could clean up there. He would have to make do with the cold water coming from his shower, a small discomfort compared to his urgent need to rid himself of the sticky feel of sweat and death that clung to him. Shivering, he washed his hair and body as fast as he could. His muscles were painfully tense.

Quickly, he shaved, the cold water making the razor irritate his face. He put on loafers, khaki pants, and a camel shirt, the colors chosen because they were muted and wouldn't draw attention to him. Wishing that the police hadn't confiscated his pistol, regretting that he hadn't bought two, he picked up a shopping bag of clothes that he had taken from Beth's bedroom closet after he had made his phone call at her house. He tried not to look at the dried blood on his hallway floor as he carried the bag into his living room, where Officer Sanchez was waiting.

'I need to go to the hospital to visit my friend,' Decker said.

'I'll drive you.'

The stocky policeman went past the courtyard and into the

driveway. After looking around, he gestured that it was all right for Decker to come out and get in the police car. Troubled by a group of curious onlookers who were gathered on the road, pointing toward his house, Decker didn't feel reassured, but Sanchez's precaution was better than nothing. If only I had a gun, Decker thought.

He wasn't fooled by the explanation that Esperanza had given for putting Decker under police guard. Sanchez wasn't staying with Decker only to provide protection; the policeman's presence also guaranteed that Decker wouldn't suddenly leave town before Esperanza got some answers. Six hours, Decker thought. The intelligence official whom Decker had spoken to on the phone had said to call back in six hours. But six hours seemed an eternity.

As Sanchez steered onto St Michael's Drive, heading toward the hospital, Decker glanced through the rear window to see if anyone was following.

'Nervous?' Sanchez asked.

'Esperanza has me jumping at shadows. Aren't *you* nervous? You seem a little heavier than when I first saw you. It looks to me like you're wearing a bullet-resistant vest under your uniform.'

'We wear these all the time.'

'Sure you do.'

At the hospital, Sanchez avoided the parking lot and stopped at an out-of-the-way door, then scanned the area before saying it was all right to go inside. On the third floor, the heavy set policeman hitched up his gunbelt and stood watch outside Beth's room while Decker went in.

9

'How are you?' Decker studied Beth in the hospital bed, his heart filled with pity and sorrow. Again he blamed himself for having been indirectly responsible for what had happened to her.

Beth managed a smile. 'A little better.'

'Well, you look *much* better.' Decker kissed her cheek, trying not to jostle the sling on her right arm, noting that the intravenous line had been removed.

'Liar,' Beth said.

'Really. You look beautiful.'

'You have a great bedside manner.'

Although Beth's hair remained gritty, the tangles had been combed from it. The pallor had faded from her tan cheeks, as had a lot of the dark areas around her eyes. The blue-gray eyes themselves had regained some of their brightness. Her loveliness was reasserting itself.

'I can't tell you how worried I was about you.' Decker touched her cheek.

'Hey, I'm tough.'

'That's an understatement. How's the pain?'

'It throbs like hell. Did you learn anything? Did the police find out who broke into your house?'

'No.' Decker avoided her gaze.

'Tell me all of it,' Beth insisted.

'I don't know what you mean.'

'I've gotten to know you better than you think,' Beth said. 'You're keeping something from me.'

' . . . This might not be the time to go into this.'

'I'm asking you not to hide things from me.'

Decker exhaled. 'The detective in charge of the investigation . . . His name is Esperanza . . . feels that this wasn't a random event, that those men broke in specifically to kill me.'

Beth's eyes widened.

'I can't imagine a reason anyone would want to kill me,' Decker lied. 'But Esperanza thinks that, well, I ought to be careful for a while until he figures out what's going on. There's a policeman with me. Outside in the hallway. He drove me here. He's sort of . . . I guess you could call him . . .'

'What?'

'My bodyguard. And . . .'

'Tell me *everything*.'

Decker looked deeply into her eyes. 'You mean too much to me. I don't want to put you in danger a second time. When you're released from the hospital, I don't think we should see each other for a while.'

'Shouldn't see each other?' Beth winced, sitting straighter.

'What if you were struck by another bullet meant for me? It's too dangerous. We've got to stay apart until Esperanza gets the answers he wants, until he says the risk is over.'

'But this is insane.'

Without warning, the door opened. Decker turned sharply, not knowing what to expect, relieved when he saw the short slight doctor whom he had met when Beth was admitted to the hospital.

'Ah,' the doctor said, adjusting his spectacles. 'Mr Decker. You must be as pleased as I am by Ms Dwyer's recovery.'

Decker tried not to reveal the intense emotions his conversation with Beth had produced. 'Yes, she's recovering better than I hoped.'

The doctor walked over to Beth. 'In fact, I'm so pleased that I'm going to release you.'

Beth looked as if she hadn't heard him correctly. 'Release me?' She blinked. 'Now? Are you serious?'

'Absolutely. Why? You don't seem happy about—'

'I'm delighted.' Beth glanced meaningfully at Decker. 'It's just that what happened has been so depressing . . .'

'Well, now you have some good news,' the doctor said. 'Resting in your own bed, with familiar things around you, you'll be at the top of your form in no time.'

'In no time,' Beth echoed, glancing again at Decker.

'I stopped by your house and brought you some clothes.' Decker gave her the shopping bag he'd been holding. 'Nothing fancy. Jeans. A pullover. Tennis shoes and socks. Underwear.' The latter reference made him feel selfconscious.

'I'll have a nurse bring you a wheelchair,' the doctor said.

'But I'm able to walk,' Beth said.

The doctor shook his head. 'Our insurance won't let you leave the hospital unless you're in a wheelchair. After that, you can do as you like.'

'Can I at least dress myself without a nurse watching?'

'With an injured arm? Are you sure you can do it?'

'Yes.' Beth checked that her hospital gown was fastened tightly, then allowed the doctor and Decker to help her out of bed. 'There. You see.' Beth stood on her own, looking slightly off balance because of the sling on her right arm. 'I can manage.'

'I'll help with your clothes,' Decker said.

'Steve, I . . .'

'What?'

'I'm not feeling very attractive at the moment. In fact, I'm so grungy I'm embarrassed.' She blushed. 'I could use a little privacy.'

'There's no need to be embarrassed. But if you want privacy, sure, I'll be waiting outside in the hallway. When you're ready, the policeman will drive us home. If you do need help, though . . .'

'You can bet I'll let you know.'

10

After Sanchez checked the parking lot, Decker nervously guided Beth through the hospital's side entrance. On guard against any threatening movements in the out-of-the-way area, Decker helped Beth from the wheelchair into the back seat of the police car, then quickly closed the door and got in the front.

'Why aren't you sitting back here with me?' Beth asked as the police car pulled away.

Decker didn't answer.

'Oh.' Her voice dropped as she realized. 'You're keeping a distance between us in case . . .'

'I'm having second thoughts about even being in the same car with you,' Decker said. 'If Esperanza's right, there'll be another attempt against me, and I don't want to put you at risk. I can't bear the thought that something might happen to you because of me.' On edge, he kept studying the cars behind him.

'And I can't bear the thought of being apart from you,' Beth said. 'Are you really determined that we shouldn't see each other until this is over?'

'If I could think of another option that was safe, I'd take it,' Decker said.

'We could run away and hide.'

Sanchez looked back at her. 'Sergeant Esperanza wouldn't appreciate that. In fact, I can guarantee he'd do everything possible to discourage you.'

'That's part of your job right now, isn't it?' Decker asked. 'To make sure I don't leave the area?'

No response.

'It might be a good idea to avoid returning along St Michael's Drive,' Decker said. 'Take an alternate route so we don't follow a predictable pattern.'

Sanchez looked strangely at him. 'You sound as if this isn't the first time you thought you were being watched.'

'An alternative route just seemed a logical precaution.' Decker turned to Beth. 'We'll let you off at your house. You told me you had business back east, that you were leaving tomorrow. This is a good time for it. I know you don't feel like traveling with your arm the way it is, but you'll be able to rest when you get to New York. In fact, it would be a good idea if you stayed with relatives when your business meetings were over. Make it a long visit. And I think you should leave sooner. This afternoon.'

Beth looked overwhelmed.

'It's the only sure way,' Decker said. 'I still can't believe Esperanza's right, but in the event that he is, someone wanting to hurt me could use you as a weapon, maybe kidnap you.'

'*Kidnap* me?'

'It has to be considered as a possibility.'

'Jesus, Steve.'

'We can keep in touch by phone, and the moment Esperanza thinks it's safe, you can come back.'

'Stay away?'

'Maybe it won't be for a long time. Maybe it'll just be a little while.'

They lapsed into an awkward silence as Sanchez pulled into Beth's driveway and parked the cruiser protectively sideways in front of the gate to her walled courtyard.

Beth winced when Decker helped her out of the back seat. While Sanchez waited in the police car, they entered the courtyard and paused beneath the shadows of the portal, looking into each other's eyes.

'This has got to be a mistake,' Beth said. 'I feel as if I'm having a nightmare and I'll wake up in your arms and none of this will have happened.'

Decker shook his head.

'Can you think of *any* reason someone would want to kill you?' Beth asked.

'I've asked myself that question a hundred times. A *thousand* times. I can't think of an answer,' Decker lied. He studied her face intensely. 'If I'm not going to see you for a while, I want to make sure I remember every detail of your face.'

He leaned close, kissing her lips, trying to be gentle, to avoid her injured shoulder.

Regardless of her wound, Beth used her free arm to hold him close against her, to kiss him as if trying to possess him, even as she winced from the pressure against her shoulder.

She rested her cheek against his, whispering urgently, 'Run away with me.'

'No. I can't.'

She leaned back, her eyes imploring as fiercely as her voice. '*Please.*'

'Sanchez just told you, the police would stop us.'

'If you truly loved me . . .'

'It's *because* I love you that I can't risk putting you in danger. Suppose we did manage to fool the police and run away. Suppose we were followed by whoever is after me. We'd always be looking over our shoulders. I won't do that to you. I love you too much to ruin your life.'

'One last time – please, come with me.'

Decker shook his head firmly.

'I'll miss you more than you know.'

'Just keep reminding yourself, this won't be forever,' Decker said. 'In time . . . with luck soon . . . we'll be together again. When you get to wherever you're going, use a payphone to call

179

me. We'll work out a way to keep in touch. And . . .' Decker breathed deeply. 'There are so many details to be settled. I'll ask Esperanza to have a policeman drive you to the airport. Also—'

Beth put a finger to his lips. 'I'm sure you'll take care of everything.' Reluctantly, she added, 'I'll phone your house when I've made flight arrangements.'

'Do you need help getting your suitcases ready?'

'Most of my stuff is already packed.'

Decker kissed her a final time.

'Remember the best day we ever had together,' Beth said.

'There'll be many more.' Decker waited until he had his last glimpse of Beth going into the house. Only after she closed the door did he turn and walk back to the cruiser.

11

'*I want to talk to you.*' Esperanza was waiting in Decker's driveway when the cruiser pulled in. His normally relaxed lean features were rigid with fury. 'I want to know why you lied to me!'

'Lied?'

Esperanza stared past Decker toward bystanders on the road. '*Inside.*'

'If you'd tell me what's bothering you.'

'*Inside.*'

Decker lifted his hands in a surrendering motion. 'Whatever you say.'

Esperanza slammed the door shut behind them after they entered. They faced each other in the living room.

'I asked you if you were holding anything back. You said you'd told me everything you could think of.' Esperanza's breathing was strident.

'That's right.'

'Well, you ought to see a doctor – you're having serious memory problems,' Esperanza said. 'Otherwise, you wouldn't have overlooked mentioning something as important as your connection with the FBI.'

'The FBI?' Decker asked in genuine surprise.

'Damn it, are you also having hearing problems? Yeah! The FBI! The head of the Santa Fe bureau called me an hour ago and said he wanted to have a little chat. What could he possibly have in mind? I wondered. Something to do with Los Alamos or the Sandia labs? A national security problem? Or maybe an interstate crime spree? So imagine my surprise when I met him at his office and he started talking about the attack on your house.'

Decker didn't trust himself to speak.

'It's a federal matter now, did you know that? *Federal*. Why, I could barely keep my mouth from hanging open when he told me all about what happened last night. He knew details only Sanchez and I and a few other policemen knew. How the hell did he get that information? It's not like he *asked* about last night, sort of professional curiosity. He didn't need to ask. He *told* me. And then he told me something else – that the FBI would appreciate it if I let them handle the case from now on.'

Decker remained still, fearing that any reaction he made would cause Esperanza to become more agitated.

'The attack on your house involves extremely sensitive matters, I was informed. Information about the FBI's interest in the attack is passed out on a need-to-know basis and I do not need to know, I was assured. If I persisted in remaining attached to the case, I would cause untold harm, I was warned.' Esperanza's eyes were ablaze with anger. 'Fine, I said. I mean, hey, I wouldn't want to cause untold harm. God forbid. I'm as good a team player as the next man. My hands are off the case.'

Esperanza stalked toward Decker. 'But that doesn't mean I can't nose around *un*officially, and it certainly doesn't mean I can't demand a private explanation from you! Who the hell *are* you? What really happened last night? Why didn't you keep me from making a fool of myself by telling me from the start to go talk to the FBI?'

Whump.

With a roar, the house shook.

12

Decker and Esperanza frowned at each other as a deafening rumble shuddered through them.

'What the—' Windows rattled. Dishes clattered. Decker felt a change in air pressure, as if cotton batting had been pushed into his ears.

'Something blew up!' Esperanza said. 'It came from—'

'Down the street! Jesus, you don't suppose—' Decker lunged toward the front door and yanked it open just as Sanchez, who had been waiting outside, ran into the courtyard.

'The house next door!' Sanchez said, pointing, agitated. 'It—'

Another roar shook them, the rumbling shockwave of a second explosion knocking Decker off balance. 'Beth!' Regaining his footing, he charged past Sanchez, through the open gate, and into the driveway. To his right, above the piñons and junipers that shielded Beth's house, black smoke billowed. Wreckage cascaded. Even from a hundred yards away, Decker heard the whoosh of flames.

'*Beth!*' Vaguely aware that Esperanza and Sanchez were next to him, Decker raced to help her. He ignored the police car. He ignored the road. His throat raw from screaming Beth's name, he chose the most direct route, charged to the right, crossed his driveway, and scrambled among piñon trees.

'BETH!' Branches scraped his arms. Sand crunched beneath his shoes. Esperanza shouted to him. But all Decker really heard was the fierce rush of his breathing as he swerved around a farther tree, the flames and dark smoke looming closer before him.

As the trees ended, he reached a waist-high wooden fence, gripped a post, vaulted a rail, and landed on Beth's property. The fiery, smoke-obscured wreckage of the house was spread before him. The bitter stench of burning wood surged into his nostrils, searing his throat and lungs, making him cough.

'BETH!' The whoosh of the flames was so loud that he couldn't hear himself scream her name. Fractured adobe bricks were strewn everywhere. He stumbled over them. Smoke stung his eyes. Abruptly a breeze caused the smoke to shift, showing him that not all of the house was on fire. A corner section at the back had not yet been engulfed. Beth's bedroom was in that section.

Esperanza grasped his shoulder, trying to stop him. Decker shoved his hand away and rushed toward the back. He squirmed over a waist-high wall, crossed a wreckage-littered patio, and reached one of the bedroom windows. The force of the explosions had blown the glass out, leaving jagged edges that he broke off with a chunk of adobe he found at his feet.

The effort made him breathe hoarsely. As smoke billowed out, he swallowed some of it, strained to control his coughing, and peered through the window. 'Beth!' Again, Esperanza grabbed him. Again, Decker shoved him away.

'Leave me alone!' Decker screamed. 'Beth needs me!' He pulled himself through the window, tumbled to the floor, and banged his shoulder on more wreckage. Smoke surrounded him. He lurched toward the bed but found it empty. Coughing more violently, he groped along the floor, hoping to find Beth if she had collapsed. He felt his way toward the bathroom, bumped against the closed door, and became excited by the thought that Beth had taken shelter there, but when he tugged the door open, he had a heartsinking chance, before the smoke swept in, to see that the bathroom's tub and shower stall were empty.

His vision blurred. He felt heat and recoiled from flames that filled the bedroom doorway. At the same time, he was pressed down by the force of other flames that roared from the ceiling. He fell to the floor and crawled, struggling to breathe. He reached the window, fought to stand, and shoved his head through the opening, trying to pull himself outside. Something crashed behind him. Heat swept over his legs. At once something else crashed. Beams must be falling, he thought in dismay. The roof's about to collapse. Heat pressed against his hips. Frantic, he pulled and pushed and fell outward through the window.

Hands grabbed him, dragging him fiercely over wreckage as flames followed Decker through the window. The hands belonged to Esperanza, who clutched Decker's jacket, jerked him to his feet, and shoved him over the waist-high wall.

Decker felt weightless. Immediately he landed hard on the opposite side of the wall, rolled, and struck the base of a piñon tree. Esperanza dropped next to him, pursued by flames that ignited the tree. As the branches crackled, fire erupting, Esperanza dragged Decker farther away.

Another tree burst into flames.

'We have to keep going!' Esperanza shouted.

Decker stared back at the house. The smoke-spewing wreckage shimmered from the intense heat. 'Beth's in there!'

'There's nothing more you can do to help her! We have to get farther away!'

Listing, Decker fought to get air in his lungs. He stifled the urge to vomit and staggered with Esperanza through smoke down the treed slope at the rear of Beth's house. Again, he stared back at the inferno. 'Christ, what am I going to do? *Beth!*' he kept screaming. 'BETH!'

SIX

1

Decker sat numbly on the hard-packed dirt of Camino Lindo, his back against the right rear wheel of a paramedic truck, breathing through an oxygen mask. The gas was dry and bitter, or maybe the bitterness was because of the smoke he had inhaled – he didn't know. He heard the oxygen hiss from a tank beside him, a paramedic checking the pressure gauge on top. He heard the rumble of engines, fire trucks, police cars, other emergency vehicles. He heard firemen shouting to each other as they sprayed water from numerous hoses onto the smoking wreckage of Beth's house.

My fault, he thought. All my fault.

He must have said it out loud, because the paramedic asked, 'What?' frowned with concern, and took the mask from Decker's face. 'Are you all right? Do you think you're going to throw up?'

Decker shook his head, the movement aggravating a monumental headache, making him wince.

'What were you trying to tell us?'

'Nothing.'

'That's not true,' Esperanza said next to him. 'You said, "My fault. All my fault." ' The detective's grime-covered face had an oval impression around his nose and mouth from an oxygen mask that he had taken away. 'Don't blame yourself. This isn't your fault. You couldn't have anticipated this.'

'Bullshit. I was worried she might have been in danger

because she was close to me.' Decker spat, his phlegm specked with soot. 'I never should have let her go home. Damn it, I never should have—'

'Hold still,' the paramedic said. He had pushed up Decker's pant-legs and was examining the skin of his calves. 'You're lucky. The fire scorched your pants but didn't set them on fire. The hair on your legs is singed. And on your arms. Your head. Another few seconds in there and . . . I'm not sure I would have been as brave.'

Decker's tone was full of self-ridicule. 'Brave. Like hell. I didn't save her.'

'But you nearly got killed trying. You did everything you could,' Esperanza emphasized.

'Everything?' Decker coughed deeply, painfully. 'If I'd been thinking, I would have insisted she stay under guard at the hospital.'

'Here, drink this,' the paramedic said.

Decker sipped from a bottle of water. Drops of liquid rolled down his chin, leaving streaks in the soot on his face. 'I should have anticipated how easy it would be for them to get into *her* house while everyone was watching *my* house. If I'd gone inside when we brought her home, the explosions would have gotten both of us.'

Esperanza's dark brown eyes became somber – what Decker had said troubled him. About to respond, he was distracted by the wailing sirens of another police car and a fire truck arriving on the scene.

Decker sipped more water, then stared toward the chaos of firemen hosing the rubble. 'Jesus.' He dropped the water bottle and raised his hands to his face. His shoulders heaved painfully as tears welled from his eyes. He felt as if he was being choked. Grief cramped his chest. 'Oh, Jesus, Beth, what am I going to do without you?'

He felt Esperanza's arm around him.

'All my fault. All my damned fault,' Decker said through his tears.

He heard an ambulance attendant whisper, 'We'd better get him to the hospital.'

'No!' Decker's voice was strained. 'I want to stay and help find the bastards who did this!'

'How do you suppose they set off the bombs?' Esperanza asked.

'What?' Bewilderment clouded Decker's senses. He tried to focus on Esperanza's question. Concentrate, he told himself. Get control. You can't find whoever did this if you're hysterical. 'Some kind of remote device.'

'Electronic detonators set off by a radio signal.'

'Yes.' Decker wiped tears from his raw red eyes. Beth, he kept thinking. Dear God, what am I going to do without you? All my fault. 'A timer wouldn't be practical. They wouldn't know what time to set it for, when anybody would be home.'

Esperanza looked more troubled.

'It would have to be somebody watching the house, holding a detonator, waiting for the right time to push the button,' Decker said. 'Maybe someone with binoculars on Sun Mountain. Maybe one of the people lingering on the road, pretending to be interested in what happened last night.'

'I have police officers talking to everybody in the area,' Esperanza said.

'Too late. Whoever pushed the button is long gone.'

'Or maybe an electronic signal in the area happened to have the same frequency the detonators were set to. Maybe the bombs went off by mistake,' Esperanza said.

'No. The detonators would have needed a sequence of two different frequencies in order for them to go off. They would have been set to frequencies that weren't common in this area.'

'You seem to know an awful lot about this,' Esperanza said.

'I read about this stuff somewhere. A lot of it's just common sense.'

'Is it?'

Someone was approaching, footsteps heavy. Decker looked up and saw Sanchez stop in front of them.

'The fire chief says the wreckage has cooled enough for him to get close,' Sanchez told Esperanza. 'According to him, there wouldn't have been so much fire unless the bombs were incendiaries.'

'I figured that much already.' With effort, Esperanza stood. His long hair was singed. His jeans and denim shirt were grimy, laced with holes made by sparks. 'What can the fire chief tell us that we *don't* know?'

'He and his crew have started searching for the body. He says, with the adobe walls and the brick and tile floors, there wasn't as much to burn as in a wood-frame house. That'll make the search easier. So far they haven't found any sign of her.'

'Is there anything else?' Esperanza sounded frustrated.

'Yes, but—' Sanchez glanced at Decker, obviously not comfortable speaking in front of him.

'What is it?' Decker came to his feet. Adrenaline shot through him. 'What aren't you saying?'

Sanchez turned to Esperanza. 'Maybe we should go over to the cruiser. There's something we need to talk about.'

'No,' Decker said. 'You're not keeping *anything* from me. Whatever you have to say, you say it right here.'

Sanchez looked uncertainly toward Esperanza. 'Is that okay with you?'

Esperanza raised his shoulders. 'Maybe Mr Decker will share what *he* knows with us if *we* share with him. What have you got?'

'Something weird. You told me to assign officers to question people in the area – neighbors who might have been outside, someone who might have been walking by, busybodies who've been hanging around, curious about what happened last night, anybody who might have seen the explosions.'

Esperanza anticipated. 'And our men found someone who can help us?'

'Well, I think it's a complication more than a help,' Sanchez said.

'Damn it, what did you learn?' Decker stepped closer. 'What are you trying to hide from me?'

'Down on Fort Connor Lane, the street below and behind these houses, a woman was looking for a lost dog. Just before the explosions, she was startled by someone hurrying down through the trees and bushes on the slope.'

'Whoever set off the bombs,' Decker said. 'Does the woman remember well enough to provide a description?'

'Yes. The person she saw was another woman.'

Decker felt as if he'd been jabbed.

'Carrying a suitcase,' the policeman said.

'What?'

'Attractive, in her early thirties, with long auburn hair, wearing jeans and a pullover. Her right arm was under the pullover, as if the arm had been injured.'

Decker put a hand against the paramedic truck. The ground seemed to shift. He felt dizzy, his legs unsteady, his sanity tilting. 'But you just described—'

'Beth Dwyer. That's right,' Sanchez said. 'The woman looking for her dog says there was a car parked on Fort Connor Lane. A man was inside. When he saw the woman with the suitcase, he hurried out, put her suitcase in the trunk, and helped her into the car. That's when the bombs went off, when they were driving away.'

'I don't understand,' Decker said. 'This doesn't make sense. How could—'

A fireman came over, taking his wide-brimmed metal hat off, dripping sweat from his soot-smeared face, reaching for a bottle of water a paramedic offered him. 'There's still no sign of a victim,' he told Esperanza.

Decker's heartbeat became sickeningly fast. His mind swirled. 'But why would . . . Beth's *alive*? What was she doing on the slope? Who the hell was in the car?'

2

It seemed impossible. Beth hadn't been killed! A welter of relief and hope coursed through him. But so did confusion and dismay about her mystifying behavior.

'How did you meet Beth Dwyer?' Esperanza asked. They faced each other in Decker's living room.

'She came to my office. She wanted to buy a house.' This can't be happening, Decker thought, slumping on his sofa.

'When was this?'

'Two months ago. In July.' I'm losing my mind, Decker thought.

'Was she local?'

'No.'

'Where did she come from?'

'Back east.' Decker's headache was excruciating.

'Which city?'

'Some place outside New York.'

'Why did she move to Santa Fe?'

'Her husband died in January. Cancer. She wanted to get away from bad memories, to start a new life.' Just as *I* wanted to start a new life, Decker thought.

'This is an expensive district,' Esperanza said. 'How could she afford to buy her house?'

'Her husband had a sizeable life-insurance policy.'

'Must have been hefty. What was his occupation?'

'I don't know.'

Esperanza looked confused. 'I assumed you were intimate.'

'Yes.'

'And yet there are several basic things about her past that you don't know.'

'I didn't want to ask too many questions,' Decker said. 'With her husband dead less than a year, I didn't want to raise disturbing memories.'

'Such as where she used to live? How disturbing would that have been for her to tell you?'

'I just didn't think to ask.' It was another lie. Decker knew exactly why he hadn't asked. In his former life, he had made it his business to elicit every possible scrap of personal information from people he had just met, never knowing when that information might prove useful. But from the moment he had arrived in Santa Fe, beginning his new life, reinventing himself, he had been determined to shut out his former calculating ways.

'Was the husband's insurance policy large enough to support her after she bought the house next door to you?'

'She earned a living as an artist,' Decker said.

'Oh? What gallery?'

'In New York.'

'But what name?'

'I don't know,' Decker repeated.

'Imagine that.'

'I met the man who runs the gallery. He came to visit. His name is Dale Hawkins.'

'When was this?'

'Thursday. The first of September.'

'How can you be so specific?'

'It was only nine days ago. I remember because that was the day Beth closed the deal on her house.' But Decker had another reason for remembering so quickly – that night, he and Beth had first made love. Beth! he mentally screamed. What in God's name is going on? Why were you running down the slope in back of your house? Who was the man waiting for you in the car?

'Mr Decker.'

'I'm sorry. I—' Decker blinked, realizing that his attention had drifted, that Esperanza had continued speaking to him.

'You said someone with a remote-control detonator must have been watching the house.'

'That's right.'

'Why didn't that person set off the bombs when you were with Ms Dwyer outside her house?'

'Unless I went inside, it wouldn't have been one hundred percent certain that the bombs would have done the job.'

'So the spotter decided to wait until you left before setting off the bombs?' Esperanza asked. 'Does that tactic make sense?'

Decker felt a chill.

'If you were the target,' Esperanza added.

'*Beth* was the target?' Decker's chill became so intense that it made him shiver. 'You're saying that this afternoon and last night, they weren't after *me*?'

'She was obviously afraid of something. Otherwise, she wouldn't have been running down the back slope of her house.'

Decker's face tingled. 'They were after *Beth*? Jesus.' Nothing in his experience – not in military special operations, not in anti-terrorist intelligence work – could compare with what he was going through. He had never felt so emotionally threatened. But then, until he came to Santa Fe, he had never put down his defensive mechanisms and allowed himself to be emotionally vulnerable.

'A while ago, you spoke about the radio frequencies used to set off bombs by remote control,' Esperanza said. 'Where did you learn so much about how to blow up a building?'

Decker wasn't paying attention. He was too busy analyzing implications. For over a year, he had been in a state of denial, convinced that all he needed to be content were a total unsuspicious openness to the present and an equally total rejection of the calculating habits of his former life. But now he embraced those habits with a resolution that startled him. He picked up the telephone book, found the listing he wanted, and urgently pressed numbers.

'Mr Decker, what are you doing?'

'Phoning St Vincent's Hospital.'

Esperanza looked baffled.

When a receptionist answered, Decker said, 'Please put me through to whatever nurses' station is responsible for room 3116.'

When someone else answered, Decker said, 'You had a gunshot victim, Beth Dwyer, who was just released. I'd like to speak to any of the nurses who took care of her.'

'One moment.'

Someone else picked up the phone. 'Yes, I helped take care of Beth Dwyer,' a pleasant-voiced woman said. 'Of course, I didn't come on duty until seven. Other nurses would have taken care of her before that.'

'This is one of the police officers investigating her shooting.'

'Hey,' Esperanza demanded, 'what do you think you're doing?'

Decker held up a hand, gesturing for Esperanza to give him a chance. 'Did she have any visitors?'

'Only a male friend of hers.'

That was probably me, Decker thought. But he was finished taking things for granted. 'What did the man look like?'

'Tall, well-built, around forty.'

'Sandy hair?'

'As I remember. He was good looking in a rugged sort of way. I didn't see anybody else.'

'What about phone calls?'

'Oh, she made plenty of those.'

'What?'

'She received several, too. The phone was ringing constantly for a while. If I was in her room, she wouldn't speak to whoever was calling until I left.'

Decker's chest felt heavy. 'Thank you,' he managed to tell the nurse. 'You've been very helpful.' Pensive, he set down the phone.

'What was *that* about?' Esperanza asked. 'Do you know the penalty for impersonating a police officer?'

'Beth made and received several calls. But to my knowledge, I'm the only close friend she has in town. So who was she calling, and who was calling her?'

'If her calls were long distance and she didn't reverse the charges, there'll be a record of the numbers she called,' Esperanza said.

'Get it. But I have a suspicion the calls were local – that she was talking to the man who was waiting on Fort Connor Lane to pick her up. When I brought her some clothes so she'd have something to wear when she left the hospital, she told me she felt so grungy she was embarrassed to get dressed in front of me. She asked me to wait outside in the corridor. Given her injury and the fact that she might have needed help, I thought it was an impractical time to be modest, but I let it go. Now it's my guess she took the opportunity to make a final call to the man and tell him she was being released – to confirm what time he'd be waiting for her. But who the hell *was* he?'

In addition to Decker's other confusing overwhelming

emotions – relief that Beth was alive, bewilderment about her behavior – a new one suddenly intruded: jealousy. Dear God, is it possible? he thought. Could Beth have had a secret lover? Could she have been seeing someone else all the time I knew her? Questions tumbled frantically through his mind. How would she have met him? Is he someone who followed her from back east? Someone from her past?

'The man who was waiting in the car – did the woman who saw him get a good enough look to provide a description?' Decker asked.

'Sanchez would know.'

As Decker started toward the front door, in a rush to get outside to where Sanchez was guarding the house, the front door opened abruptly.

Sanchez appeared, startling Decker. 'Two men who claim to be friends of yours want to see you.'

'Probably neighbors or people I work with. Tell them I'll talk to them later. Listen, there's something I need to ask you.'

'These men are very insistent,' Sanchez said. 'They emphasized that they're *old* friends of yours, very old friends. They say their names are Hal and Ben.'

3

'Hal and—' Decker tried not to show his surprise. 'Yes.' His reflexes tightened. 'I know them. Let them in.'

Hal and Ben were the two operatives who had taken him into custody in the St Regis lobby after his bitter resignation the previous year. They had questioned him about his motives, had finally decided that he wasn't a threat to security, and had allowed him to proceed to the sanctuary of Santa Fe – with an implicit warning that his anger about what had happened in

Rome had better not prompt him to tell tales out of school.

Now he had to assume that they were the investigators his former employer had sent in response to his emergency telephone call about the attack on his house. As they appeared in the doorway, Decker noted that they didn't look much different than the last time he had seen them – trim and tall, about one hundred and ninety pounds and six feet, close to Decker's age, forty-one, their features hard, their eyes wary. About the only distinction between them was that Hal's hair was dark brown and combed straight back while Ben's was red and cut short. They wore jackets, khaki pants, and sturdy street shoes. After scanning the living room, they assessed Esperanza and focused on Decker.

'What's going on?' Hal asked. 'Why the policeman outside? What happened down the road?'

'It's a long story. This is Sergeant Esperanza. Sergeant, meet Hal Webber and Ben Eiseley.' The last names were fictitious, matching false identification that Decker knew they customarily carried. 'We hung around with each other when I worked in Virginia. They told me they planned to come out this way one of these weekends, but I guess it slipped my mind that it was going to be Fiesta weekend.'

'Sure,' Esperanza said, obviously not buying the story. He shook hands with them, comparing their trim-hipped, strong-shouldered build to Decker's similar physique. 'Are these more real-estate salesmen who know about setting bombs off by remote control?'

Hal looked puzzled. 'Bombs? Is that what happened next door? The place exploded?'

'Sergeant, would you give me a moment to be alone with my friends?' Decker started to guide Hal and Ben toward a door that led to a small barbecue area off the kitchen.

'No,' Esperanza said.

Decker stopped and looked back at him. 'Excuse me?'

'No. I *won't* give you a moment to be alone with them.' Esperanza's weathered face hardened. 'From the start, you've been evasive and uncooperative. I won't tolerate it any longer.'

'I thought you said you'd been asked by the FBI to stay away from the case.'

'The attack on your house. Not the explosions next door.'

'The FBI?' Ben asked, puzzled.

'Whatever you need to tell these men to bring them up to speed, you tell them in front of me,' Esperanza said. 'Bring *me* up to speed.'

'The FBI?' Ben said again. 'I don't get it. What does the FBI have to do with this?'

'Sergeant, I really do need to speak to these men alone,' Decker said.

'I'll arrest you.'

'On what charge? A good lawyer would have me out of jail by tonight,' Decker said.

'On Saturday of Fiesta weekend? Your lawyer would have a hell of a problem finding a judge to listen to him,' Esperanza said sharply. 'You wouldn't be out of jail until tomorrow, maybe Monday, and I don't think you want to lose that much time. So pretend I'm not here. What do you want to tell these men?'

Time, Decker thought, anxious. I've got to start looking for Beth right away. I can't afford to lose two days. Frantic, he felt torn between conflicting motives. Until now, he had been determined to protect his former employer from being implicated in the investigation, but other, more urgent priorities now insisted – he had to find Beth; he had to find out who wanted to kill her.

'I used to work for the US government.'

'Hey, be careful,' Ben told Decker.

'I don't have a choice.'

'The government?' Esperanza came to attention. 'You're talking about—'

'Nothing I can't deny,' Decker said. 'These men were associates of mine. They're here to help find out if the attack last night had anything to do with sensitive matters I was involved with.'

'Take it easy,' Hal told Decker.

'That's as specific as I'm going to get,' Decker told Esperanza, his gaze intense.

Esperanza's gaze was equally intense. Slowly, the detective's lean features became less rigid. He nodded.

Decker turned to Hal. 'You got here sooner than I expected.'

'We were in Dallas. We had the company jet. It's less than a two-hour flight.'

'Thanks for coming.'

'Well, it seemed the only way,' Ben said. 'We were told telephone contact with you wasn't secure. We wanted to touch base, clear up some confusion about something you said when you reported the attack, and then get in touch with the local feds.'

'Which you've already done,' Esperanza said. 'Talked to the FBI.'

'No,' Hal said with concern.

'Not in person but over the phone,' Esperanza said.

'No,' Hal said with greater concern.

'But the head of the local FBI office spoke to me this morning and made an official request to take over investigating last night's attack,' Esperanza said.

'You mentioned that earlier, but I didn't understand what you were talking about,' Ben said. '*No one* on our end has talked to the feds yet. We wanted a first-hand look before deciding if we had to involve them.'

Decker felt a deepening premonition, a quickening throughout his nervous system.

Esperanza anticipated the question for which Decker

urgently needed an answer. 'Then, if *you* didn't ask for federal intervention, who in God's name did?'

4

Steering sharply from Old Santa Fe Trail onto Paseo de Peralta, Sanchez drove the police car as quickly as he could without sounding the siren in the congestion of downtown Fiesta traffic. Stark-faced, Hal sat in front with him. Conscious of his rapidly beating heart, Decker hunched between Ben and Esperanza in the back.

Esperanza finished a hasty conversation on a cellular telephone, then pressed a button that broke the connection. 'He says he'll be waiting for us.'

'What if he doesn't tell us what we want to know?' Decker asked.

'In that case, I'll have to make some phone calls to Virginia,' Ben said. 'Sooner or later, he *will* tell us. I guarantee it.'

'Sooner,' Decker said. 'It better be sooner. It's been two hours since Beth ran down that slope and got in that car. She could be in Albuquerque by now. Hell, if she went directly to the airport, she could be on a plane to anywhere.'

'Let's find out.' Esperanza pressed buttons on the cellular phone.

'Who are you calling?'

'Security at Albuquerque's airport.'

'What if she used the airport in Santa Fe?' Hal asked.

'I'll call there next. The local airport has only a few small passenger flights. Prop jobs. It won't be hard to find out if she was on one of them.'

Someone answered on the other end of the line – Esperanza started talking.

Meanwhile, Decker turned to Ben. For a disturbing moment, he suffered a kind of double focus in which he was still being questioned by Ben and Hal as they drove him through Manhattan the previous year. Or maybe that debriefing had never stopped and what he was going through now was a waking nightmare.

'Ben, when you arrived at my house, you said you wanted to clear up some confusion about something I mentioned when I reported last night's attack. What were you talking about?'

Ben pulled a piece of paper from his pocket. 'This is a faxed transcript of part of your phoned-in report.' Ben ran a finger down the page. 'The case officer you spoke to said, "But you're not our responsibility any longer." You replied, "Hey, you sure thought I was when I quit. You were all over me. I figured your security checks would never stop. Damn it, two months ago, you were still keeping me under surveillance." '

Decker nodded, feeling a swirl of *déjà vu* as his words were read back to him. 'So what's the problem?'

'The case officer didn't comment at the time, but he had no idea what you meant by your last statement. He doublechecked your file. No one from our organization has been maintaining surveillance on you.'

'But that's not true,' Decker said. 'Two months ago, I saw a team. I—'

'At the start, when you first came to Santa Fe, we kept a watch on you, yes,' Ben said. 'But then it seemed easier and cheaper to monitor your financial records. If you suddenly had more money than your new occupation could explain, we would have been all over you, wondering if you'd been selling secrets for cash. But everything about your income has been copacetic. You seemed to have gotten over your attitude toward the problems that made you quit. There wasn't any need for visual surveillance. Whoever was watching you, the team definitely wasn't from us.'

'You expect me to believe Brian McKittrick decided to watch me on his free time when he wasn't working for you?'

'Brian McKittrick?' Hal asked sharply. 'What are you talking about?'

'*I told you I saw him.*'

'Two months ago?'

'McKittrick was in charge of the surveillance team,' Decker said.

'But McKittrick hasn't worked for us since February.'

Decker was speechless.

'His father died in December,' Ben said. 'With no one to protect the son, your complaints about him began to sink in. He screwed up on two other assignments. The organization dumped him.'

Esperanza put his hand over the mouthpiece on the cellular phone. 'Can you guys keep it quiet? I can hardly hear. Luis?' He leaned forward toward Sanchez. 'The Albuquerque police want to know if we've got a description of the car Beth Dwyer drove off in. Did the eyewitness give you one?'

'The old lady didn't know much about cars.' Sanchez steered around a crowded curve on Paseo de Peralta. 'She said it was big, it looked new, and it was gray.'

'That's all?'

'Afraid so.'

'Swell. Just swell,' Esperanza said. 'What about the man who was driving? Did she get a look at him when he hurried out to put Beth Dwyer's suitcase in the trunk?'

'When it comes to noticing *people*, this woman has twenty-twenty vision. The guy was in his early thirties. Tall. Built solidly. Reminded her of a football player. Square jaw. Blond hair.'

'Square jaw? Blond—' Decker frowned.

'What's wrong?'

'Reminded her of a football player? That sounds like—'

'You know somebody who looks like that?'

'It can't be.' Decker felt breathless. What he'd just heard didn't make sense. *Nothing* made sense. 'Brian McKittrick. The description fits Brian McKittrick. But if he isn't working for *you*,' Decker told Ben, 'who *is* he working for?'

5

Decker didn't wait for Sanchez to brake to a full stop in a no-parking zone before he rushed out of the police car toward a long, three-story-high, clay-colored government building. Flanked by Esperanza, Hal, and Ben, he ran up wide concrete steps to a row of glass doors, in the middle of which a fortyish man of medium height and weight, with well-trimmed hair and short sideburns, waited for them outside. The man wore slacks and a blue sport coat. A pager was hooked to his belt. He carried a cellular telephone.

'This better be good. I was at a Fiesta party.' The man pulled out a set of keys and prepared to unlock one of the doors. His sober gaze was directed toward Esperanza, who hadn't had an opportunity to change his singed soot-covered shirt and jeans. 'What happened to you? On the phone, you said this has something to do with what we discussed this morning.'

'We don't have time to go up to your office,' Decker said. 'We're hoping you can tell us what we need right here.'

The man lowered his keys from the door and frowned. 'And just who are *you*?'

'Stephen Decker – the man whose house was attacked,' Esperanza said. 'Mr Decker, this is FBI senior resident agent John Miller.'

Decker immediately asked, 'Why did you intervene in

Sergeant Esperanza's investigation of the attack?'

Miller was caught by surprise. He took a moment before replying, 'That's confidential.'

'It looks as if the attack wasn't against me but against a woman I've been seeing. My neighbor. Her name is Elizabeth Dwyer. She calls herself Beth. Does that name mean anything to you?'

This time, Miller didn't pause. 'I'm not prepared to discuss the matter.'

'Her house blew up this afternoon.'

Miller reacted as if he'd been slapped. 'What?'

'Have I finally got your attention? Are you prepared to discuss the matter *now*? Why did you intervene in the investigation about the attack on me?'

'Elizabeth Dwyer's house blew up?' Startled, Miller turned toward Esperanza. 'Was she there? Was she killed?'

'Apparently not,' Esperanza said. 'We haven't found a body. Someone who looked like her was seen getting in a car on Fort Connor Lane a few seconds before the explosions.'

'Why didn't you tell me this when you called?'

'I'm telling you now.'

Miller glared. 'I don't like being manipulated.'

'And I don't like being shot at,' Decker interrupted. 'Who's trying to kill Beth Dwyer? What do you know about a man named Brian McKittrick? How are you mixed up in all this?'

'No comment,' Miller said flatly. 'This conversation is over.'

'Not until you give me some answers.'

'And if I don't?' Miller asked. 'What are you going to do if I *don't* give you answers?'

'Doesn't it matter to you that Beth's life is in danger?'

'Whether it does or not is none of your business.'

Decker felt heat surging through his veins. As he returned the agent's glare, he wanted to slam Miller against the door. Beth!

he kept thinking. Whoever wanted to kill her might have caught up to her by now. But this son of a bitch didn't seem to care.

'Well?' Miller asked.

Decker took a step backward. He told himself to calm down. He told himself that it wouldn't do Beth any good if he got himself arrested for assaulting an FBI agent. Calm down, he repeated, his chest heaving.

'Smart,' Miller said.

'We need to talk about this,' Esperanza said.

'No,' Miller said, 'we don't. Excuse me. I have several important phone calls to make.' He opened the door and walked into the building. With an angry glance through the window, he locked the door, then turned away.

'When this is over, he and I *will* talk,' Decker said.

6

As Decker got out of the police car in his driveway, he peered dismally up Camino Lindo toward the remaining fire trucks and the smoking ruin of Beth's house. Onlookers crowded the side of the road. A TV crew had a camera aimed toward the wreckage.

'Sorry.' Remaining in the police car, Esperanza made a gesture of futility.

Heartsick, Decker was too preoccupied to respond.

'I'll keep working on him,' Esperanza said. 'Maybe he'll let something slip.'

'Sure,' Decker said without conviction. He had never felt so helpless. Hal and Ben stood next to him.

'I'll keep prodding the Albuquerque police and airport security,' Esperanza said.

'Maybe Beth and McKittrick drove toward Denver or

Flagstaff,' Decker said. 'Hell, there's no way to guess *which* way they went.'

'Well, if I hear anything, I'll let you know. Just make sure you return the favor. Here's my card.' Esperanza wrote something on it. 'I'm giving you my home telephone number.'

Decker nodded.

The dark-blue police car pulled away, turned to avoid the congestion of fire trucks and onlookers at Beth's house, and went back the way it had come.

Squinting from the westerly sun, Decker watched the cruiser raise dust as it receded along Camino Lindo.

'He's not obligated to tell us anything,' Hal said. 'In fact, he has to be suspicious about us. Certainly, he can't just take our word that we're somehow connected to the intelligence community.'

'Affirmative,' Ben added. 'Right now, he'll do everything he can to check our backgrounds. Not that he'll learn anything.'

'At least, he knew enough not to identify you as intelligence officers to that FBI agent,' Decker said. 'Given the FBI's turf wars with other agencies, Miller would have revealed even less than he did.'

'Even less? Hey, he didn't tell us *anything*,' Hal said.

'Not true.' Decker watched the police car completely disappear, then turned to open his courtyard gate. 'Miller's interest in Beth confirms that she was the real target, and when I mentioned Brian McKittrick, I saw a look of recognition in Miller's eyes. Oh, he knows something, all right. Not that it does *us* any good.'

Hal and Ben looked uncomfortable.

'What's the problem?' Decker asked.

' "Us",' Hal said.

'What do you mean?'

'We were sent here to do damage control if what happened

last night was related to any of your former assignments,' Ben said.

'And?'

'It wasn't.' Ben looked down, scuffing the gravel driveway with his shoes. 'Whatever Beth Dwyer's problem is, *your* problem is personal. We're not authorized to help you.'

Decker didn't say anything.

'As soon as we report in, we'll be recalled,' Ben said.

Decker still didn't say anything.

'Honestly,' Hal said, 'it's out of our hands.'

'Then, damn it, get in your car and leave,' Decker said. 'I'll do this without you.'

'How?'

'There has to be another way. Whatever it is, I'll find it. Get out of here.'

'No hard feelings?' Hal asked.

'Do I sound like I have hard feelings?' Decker said bitterly. He entered his courtyard and slumped on a bench beneath the portal, murmuring despondently, thinking, If Esperanza doesn't learn anything from the Albuquerque airport, if he decides to hold back on anything he does learn . . . The words 'dead end' passed through Decker's mind. He automatically applied their literal meaning to Beth. Was she being threatened at this moment? Why was she with McKittrick? Why had she lied? 'Something.' Decker impatiently tapped his right hand against the bench. 'There has to be something I've missed, another way to connect with her.'

Decker heard footsteps enter the courtyard. He looked up to find Hal standing next to him.

'Did she ever mention that she'd like to go to any particular place?' Hal asked.

'No. Only that she wanted to close the door on her life back east. I thought you were leaving.'

'No rush.'

'Isn't there?' Frustrated, Decker imagined Brian McKittrick driving Beth along Fort Connor Lane as she felt the rumble of the explosions that blew her house apart on the street above her. If only the old woman who had seen the car drive away had gotten the license number. Numbers, he was thinking. Maybe the record of the telephone calls Beth made from her hospital room would provide a direction in which to search.

Or calls she made from her *home* phone, Decker thought. I'll have to remind Esperanza to check on that. But Decker's skepticism about Esperanza continued to make him uneasy. What if Esperanza holds back information?

'There has to be another way,' Decker said again. 'What alternatives are there to trace her? It can't be through her paintings. She never told me the name of the New York gallery she used. There are hundreds and hundreds of galleries there. Given the time pressure, it would take too long to contact every one of them. Anyway, for all I know, the gallery was a lie and Beth never sold *any* paintings. The only proof was the art dealer I met, Dale Hawkins, and he might not have been who Beth said he was. If only I'd thought to make a note of the license number on the car he parked outside her house. But I didn't have a reason to be suspicious.'

When Decker looked up, Hal and Ben were watching him strangely. 'Are you okay?'

'What do you mean?'

'You're gesturing and muttering to yourself.'

'The car,' Decker said.

'Excuse me?'

'The car Hawkins was driving. That's it!'

'What are you talking about?'

'Dale Hawkins was driving a rental.' Decker stood, excited. 'When I passed the front window, I looked in and saw the envelope for the rental agreement on the front seat. I'm pretty sure it was Avis. And I'm *very* sure the date was September first because that was when Beth closed the deal on her house. A blue Chevrolet Cavalier. If Dale Hawkins flew into Albuquerque as he claimed, he would have rented the car at the airport. He would have needed to show his driver's license and a credit card. I can find out his home address.' Decker's excitement suddenly was smothered. 'Assuming Esperanza tells me what he learns from the car rental company.'

Decker looked long and hard at Hal and Ben.

'I'm probably going to regret this,' Hal said.

'What are you talking about?'

'I guess I can wait a while to let headquarters know that what happened last night has nothing to do with business.'

'You're going to help me?'

'Do you remember when the three of us worked together in Beirut?' Hal asked unexpectedly.

'How could I forget?'

On March 16, 1984, the Shiite terrorist group, Hizbullah, had kidnapped CIA station chief, William Buckley. Decker, Hal, and Ben had been part of a task force, trying to find where Buckley was being held prisoner. Decker's part in the search had lasted until September when he had been transferred to anti-terrorist activities in Germany. The intensity of those hot summer months and the determination of the task force were seared in his memory. Buckley was never located. A year later, on October 11, 1985, Hizbullah announced Buckley's death.

'Down the street from the task force headquarters, there was a little zoo,' Hal said. 'Do you remember *that*?'

'Certainly. I don't know how many animals the zoo had before the civil war broke out, but when we arrived, the only ones left were a leopard, a giraffe, and a bear. The bear hadn't adjusted to the climate. It was pathetic.'

'Then a sniper from one of the factions decided to make a game of shooting at whoever went out to feed the animals. The sniper killed the caretaker. In the next two days, he popped off four volunteers. The animals began to starve.'

'I remember that, too.' Decker felt a constriction in his throat.

'One night, you disappeared. When you came back in the morning, you said you were going to take food and water out to the animals. I tried to stop you. I warned you the sniper would like nothing better than to kill an American. You told me you had taken care of the sniper. He wasn't going to be a problem any longer. Of course, another sniper might have replaced him and shot at you, but that didn't seem to bother you. You were determined to make sure the animals weren't suffering.'

The courtyard became silent.

'Why did you mention that?' Decker asked.

'Because *I* thought about going out to track down that sniper,' Hal said. 'But I never worked up the nerve. I envied you for having done what *I* should have. Funny, huh? Beirut was a pit of human misery, but we were worried about those three animals. Of course, it didn't make any difference. A mortar shell killed them the next day.'

'But they didn't die hungry,' Decker said.

'That's right. You're a stand-up guy. Show me where the nearest payphone is,' Hal said. 'I'll tell headquarters we're still looking into things. I'll ask them to use their computer network to find out who rented a blue Chevrolet Cavalier from Avis at the Albuquerque airport on September first. There was probably more than one Cavalier. A good thing it's not a big airport.'

'Hal?'

'What?'

'. . . Thanks.'

7

Decker struggled with painful emotions as he stared out the rear window of the Ford Taurus that Hal and Ben had rented when they drove up from Albuquerque earlier in the day. That seemed an eternity ago. What he saw through the car's rear window was the diminishing vista of the Sangre de Cristo mountains, of yellowing aspen in the ski basin, of adobe houses nestled into foothills, of piñons and junipers and the crimson glow of a high-desert sunset. For the first time since he had arrived more than a year ago, he was leaving Santa Fe. Oh, he had driven out of the city limits before – to go fishing or white-water rafting or on sightseeing expeditions to Taos. But those day trips had somehow seemed an extension of Santa Fe, and after all, they had been brief, and he had known that he would soon be coming back.

Now, however, he was truly leaving – for how long he had no idea, or whether he would in fact be coming back. Certainly, he wanted to come back, with all his heart, the sooner the better, but the issue was, would he be *able* to come back? Would the search upon which he had embarked create pitfalls that *prevented* him from coming back? Would he *survive* to come back? During his numerous missions in military special operations and later as an intelligence operative, he had remained alive in part because he had a professional's ability to distinguish between acceptable risks and foolhardy ones. But being a professional required more than just making judgments based on training, experience, and ability. It demanded a particular attitude – a balance between commitment and objectivity. Decker had resigned from intelligence work because he no longer had the commitment and was sick of an objectivity that left him feeling detached from everything around him.

But he definitely felt committed now, more than at any time

in his life. He was totally, passionately, obsessively determined to find Beth. His love for her was infinite. She was the focus of his life. He would risk anything to catch up to her.

Anything? he asked himself, and his answer was immediate. Yes. Because if he wasn't able to find Beth, if he wasn't able to resolve the overwhelming tensions that seized him, he wouldn't be able to continue with anything else. His life would have no meaning. He would be lost.

As he peered morosely out the Taurus's side window, noting how the sunset's crimson had intensified, almost blood red, he heard Hal in the front seat saying something, repeating his name.

'What is it?'

'Do people around here always drive this crazy, or is it just because of the holiday weekend?'

'No. Traffic's always this crazy,' Decker said, only partly attending to the conversation.

'I thought New York and Los Angeles had terrible drivers. But I've never seen anything like this. They come up right behind my rear bumper at sixty-five miles an hour. I can see them in my rearview mirror glaring at me because I'm not going eighty. They veer out into the passing lane without using their signal, then veer back into *my* lane, again without signaling, this time almost scraping my *front* bumper. Then they race ahead to crowd the next car. Sure, in New York and Los Angeles, they crowd you, too, but that's because everybody's in gridlock. Here, there's plenty of space ahead and behind me, but they *still* crowd you. What the hell's going on?'

Decker didn't answer. He was peering through the back window again, noting that the foothills and adobe houses had gotten even smaller. He was beginning to feel as if he were plummeting away from them. The race track flashed by. Then the Taurus began the climb to the peak of La Bajada hill and the start of the two-thousand-foot southward drop toward Albuquerque.

'Saturday night,' Hal said. 'The guy might not be home.'

'Then I'll wait until he comes back,' Decker said.

'We'll all wait,' Ben said.

Emotion made it difficult for Decker to speak. 'Thanks. I appreciate this.'

'But I don't know how long I can keep stalling headquarters,' Hal said.

'You've already been a great help.'

'Maybe. We'll soon find out if what I learned really does help.'

When Hal had driven to a payphone in Santa Fe, he had requested information from his employer's computer system. The system had covert links to every civilian data bank in the United States and with remarkable speed was able to inform Hal that while several blue Chevrolet Cavaliers served as rental cars at the Albuquerque airport, all but one had been rented prior to Thursday, September 1. The remaining Cavalier had indeed been rented on September 1, at 10:13 in the morning, but the name of the renter had not been Dale Hawkins, as Decker had hoped. Instead, the name had been Randolph Green, and his address had not been in or around New York City, as would have been the case for Dale Hawkins, but rather the address had been in Albuquerque itself.

'Randolph Green,' Hal said, driving farther from Santa Fe, almost to the crest of the hill. 'Who do you suppose he is?'

'And why does a man who lives in Albuquerque go out to the airport to rent a car?' Decker turned from the diminishing crimson sunset. 'That's what makes me think we're on the right track.'

'Or at least the only track that's promising,' Ben said.

'But why would Beth lie about his name?' Decker shook his

head. In a way, the question was naive – he already knew part of the answer. Beth had lied for the same reason she hadn't told him she thought *she* was the real target of last night's attack, for the same reason she hadn't told him that Brian McKittrick would be waiting on Fort Connor Lane to pick her up. Throughout her relationship with me, Decker thought, she's been hiding something. The relationship itself had been a lie.

No! he insisted. It *can't* have been a lie. How could anything that powerful have been a sham? Wouldn't I have seen the deception in her eyes? Wouldn't I have noticed hesitancy or calculation, *something* in her manner that would have given her away? I used to be a master of calculation. She couldn't possibly have fooled me. The emotion she showed toward me was real, the tenderness, the passion, the caring, the . . . Decker was about to use the word 'love' when it occurred to him that he couldn't recall an occasion when Beth had told him directly that she loved him. He had said it to her often enough. But had she ever initiated the statement or echoed it when he said it to her? Trying as hard as he could, he was unable to remember.

Other memories came readily – the first time he and Beth had made love, sinking to the brick floor of her studio, uncertain, tentative, awestruck, wanting, caressing, exploring. That, also, had been on September 1, after he had met 'Dale Hawkins', after Beth had shown Decker her paintings. An avalanche of doubting questions threatened to crush Decker's sanity. Had Beth actually painted them? Was Beth Dwyer her true name? Was her husband in fact dead? For that matter, had she ever been married? What was her relationship with Brian McKittrick? It couldn't possibly be a coincidence that McKittrick knew *both* Decker and Beth.

Madness, Decker thought. Sweat beaded on his upper lip. He felt off balance. Nothing was as it seemed. Everything he had taken for granted was called into question. He had a persistent sense of falling and almost wished that he had never resigned from intelligence work. At least, back then, he had known the rules. Deception was the norm, and he had never been fooled by the lies presented to him. Now, in his determination to believe that life didn't have to be based on deception, he had finally been deceived.

Then why, he asked himself, did he feel so determined to catch up to Beth? To protect the woman he loved? Or was his motive the need to demand explanations from the woman who had lied to him? Confusion was the only thing about which he was certain – and the fact that, for whatever reason, he would never rest until he found Beth. He would die trying.

Ben was talking to him again. 'When that detective – what's his name? Esperanza? – figures out you've left town, he'll be mad as hell. He'll have the state police looking for you.'

'For all of us,' Hal added. 'He saw this rental car parked in front of Steve's house. He can describe it.'

'Yes,' Decker said. 'He'll come looking for me.'

The Taurus crested the hill and began the long descent toward Albuquerque. As Santa Fe vanished, Decker turned to study the dark uncertainties that faced him.

SEVEN

1

After the Hispanic-pueblo design of the buildings in Santa Fe, the peaked roofs and brick or wood exteriors of the conventional structures in Albuquerque seemed unusual. While Santa Fe had a few Victorian houses, Albuquerque had many, and they too looked unusual to Decker, as did the even more numerous ranch houses, one of which was Randolph Green's.

It took an hour to find the address. Decker, Hal, and Ben had to stop at three different service stations off Highway 25 before they found one that had a map of Albuquerque. The map wasn't as detailed as they would have liked and they had to drive slowly, watching for street signs, but they finally reached their destination in the flatlands on the west side of the city. Chama Street consisted of modest ranch houses, whose lawns, shade trees, and hedges made Decker feel as if he'd been transported into a midwestern suburb. Again he had a dizzying sense of unreality.

'That's the address,' Hal said, driving past a house that seemed no different from any of the others.

The time was after ten p.m. Sunset had ended quite a while ago. Except for widely spaced street lights and a few illuminated windows in homes, the neighborhood was dark, residents presumably out enjoying their Saturday night. Green's house had a light on in a room at the back and on the porch.

'Maybe he's home – maybe he isn't,' Ben said. 'Those lights

might be intended to discourage burglars.'

'Drive around the block,' Decker said. 'Let's make sure there aren't any surprises.'

There weren't. The neighborhood appeared as perfectly ordinary as Green's house.

'Maybe we've made a mistake,' Hal said. 'This doesn't exactly seem like a hotbed of danger.'

'It's the only lead we've got.' Decker struggled to maintain hope. 'I want to ask Green why he had to go all the way to the airport to rent a car.'

Hal parked down the street.

Decker waited until the Taurus's headlights had been extinguished before he got out. He wanted the cover of darkness. But as he started to walk back toward Green's house, Hal opened the trunk.

'Just a minute,' Hal told him softly, and handed him something. Decker recognized the feel of a packet of lockpick tools.

Then Hal handed him something else, and Decker definitely didn't need to ask him what *it* was. The feel of the object was all too familiar – a semiautomatic pistol.

'Nine millimeter,' Hal said even more softly. 'A Beretta. Here's a sound suppressor for it.' Hal was taking items out of a suitcase. Ben was helping himself.

'But how did you get through airport security?'

'Didn't need to.'

Decker nodded. 'I remember now. Back at the house, you mentioned you'd used a company jet.'

'All set?' Ben asked.

After glancing around to make sure he wasn't seen, Decker removed the pistol's magazine, checked that it was fully loaded, replaced the magazine, and worked the slide on top of the weapon, inserting a round into the firing chamber. Carefully, he lowered the pistol's hammer, didn't bother to engage the safety catch, and shoved the weapon under his belt, concealing it beneath a tan windbreaker that he had put on along with dark sneakers, fresh jeans, and a clean denim shirt. Although he had done his best to shower off the soot in his hair and on his skin, the cold water had not done a good job. He still had a faint odor of smoke about him. 'Ready.'

'How do you want to do this?' Ben asked. 'If Green's at home, he might not be by himself. He might have a family. He might be innocent. Or he might be rooming with a bunch of guys who love to sit around with automatic weapons. In either case, we can't just barge in.'

'Watch the house from here. I'll have a look,' Decker said.

'But you might need backup.'

'You said yourself this isn't business. Since this is *my* show, I'll take the risk.'

'We're not doing this for business reasons.'

'Believe me, if I need help, I'll let you know.'

As Hal shut the trunk, Decker walked with deceptive calm along the shadowy sidewalk, warily scanning the houses on both sides of the street as he approached Green's. No one was in sight. He passed Green's house, turned left onto the yard of the house beyond it – that house was completely dark – and moved along a wooden fence, staying low until he reached the back. He had been concerned that there might be a dog at this house or at Green's, but neither backyard had a dog house and he didn't hear any barking. The night was still. While he worked to control his tension, he smelled the unfamiliar sweetness of new-mown grass.

The light at the back of Green's house came from a window, sending a rectangular glow into the murky backyard. No figures moved inside the house. From Decker's position, he had a view of the back of Green's single-car garage. Moving slowly to minimize any slight noise he made, he climbed the waist-high fence and dropped to the opposite lawn. Immediately he pressed himself against the back of the garage, blending with shadows. When no one responded to his entry into the yard, he peered through the garage's back window, the light at the rear of Green's house allowing him to see that the garage was empty.

Immediately he crept toward bushes at the back of the house and stooped beneath a dark window, listening for voices, music, a television show, anything to indicate that someone was inside. Silence. Satisfying himself that a hedge and some trees concealed him from the house in back of this one, he emerged from shadows and warily listened at Green's back door. No sounds from within. He approached the illuminated window and listened beneath it. Nothing.

He assessed the situation. If Green lived alone, the empty garage suggested he had gone out. But what if Green shared the house with others and not everyone had left? Or what if Green didn't have a car and that was why he had rented the Cavalier on September 1?

Damn it, I don't have time to rethink everything, Decker told himself. I've got to find Beth! In his former life, he would have backed off and maintained surveillance on the house, waiting until he had a chance to confront Green under controllable circumstances. But this was Decker's *present* life, and his heart pounded with the certainty that Beth was in danger, that she needed his help. There had to be an explanation for why she had lied to him. For all he knew, at this very moment she was about to be killed in Green's house.

He hadn't seen any signs warning potential intruders that the house was equipped with a security system. Usually, such signs were displayed in prominent areas. None of the windows in back had a 'protected by' sticker. On the off chance that Green had forgotten to lock the back door, Decker tried it. No luck. He reached into his jacket pocket, pulled out the packet of lockpick tools, and in thirty seconds had freed the lock. He could have done it much quicker, but he had to work cautiously, making as little noise as possible so as not to alert anyone who might be inside. He was suddenly conscious of the irony that last night someone else had tried to be cautious while picking *his* lock.

Drawing the Beretta, he crouched, opened the door, and aimed toward what he discovered was a small kitchen. The light he had seen was above the sink. As quickly as soundlessness would allow, he crept through the otherwise dark house, checking every room, grateful that there was only one level and that the house didn't have a basement. He found no one.

He went out through the rear door, emerged onto the murky front sidewalk without being noticed, and in five minutes was back inside, this time accompanied by Hal and Ben. The moment Decker locked the door behind them, he said, 'So let's find out who the hell Randolph Green is. When I searched earlier, I didn't find any children's clothing or toys. I didn't find any dresses. Green lives alone or with a man.'

'I'll search the master bedroom,' Hal said.

'If there's another bedroom, I'll take it,' Ben said.

'There is,' Decker said. 'And I'll take the study.'

'Maybe not.' Hal frowned.

'What's wrong?'

'Headlights coming into the driveway.'

2

Decker felt a shock. Through a side window in the kitchen, he saw the gleam of approaching headlights and heard a car engine. The vehicle wasn't close enough for anyone inside it to have a direct view into the kitchen, but it *would* be that close in a matter of seconds. Decker, Hal, and Ben ducked below the window and peered around hurriedly.

'Let me handle this. Don't let anyone see your faces unless it can't be avoided,' Decker said. 'If this turns out to be nothing, I don't want you identified for breaking and entering.' He retreated through an archway on the right, concealing himself in the darkness of the living room. Hal and Ben took a hallway on the left that led to the study and the bedrooms.

Outside, what sounded like a garage door made a rumbling noise. A few seconds later, the car engine stopped. The garage door made another rumbling noise.

Pressed next to a bookshelf in the living room, Decker felt sweat trickle down his chest as he listened to the rasp of a key in the back door's lock. The door was opened. A single pair of footsteps came in. The door made a scraping sound as it was shut. The lock was twisted back into place – and Decker stepped into the kitchen, ready with his handgun.

His reaction to the person he saw was a mixture of relief, confusion, and anger. Decker was well aware that his determination had led him to take risks that he never would have considered in his former life. There was every possibility that Randolph Green was a perfectly law-abiding citizen, that it was only coincidence that the man had rented a blue Chevrolet Cavalier from the Albuquerque airport on September 1. In that case, what if Green panicked at the sight of Decker's handgun? What if something went horribly wrong and Green was fatally injured? Even if Green wasn't injured, Decker had broken the law by invading Green's home, and Decker didn't have his former employer to convince the local police to overlook the crime if he was caught.

His misgivings vanished as the man who had just entered the kitchen swung in surprise toward the sound of Decker's footsteps. Stunned by the sight of Decker's pistol, the man lunged his right hand beneath the navy blazer he wore. Decker got to him before he had a chance to pull a revolver all the way free. Kicking the man's legs from under him, Decker simultaneously yanked the man's right hand toward the ceiling, twisted the man's wrist sharply, and pried the revolver from his grasp.

The man grunted in pain as he hit the floor. Decker slid the revolver away and hurriedly searched the man while pressing the Beretta against the man's forehead. Reassuring himself that the man had no other weapons, Decker took the man's wallet and stepped back, continuing to aim the Beretta down at him. At the same time, he heard urgent footsteps in the corridor at his back as Hal and Ben rushed into the room.

'Are you okay?' Ben aimed his own Beretta.

'As okay as I can be, considering how pissed off I am.' Decker gestured down toward the slender fiftyish man with soft features and thinning, partially gray hair. The only detail that had changed since Decker had last seen him was that the man's skin had been pale ten days ago but now had some color from the desert sun. 'Let me introduce you to the art dealer who claims to sell Beth's paintings – Dale Hawkins. Long time no see, Dale. How's business?'

Hawkins glared up from where he was sprawled on the floor. 'What the hell do you think you're doing? Do you have any idea—'

Decker kicked him. When Hawkins finished groaning, Decker said, 'I asked you a question, Dale. How's business? It must not be too good if you had to leave your gallery in New York? Or is your real name Randolph Green? I'm really confused about all this, Dale, and when I get confused, I get angry. When I get angry, I—'

Decker pulled out a kitchen drawer and dropped its heavy contents on him, making Hawkins groan and clutch his arm.

'Talk to me, Dale. Eventually you will, so you might as well save yourself a world of hurt in the meantime.'

'You don't know what—'

When Decker threw a toaster at Hawkins, it struck his thigh. The man contorted his face in pain, not knowing which part of his body to clutch.

'Don't make me impatient.' Decker poured water into a pot, set it on the stove, and turned on the burner. 'In case you're wondering, that isn't for coffee. Ever had a third-degree burn? They say scalding is the worst. I'm really serious about this, Dale. Pay attention. What . . . is . . . your . . . connection . . . to . . . Beth . . . Dwyer?'

Hawkins continued to hold his thigh in pain. 'Look in my wallet.'

'What?'

'My wallet. You've got it in your hand. Look in it.'

'There's something about Beth in here?' Not wanting to take his eyes off Hawkins, Decker tossed the wallet to Ben. 'See what he's talking about.'

Ben opened the wallet, studied its contents, and frowned.

'What's the matter?' Decker asked. 'He lied? There's nothing about Beth?'

'Not that I can find.' Ben looked extremely troubled. 'But assuming that this ID isn't bogus, Randolph Green is his real name.'

'So? What's the problem?'

'According to this—' Ben held up a badge. 'He's a United States marshal.'

3

'*A marshal?*' Decker's thoughts swirled. 'No. That doesn't

make sense. What would a US marshal have to do with—?'

'Quiet,' Ben said.

'What's—?'

'I heard something.' Ben stared toward the window in the back door. 'Jesus.' He raised his pistol. 'Get down! Someone's outside!' In that instant, he jerked backward, his forehead spraying blood from the force of a gunshot.

Decker flinched, his ears ringing from the blast that shattered the window on the back door. Sensing Hal dive to the floor, Decker did the same, aiming toward the back door, frantically shifting his aim to the window above the kitchen sink, then to the windows on each side of the room. Shocked, he couldn't allow himself to react to Ben's death. Grief would come later, *strong* grief, but for now, training controlled him. He had only one imperative – to stay alive.

Squirming fiercely backward, hoping to seek cover in the darkness of the living room, Decker shouted at the man whom he still thought of as Dale Hawkins. 'Who's shooting at us? Tell them to hold their fire!'

But Hawkins had a look of absolute incomprehension.

Decker heard angry voices beyond the back door. He heard glass shatter at the front. As he spun to aim in that direction, intense detonations threatened to burst his eardrums. One, two, three, four. Almost passing out, Decker shoved his hands to his ears and then his eyes, desperate to shield them, because the concussions were matched by blinding flashes that seared past his eyeballs into his brain.

Moaning reflexively, unable to stop his nervous system's automatic response to such intense pain, he fell to the floor, powerless against the flash-bang grenades that were intended to disable without permanently harming. In a turbulent recess of his mind, Decker knew what was happening – he had used flash-bangs on many occasions.

But knowledge was no defense against primal panic. Before he had a chance to overcome his pain and reacquire his presence of mind, his gun was kicked from his hand. Deaf and blind, he was grabbed and yanked to his feet. He was shoved out a door. He fell on a sidewalk and was dragged to his feet. Hands pushed him off a curb. Suddenly weightless, he was thrown to the right. He landed hard on a metal floor, felt other bodies being hurled in with him, and vaguely realized that he must be in a vehicle. A van, he thought, dazed. The metal floor tilted as men scrambled in. With several jolts, doors were slammed. The van sped away.

4

'You searched them?' a gruff voice demanded.

'In the house.'

'Do it again.'

'But we've got all their weapons.'

'I told you, do it again. I don't want any more surprises.'

Disoriented, Decker felt hands pawing over him, rolling him over, pressing, probing. His traumatized vision had begun to correct itself. His ears rang painfully so that the voices he heard seemed to come from a distance.

'He's clean,' another gruff voice said.

'So are the others.'

'Okay,' the first voice said. He sounded as if he had gravel stuck in his throat. 'It's time for show and tell. Hey.'

The van made a swerving motion, presumably turning a corner. Its engine roared louder. Decker had the sensation of increased speed.

'Hey,' the gravelly voice repeated.

Decker felt movement beside him.

'That's right. You. I'm talking to you.'

Decker scrunched his eyelids shut, then opened them again, blinking, his sight improving. Bright spots in his vision began to dissolve. They were replaced by oncoming headlights that glared through a windshield. A *lot* of headlights. Freeway traffic. Decker saw that he had been right to believe he was in a van. The rear compartment in which he lay had no seats. Three men with handguns faced him. They were crouched at the front end of the vehicle. Beyond them were a driver and a man in the passenger seat, who had his head turned, staring back.

'Yes, *you*,' the man with the gravelly voice repeated. Flanked by gunmen, he was husky with thick dark hair and a sallow complexion, olive-like. In his thirties. Wearing expensive shoes, well-cut slacks, a designer shirt, and a tailored windbreaker, all of them dark. Decker noted that the other men in the van had a similar appearance.

Ready with his weapon, the man leaned forward and nudged someone lying next to Decker. When Decker looked, he saw that it was the man he thought of as Dale Hawkins.

'You, for Christ's sake,' the man said. 'Sit up. Pay attention.'

Dazed, Hawkins pushed himself to a sitting position and slumped against the side of the van.

Although the ringing was still painful, Decker's eardrums felt less compromised. He was able to hear the driver complain, 'Another one! Jesus, these drivers are nuts. What are they, drunk? They think this is Indianapolis. They keep cutting in front of me. Any closer, they'd have my front bumper as a souvenir.'

The man who seemed in charge didn't pay attention to the driver but instead kept staring at Hawkins, who was on Decker's left. On Decker's right, Hal sat up slowly.

'So this is how it works,' the husky man said. 'We know Decker has no idea where the woman is. Otherwise, he wouldn't be running around trying to find her. But he must think *you* know where she is.' The man gestured forcefully toward Hawkins. 'Otherwise he wouldn't have driven all the way from Santa Fe to Albuquerque to break into your house and question you when you came home.'

The roiling breathless effects of adrenaline seized Decker's body. Everything was happening terribly fast, but despite the light-headedness and nausea that resulted when neither a fight nor flight response was possible, Decker struggled to keep his presence of mind, to pay attention to as many details as he could.

He continued to be struck by the man's dark eyes, strong features, and olive-like complexion. Italian, he decided. The group was Italian. The same as last night. Rome. This all goes back to what happened in Rome, he thought with a chill. But how?

'I'll make it simple for you,' the man in charge told Hawkins. 'Tell *me* what Decker wanted you to tell him.'

With a curse, the van's driver swerved sharply as another car cut in front of him.

'Where is Diana Scolari?' the man in charge asked.

For a moment, Decker was certain that his traumatized eardrums were playing tricks on him, distorting the sound of words. Beth Dwyer. Surely that's what the man had asked. Where is Beth Dwyer? But the movement of the man's lips did not match Beth's name. Diana Scolari. *That* was the name the man had used. But who the hell was Diana Scolari?

'I don't know,' Hawkins said. His skin had turned gray with fear. His speech was forced as if his mouth was dry. 'I have no idea where she is.'

The man in charge shook his head with disappointment. 'I told you I wanted to make this simple for you. I asked you a question. You're supposed to give me the answer I need. No muss, no fuss.'

The man picked up a tire iron, raised it, and whacked it against Hawkins's shin.

Hawkins screamed, clutching his leg.

'And if you do what you're told, no pain,' the man in charge said. 'But you're not cooperating. Do you honestly expect me to believe that the US marshal –' He held up Hawkins's badge. '– assigned to make sure that Diana Scolari settles herself into Santa Fe doesn't know where she's run to?' The man whacked the tire iron near Hawkins's other leg, causing the floor to rumble, making Hawkins wince. 'Do you think I'm that stupid?'

Hawkins's throat sounded parched as he insisted, 'But I wasn't the only one. There was a team of us. We took turns checking in with her, so none of us would stand out. I haven't seen her since the first of the month.'

The husky man again whacked the tire iron against the metal floor. '*But you knew she ran off today.*'

'Yes.' Hawkins swallowed with difficulty.

Whack! The tire iron struck the floor yet again. 'Which means you've been in contact with the rest of the team. Do you expect me to believe you weren't told where the rest of the team has got her holed up?'

'That information is on a need-to-know basis. They told me I didn't need to know.' Hawkins's voice sounded like sandpaper.

'Oh, did they really? Well, that's too bad for you, because if you don't know anything, you're useless, and I might as well kill you.' The man pointed his handgun at Hal. 'I know who Decker is. But who are *you*?'

'Nobody.'

'Then what good are you?' The man's weapon had a sound suppressor. The pistol made the muffled report of a hand striking a pillow.

Hal fell back and lay still.

Decker's heartbeat lurched.

The sudden silence in the van was emphasized by the roar of traffic outside. The driver swerved, avoiding a car that changed lanes without warning. 'These jerks. I don't believe it. They think this is a stockcar race. They're out of their minds.'

The husky man continued to ignore the driver, concentrating hard on Hawkins. 'Do I have your full attention now? One down. Next comes Decker. And after that, guess who?'

'You'll kill me anyway,' Hawkins said. 'Why should I tell you anything?'

'Hey, if you cooperate, we'll tie you up and stick you in a shed somewhere. We need to keep you quiet only until Monday. After that, it won't matter.'

'How do I know I can believe you?'

'Look at this face. Would it lie to you?'

'What happens Monday?' Decker asked. He remembered that Beth had planned to fly east on Sunday.

'Did I ask you to butt in?' the husky man demanded.

Decker shook his head.

'You're already on my list,' the gunman said. 'If it hadn't been for you, we would have gotten the bitch last night. We would have been back in Jersey by now. The boss wouldn't have gone ballistic at us for missing her again this afternoon. We wouldn't have to be spending our Saturday night driving around goddamn Albuquerque with you two.'

The reference to New Jersey increased the burning in Decker's stomach. It was absolutely clear to him that the gunman would not have revealed any personal detail unless, despite his promises to the contrary, he had every intention of killing Decker and Hawkins.

The gunman pressed his pistol against Hawkins's forehead. 'Maybe you still haven't grasped the situation. Maybe you don't realize what my boss will do to me if I don't solve his problem.'

'Please,' Hawkins said. 'Listen to me. I don't know what to

tell you. At the end of August, I was transferred from Philadelphia to Albuquerque. Diana Scolari was my first assignment in this area. Other marshals were already involved. *They* knew the details. I wasn't in the loop.'

At once Decker thought he might have found a way to postpone his execution. '*I* know her better than Hawkins does.'

The gunman swung his pistol toward Decker's face. 'Didn't I tell you about butting in?'

Decker nodded.

'If you know so damned much about her, why don't you know where she's gone? We had orders to tail you. After the bunch of you left the house to drive to the FBI office, Rudy here put a homing device under the back bumper of the car your friends rented, the one you drove to Albuquerque tonight. We've been following you. It's obvious you're running around looking for her.'

Decker didn't respond.

'Say something!' the gunman barked.

'If I knew what this was about, I might be able to remember something she said, something she let slip, something that gives away where she might have gone,' Decker said.

'And out of the goodness of your heart, you'd tell me.'

'To get out of this alive. Hey, I'm as pissed off at her as *you* are,' Decker said.

'Man, I doubt it.'

The van swerved again.

'She lied to me,' Decker said. 'Diana Scolari? She told me her name was Beth Dwyer. She told me her husband died from cancer back in January. She told me she'd come to Santa Fe to start a new life.'

'Oh, her husband died all right,' the gunman said bitterly. 'But it wasn't from cancer. She blew his brains out.'

Surprise made Decker gape. 'What?'

'She's a better shot than I am. She ought to be. Joey taught her.'

Joey? Decker thought. He wanted urgently to ask who Joey was, but he didn't dare, needing to seem to be giving information rather than getting it.

'And how did she tell you she could afford that house?' the gunman asked.

'Her husband's insurance police.'

The gunman laughed once, angrily. 'Yeah, Joey had an insurance policy, all right. It was in hundred-dollar bills in several bags in his safe at the house. Over two million dollars. After she blew his brains out, she took everything.'

The van swerved sharply, making everybody lurch.

'Hey!' The gunman turned in fury toward the driver. 'If you can't handle this thing, Frank will.'

'I'm telling you,' the man behind the wheel said, 'I've never seen drivers like this. Everybody's got these big pickup trucks, and they cut in front of me like it's some kind of game to see how close they can get without hitting me. This makes the Long Island Expressway seem like a drive in the country.'

'Just do what you're told. I'm sick of screwups. That's all this rotten job has been. One long screwup.'.

As the gunman swung back toward Decker, Decker didn't show his startled reaction when he felt slight movement next to him. On his right. From Hal. Concealed by the shadows at the rear of the van, Hal pressed a finger against the side of Decker's ankle to show that the gunshot hadn't killed him. Decker could think of only one reason Hal would do that – to warn Decker that Hal might try something.

The gunman aimed his pistol at Decker. 'So, all right, loverboy. I'm a reasonable man.'

One of his companions snickered.

'Hey, I am,' the gunman said. 'Give me a little credit. So

here's my proposition. On the odd chance that you had a suspicion you wanted confirmed by this marshal, I'll give you thirty seconds to give me your best guess where she is. Make it good. Because if you don't sell me, it's bye-bye. Maybe by then this marshal will have figured out how serious I am.'

Sweat streaked Decker's face. 'She told me she was going back to New York on Sunday.'

'Of course. To testify on Monday. Twenty-five seconds left.'

'Then you know where to try to intercept her – wherever she's testifying.'

'Decker, after two attempts on her life, the feds won't risk exposing her now until she's got as much security as the president. The point is to get to her while they're still confused, *before* they get organized. Twenty seconds.'

I have to do something, Decker thought, frantic. I can't just let him shoot me. I have to—

His reflexes tightened as something made a muffled shrill noise in the gunman's windbreaker. A cellular telephone.

The gunman muttered, taking out a small slim telephone, pressing a button. 'Yeah, who is this?' The gunman listened. 'Damn it, Nick's going to be furious. We missed her again. The police radio said she got out of the house before it blew up. We're trying to find her . . . *You?* She went to *you*? Where did you take her? Well, I'll be . . . That close to home. Did you phone Nick? Will he take care of it? I don't mind telling you I was getting nervous . . . . We'll catch the first plane back. In the meantime, I've been talking to an old pal of yours, asking him if he has any last words. Anything you want to pass on? . . . Right.' With a grin, the gunman handed the phone to Decker.

Confused, Decker took it. ' . . . Hello?'

The voice on the other end was one that he hadn't heard in over a year, but its sullen tone was instantly recognizable. 'Decker, I wish to God I could be there to see you get it.'

'*McKittrick?*'

'You ruined my life,' the voice said.

'Listen to me.'

'You destroyed my career.'

'No. That isn't true. Tell these guys to take me to where you are. We need to meet. We need to talk about this,' Decker said.

'My father would have been proud of me.'

'McKittrick, I need to know about Beth.'

'But you had to interfere. You had to prove how smart you are.'

'Where is she?'

'You wanted all the credit.'

'*Why did she run away with you? What have you done with her?*'

'Nothing compared to what I'm *going* to do. And what those men do to *you* – I hope they make it last a long time.'

'McKittrick!'

'*Now* who's so damned smart?'

Decker heard a click, dead air, a dial tone. Slowly, in despair, he lowered the telephone.

The gunman kept grinning. 'Before I gave you the phone, your old buddy said to tell you, "*Arrivederci, Roma*." ' He laughed and raised his pistol. 'Where was I? Fifteen seconds? Ten? Oh, to hell with it.'

But as the gunman's finger tightened on the trigger, Hal managed sufficient strength to make his move. Despite his wound, he kicked his foot up, deflecting the weapon. The muffled report of the pistol sent a bullet bursting through the van's roof.

Decker threw the telephone as hard as he could, striking the gunman between the eyes. At the same time, he lunged for the pistol, knocking the husky man off balance, jolting against the two men who flanked him. In the confinement of the van, bodies slammed against bodies.

'What's going on back there?' The driver looked over his shoulder toward the commotion. The van swerved.

Bodies lurched against each other. Decker kicked one of the gunmen in the groin while he struggled for the husky man's pistol. At once someone else was struggling next to him. Hawkins. The marshal struck one of the gunmen in the face and fought to pry his weapon away. In front, the gunman in the passenger seat started climbing over the low barrier to get to the back. The husky man fired again, another bullet bursting through the roof, as Decker shoved and the entire group thrust forward. The press of bodies knocked the gunman in front back into the passenger seat. The struggling bodies thrust even farther forward, toppling over the barrier, sprawling into the front, squeezing the driver against the steering wheel.

'No!' the driver screamed as the van struck the rear of a pickup truck. He stomped the brake pedal and tried to swing the steering wheel to avoid hitting the truck again, but the weight of several squirming men wedged him against the steering wheel and he didn't have the leverage to turn it. Out of control, the driver could only watch in horror as the van veered into the next lane, broadsided a car, tipped, fell onto its right side, slid forward, grazed another vehicle, and careened violently to the side of the freeway, striking barrels, smashing through a barrier, shattering the windshield, walloping to a dizzying sickening stop.

Decker's breath was knocked out of him. He lay motionless among a jumble of other motionless men, stunned, seeing double for a moment. He wondered why he was blinking up at the van's left side instead of the ceiling, then realized that the van had overturned and the left side *was* the ceiling. Time seemed to have halted. With a shock, it resumed, fear urging him into action as he smelled gasoline. The fumes were cloyingly thick. My God, he thought, the gas tank must have ruptured.

He groped to move, pushing a body off him. Fear propelled him. Headlights gleamed through the broken windshield. Hal. Have to get Hal out with me. Have to find Hawkins. With a start, he realized that it was Hawkins he had pushed off him and that Hawkins's blank gaze in tandem with the grotesque position of his head made it obvious his neck was broken. Hal! Where is—? One of the gunmen groaned. As Decker searched for Hal, his mind cleared enough for him to understand that the front doors were jammed with bodies and that the van had fallen onto its side door. Amid overpowering gasoline fumes, feeling trapped, Decker prayed that the back doors hadn't been jammed.

Another gunman groaned. One of them weakly raised an arm. Decker groped on his hands and knees toward the back and found himself staring down at Hal, whose mouth – revealed by headlights rushing past the broken windshield – was open, trickling blood.

His eyes were open also, sightless. But maybe he's just knocked out! Maybe he's not dead! Decker fumbled to try to find a pulse, not succeeding.

With a curse, one of the gunmen gained more strength. Simultaneously Decker smelled something else besides gasoline. Smoke. The van was hazy with it, making Decker cough. The van's going to blow up, he realized, and scrambled toward the back doors. His abrupt movement caused the van to tilt toward the rear. Why? What was it resting on? He reached the back doors. Because the van was on its side, the doors were horizontal. Gripping the bottom latch, turning it fiercely, he exhaled in triumph when it moved, grateful that it wasn't jammed. He pushed the bottom door open and squirmed out onto it, again feeling the van tilt. Unexpectedly he slid downward. In a frenzy, he grabbed the edge of the back door just before he would have tumbled toward the headlights of cars speeding below him.

He gasped as he understood that the van must have crashed through barriers on a section of the freeway that was being repaired. That section was on a bridge. The back end of the van projected into space, delicately balanced on the sideless rim of the bridge. He was dangling over a busy underpass, oncoming traffic roaring beneath him. If he let go, he would probably break his legs when he hit the highway twenty feet below him. Not that the pain would matter. He would be killed an instant later when a vehicle struck him.

He struggled to pull himself back up, but, responding to each of his motions, the van bobbed. It threatened to tilt all the way over and topple with him onto the underpass, crushing him. His heart pounded so fast that it made him nauseous. He stopped his frenzied attempt to climb back into the overturned van and instead hung motionless from the horizontal back door, calculating whether he could reach beneath the back of the van and clutch the rim of the bridge, whether he could grope along the bridge until he came to the side. Beneath him, wreckage blocked one of the lanes. Horns blared as the traffic in the blocked lane swerved between vehicles in the open lane. Meanwhile, the van bobbed again as a sound above him made him flinch.

The sound came from labored breathing as someone crawled to the back of the van. The husky man who had interrogated him peered down in stupefaction, his face covered with blood. Obviously disoriented, the man seemed paralyzed by the rush of headlights beneath him. Then the man saw Decker hanging from the open rear door, and his senses returned to him. He pawed at his clothes, evidently looking for his pistol. Realizing he had dropped it, he swung toward the van's interior. Again, the van bobbed.

Whump. A bright flickering light burst into view at the front. Fire! Decker thought. The gasoline had ignited. Any second, the fuel tank would explode. The van would blow apart in flames. The husky man quickly reappeared, pursued by the fire spreading rapidly toward him. In panic, he started to climb out onto the open door, then seemed to realized that the door wouldn't hold both Decker and himself. Screaming, he raised a pistol he had picked up, aiming at Decker.

No choice, Decker thought. He peered down, saw a transport truck passing beneath him, released his grip, and plummeted as the gunman shot at him. At the same time, the fuel tank erupted, flames enveloping the gunman. Then all Decker saw was the moving transport truck beneath him. Its driver had been forced to reduce speed as he avoided the wreckage in one lane, squeezing between vehicles in the next lane. With a gasp, Decker struck the sixteen-wheeler's roof and instinctively buckled his knees as he had been taught in jump school. If he hadn't rolled, if he had somehow remained upright, his chest and head would have been whacked against the top of the overpass. Coming out of his roll, propelled by the force of his fall and the momentum of the truck, Decker slammed his hands against the roof of the truck and clawed to find a seam, a ridge, *anything* to stop him from sliding. The rumbling darkness of the tunnel contributed to his dizziness. He felt his feet slipping off the back of the truck. Behind him, vaguely, he had the sense of a flaming body that streaked from the bridge and hit the highway, more horns blaring, the crunch of impact. But all he paid attention to was the speed with which his knees, thighs, groin, and chest slid off the back of the transport truck. He pressed his fingers harder against the roof, felt himself about to fly into space, imagined his impact on the freeway just before the crushing force with which the vehicle behind him would strike him . . . and then he snagged the top edge of the truck's rear door. Immediately his left hand lost its grip. He clung more desperately with his right, again snagged his left hand onto the top edge of the door, banged his knees against the center of the door, and touched the huge latch with the bottom of his left sneaker.

The truck sped from the tunnel. Decker heard an explosive crash behind him. Even without looking back, he knew what had happened. The burning van had cascaded off the bridge and struck the remaining open lane on the freeway. Horns blared. Metal crashed against metal. Glass shattered.

The truck's speed diminished, its driver veering off the freeway toward a breakdown lane. The sideview mirrors must have shown the driver the flames and explosion on the lane behind him. Now he was pulling over to stop and see what had happened. The more the truck reduced its speed, the better Decker was able to hang on. The moment the truck eased to a halt, Decker released his grip and dropped to the gravel at the side of the freeway. He vaulted the freeway's guardrail and disappeared into the darkness near a used-car lot before the driver walked to the rear of the truck and stared back toward the inferno.

5

'I'll pay you to drive me to Santa Fe.'

Decker was outside a convenience store/gas station. Amid the harsh glare of arc lights, he spoke to three street kids who had just returned to their bright red, dark-windowed, low-slung Ford, carrying two twelve-packs of beer.

'Man, we're busy,' the first kid said.

'Yeah, we're havin' a party,' the second kid said.

'Yeah, we're drivin' around, havin' a party,' the third kid said.

As one, the three of them snickered.

'You'll be able to have a much better party with the hundred dollars I'm willing to pay for a ride to Santa Fe,' Decker said.

The three kids scowled at him.

'A hundred?' the first kid asked.

'You heard me.'

'It ain't enough,' the second kid said.

'What *is* enough?'

'*Two* hundred,' the third kid said.

Again, they all snickered.

'All right,' Decker said.

The three kids scowled harder.

'Hey, what happened to you?' the first kid asked.

'I was in a car accident.'

'Looks more like you were in a fight,' the second kid said.

'Like you *lost* the fight,' the third kid said.

They bent over, laughing.

'Let's see your money,' the first kid said.

Decker showed them the cash he had gotten from his bank's automatic teller machine before leaving Santa Fe earlier in the day. 'So are you giving me a ride, or aren't you?'

'Oh, yeah, we're givin' you a ride, all right,' the second kid said.

But half the distance to Santa Fe, they turned off the Interstate onto a murky side road.

'What's this?'

'A detour.'

'Short cut.'

'Rest stop.'

They snickered uncontrollably as they showed him their knives.

'Give us your money, man,' the first kid said.

'Not just the two hundred,' the second kid added.

'*All* of it,' the third kid demanded.

'You picked the absolutely worst time to do this,' Decker said.

He broke their arms, legs, and jaws. Leaving them unconscious in the darkness of the desert, he got in the car and revved the engine, roaring back toward the Interstate, racing toward Santa Fe.

6

Beth. Decker was hunched over the Ford's steering wheel, gripping it tightly, staring fiercely ahead toward the dark freeway. Beth. His foot was heavy on the accelerator. Although he was determined not to attract the attention of the police by driving faster than the sixty-five-mile-an-hour speed limit, he was appalled to discover that he was doing seventy-five every time he glanced down at the speedometer. He had to go slower. If he was stopped in a stolen car . . .

Beth, he kept repeating. Why did you lie to me? Who *are* you? Who on earth is Diana Scolari?

A clock on the Ford's dashboard told Decker that the time was shortly after one in the morning, but he felt as if it was much later. His head throbbed from fatigue. His eyes were raw, as if sand had been thrown into them. More, his body ached from the bruises and scrapes he had suffered during the fight in the van and the subsequent accident. Dropping onto the transport truck had jolted him to his core. For the past year, he had deluded himself that by exercising regularly, jogging and playing tennis for example, he had kept in adequate physical condition. But now he realized that he had been coasting. He hadn't been maintaining a professional level of preparedness.

For what? he raged. I left that life behind me. I reinvented myself. What did I need to be prepared for?

Everything! he insisted as he sped past a pickup truck, his headlights blazing. I was crazy to let my guard down! *Beth*, he inwardly screamed.

Or maybe he screamed Beth's name out loud. His throat felt strained, his vocal cords tense. *Why did you lie to me?* Shot your husband? Took two million dollars from a safe your husband had in the house? What the— Had the gunman told the truth? Was *anybody* telling the truth? What about McKittrick? How was he involved in this?

Now he definitely *was* screaming Beth's name out loud, the angry outburst amplified by the Ford's interior. As he urged the Ford up the long dark curve of La Bajada hill, exhaustion and pain caused him to be overwhelmed by the confusion of emotions surging through him. He couldn't separate them, couldn't tell them apart. Was it love he felt, the certainty that there had to be a valid explanation, that Beth would provide the explanation, convincing him when he found her? Or were his emotions the opposite – hate, anger, betrayal? Did he want to save Beth?

Or did he want to catch up to her and punish her?

The Ford rushed to the crest of the hill, and in turmoil, he suddenly faced the lights of Santa Fe. The English translation of the city's Spanish name struck him with its bitter irony: holy faith. He had to have – he prayed for – faith.

EIGHT

1

Decker's house seemed like a stranger's. Having wiped his fingerprints from the stolen car and left it on a dirt road off Old Pecos Trail, he ran wearily through the darkness toward his home, but despairingly he felt no identification with it. For the past year and a quarter, it had been his sanctuary, the symbol of his new life, and now it was merely a place, no different from the apartment he had given up in Alexandria, Virginia.

Wary, he checked for surveillance on it, detected none, but still felt the need to be cautious, approaching up the piñon-treed slope behind it, as last night's attackers had done. Fumbling with his key in the gloom beneath a rear portal, he unlocked his back door and eased inside. In case the police might drive by and see any lights he turned on, he didn't reach for a switch, just quickly locked the door behind him and used the moonlight streaming through the wall of windows at the back to guide him into his ravaged bedroom. Litter was everywhere. The stench of cordite remained. *That* now was the symbol of his life.

For the third time in less then twelve hours, he took a cold shower and put on fresh clothes. *This* time, he packed a small travel bag. He gathered his few items of jewelry – a gold bracelet, a gold chain, a jade ring. He never wore these. They were a vestige from his former life, objects that he could barter if he ran out of money in an emergency. The same was true for the pouch of twelve gold coins that he had thrown disgustedly into a drawer when he moved in. He had intended to cash them in or store them in a safe-deposit box but had not gotten around to doing either. Now he added his jewelry to the coins in the pouch and set the pouch among the clothes in his travel bag.

Almost ready. He carried the bag to the door that led to his garage. That door was off the kitchen. He grudgingly paused to open the refrigerator, slap together and wolf down a ham-and-cheese sandwich, and gulp what was left in a carton of skim milk. Wiping drops from his mouth, he went into his study and checked his answering machine in hopes that there would be a message from Beth. What he heard instead were reporters wanting to talk to him about the attack on his house and the bombing next door. Several friends from work had also left messages, surprised about what they had learned on the news. There were a half dozen messages from Esperanza. 'Decker, as soon as you hear this, phone me. I've been trying to get in touch with you. By God, if you've left town . . .' Solemn, Decker returned to the kitchen, picked up his travel bag, and went out to his garage. His Jeep Cherokee's powerful engine starting without hesitation, he roared away into the night.

2

'Uh. Just a . . . What time is . . . ?'

Holding his carphone to his ear as he drove, Decker said, 'Esperanza?'

'*Decker*?' The detective's groggy voice immediately sounded alert. 'Where have—'

'We need to talk.'

'You're damned right we need to talk.'

'Your home phone number is on the business card you gave me but not your address. How do I get to where you live?'

Decker listened. 'Yes, I know where that is.'

Eight minutes later, Decker pulled into a dimly lit trailer court on the south side of town, the sort of unglamorous district that tourists roaming the glitzy shops on the Plaza weren't aware existed. A pickup truck and a motorcycle were parked on a shadowy dirt driveway next to a trailer. Yuccas studded the gravel area in front. A flower garden hugged the front wall. Esperanza, wearing black sweat pants and a top, his long dark hair hanging to his shoulders, sat under a pale yellow light that illuminated three concrete steps that led up to the metal front door.

When Decker started to get out of the Jeep, Esperanza gestured for him to stay put, walked over, and climbed in, shutting the passenger door. 'Your phone call woke my wife.'

'Sorry.'

'That's what *I* said. It didn't help the problems she and I are having.'

Esperanza's personal remark came as a surprise. Decker had been so preoccupied by his own problems that he hadn't thought about what kind of life Esperanza had outside his job. The detective seemed so objective and professional, he gave the impression he was like that twenty-four hours a day. Decker would never have guessed that the man had problems of his own.

'She keeps telling me I don't earn enough for the risks I take and the hours I put in,' Esperanza said. 'She wants me to quit the force. Guess what she wants me to be? You'll love the coincidence.'

Decker thought a moment. 'A real-estate broker?'

'Give the man a cigar. Do *you* get calls in the middle of the night?'

Decker shook his head.

'But in your former line of work, I bet you did. And for damned sure, *tonight* you did. I went over to your house several times. You weren't around. I kept phoning. All I got was your answering machine. Funny how a person can jump to conclusions. I had a notion you'd left town. If you didn't show by tomorrow morning, I was going to put out an APB for you. Where the hell have you been?'

'Out walking.'

'Since four in the afternoon? That's almost ten hours.'

'I stopped and sat a while.'

'*Quite* a while.'

'I had a lot to think about.'

'Like what?'

Decker looked squarely into Esperanza's eyes. 'I'm going after her.'

Esperanza's gaze was equally challenging. 'Even though I want you here in case I have more questions?'

'I've told you everything I can. This is a courtesy visit. So there aren't any misunderstandings. So you know exactly what I'm up to. *I'm going after her.*'

'And where exactly do you think she's gone?'

Decker ignored the question. 'I'm telling you my plans because I don't want you to put out that APB you mentioned. I don't want to have to worry that the police are looking for me.'

'And in exchange? Why on earth should I agree to this?'

Decker ignored those questions, too. 'Did the Albuquerque airport mention any sign of Beth and McKittrick?'

Esperanza stared at him in amazement, then broke out into bitter laughter. 'You really expect me to help? From the start, you told me as little as possible, but I'm supposed to share what I know?'

'Do whatever you want.'

'I intend to. Right now, what I want is for you to come into the house.'

Decker straightened. 'You expect me to stay here while you

phone for a patrol car to take me to the station?'

'No. I expect you to stay while I get dressed. Wherever *you're* going, *I'm* going. Whether you like it or not, you've got company. I'm tired of being jerked around. You obviously know a lot more than you're letting on. From now on, you and I are going to be like Siamese twins until you give me some answers.'

'Believe me, I wish I had them.'

'Get out of the car.' Esperanza opened his passenger door.

'Her real name isn't Beth Dwyer,' Decker said. 'It's Diana Scolari.'

Esperanza froze as he was getting out.

'Does that name mean anything to you?' Decker asked.

'No.'

'US marshals were watching her. She was supposed to fly to New York and testify about something on Monday. I can think of only one explanation that fits.'

'The Federal Witness Protection Program.'

'Yes.'

Esperanza got back into the Cherokee. 'When did you find this out?'

'Tonight.'

'How?'

'You don't want to know. But if you're serious about helping, there's a man you can tell me how to find.'

3

Decker rang the bell a fourth time, banged on the door, and was pleased to see a light come on inside the house. He and Esperanza had tried phoning, but after four rings, they had gotten only an answering machine. Assuming the man Decker needed to talk to hadn't left town in the twelve hours since they had last seen him, they had decided to go directly to where Esperanza knew he lived. It was a modest adobe on a side street off Zia Road, a low wall enclosing well-tended shrubs. Like many districts in Santa Fe, there weren't any street lights. Taking care to step back from the door when its overhead light came on, showing themselves so they wouldn't seem to be threatening, Decker and Esperanza waited for the door to open.

FBI Agent John Miller challenged them from the shadows behind an open window. '*Who's out there? What do you want?*'

'It's Sergeant Esperanza.'

'Esperanza? Why the— It's almost four in the morning. What are *you* doing here?'

'I have something I need to talk to you about.'

'Can't this wait until a decent hour?'

'It's urgent.'

'That's what you said this afternoon. I haven't forgotten how you tried to set me up.'

'You'll be setting *yourself* up if you don't listen this time.'

'Who's that with you?'

'The man who was with me this afternoon.'

'Shit.'

More lights came on in the house. The scrape of a lock being turned was followed by the creak of the front door as Miller opened it. He wore boxer shorts and a T-shirt that showed his athletically lean arms and legs. His rumpled hair and whisker stubble contrasted with his bureaucratically neat appearance the previous afternoon. 'I have a guest,' he said. Blocking the entrance to the house, he pointed toward a closed door at the end of a short hallway. Miller was divorced, Esperanza had told Decker. 'She's not used to people pounding on the door at four in the morning. This had better be good.'

'I want to know about Diana Scolari,' Decker said.

'Who?' Miller gave him a deadpan.

'Diana Scolari.'

Miller pretended to look confused. 'Never heard of her.' He started to close the door. 'If that's all you came here about—'

Decker blocked the door with his shoe. 'Diana Scolari is Beth Dwyer's real name.'

Miller stared down at where Decker's shoe blocked the door. 'I don't know what you're talking about.'

'She's in the Federal Witness Protection Program.'

Miller's eyes changed focus, sharper, more alert.

'That's what the attack on *my* house and the explosions at *her* house were about,' Decker said.

'I still don't know what you're getting at.'

'Granted, the FBI isn't as directly involved with the Witness Protection Program as it used to be,' Decker said. 'The US Marshals Service is mostly in charge. But you and they work closely enough together that they would have told you if they were relocating a major witness to Santa Fe. On the other hand, the local police would *not* have been told. It *wasn't necessary* for them to be told. The fewer people who knew the better.'

Miller's features became harder. 'Assuming what you say is correct, why should I admit anything to *you*?'

'Brian McKittrick,' Decker said.

Miller stopped trying to close the door.

'He's the man who picked up Beth when she ran from her house just before it blew up,' Decker said.

Miller's suspicion was obvious. 'How do you know this man?'

'I used to work with him.'

'That's a stretch. You're telling me you used to be a US marshal?'

'Marshal?' Decker didn't understand what Miller was referring to. At once the implications struck him. '*McKittrick is a US marshal?*'

Having unintentionally given away information, Miller looked chagrined.

'No,' Decker said. 'I never worked for the Marshals Service.' Pressed for time, he had to take Miller by surprise. 'I knew McKittrick when we worked together in the CIA.'

It had the appropriate effect. Startled, Miller assessed Decker with new awareness. He turned to Esperanza, then looked at Decker again, and gestured for them to come in. 'We need to talk.'

4

Like the exterior of the house, Miller's living room was modest: a plain sofa and chair, a small coffee table, a twenty-inch television. Everything was scrupulously clean and ordered. Decker noticed a .38 revolver on a bookshelf and suspected that Miller had been holding it when he peered out his window to see who was pounding on his door.

'I don't suppose you can prove you worked for the agency,' Miller said.

'Not at the moment. We didn't exactly use badges and business cards.'

'Then why should I believe you?' Miller frowned toward Esperanza. 'Do *you* believe him?'

Esperanza nodded.

'Why?'

'You haven't been with him since this time yesterday. The way he handles himself in a crisis, it's obvious he's a professional, and I don't mean at selling real estate.'

'We'll see.' Miller returned his attention to Decker. 'What do you know about Brian McKittrick?'

'He's the most fucked-up operative I ever worked with.'

Miller stepped closer.

'Wouldn't obey orders,' Decker said. 'Thought his team members were scheming against him. Took serious action without permission. Exceeded his authority at every opportunity. The assignment I shared with him ended as a disaster because of him. Numerous casualties. It was almost an international incident.'

Miller studied him, as if debating how candid he wanted to be. At last, exhaling, he sat wearily in the chair opposite Decker. 'It's not giving anything important away if I admit I've heard rumors about McKittrick. Nothing to do with the CIA. I didn't know anything about that. His behavior as a marshal. That's what I heard rumors about. He's a hot dog. Thinks he knows better than his superiors. Doesn't obey the chain of command. Violates procedure. I never understood how he got into the Marshals Service.'

'I can make a good guess,' Decker said. 'The agency must have given him first-rate recommendations when they let him go. In exchange for his not embarrassing them by revealing details about the disaster he was involved in.'

'But if McKittrick caused the disaster, he would have been harming himself if he talked about it.'

'Not if he convinced himself he wasn't to blame,' Decker said. 'McKittrick has a reality problem. When he does something wrong, he manages to delude himself that it's always someone else's fault.'

Esperanza leaned forward. 'You sound especially bitter about that.'

'*I* was the one he blamed. I resigned from government work because of him – and now the son of a bitch is back in my life.'

'By coincidence.'

'No. I can't believe it's a coincidence that Beth just happened to buy the house next to mine. Not if McKittrick was in charge of her protection. The only way the scenario makes sense is if McKittrick kept tabs on me after I quit the agency. He knew I was in Santa Fe. He had a witness to relocate. He did a little more investigating and found out the house next to mine was for sale. Perfect. Why not put Beth next to me? She'd have a next-door neighbor as extra protection, an unwitting bodyguard.'

Miller thought about it. 'The tactic might have been cynical, but it does make sense.'

'Cynical doesn't begin to describe it. I was *used*,' Decker said. 'And if I'm not mistaken, *Beth* was used. I think McKittrick went over to the other side.'

'*What?*'

Decker vividly remembered his telephone conversation with McKittrick. 'I think McKittrick told the mob how to find her, provided they killed me in the bargain. I think he blames me for the CIA's decision to kick him out. I think he's a sick bastard who planned to ruin my life from the moment he was assigned to help turn Diana Scolari into Beth Dwyer.'

5

The small living room became silent.

'That's a serious accusation.' Miller bit his lower lip. 'Can you *prove* any of this?'

'No.' Decker didn't dare tell him about what had happened in the van.

'How did you find out that Beth Dwyer's real name is Diana Scolari?'

'I can't tell you.'

'Why not?'

Decker didn't respond.

'Listen very carefully.' Miller stood. 'You are in possession of information indicating there was a serious breach of security in the protection of an important government witness. I am ordering you to tell me how you came by this information.'

'I'm not at liberty to say.'

Miller glared. 'I'll teach you about liberty.' He picked up the telephone. 'You'll be giving up your liberty for quite a while until you tell me what I want to know.'

'No. You're making a mistake,' Decker said.

Miller glared harder. '*I'm* not the one who's making a mistake.'

'Put down the phone. Please. All that matters is saving Beth's life.'

Miller swung toward Esperanza. 'Do you hear this bullshit?'

'Yes. For the past twenty-four hours, he's been playing mindgames on me,' Esperanza said. 'What worries me is, he's beginning to make sense. Beth Dwyer's safety *is* the priority. If Decker cut corners to get his information, I'm prepared to deal with that later, provided it doesn't compromise me.'

'Plausible deniability,' Decker said.

'What?'

'That's what we used to call it in the agency.'

'How about calling it "accessory to a felony"?' Miller asked.

'Tell me what Beth Dwyer was going to testify about.'

Miller wasn't prepared for the abrupt change of topic.

'Did she really shoot her husband in the head and get away with two million dollars of mob money?' Decker asked.

Miller gestured fiercely. 'Where the hell did you learn this stuff?'

But Decker ignored the outburst. He was too busy recalling something the gunman had said on the telephone. ('*Nick's going to be furious.*')

'A man called Nick is involved,' Decker said. 'Do you know who that is? What's his last name?'

Miller blinked in astonishment. 'It's worse than I thought. There'll have to be a complete review of witness-relocation security procedures.'

'Beth's in danger,' Decker said with force. 'If we share what we know, we might be able to save her life.'

'Diana Scolari.'

'I don't know anything about Diana Scolari. The woman I care about is Beth Dwyer. *Tell me about her.*'

Miller stared toward the darkness beyond his window. He stared at his hands. He stared at Decker. 'Diana Scolari is the wife – or used to be the wife until someone shot the son of a bitch in the head – of Joey Scolari, the chief enforcer for the Giordano family in New York City. We estimate that Joey was responsible for at least forty mob executions during his eight-year tenure. He was a very busy man. But he didn't complain. The money was excellent and, just as important, he loved his work.'

Decker listened, distressed.

'Three years ago, Joey met the woman you know as Beth Dwyer. Her unmarried name was Diana Berlanti, and she was working as an activity director on a cruise ship in the Caribbean, where Joey had decided to put himself on display to give himself an alibi while one of his lieutenants eliminated a problem back in New York. Diana attracted his attention. Understand, he was a good-looking guy, stylish dresser, knew what to say to women. They normally fell all over him, so it wasn't any surprise that Diana didn't tell him to get lost when he started making advances. One thing led to another. They were married three months later. The courtship was convenient for him. He arranged it so they kept going back to the Caribbean. It gave him a chance to have a natural-seeming reason to visit certain islands that have banks with numbered accounts and no objection to laundering money. Same with the honeymoon.'

Decker felt sick.

'It's important to emphasize that, according to Diana, she had no idea of Joey's real occupation. She claims he told her he was in the restaurant business – which is true enough; Joey did own several restaurants as part of the same money-laundering scheme. Anyhow, time passed, and – no surprise, Joey's attention span was limited – he started to get tired of her. For a while, they lived in his penthouse in the city, but when he needed the place for his extracurricular activities, he put Diana in a big house with walls around it across the river in one of those mob bedroom communities in New Jersey. Plenty of guards. To keep her safe, he claimed. Actually they were to keep her from going back to the penthouse and catching him with his girlfriends. But an equally important reason for the guards was to make sure she didn't get any ideas about moving out after the numerous times he beat her up.'

Decker's temples throbbed.

'And I mean he beat her up *a lot*,' Miller said. 'Because Diana had started asking questions not only about his fidelity but also about his business. You know how intelligent she is. It didn't take her long to realize what Joey really did, what kind of monster he was. So now she had a big problem. If she tried to leave – and there wasn't much hope of success with so many guards – she was certain he'd kill her. If she stayed and he suspected she was noticing too much, he'd kill her also. Her temporary solution was to pretend to lose interest in his women and his business, to pretend to be compliant. She spent her days doing what under other circumstances would have given her a great deal of pleasure – painting. Joey got a kick out of that, found it amusing. Sometimes, after he beat her up, he would build a big fire in the den and force her to watch him burn her favorite paintings.'

'Jesus,' Decker said. 'Why did the bastard marry her?'

'Obviously for the pleasure of possessing someone he could

hurt. As I said, Joey was a monster. Until nine months ago, in January, when someone solved her problem by blowing Joey's brains out. Or maybe *she* did it. There are two conflicting stories. Diana claims she was outside in the back of the estate, painting a winter scene, when she heard a shot in the house. Cautious, not knowing what to expect, she took her time going inside. Her assumption was that whatever had happened, Joey and the guards would take care of it. Her first surprise was to find the guards gone. Her second surprise was to find Joey dead in his study, his brains across his desk, his safe open. That safe normally held a considerable amount of cash, she knew. She'd seen bags of it delivered from time to time. She'd caught a glimpse of Joey putting it away. She'd overheard references to amounts. Her best guess was that two million dollars was missing. The implications of that didn't strike her at the time. All she cared about was taking the opportunity to escape. She didn't even bother to pack, just threw on an overcoat, grabbed Joey's keys, and drove away.'

'To the Justice Department,' Decker said.

'What other direction did she have? She knew the mob would be looking for her after she disappeared. But she figured their motive would be to keep her from talking. She didn't realize until later that Joey's godfather blamed her for the death, that the mob figured *she* killed Joey and took the money. It was a matter of family pride now. *Blood* pride. Revenge.'

Decker nodded. 'So the Justice Department spent months debriefing her, relocated her with a new identity in Santa Fe, and finally summoned her back to New York to testify.'

'Under protection.'

'You mean *McKittrick's* protection.'

'Unfortunately.'

'What a goddamn mess,' Esperanza said.

'You still haven't told me who Nick is,' Decker said.

'Nick Giordano, the head of the family, Joey's godfather. Joey's birth father was Nick's best friend. When Joey's parents were killed in a mob attempt to kill Nick, Nick raised Joey as his own. That's what I meant about blood pride. To Nick, it's a matter of personal honor – family in the strictest sense – to find and punish her. Now it's *your* turn,' Miller said. 'How is what I just told you going to help save Diana Scolari's life?'

Decker didn't speak for a moment. 'It looks like I have only one choice.'

'What are you talking about? *What* choice?'

'I'm suddenly very tired. I'm going home.'

'How the hell is *that* going to help your girlfriend?'

'I'll phone you when I wake up. Maybe you'll have more information by then.' Decker turned toward Esperanza. 'I'll drop you off.'

6

'Don't bother taking me home,' Esperanza said as Decker put the Cherokee into gear and sped from Miller's house.

'Then where do you want me to take you?' Decker veered around a shadowy corner.

'Just figure I'm along for the ride.'

'What do you think that will accomplish?'

'Maybe I'll keep you out of trouble,' Esperanza said. 'Where are your friends?'

'Friends?' The thought of Hal and Ben made Decker's mouth taste of ashes.

'You sound as if you don't really have many.'

'I have a lot of acquaintances.'

'I was referring to the two men who showed up at your house this afternoon.'

'I know who you're referring to. They left town.' The taste of ashes was matched by an aching sensation – in his chest and at his eyes.

'So soon?' Esperanza asked. 'After they went to all the trouble to get here so quickly?'

'My former employer decided what was happening here had nothing to do with business.' The murky streets were almost deserted. Headlights blazing, Decker pressed his foot on the accelerator.

'Do you think it's a good idea exceeding the speed limit with a police officer in the car?'

'I can't think of anyone I'd rather exceed it with. If a cruiser stops us, show your badge – explain we're on the way to an emergency.'

'I lied to you,' Esperanza said. 'I did have the State Police and the Albuquerque PD looking for you.'

Decker felt a cold spot on his spine.

'I gave them the license number and the description of the Taurus your friends were driving. The car was found near a crime scene on Chama Street in Albuquerque around eleven o'clock tonight. The neighbors complained about what they thought were gunshots and explosions. Turned out the neighbors were right. A man whose ID referred to him as Ben Eiseley was found shot to death on the kitchen floor of the house the neighbors complained about. We have no idea where Hal is.'

For an instant, Decker could no longer repress his grief. The memory of the shocked expression on Ben's face as the bullet struck him, blood spewing from his head, seized Decker. Suddenly it was as if he had never come to Santa Fe, as if he had never tried to distance himself from his former life. He thought about how Hal had been shot in the chest and yet had still managed the strength to kick the man who had shot him. This wasn't their fight! Decker thought. I should have insisted they back off. But I asked for their help. They died because of me. It's my fault!

'They must have been given another assignment while they were out here,' Decker said as calmly as he could.

'You don't seem affected by what happened to Ben.'

'In my own way.'

'I've never met anyone like you,' Esperanza said. 'Aren't you curious about what he was doing there and where his partner is?'

'Let me ask *you* a question,' Decker said angrily. 'Why did you wait so long to tell me you'd put out a police alert about me?'

'I wanted the right moment. To make a point. You need me,' Esperanza said. 'Security at the Albuquerque airport has your name. The officers are watching for a man of your description. The minute you try to buy a ticket, you'll be stopped. If you want to fly to New York, you need me to call off the alert, and I charge a price for doing that. You're going to have to let me come along.'

'Fly to New York? What makes you think I—'

'Decker, just once, for Christ's sake, quit playing mindgames with me, will you?'

'Why would you want to go to New York?'

'Let's say tomorrow's my day off and and my wife and I could use a little distance from each other.' Esperanza gestured with frustration. 'Or let's say being with you is a definite learning experience, and I'm not ready to let the classes end. Or maybe, let's say – and this is really far out – let's say I'm a cop because I'm a sucker for helping people. Dumb idea, huh? Right now, I can't think of anybody who needs help more than Beth Dwyer. I want to help you save her. I've got a feeling you're the only person who really knows how to do that.'

7

The roar of the eastward-bound jet vibrated through the fuselage. Sunlight blazed through the window, making Decker's weary eyes feel stabbed. As flight attendants came down the aisle, handing out coffee and a sweet roll, his stomach pained him, reminding him of the stomach problems that he used to have when he was an operative. It's all coming back, he told himself.

Esperanza sat next to him, the only other passenger in the row. 'I regret I've never met Beth Dwyer. She must be very special.'

Decker stared out the window at the high-desert landscape he was leaving, the mountains, the arroyos, the Rio Grande, the green of piñon trees against the yellow, orange, and red of the land. He couldn't help being reminded of his ambivalent feelings when he had first arrived, his concern that he might have been making a mistake. Now, after more than a year, he was flying away, and again he felt ambivalent, again wondered if he was making a mistake.

'Yes,' Decker said, 'very special.'

'You must love her very much.'

'That depends. It may be –' Decker had trouble speaking. '– that I also hate her.'

'Hate?'

'She should have told me about her background,' Decker said.

'At the start, she probably thought it was none of your business.'

'And what about later, after she and I were involved?' Decker insisted.

'Maybe she was afraid to tell you, afraid you'd react as you're reacting now.'

'If she loved me, she would have trusted me.'

'Ah,' Esperanza said. 'I'm beginning to understand. You're worried that maybe *she* doesn't love *you*.'

'I've always let business control my personal life,' Decker said. 'I have never been in love, not truly. Until I met Beth Dwyer, I had never allowed myself to experience—' Decker hesitated. 'Passion.'

Esperanza furrowed his brow.

'When I did commit, when I gave myself, it was totally. Beth became the absolute focus of my life. If I was merely a convenience to her . . .' Decker's voice dropped toward despair.

'Suppose you do find out that she didn't care about you, that you *were* just an unwitting bodyguard. What will you do about it?'

Decker didn't answer.

Esperanza persisted. 'Would you still save her?'

'In spite of everything?'

'Yes.'

'In spite of all my suspicions, all my fear that she betrayed me, my anger because of my fear?'

'Yes.'

'I'd go through hell for her. God help me, I still love her.'

NINE

1

It was raining when Decker arrived in New York, a strong steady downpour that was one measure of how foreign Manhattan felt to him after New Mexico's arid climate. The unaccustomed humidity was palpable. After having lived for fifteen months at almost a mile and a half above sea level, he felt an atmospheric pressure that reinforced the emotional pressure inside him. Accustomed to being able to see for hundreds of miles, he felt constricted by skyscrapers. And by people: the total population of New Mexico was one and a half million, but that many people lived within the twenty-two square miles of Manhattan alone, and that didn't count the hundreds of thousands who commuted to the island to work, with the consequence that Decker was conscious – as he had never been until he experienced New Mexico's peace and expansiveness – of New York's intense noise and congestion.

Esperanza stared in fascination out the taxi's rain-beaded windows.

'Never been here?' Decker asked.

'The only big cities I've been to are Denver, Phoenix, and Los Angeles. They're low. They sprawl. Here, everything's jammed together, crammed on top of each other.'

'Yeah, we're not in the wide open spaces any longer.'

The taxi let them off at the Essex Street Market on the Lower East Side. The large brick building was closed. As Decker carried his travel bag into the shelter of one of the doorways, his headache increased. Although the sleep he had managed to get on the airplane had not been enough to relieve his weariness, nervous energy kept him going. Fear for Beth fueled him.

Esperanza peered into the deserted market, then glanced at the shops on the other side of the street. 'Is our hotel in this area?'

'We don't have one. We don't have time to check into one.'

'But you made a phone call at the airport. I thought you were making a reservation.'

Decker shook his head; the movement aggravated his headache, but he was too obsessed to notice. He waited until the taxi drove out of sight. Then he left the market's doorway and began walking north through the rain. 'I was making an appointment with someone.'

'Nearby?'

'A couple of blocks.'

'Then why didn't you let the taxi take us straight to him?'

'Because I didn't want the taxi driver to know my business. Look, I'm afraid this isn't going to work. There's too much to explain, and not enough time,' Decker said impatiently. 'You've been very helpful. You called off the New Mexico police alert on me. You got me through airport security in Albuquerque. I wouldn't be here without you. Thank you. I mean that. Really. But you have to understand – our partnership ends right here. Take a taxi to midtown. Enjoy the city.'

'In the rain?'

'See a show. Have a nice meal.'

'I kind of doubt New York meals come with red and green salsa.'

'Give yourself a little vacation. Then fly back tomorrow morning. Your department must be wondering where you've gone.'

'They won't know I've left. I told you, this is my day off.'

'What about tomorrow?'

'I'll call in sick.'

'You don't have jurisdiction here,' Decker said. 'Do yourself a favor. Get back to New Mexico as soon as possible.'

'No.'

'You won't be able to follow me. Two minutes from now, you won't have any idea how I got away from you.'

'But you won't do that.'

'Oh? What makes you think so?'

'Because you can't be sure you won't need me.'

2

The bar – on First Avenue, near Delancey – looked to be on the verge of going out of business. In its windows, liquor advertisements had faded almost to illegibility. The windows themselves were so grimy that they couldn't be seen through. Several letters in its neon sign were burned out, so that instead of BENNIE'S, it now read BE E'S. A derelict holding a whiskey bottle in a paper bag slumped on the sidewalk next to the entrance, mindless of the downpour.

Frustrated by the rush of time, Decker crossed the street toward the bar. He was followed by Esperanza, whose cowboy hat had been replaced by an inconspicuous Yankees baseball cap that they had bought from a souvenir stand along the way. His long hair had been tied back so that it, too, was less noticeable. About to go into the bar, Decker made Esperanza pause at the entrance, letting the derelict, who wasn't a derelict, get a good look at them.

'Bennie's expecting us,' Decker said.

The derelict nodded.

Decker and Esperanza went into the bar, which was hazy with cigarette smoke. Given its shabby exterior, the place was surprisingly busy, its noise level high because of a football game on a big-screen television.

Decker went directly to the husky bartender. 'Is Bennie around?'

'Ain't seen him.'

'I phoned earlier and made an appointment.'

'Says who?'

Decker used the pseudonym, 'Charles Laird.'

'Why didn't you say so?' The bartender gestured toward the far end of the counter. 'Bennie's waiting for you in his office. Leave your bag with me.'

Decker nodded, handing him the small suitcase, putting twenty dollars on the counter. 'This is for the beer we didn't have.'

He led Esperanza toward the closed door at the end of the counter, then halted.

'What's the matter?' Esperanza asked. 'Why don't you go ahead and knock?'

'There's a formality we have to get through first. I hope you don't mind being groped.'

Four broad-shouldered men turned from playing pool at a table next to the door. Eyes cold, they searched Decker and Esperanza roughly and thoroughly. With a final check of both men's ankles, not finding any microphones or weapons, they nodded curtly in dismissal and went back to playing pool. They didn't find anything suspicious because, at Decker's insistence, Esperanza had left his badge and handgun locked in Decker's Jeep Cherokee at the Albuquerque airport. Decker was determined that, if he and Esperanza had to do any shooting, it wouldn't be with a weapon that could be traced to either of them.

Only now did Decker knock on the door. Hearing a muffled voice behind it, he opened it and faced a narrow cluttered office, in which an overweight man with a striped shirt, a bow-tie, and suspenders sat at a desk. The man was elderly. He had a bald head and a silvery mustache. A polished-brass cane lay across the top of his desk.

'How are you, Bennie?' Decker asked.

'On a diet. Can't seem to lose this weight. Doctor's orders. And what about you, Charles?'

'I've got trouble.'

Bennie nodded wisely, each movement of his head squeezing his double chins together. 'No one ever comes to me otherwise.'

'This is a friend of mine.' Decker indicated Esperanza.

Bennie listlessly raised a hand.

'My friend has to make a phone call.'

'Right over there.' Bennie pointed to a payphone in a corner.

'It's still linked to a payphone in Jersey City?'

'That's where anyone tracing the call will think you are,' Bennie said.

Decker gestured to Esperanza that it was okay for him to make the call. As agreed, it would be to Miller in Santa Fe to find out if there was any news about Beth and McKittrick. Decker had phoned him several times en route, desperate to know if Beth was still alive. So far, there wasn't any news.

'Sit down,' Bennie told Decker as Esperanza put coins in the payphone. 'How can I help?'

Decker positioned himself in a chair across from Bennie, knowing that a shotgun was under the intervening desk. 'Thank you. You were always cooperative when I needed help before.'

'It amused me,' Bennie said. 'A change of pace, doing something for my government.'

Decker understood. Although it was commonly thought that the CIA had a mandate limiting it to overseas operations, the fact was that it maintained offices in various major American cities and did on occasion carry out domestic operations, but in theory not without first obeying a presidential order to alert the FBI. It had been with the cooperation of the Bureau that Decker had consulted with Bennie three years earlier and been given a fake identity as a mob member associated with Bennie. The purpose was to enable Decker to infiltrate a foreign terrorist network that was trying to disrupt the United States by using organized crime to flood the country with fake hundred-dollar bills.

'I'm sure the government was most appreciative,' Decker said.

'Well, it doesn't come around and bother me anymore.' Bennie shrugged listlessly. 'And after all, it *was* in my self-interest. What's bad for the economy is bad for *my* business, too.' He smiled slightly.

'This time, I can't offer you incentives, I'm afraid.'

'Oh?' Bennie looked suspicious.

'I don't have anything to do with the government these days. I have a personal favor to ask you.'

'Favor?' Bennie grimaced.

In the background, Decker heard Esperanza speaking into the payphone, his tone somber as he asked questions.

'What kind of favor?' Bennie obviously dreaded the answer.

'I need to know how to contact Nick Giordano.'

Bennie's cheeks normally had a touch of pink. Now they turned pale. 'No. Don't tell me any more. I don't want to be involved with any involvement *you* have with Nick Giordano.'

'I swear to you, this has nothing to do with the government.'

Bennie's formerly listless gestures were now animated. 'I don't care! I don't want to know anything about it!'

Decker leaned forward. 'And I *don't want* you to know anything about it.'

Bennie stopped suddenly in mid-gesture. '*Don't want* me to know?'

'All I'm asking for is a simple piece of information. How do I get in touch with Nick Giordano? Not the owner of the restaurant where he likes to eat. Not one of his lieutenants. Not his attorney. *Him. You* won't have to introduce us. *You* won't be directly involved in any way. I'll take the responsibility for making contact. Giordano will never know who told me how to get in touch with him.'

Bennie stared at Decker as if trying to understand a foreign language. 'What possible reason would make me want to do this?'

Esperanza's telephone conversation ended. He turned toward Decker.

'Any news?' Decker's stomach cramped.

'No.'

'Thank God. At least, she hasn't been reported dead. I've still got hope.'

'She?' Bennie raised his thick eyebrows.

'A friend of mine. I'm trying to find her. She's in trouble.'

'And Nick Giordano can help get her *out* of trouble?' Bennie asked.

'He definitely has the power to do that,' Decker said. 'That's what I need to talk to him about.'

'You still haven't given me a reason to help you.'

'I love this woman, Bennie. I want you to do this because I love her.'

'You're making a joke, right?'

'Am I laughing?'

'Please. I'm a businessman.'

'Then here's another reason. Nick Giordano has a special interest in this woman. He thinks she killed Joey Scolari.'

Bennie flinched. 'You're talking about *Diana* Scolari? Joey's

277

wife? Jesus, Nick has everybody looking for her.'

'Well, it might be I can help him find her.'

'Make sense. If you love her, why would you turn her over to Nick?'

'So she won't have to run for the rest of her life.'

'Of course not. She'll be dead. You're still not making sense.'

'Then maybe *this* will make sense,' Decker said. 'If Nick Giordano is happy with the way my conversation with him turns out, he might want to reward anybody who showed the good judgment to make the conversation happen.'

Bennie scowled, calculating.

3

The phone on the other end rang only once before a man's raspy voice said, 'You'd better have a damned good reason for calling this number.'

Immediately Decker heard the beep of an answering machine and dictated his message. 'This is Steve Decker. My name ought to be familiar to you. Your people were watching me in Santa Fe. I have something important I need to discuss with Mr Giordano. It concerns Diana Scolari and the murder of her husband. It also concerns a US marshal named Brian McKittrick. I'll call back in thirty minutes.'

Decker put the phone back on its hook and stepped from the littered glass booth into the dusky rain, approaching Esperanza who stood in the doorway of a closed appliance store.

'Getting tired of following me?'

'Not when you're taking me to such interesting places.'

4

The flower shop was on Grand Street. OPEN SUNDAYS AND HOLIDAYS, a sign on the door announced. A bell rang when Decker opened the door and stepped into the shop. The funeral-home scent of flowers surrounded him. Curious, Esperanza glanced around at the closed-circuit television cameras above the abundant colorful displays, then turned toward the sound of footsteps.

A matronly middle-aged woman, wearing gardener's gloves and a smock, came out of a back room. 'I'm sorry. It's almost seven. My assistant was supposed to lock the door. We're closed.'

'I guess I lost track of the time,' Decker said. 'It's been a while since I did business with you.' He picked up a pen and a business card on the counter, wrote something, then showed it to the woman. 'This is my account number, and this is how my name is spelled.'

'One minute while I examine our records.'

The woman returned to the back room and closed the door behind her. A mirror next to that door was two-way, Decker knew. An armed man watched him from behind it, he also knew, just as two other armed men in the basement watched the monitors of the closed-circuit cameras.

Not letting his troubled thoughts show, he pretended to be interested in various attractive corsages that were visible behind the glass doors of a cooler. He was appalled by the disarming ease with which he was slipping back into his former life.

Esperanza glanced at his watch. 'Ten minutes until you have to make that phone call.'

The woman came back into the display room.

'Mr Evans, our records show that you left a deposit with us two years ago.'

'Yes. I've come to close out the account.'

'Our records also show that you always ordered a particular type of flower.'

'Two dozen yellow roses.'

'Correct. Please, step into our display room.'

The small room was to the left of the counter. It had photographs on the walls, showing the numerous flower arrangements the shop could provide. It also had a plain table and two wooden chairs at which Decker and Esperanza sat after Decker closed and locked the door. Esperanza parted his lips to say something but was interrupted when the matronly woman came in through another door, set a briefcase on the table, and left.

The moment the door clicked shut, Decker opened the briefcase. Esperanza leaned forward, seeing objects cushioned within niches cut into plastic foam: a Walther .380 pistol, an extra magazine, a box of ammunition, and two small electronic objects, the purpose of which wasn't obvious.

Decker couldn't subdue his self-loathing. 'I hoped I had touched this stuff for the last time.'

5

'You'd better have a damned good reason for calling this number.'

Beep.

'This is Steve Decker again. I have something important I need to discuss with Mr Giordano. It concerns Diana Scolari and—'

A man picked up the phone on the other end. His voice had the arrogant tone of someone accustomed to giving orders. 'What do you know about Diana Scolari?'

'I need to speak to Mr Giordano.'

'*I'm* Mr Giordano,' the man said angrily.

'Not *Nick* Giordano. Your voice sounds too young.'

'My father doesn't take calls from people he doesn't know. Tell me about Diana Scolari.'

'And Brian McKittrick.'

'Is that name supposed to mean something to me?'

'Put your father on.'

'Anything you have to say about Diana Scolari, you can say to *me*.'

Decker hung up, waited two minutes, then put additional coins in the payphone and pressed the same numbers.

This time, there wasn't an answering machine. Instead, halfway through the first ring, a hoarse elderly male voice said, 'Nick Giordano.'

'I was just talking to your son about Diana Scolari.'

'And Brian McKittrick.' The voice sounded strained. 'My son says you also mentioned Brian McKittrick.'

'That's right.'

'How do I know you're not a cop?'

'When we meet, you can search me to make sure I'm not wearing a wire.'

'That still won't mean you're not a cop.'

'Hey, if you're that paranoid, maybe there's no point in trying to arrange a meeting.'

For a moment, the line was silent. 'Where are you?'

'Lower Manhattan.'

'Stand on the Fifth Avenue side of the Flatiron Building. A car will be there to pick you up in an hour. How will the driver know it's you?'

Decker glanced at Esperanza. 'I'll be holding two dozen yellow roses.'

6

In a coffee shop just down Fifth Avenue from the Flatiron Building, Decker stayed silent until the waiter brought their order and left. They had chosen a far corner table. The place wasn't busy. Even so, Decker made sure no one was looking in his direction before he leaned down, opened his travel bag, and removed a small object that he had earlier taken from the briefcase at the flower shop. The object was metal, the size of a match box.

'What *is* that thing?' Esperanza asked.

'It sends out a homing signal. And this –' Decker reached into his travel bag and withdrew a metal box the size of a pack of cigarettes '– receives it, as long as the signal doesn't come from farther than a mile. Traffic moves south on Fifth Avenue past the Flatiron Building. You'll be waiting in a taxi north of here – at Madison Square Park. After I get into the car Giordano sends for me, give me fifteen seconds so you won't be obvious, then follow. The receiver operates visually. This needle points to the left, right, or straight ahead, depending on which direction the signal is coming from. This gauge tells you from one to ten how close you are, ten being the closest.' Decker flicked a switch and put the receiver ahead of the transmitter. 'Yes. The system's working. Take the receiver. If something goes wrong, our rendezvous is in front of this coffee shop at the top of each hour. But if I don't show up by six tomorrow night, get back to Santa Fe as fast as you can.' Decker glanced at his watch. 'It's almost time. Let's go.'

'What about your bag?'

'Keep it.' The bag contained the pistol, the spare magazine, and the box of ammunition. Decker knew he'd be searched. There was no way he was going to spook Giordano by trying to carry a weapon to a meeting with him. 'Ten minutes after I arrive at wherever I'm being taken, phone the number Bennie gave me. Ask to speak to me. Make it sound as if bad things will happen if I don't come to the phone.'

'And?'

'Follow my lead when I talk to you.'

They reached the exit from the coffee shop.

'You won't have any trouble catching a cab around here.'

'Decker.'

'What?'

'Are you sure about this?'

'No.'

'Then maybe there's another way.'

'The last thing I want to do is go out there. But I'm running out of time. Maybe I've *already* run out of time. I don't know where else to go except straight to the source of the problem.'

Esperanza hesitated. 'Good luck.'

'Beth needs it more than me.'

'But what if—'

'They've already killed her?'

'Yes.'

'Then what happens to me doesn't matter.'

A minute later, during which Decker hoped that Esperanza had time to hail a cab, he stepped into the darkening rain and turned right, walking toward the Flatiron Building. Worried about what McKittrick might be doing to Beth, Decker couldn't help being reminded of the similar rain that had fallen the night McKittrick shot his father in Rome.

He reached the Flatiron Building five minutes ahead of schedule and stood in the shelter of another doorway, holding the yellow roses in plain view. His emotions were complicated: various levels of doubt, fear, and apprehension. But only the doubt applied to himself. The rest were outwardly directed: fear for Beth, apprehension about what might already have happened to her. But most of all, he felt seized with determination. It was the first time he had ever engaged in a mission in which the mission truly meant more to him than his own life.

He recalled something Beth had told him two nights earlier,

Fiesta Friday, after they had left the film producer's party and driven back to Decker's house – their last moment of normalcy, it seemed at the time, although Decker now realized that *nothing* about their relationship had been normal. Moonlight through his bedroom windows had gleamed on them, making their bodies resemble ivory, while they made love – the bittersweet memory made him feel hollow. Afterward, as they lay next to each other, side by side, Decker's arms around her, his chest against her back, his groin against her hips, his knees against hers, legs bent, in a spoon position, she had lapsed into so long a silence that he thought she had fallen asleep. He remembered inhaling the fragrance of her hair. When she spoke, her hesitant voice had been so soft that he barely heard it.

'When I was a little girl,' she murmured, 'my mother and father had terrible fights.'

She lapsed into silence again.

Decker waited.

'I never knew what the fights were about,' Beth had continued softly, not without tension. 'I still don't. Infidelity. Money problems. Drinking. Whatever. Every night, they screamed at each other. Sometimes it was worse than just screaming. They threw things. They hit each other. The fights were especially horrible on holidays. Thanksgiving. Christmas. My mother would prepare a big meal. Then, just before dinner, something would happen to make them start yelling at each other again. My father would storm out of the house. My mother and I would eat dinner alone, and all the while she would tell me what a rotten bastard he was.'

More silence. Decker knew enough not to prompt her, sensing that whatever she wanted to say was so private she had to reveal it at her own pace.

'When the fights got worse than I could bear, I begged my parents to stop. I pushed at my father, trying to get him to stop

hitting my mother. All that did was make him turn against *me*,'
Beth finally continued. 'I still have a mental image of my
father's fist coming at me. I was afraid he would kill me. This
happened at night. I ran into my bedroom and tried to figure out
where to hide. The shouts in the living room got louder. I stuffed
my pillows, one in front of the other, under my bed covers to
make it seem as if I was sleeping there. I must have seen that
trick on television or something. Then I crawled under the bed,
and that's where I slept, hoping I was protected from my father
if he came in to stab me. I slept that way every night after that.'

Beth's shoulders heaved slightly, in a way that made Decker
think she was sobbing. 'Was *your* childhood like that?' she
asked.

'No. My father was a career soldier. He was rigid, very much
into discipline and control. But he was never violent with me.'

' Lucky.' In the darkness, Beth wiped at her eyes. 'I used to
read stories about knights and fair ladies, King Arthur, that sort
of thing. I kept dreaming that I was in those stories, that I had a
knight to protect me. Even as a kid, I was good at drawing. I
used to make sketches of what I thought the knight would look
like.' Covers rustling, Beth turned to him, her face now in
moonlight, tears glinting on her cheeks. 'If I could draw that
knight again, he'd look like you. You make me feel safe. I don't
need to sleep under the bed anymore.'

Two hours later, the hit team had broken into the house.

7

Rain gusting at Decker's face brought him out of his memory.
Racked with emotion, he studied the traffic that sped through
puddles past the Flatiron Building. Conflicting questions
tortured him. Had the story Beth told him been true, or had she

been setting her hook deeper, lying to elicit more sympathy from him, programming him to protect her regardless of the threat? It came down to what he had been brooding about since yesterday when he had learned that she had deceived him about her background. Did she love him, or had she been using him? He *had* to know. He *had* to find her and learn the truth, although if the truth wasn't what he wanted to hear, he didn't know what he would do, for the fact was, *he* loved *her* completely.

Headlights piercing the rain, a gray Oldsmobile veered out of traffic and stopped at the curb before him. The car's back door opened and one of Giordano's soldiers got out, indicating with a stiff motion of his head that he wanted Decker to get in the car. Muscles compacting, determination strengthening, Decker approached him, holding a bunch of roses with each hand.

'That's right.' The man, who had a large chest, broad shoulders, and a suit that was too tight, smirked. 'You keep your hands around those flowers while I search you.'

'On the street? With that police car coming?'

'Get in the car.'

Calculating, Decker saw that there were two men in the front and another man in the back. As he got in, feeling the first man coming after him, pressing against him, he kept the matchbox-sized transmitter along with the stems of the flowers in the palm of his right hand. As the driver pulled away from the curb, tires splashing, the man in the passenger seat aimed a pistol at Decker. The two men in back searched him.

'He's clean.'

'What about those flowers?'

The men pulled the roses from Decker's clenched hands, so preoccupied that they didn't notice the small transmitter he continued to conceal in his cupped right palm.

'Whatever you want with the boss, it better be good,' one of the men said. 'I've never seen Nick this pissed off.'

'Hey, what stinks in here?' another man asked.

'It's them flowers. They smell like a cheap funeral.'

'Maybe *this* guy's funeral.' The man on Decker's left chuckled as he rolled down the window and tossed out the battered roses.

8

Throughout the drive, Decker didn't speak. For their part, the men ignored him. As they talked among themselves about football, women, and casinos on Indian reservations – safe topics, nothing that would incriminate them – Decker kept wondering if Esperanza had managed to follow in a cab, if the transmitter and the receiver were working, if the driver would notice he was being tailed. He kept telling himself that he had to have faith.

The time was just after eight p.m. The rain had thickened, dusk becoming night. Headlights piercing the downpour, the driver took several streets at random as an evasion tactic, then proceeded north on the crowded Henry Hudson Parkway, eventually turning west onto the George Washington Bridge. On the New Jersey side, he headed north again, this time on the Palisades Parkway. An hour after picking up Decker, he turned left into the sleepy town of Alpine.

The men in the car sat tensely straighter as the driver went through the almost non-existent downtown area, then steered to the right, took several more turns, and at last came to a quiet, thickly treed, tastefully but brightly lit section of large houses on half-acre lots. High fences made from wrought iron topped with spikes separated the lots. The car pulled into a driveway and stopped before an imposing metal gate, where the driver leaned out into the rain and spoke into an intercom. 'It's Rudy. We've got him.'

The gate parted to the right and left, providing a gap through which the driver proceeded. Glancing back through the rain-beaded rear window, Decker saw the gate close as soon as the Oldsmobile had cleared it. He didn't see any headlights of a taxi that might be following. The car went along a curved driveway and stopped before a brick three-story home with numerous gables and chimneys. After the low, round-edged, flat-roofed adobe houses that Decker was used to, the mansion seemed surreal. Arc lights illuminated the grounds. Decker noted that the trees were a distance from the house and that all the shrubs were low. Any invader who managed to get past what Decker assumed were state-of-the-art intrusion detectors along the fence wouldn't have any cover as he tried to reach the house.

'Showtime,' the man on Decker's left said. He opened his door, got out, and waited for Decker. 'Move it. Don't keep him waiting.'

Decker didn't say a word when his arm was grabbed. In fact he welcomed the gesture. It gave him an excuse to pretend to trip as he was tugged through the rain toward the wide stone steps that led into the house. Falling near a bush, he slipped the small homing device under it, then let the man pull him to his feet and into the house. His heart seemed surrounded by ice.

The first thing he noticed was an armed guard in a corner of the spacious, marble-floored foyer. The second thing he noticed was a pit bull behind the guard. After that, he barely had time to look for other possible exits as he was hurried along an oak-paneled hallway, through double doors, and into a thickly carpeted study.

The wall opposite Decker had leather-bound books. The wall to the right had framed family pictures. The wall to the left had glass cabinets, in each of which were vases. The center of the room was dominated by a wide antique desk, behind which a compact man of about seventy, wearing an expensive dark-blue suit, exhaled cigar smoke and squinted at Decker. The man had severely pinched features, dominated by a cleft chin and a furrow down each cheek. His deep tan emphasized his short but thick white hair.

Sitting in front of the desk, turning to look at Decker, was a man in his thirties, but the contrast involved more than age. The younger man wore trendy clothes that seemed garish compared to the elderly man's conservative suit. The younger man wore conspicuous jewelry whereas the older man had none to be seen. The younger man looked less fit than the older man, his body slightly puffy as if lately he had given up exercise in favor of drinking.

'Did you search him?' the elderly man asked the guards who had brought in Decker. The raspy voice sounded like the one Decker had heard on the phone, the man who claimed to be Nick Giordano.

'When we picked him up,' a guard said.

'I'm still not satisfied. This guy's clothes are wet. Get him a robe or something.'

'Yes, sir.'

Giordano assessed Decker. 'Well, what are you waiting for?'

'I don't understand.'

'Take off your clothes.'

'What?'

'You've got a hearing problem? Take off your clothes. I want to make sure you're not wearing a wire. Buttons, belt buckles, zippers, I don't trust any of them, not when it comes to a guy who used to be a spook.'

'Brian McKittrick must have told you a lot about me.'

'The son of a bitch,' the younger man said.

'Frank,' Giordano said in warning. 'Shut up until we know he's not wired.'

'You're actually serious about my clothes?' Decker asked.

Giordano didn't answer, only glared.

'If this is how you get your kicks.'

'Hey.' The younger man stood angrily. 'You think you can come into my father's home and insult him?'

'Frank,' Giordano said again.

The young man was poised to slap Decker's face. He stared at his father and backed away.

Decker took off his sports coat.

Giordano nodded. 'Good. It's always smart to cooperate.'

As Decker took off his shirt, he watched Giordano walk over to the vases in their glass cabinets.

'Do you know anything about porcelain?' Giordano asked.

The question was so unexpected that Decker shook his head in confusion. 'You mean like bone china?' Grim, Decker removed his shoes and socks.

'That's one type of porcelain. It's called bone china because it's made from powdered bones.'

Even grimmer, Decker unbuckled, unzipped, and took off his pants. His exposed skin prickled.

'Everything,' Giordano ordered.

Decker slipped off his briefs. His testicles shrank toward his groin. He stood with as much dignity as he could muster, keeping his arms at his sides. 'What's next? A cavity search? Do you do it personally?'

The younger man looked furious. 'You want one, big mouth?'

'Frank,' Giordano again repeated in warning.

A guard came in with a white terry-cloth robe.

'Give it to him.' Giordano gestured with his cigar. 'Take his clothes to the car.'

As the man obeyed, Decker put on the robe. Its hem came down to his knees, its wide sleeves just below his elbows. Tying its belt, he was reminded of the *gi* he had worn when he learned martial arts.

Giordano picked up a vase that had the shape of a heron, the bird's head upright, its beak open. 'Look at how light seems to shine through it. Listen when I tap it with my finger. It resonates, almost like crystal.'

'Fascinating,' Decker said unenthusiastically.

'A hell of a lot more than you know. These vases are my trophies,' Giordano said. 'They warn my enemies –' His face became flushed. '– *not to fuck with me.* Bone china. Powdered bones.' Giordano held the bird-shaped vase close to Decker. 'Say hello to Luigi. *He* tried to fuck with me, so I had his flesh burned off with acid, then his bones ground up and made into this. I put him in my trophy case. Like everyone else who tried to fuck with me.' Giordano hurled the vase toward the room's large fireplace, the porcelain shattering.

'Now Luigi's just garbage!' Giordano said. 'And *you'll* end up just like him if *you* try to fuck with me, too. So answer this question very carefully. *What do you have to tell me about Diana Scolari?*'

9

The shrill ringing of a phone punctuated the tension in the room.

Giordano and his son exchanged troubled glances.

'Maybe it's McKittrick,' Frank said.

'It damned well better be.' Giordano picked up the phone. '*Talk to me.*' He frowned. 'Who the hell—' He stared at Decker. '*Who?* What makes you think he's—'

'That'll be for me,' Decker said. 'It's a friend of mine,

checking on my welfare.' He took the phone from Giordano and spoke into it. 'So you found the place all right.'

'Almost didn't,' Esperanza's somber voice said on the other end. 'It was tough staying far enough back so your driver wouldn't see the taxi's headlights. It was also tough finding a phone.'

'Where are you?'

'Outside the post office – on what passes for the main drag.'

'Call back in another five minutes.' Decker set the phone on its cradle and turned to Giordano. 'Just a precaution.'

'You think some guy on the phone is going to save your ass if I think you're out of line?'

'No.' Decker shrugged. 'But before I died, I'd have the satisfaction of knowing that my friend would get in touch with other friends and you'd soon be joining me.'

The room became silent. Even the rain lancing against the French doors seemed suddenly muted.

'Nobody threatens my father,' Frank said.

'That stuff about Luigi sure sounded like your father was threatening *me*,' Decker said. 'I came here in good faith to discuss a mutual problem. Instead of being treated with respect, I was forced to—'

'Mutual problem?' Giordano asked.

'Diana Scolari.' Decker paused, focusing his emotion. Everything depended on what he said next. 'I want to kill her for you.'

Giordano stared.

Frank stepped forward. 'For what she did to Joey, there are *plenty* of us who want to kill her.'

Decker's expression remained rigid. He didn't dare show the relief that flooded through him. Frank had used the present tense. Beth was still alive.

'You expect me to believe you want to kill her after you've been screwing her?' Giordano asked.

'She lied to me. She used me.'

'Too damned bad.'

'For her. I'm going to find her. I'm going to give her what she deserves.'

'And we're supposed to tell you where she is?' Frank asked.

'And where *Brian McKittrick* is. *He* used me, too. *He* set me up. It isn't the first time. He's going to pay.'

'Well, you can get in line for him, as well,' Frank said. 'A lot of us are looking for *both* of them.'

'Looking for— I thought he was working for you.'

'That's what *we* thought. He was supposed to report in yesterday. Not a word. Is he back working for the US Marshals Service? If she shows up in that courtroom tomorrow—'

'Frank,' Giordano said, 'how many times do I have to tell you to shut your mouth?'

'You don't have any secrets from me,' Decker said. 'I know she's supposed to testify against you tomorrow. If I could find out where she is, I'd solve your problem for you. She'd let me get close enough to—'

The phone rang again.

This time, Giordano and Frank kept their full concentration on Decker.

'That'll be your friend again,' Giordano said. 'Get rid of him.'

Decker picked up the phone.

'Give me Nick,' a New-England-accented voice demanded smugly.

Brian McKittrick.

10

Time seemed suspended.

As Decker's pulse faltered, he urgently lowered his voice,

hoping that McKittrick wouldn't recognize it. 'Is the woman still alive?'

'You're damned right. And she's going to stay that way unless I get a million dollars by midnight. If I don't get the money, she goes into that courtroom tomorrow.'

'Where are you?'

'Who *is* this? If I don't hear Nick's voice in ten seconds, I'm hanging up.'

'No! Wait. Don't do anything. Here he is.'

Decker handed the phone to Giordano, whose eyebrows were raised in question. 'It's McKittrick.'

'*What?*' Giordano grabbed the phone. 'You son of a bitch, you were supposed to call me yesterday. Where——? Stop. Don't answer right away. Is your phone secure? Use that voice scrambler I gave you. Turn it on.' Giordano flicked a switch on a black box next to his phone – a voice scrambler presumably calibrated to the same code as McKittrick's scrambler. 'Now talk to me, you bastard.'

Decker stepped away from the desk. Frank and the guards, the fourth member of whom had come back, were riveted by Giordano's savage expression as he shouted into the phone.

'*A million dollars?* Are you out of your mind? I already paid you two hundred thousand . . . It wasn't enough? Is your *life* enough? I told you what I do to smart guys who try to mess with me. Here's the best deal anybody ever offered you. Do the job you promised. Prove to me you did it. *I'll forget this conversation happened.*'

To the left of the guards, parallel to them but not wanting to arouse their suspicions by stepping behind them, Decker scanned the room and focused his attention on the fireplace.

Giordano listened to the phone, shocked. 'You dumb bastard, you're really serious. You're going to hold me up for a million bucks . . . I *don't need reminding* her testimony can put me away for life.' Giordano's expression became even more fierce. 'Yes, I know where that is. But midnight's too soon. I need more time. I need to . . . I'm not stalling. I'm not trying to doublecross you. All I want is to solve my problem. I'm telling the truth. I'm not sure I can get the money by midnight . . . Here's a gesture of good faith. The guy you talked to at the start of your call – he's the guy you wanted us to take out in Santa Fe as part of the deal. Your buddy, Steve Decker.'

As Giordano and everyone else in the room looked at him, Decker's reflexes tightened.

'He paid us a visit. Called me up and wanted to come over for a heart-to-heart. He's standing right in front of me. Want to come over and visit? . . . No? Don't you trust me? . . . Okay, here's my offer. We'll do him for you. You prove the woman's dead. I'll prove Decker's dead. You'll get the million. But I can't get you the money by midnight.' Giordano scowled. 'No. Wait. Don't.' He slammed the phone onto its cradle. 'Bastard hung up on me. Midnight. Says midnight or it's no deal. Thinks I'll pull a fast one if I've got more time.'

'Where are we supposed to meet him?' Frank asked angrily.

'The scenic lookout two miles north of here.'

'In Palisades State Park?'

Giordano nodded. 'The bastard's right here in the neighborhood. We leave the money and Decker behind the refreshment stand.'

'And McKittrick leaves the woman?'

'No. He says he *won't* do the job until he's positive we don't try to follow him after he leaves with the money.'

'Shit.'

Giordano turned toward the wall of leather-bound books. He pressed a portion of the wall, releasing a catch.

'You're actually going to give him the money?' Frank asked.

'What choice do I have? I don't have time to second-guess

him. Diana Scolari can't be allowed to go into that courtroom tomorrow. I'll deal with McKittrick later. He can't hide forever. But right now—' When Giordano tugged, the large bookshelf slid away from the wall, revealing a safe. He quickly worked the combination, yanked open the door, and pulled out bundles of cash, setting the rubber-banded packets onto the desk. 'There's a briefcase in that closet.'

'Suppose McKittrick takes the money and *still* lets her testify.' Frank went for the briefcase. 'Or suppose he asks for more cash tomorrow morning.'

'Then I'll give him more cash! I won't spend the rest of my life in prison!'

'We can try to follow him,' Frank said. 'Or we can grab him when he shows up to get the money. Believe me, *I'll* make him tell us where the woman is.'

'*But what if he dies before he talks?* I can't take the risk. I'm seventy years old. Prison would kill me.'

For the third time, the phone rang.

'Maybe that's McKittrick again.' Giordano grabbed it. 'Talk to me.' He frowned toward Frank. 'I can't understand a word he's saying. He must have turned his scrambler off.' Furious, Giordano switched his own scrambler off, then blurted into the phone, 'I told you . . . Who? Decker? For Christ's sake, he isn't here anymore. Quit calling about him. He's gone. One of my men drove him back to the city . . . Shut up and listen. *He's gone.*'

Giordano slammed down the phone and told Decker, 'So much for your insurance policy. Think you can threaten *me*, huh?' He turned to the guards. 'Take this prick out to the cliffs and do him.'

Decker's stomach felt frozen.

'Just before midnight, dump him behind the refreshment stand at the scenic overlook. Frank'll be there by then with the money,' Giordano said.

'*I'll* be there?' Frank asked in surprise.

'Who else am I going to trust with the money?'

'I thought *we* were taking it.'

'Are you nuts? *You're* not the one who might be indicted tomorrow. If I get caught being involved in this . . . Hey,' Giordano told the guards, 'what are you hanging around for? I said take him out and do him.'

The pressure in his chest intensifying, Decker saw one of the guards reach beneath his suit coat to pull out a gun. Decker's body was like a spring wound to its tightest coil. The coil was suddenly released. While Giordano had been arguing with McKittrick on the phone, Decker had choreographed what abruptly happened now. Next to the fireplace, he had noticed a set of tools. With eyeblink speed, he grabbed the long thin heavy log pick and whipped it around, striking the guard in the throat. The guard's larynx made an audible crack. His windpipe swelling shut, in agony, unable to breathe, the guard dropped his pistol and clutched his throat. He fell back against another guard, who was already dead, falling from the impact with which Decker had struck the top of his skull with the metal tool. As a third guard tried to pull a pistol from beneath his suit, Decker threw the pick with such force that it speared the guard's chest. The next thing, Decker was diving to the floor, grabbing the pistol that the first guard had dropped, shooting the fourth guard, shooting Giordano, shooting . . .

But the only other target was Frank, and Frank wasn't in the room any longer. Using the hanging draperies to protect himself from broken glass, Frank had lunged against a French door, smashed through its windows, and disappeared past the draperies into the storm. Decker fired but missed. He barely had time to register that the briefcase was gone from the desk before the guard who had been speared managed to brace himself against a chair and aim his pistol.

Decker shot him. Decker shot the guard who had been at the front door and now rushed into the room. Decker shot the pit bull who charged in after him. He had never felt such a fury. Pausing only for the second it took him to flick off the lights, he ran toward the French doors. Wind gusted through the broken glass, billowing the draperies into the room. He thought of the arc lights outside and the lack of cover near the house. He imagined Frank aiming from behind one of the few large trees that Giordano's security staff had permitted. Even if Decker managed to shoot out the arc lights, his white robe would be an obvious target in the darkness. He tugged it off and threw it on the floor. But his skin, although tan, was pale compared to the night. His body, too, would be an obvious target in the darkness.

What am I going to do? It'll soon be midnight. I have to get to that scenic lookout. Grabbing a second pistol from one of the fallen guards, Decker spun and rushed into the hallway. At the same moment, to the right, a guard burst into the hallway through a door at the back. Decker shot him.

Rain swept in through the open door. Decker reached the exit, pressed himself next to the door, and peered toward the arc-lit grounds at the back of the house. Seeing no sign of Frank, he ducked back out of sight and flinched as a bullet from out there blasted away part of the doorjamb. He noticed a row of light switches and flicked them all, sending this portion of the house and the grounds into darkness.

Immediately he charged through the open door and raced across rain-soaked grass toward a series of low shrubs that he had seen before he shut off the arc lights. The rain felt shockingly cold on his nakedness. He dropped flat behind the first shrub and squirmed forward as a bullet tore up lawn behind him. He reached another shrub, and unexpectedly, his chest and groin were no longer pressed against soft grass. Instead, he was in a flower bed, crawling across stalks and mud. The stalks scraped his skin. Mud. He smeared it onto his face. He rolled in it, trying to coat himself, to conceal his skin. He knew that the rain would soon wash off the camouflage. He had to move quickly.

Now! He surged to his feet, almost falling on the slick grass as he scrambled toward the cover of a large tree. The tree seemed to expand, its trunk becoming double. A figure whirled in surprise, lurching away from the trunk. As Decker dove to the spongy lawn, the figure fired toward where Decker had been, the muzzle flash disorienting, the bullet zipping above Decker. Decker shot three times, saw the figure drop, and darted closer, taking cover behind the tree.

Had he shot Frank? Staring toward the fallen man, he could see enough to determine that the man wore a suit. Frank had not.

Where *is* he? The shots will alarm the neighbors. The police will soon be here. If I don't get my hands on Frank before then, I'll never have the chance. I've got to get away from here before the police arrive. I can't save Beth if I'm in jail.

From the other side of the house, he heard a rumble, a garage door opening. Frank isn't hiding out here, waiting to shoot me! Decker realized. He ran for the garage!

Decker knew that there might be other guards, that they might be aiming at him from the darkness, but he couldn't let that hold him back. He didn't have time for caution. With the father dead, there was no certainty that Frank would go through with the plan to give McKittrick the money. What would be the point? Beth's testimony wasn't against Frank. He might keep the money and tell McKittrick to do whatever he wanted with Beth. She wasn't important anymore. McKittrick would have no choice except to kill Beth to keep her from telling the authorities about him.

Hearing a car engine, Decker raced toward the open back door of the house. Someone shot from the darkness, a bullet walloping next to Decker as he rushed into the house, but he didn't return fire. His only thought was to reach the front and hope to get a shot at Frank when he drove past toward the gate. He threw open the door and crouched naked, aiming.

Headlights flashed. A large dark sedan, a Cadillac, rushed past, a blur in the rainswept night. Decker fired, hearing glass shatter. The car roared toward the gate. Decker fired again, hearing a bullet puncture metal. Abruptly he heard another sound: the drone of the gate as it started to open. And yet another sound: sirens in the distance.

The Oldsmobile remained in front of the house, where the gunmen had left it after bringing Decker from Manhattan. As the Cadillac's taillights receded toward the gate, Decker raced down the steps toward the Oldsmobile. He yanked open the driver's door, stared in frantic hope, and saw that the key had been left in the ignition.

The interior light made him a target. Stooping to get in and slam the door to shut off the light, he heard footsteps behind him. Caught off balance, he spun, aiming toward the open front door, where the hulking shadows of two guards suddenly loomed into view, their handguns raised. At the same time, he was terribly conscious of urgent footsteps on the opposite side of the Oldsmobile. Another guard! He was trapped. The guard on the opposite side of the car shot at him, his handgun roaring once, twice, bullets zipping over Decker's head, and Decker didn't have a chance to pull the trigger of his own weapon before the two guards at the open front door lurched backward. Two more shots dropped them, and with a shock, Decker understood that it wasn't a guard on the opposite side of the Cadillac. It was—

Esperanza shouted, 'Are you all right?'

'Yes! Get in! You're driving!'

'*What happened to your clothes?*'

'No time to explain! Get in and drive!'

Hearing the fast-approaching sirens, Decker scurried toward a bush on the right side of the front steps.

'Where are you going?' Esperanza shouted, throwing Decker's travel bag into the Olds, sliding behind the steering wheel.

Decker fumbled beneath branches. He scrabbled and clawed to find what he was looking for, finally snagging it: the tiny transmitter that he had hidden under the bush when he had pretended to fall after his arrival here. He opened the Oldsmobile's rear door and leapt in, yelling, 'Frank Giordano's in the car that just left! We have to catch up to him!'

Before Decker could slam the door behind him, Esperanza had started the car, put it into gear, and stomped the accelerator, swerving along the curved driveway toward the front gate. The gate was closing. Beyond it, the Cadillac's taillights disappeared to the right. To the left, the sirens were louder. Straight ahead, the gap between the right and left portions of the gate became narrower.

'Hang on!' Esperanza shouted. The Oldsmobile roared into the gap. The left portion of the gate scraped along the car's side. The right portion struck the car's other side, and for an instant, Decker feared that the car would be jammed to a stop. Instead, when Esperanza stomped even harder on the accelerator, the Oldsmobile rocketed through the opening with such force that the two portions of the gate were twisted and yanked off their moorings. Decker heard them clatter on the wet pavement behind him. Esperanza swung the steering wheel. Tires skidding through puddles, throwing up water, the Oldsmobile slid sideways onto the murky road, straightened, and roared after the Cadillac.

'Damned good!' Decker said. Shivering, he remembered that Giordano had told a bodyguard to put his clothes in the car.

Checking the back seat, he found them.

'Comes from learning to drive on mountain roads,' Esperanza said, speeding after the Cadillac. 'When I was thirteen.'

Decker pulled on his underwear and trousers, chilled by their dampness. Simultaneously he stared out the rear window in search of the flashing lights of police cars. Despite the nearness of the sirens, the night remained dark. Without warning, the night became even darker as Esperanza extinguished the Oldsmobile's lights.

'No point in letting our taillights tell the police where we're headed,' Esperanza said.

A half block in front, the Cadillac's brake lights came on as Frank swerved to the left around a corner. The moment he disappeared, flashing lights sped into view behind Decker. Sirens wailing, police cars stopped at Giordano's estate.

'They haven't spotted us yet, but they will,' Decker said, hastily putting on his shirt. 'They'll see our brake lights the moment you slow down to go around that corner.'

'Who said anything about slowing down?' Esperanza slid into the intersection, steering furiously, almost careening over the curb, straightening, vanishing from the police cars. 'I used to do a little drag racing. When I was fourteen.'

'What did you do when you were *fifteen*? Race in demolition derbies?' Decker reached for his shoes and socks. 'Jesus, except for the Cadillac, I can't see a thing. You'd better turn on the headlights now.'

Narrowly missing a car parked at the side of the road, Esperanza breathed out sharply. 'I agree.' The lights came on. 'That doesn't help much. How do you work the windshield wipers on this thing? Is this the switch? No. How about *this* one?' The wipers started flapping.

Ahead, the Cadillac swerved to the left around another corner.

Esperanza increased speed, braked at the last minute, and veered through the intersection. Midway through the turn, streaking through a puddle, his tires lost their grip on an oily section of pavement. He jolted up on the curb, scraped past a light pole that snapped off the right sideview mirror, and lurched back onto the street.

'No, when I was fifteen, I was *stealing* cars, not racing them,' Esperanza said.

'How did you show up at the house?'

'When the guy on the phone told me you were gone, I knew there was trouble. I checked the receiver you gave me. The homing signal was constant, so I figured the guy was lying and you were still at Giordano's place. But whatever was going on, I was useless in that phone booth. So I had the taxi drive me to the house. That's when I heard shots from inside.'

'When we left, I didn't see the taxi outside.'

'The driver thought there was something suspicious about me. He spotted the receiver and kept asking me if I was following somebody. The second he heard the shots, he made me pay him, ordered me to get out of the cab, and sped away. The only thing I could think to do was climb the fence and find out what was going on.'

'And take the pistol from my travel bag.'

'A good thing for you I did.'

'I owe you.'

'Don't worry – I'll figure out a way for you to repay me. Tell me what happened at the house.'

Decker didn't answer.

Esperanza persisted. 'What was the shooting about?'

'I have to keep reminding myself you're a policeman,' Decker said. 'I'm not sure it's a good idea to go into details.'

With the next sharp turn, the Cadillac led them onto the town's deserted main road. They sped through the rain past the few shops in the shadowy business area.

'In a minute, he'll be on the Interstate,' Decker said.

'I can't catch up to him before that.' Esperanza tried to increase speed but almost lost control of the Olds. 'Is Nick Giordano dead?'

'Yes.' Decker's mouth was dry.

'Self-defense?'

'That's definitely what it felt like to me.'

'Then what's the problem? Are you worried that the police will think you went out there intending to kill him? That you planned to get rid of him from the moment you left Santa Fe?'

'If that thought occurred to you, it'll occur to *them*,' Decker said.

'It would certainly be a direct way of solving Diana Scolari's problems.'

'Beth Dwyer. Her name's Beth Dwyer. I'm trying to save Beth Dwyer. *Up ahead*.' Decker pointed urgently toward a swiftly moving stream of glaring headlights. '*There's the entrance to the Interstate*.'

The Caddy's brakelights flashed as Frank Giordano slowed, trying to navigate the curve that would lead him down the Interstate's access ramp. He braked too hard and lost control of the car. The Caddy spun violently.

'Jesus,' Esperanza said. The Oldsmobile hurtled toward the spinning Caddy, which magnified with alarming speed. 'We're going to hit him!'

Esperanza tapped the brakes. They gripped but not enough. He tapped them again, then pressed them, speeding nearer to the Caddy. At once a gust of wind hit the Olds, and Esperanza lost control on the rain-slick pavement. The car drifted, its back end suddenly at the front. It spun.

Decker had the disorienting vision of the ever-larger spinning Caddy appearing like flashes of a strobelight through the Olds's front windshield, it too spinning. At once the Caddy wasn't there anymore. It must have gone off the road, Decker thought, frantic. Simultaneously the Oldsmobile lurched. The texture of the surface beneath the car became soft and mushy. Grass! The Olds's right rear fender struck something. Decker's upper and lower teeth were knocked together. Outside, metal crumbled. A taillight shattered. The Olds jerked to a stop.

'Are you okay?' Esperanza's voice shook.

'Yes! *Where's Giordano?*'

'I see his headlights!' Esperanza gunned the engine, urging the Olds away from the tree it had spun into, fishtailing across the edge of a muddy field, aiming toward the Interstate's access ramp. Ahead, the Caddy roared out of a ditch and sped toward the chaos of traffic on the Interstate.

'You killed the father.' Esperanza's breathing was strident. 'If you kill the son, Beth Dwyer's problems are over. There's no one to pay off the contract on her. Giordano's men will stop hunting her.'

'You sound like you don't approve of my methods.'

'I'm just making observations.'

Ahead, Giordano sped onto the Interstate, forcing other cars to veer out of his way. Horns blared.

'Giordano has a million dollars in that car,' Decker said.

'*What?*'

'It's a payoff to Brian McKittrick, the price for killing Beth. Ninety minutes from now, he expects it to be delivered to him.'

Esperanza raced onto the Interstate after the Cadillac. 'But what if it isn't? Maybe he'll let her go.'

'No. McKittrick's crazy enough to kill her out of spite,' Decker said. 'The money has to be delivered to him. Maybe I can use it to get him to lead me to Beth. As it is, Frank obviously has no intention of delivering the money. He's heading south. The drop-off site is a couple of miles north of here.'

Despite the downpour, Esperanza risked pushing the accelerator to seventy, veered into the passing lane, and surged forward, approaching the Cadillac five cars ahead in the right lane. Rain pelted the windshield. The wipers could hardly clear it. Unable to go faster because of the car ahead of him, Giordano veered into the passing lane and accelerated. The Cadillac's spray struck the Oldsmobile's windshield and made it impossible for Esperanza to see. With a curse, he swerved into a break in traffic in the right lane, only four car lengths away now.

Inexplicably Giordano slowed, dropping back. In a moment, the Cadillac was parallel to the Oldsmobile. The Cadillac's passenger window was down. Giordano raised his right arm.

'He's going to shoot!' Decker yelled.

Esperanza tapped the brakes. When Giordano fired, the Olds had dropped back just enough that the bullet passed in front of the windshield.

Giordano reduced speed more, dropping back farther, trying for another shot.

Decker lunged toward the floor to grab the pistol that he'd thrown into the car when they left Giordano's house. Giordano fired. The bullet punched a hole in the driver's-side window, zipped past Esperanza's head, and crashed through the far side window in the back. In front, a section of the safety glass disintegrated into jagged pellets, spraying Esperanza's face.

'I can't see!' Esperanza shouted.

The Olds wavered.

Giordano aimed again.

Decker fired. The report inside the closed space was agonizing, like hands being slammed against Decker's ears. There hadn't been time to open the back window. The bullet blasted a hole in the glass, passed through Giordano's open front window, and blew a chunk out of his windshield. Giordano flinched and, instead of firing, had to use both hands to correct his steering.

The Olds wavered again as Esperanza struggled to see. Decker bent frantically over the front seat and grabbed the steering wheel. About to hit a car in front, he swung sharply to the left, crossed into the passing lane, and slammed against Giordano's Cadillac.

'Keep your foot on the accelerator!' he yelled to Esperanza.

'*What are you doing?*' In a sightless frenzy, Esperanza pawed chunks of glass from around his eyes.

Bent over the front seat, Decker steered harder toward the Caddy, walloping against it. He thought he heard Giordano scream. The third time Decker whacked the Caddy, he forced it off the road. In terror, Giordano veered toward the grassy centerstrip, hurtled down a slight embankment, and surged up an incline toward approaching headlights in the opposite lanes.

Decker followed, almost parallel to the Caddy, feeling a jolt as the Olds left the Interstate. He cringed from the loose feel of the steering on rain-soaked grass. His stomach dropped as the Oldsmobile rose, and suddenly he was streaking diagonally past headlights speeding toward him.

'Brake!' Decker yelled to Esperanza. '*Hard*!'

The Olds had hurtled across two lanes of traffic before the brakes engaged. The wheels skidded, shrieking across wet pavement, throwing up gravel on the shoulder. Horns blaring, traffic rushed past. Ahead, Giordano skidded sideways, crushed bushes, snapped through saplings, and disappeared down a rainswept slope.

Decker swung the steering wheel in a furious effort to avoid going straight down the slope. He had no idea how steep the drop was or what would be at the bottom. All he did know was that they had to reduce speed even more. 'Keep your foot on the brake!' he yelled to Esperanza.

The Olds skidded nearer to the drop. Veering, Decker swung the steering wheel harder, gravel flying. Afraid that the Olds would flip over, he was equally afraid of a head-on impact against a tree. The Olds spun, its tail end pointing toward the slope where the Caddy had disappeared, and suddenly halted, banging Decker's ribs against the seat he leaned against.

'Jesus,' Decker said. 'Are you all right?'

'I think so.' Esperanza pawed more chunks of glass from his blood-smeared face. 'I'm starting to see. Thank God, my eyes weren't cut.'

'I'm going after him!' Decker grabbed his pistol and raced from the Olds, assaulted by cold lancing rain. Vaguely aware that headlights were pulling off the Interstate behind him, a car stopping to investigate what seemed to be a terrible accident, he ignored the distraction and studied the dark wooded slope.

The Caddy's headlights blazed upward from it, as if the car had twisted going down the slope and was now resting on its back end. Decker didn't dare make himself a clear target by going straight ahead and exposing himself to the Caddy's headlights. Instead, he hurried to the right, entered the darkness of the rainswept trees, and climbed warily down a steep slippery slope. After what he judged to be thirty feet, he reached the bottom, turned left, and crept toward the glow of the Caddy's upended headlights, ready with his pistol.

11

Branches snapped. Rain hissing down through the thickly leaved trees obscured the sound. Decker listened harder. There! Another branch had snapped. Near the car.

Decker crouched, trying to blend with the undergrowth. A shadow moved through the trees. Partially silhouetted by the illumination from the Caddy, a man lurched into view. He held his stomach and bent forward, stumbling. Groaning, the figure lost his balance and staggered to Decker's right, away from the lights of the car, swallowed by the dark woods, but not before Decker saw that what the man had been clutching wasn't his stomach but instead the briefcase.

Decker crept through the trees after him. Although he didn't have much time, he didn't dare hurry. He couldn't afford to make mistakes. At once other noises unnerved him: voices behind him, on the top of the slope. Risking a glance backward, Decker saw rain glinting through several flashlight beams that were aimed down toward the Cadillac. A car had stopped as he went down the slope. Other vehicles must have stopped, also. He could only pray that one of them had not been a police car.

Shifting deeper into the woods, Decker followed the route he thought Giordano had taken. Behind him, people climbed awkwardly down the slope, shuffling through bushes, bending branches, talking loudly. The commotion they made prevented Decker from hearing any noises that Giordano might make ahead of him. He had to avoid the flashlights, stooping, trying to conceal himself in the undergrowth, searching. The money, he thought. I can't get to Beth if I don't have the money.

He took a tentative step forward into the darkness and at once felt nothing beneath his shoe. Another slope. About to fall, his momentum tugging him over, he grabbed a tree and dangled, then struggled back onto a slippery stretch of rock. Rain streamed down his neck, his clothes clinging coldly to him. He breathed deeply, trying to steady himself. He had no way of knowing how far down the drop went, but its pitch was extremely steep. If Giordano had toppled over, it would be impossible to climb down and find him in the dark.

Back at the Cadillac, the flashlights scanned the trees. They'll spread out and try to find the driver, Decker thought. If Giordano didn't go over the edge, if he's still alive, he'll move as far from those flashlights as he can. But which way? Forced to make an arbitrary decision, Decker turned to the right.

If not for the chest-high branch that he had to stoop under, the rock that Giordano clutched would have struck Decker's skull instead of his bent-over back. The pain of the blow was matched by its surprise. Dazed, Decker was knocked to the ground, dropping his pistol. In a frenzy, Giordano attacked from the darkness. Decker rolled, feeling the fierce rush of air as the rock passed his head and struck the wet ground with a muffled wallop. He kicked, knocking Giordano's legs from under him. Giordano's full weight landed on him, almost knocking his wind out. Squirming, Decker felt the edge of the steep slope next to him. As Giordano raised the rock to strike it at Decker's face, Decker grabbed Giordano's wrist to stop the blow. At the same time, he felt the ground give way beneath him. He and Giordano were suddenly in the air, falling through the darkness, striking an outcrop, rolling, falling again. With shocking abruptness, they jolted to a stop.

Despite being out of breath, Decker couldn't allow himself to hesitate. He struck at Giordano, who lay next to him, but in the dark, his blow glanced off Giordano's shoulder. Giordano had kept his grip on the rock, and although his aim was hampered by the darkness, he managed to graze Decker's ribs, almost doubling him over. The additional pain made Decker furious. He came to his feet and chopped with the side of his hand, but Giordano stumbled back, avoiding the blow, and swung with the rock. Decker felt the brush of wind as the rock barely missed his face. Wanting to get close to block the next blow, he lunged through the darkness, thrust Giordano back, and heard him gasp when they struck something. Giordano stiffened, his arms outstretched. He trembled. His breath sounded like a leak coming out of an innertube. Then his arms sank, his body becoming motionless, and the only hiss was that of the rain.

Decker didn't understand. Straining to catch his breath, he braced himself to continue the struggle. Slowly, he realized that Giordano was dead.

But somehow the body was still standing.

'I told you I heard something!' a man yelled. Flashlight beams arced through the storm-shrouded trees. Footsteps pounded close to the rim of the slope down which Decker had fallen.

I can't let them see him! Decker thought. He rushed toward where Giordano remained eerily upright. Tugging, he felt resistance and understood sickly that Giordano had been impaled on the jagged stump of a broken-off branch.

The voices and footsteps rushed closer. Have to get him out of sight, Decker thought. Lowering Giordano's dead weight to the ground, about to drag him deeper into the murky trees, Decker became paralyzed by a flashlight beam that caught him squarely as it glared down from the bluff.

'Hey!' a man yelled.

'I found him!' Decker shouted. 'I thought I heard a noise down here! I managed to climb down! I found him!'

'Holy—' another man yelled, aiming a flashlight. 'Look at all the blood!'

'*Can you find a pulse? Is he alive?*' someone else yelled.

'I don't know!' Decker shouted. The glare of the flashlights hurt his eyes. 'I think what I heard was him falling! The drop must have killed him!'

'But there's a chance he might be alive! We have to get an ambulance!'

'His neck might be broken! We don't dare move him!' Rain streaked down Decker's face. 'Is anybody up there a doctor?'

'We need an ambulance!'

Guided by their flashlights, several men were working down past trees on the muddy slope.

'Why did he come this way?' A man reached the bottom. 'Couldn't he see the Interstate back there?'

'He must have banged his head in the wreck!' Decker said. 'He was probably delirious!'

'Jesus, look at him!' One of the men turned away.

'He must have hit something when he fell!'

'*But what about the woman he was with?*' Decker said.

'*Woman?*'

'I heard her voice!' Decker said. 'She sounded like she was hurt! Where *is* she?'

'Everybody!' a man yelled. 'Keep looking! Someone else is out here! A woman!'

The group split apart, scanning their flashlights, quickly searching.

Taking advantage of the chaos, Decker retreated into the darkness. He climbed the slope, slipping in the mud, grabbing exposed tree roots, bracing his shoes on outcrops of rock. Any minute, the group would wonder what had become of him. He had to get away before they suspected he wasn't part of the search team. But I can't leave without Giordano's briefcase. It wasn't with him when he fell. Where *is* it? If the searchers get their hands on the money, there's no way I can save Beth.

Heart pounding, Decker reached the top and spotted more flashlight beams near the wrecked Cadillac. Temporarily he was concealed by undergrowth, but the searchers might soon investigate this area. Breathing hard, he crouched, trying to get his bearings. Where had Giordano attacked him? Was it to the right or the left? Decker swung to stare down toward what in the darkness he could barely tell was Giordano's body. He replayed the struggle at the bottom of the slope. He calculated where they had landed. To reach that area, they would have had to fall from Decker's left. Giordano must have attacked from—

Decker squirmed on his hands and knees through the underbrush. At the same time, flashlights started coming in his direction. No! Decker thought. He had never felt such a powerful surge of adrenaline. He didn't think his pulse had ever been so rapid. Pressure built behind his ears. The briefcase. Have to find the briefcase. Need the briefcase. Can't save Beth without the briefcase.

He had almost crawled past it before he realized what he had touched. Fearing that his heart would surely burst from relief, he grabbed the briefcase. At the same time, his foot nudged something behind him near the edge of the slope. His pistol. He had dropped it when Giordano struck him with the rock. As he shoved the pistol into his jacket, he dared to hope that things might actually work out. He still had a chance to save Beth.

But not if the flashlights came any closer. What if one of them belonged to a policeman? His clothes smeared with mud, Decker crawled farther through the undergrowth, straining not to make noise. He came to where he thought he had initially descended into the trees. Staring behind him, he waited for the flashlights to shift toward an area away from him. The first chance he got, he crept swiftly up through the trees and paused at the edge of the Interstate. Vehicles rushed by in the rain, tires hissing, headlights glaring. On the shoulder, several cars had stopped. Most of them were empty, their occupants presumably having gone into the trees to help search for survivors of the wreck. One of the cars was a police cruiser, Decker saw in dismay, but it too was empty, although probably not for long.

The police car was next to the Oldsmobile. Esperanza sat in the Olds, slumped behind the steering wheel. Even from a distance, it was obvious that his face was bloody. I can't wait any longer, Decker thought. He quickly emerged from the trees, tried to use his body to shield the briefcase from anyone looking at him from the trees, and walked swiftly along the side of the Interstate.

Esperanza straightened as Decker got in the Olds.

'Can you see to drive?'

'Yes.'

'Go.'

Esperanza turned the ignition key, put the Olds in gear, and sped out into traffic. 'You look like hell.'

'I wasn't dressed for the occasion.' Decker stared behind him to see if they were being followed. It didn't seem so.

'I wasn't sure when or if you'd come back,' Esperanza said.

'And *I* wasn't sure if you'd stay with the car. You did the right thing.'

'I'd make a good getaway driver. In fact, I *was* a good getaway driver.'

Decker looked at him.

'When I was sixteen,' Esperanza said. 'You've got the briefcase.'

'Yes.'

'What about Frank Giordano?'

Decker didn't answer.

'Then Beth Dwyer has one less problem.'

'It was self-defense,' Decker said.

'I didn't suggest otherwise.'

'I needed the briefcase.'

314

'A million dollars. With that kind of money, some men wouldn't think about saving anybody.'

'Without Beth, I wouldn't save *myself.*'

TEN

1

'Jesus, Decker, this is crazy. If you're not careful, you'll end up killing yourself,' Esperanza tensely murmured, lower than a whisper. 'Or else you're giving McKittrick the chance to do it for you.' But they had argued about Decker's intentions for the last hour, and Decker had made clear his determination. This was the way McKittrick expected the dropoff to happen, and by God, this was the way it was *going* to happen.

Decker felt Esperanza lean into the back seat of the Oldsmobile. He felt Esperanza grab his shoulders and tug him out into the rain. His instructions to Esperanza had been to avoid being gentle, to be as rough as someone would expect a hitman to be with the corpse of someone he had just killed.

Esperanza obeyed, making no attempt to ease the impact of Decker's body onto the ground. Pain jolted through him, but he didn't show it, just remained limp as Esperanza dragged him through a puddle. Although Decker kept his eyes shut, he imagined the scene: the battered Oldsmobile next to the refreshment building at the scenic lookout. A little before midnight, in the rain, it was very unlikely that any motorists would have stopped to admire the view from the Palisades. In good weather, the view from the lookout showed the lights of boats on the Hudson and the expansive glow of Hastings and Yonkers across the river, but in bad weather like this, it would show only gloom. On the off-chance that a driver might pull in

319

to rest for a few minutes, Esperanza had parked the Oldsmobile sideways toward the entrance to the lookout, preventing anyone on the Interstate from seeing what appeared to be a corpse being dragged around to the back of the refreshment building.

Decker heard Esperanza grunt, then felt the squishy impact as Esperanza dropped him into a muddy puddle. Limp, he allowed his body to roll and ended on his left side in the puddle. Peering through half-open eyelids, he saw what appeared to be garbage cans in the darkness behind the building. He heard Esperanza run through the puddle back to the car and quickly return. He saw Esperanza set the briefcase against the rear of the building. Then Esperanza disappeared. In a moment, Decker heard car doors being shut, an engine revving, the splash of tires as Esperanza drove away. The engine became fainter. Then all Decker heard was the distant drone of traffic on the Interstate and the pelt of rain on the clear plastic bag tied over his head.

'Giordano's deal with McKittrick was the money and my corpse,' Decker had insisted while he and Esperanza drove anxiously from town to town, worried about the time they were losing, desperate to find a convenience store. They had started their search at ten-thirty. Then the time was eleven, then eleven-fifteen. 'We have to be there by midnight.' Twice, the stores they did find open had not had all the materials Decker needed. At eleven-thirty, they had finally gotten what they needed. Esperanza had parked on a deserted country lane and done what was necessary.

'Why can't I leave the money along with a note, supposedly from Giordano, that says he won't kill you until McKittrick makes good on his promise?' Esperanza had tied clothes-line rope around Decker's ankles.

'Because I don't want to do anything to make him suspicious. Be sure the knots are in plain view. It'll be dark behind that building. I want it to be obvious to him that I've been tied up.'

320

'But this way, if he isn't convinced you're dead, you won't have a chance to defend yourself.' Esperanza tied Decker's arms behind his back.

'That's what I'm hoping will convince him. He won't believe I willingly made myself completely vulnerable to him.'

'Does this knot hurt?'

'It doesn't matter whether it hurts. Make it real. Make it look as if I couldn't possibly be alive and not show any reaction to the way I've been tied. *He has to believe I'm dead.*'

'You *might be* dead by the time he gets to you. Decker, this plastic bag scares the hell out of me.'

'That's the point. It might even scare *him*. I'm counting on it to be the finishing touch. Mark me up. Hurry.'

Needing something that looked like blood, Decker had used what a pathologist once explained to him were the easiest materials to obtain to fake it – colorless corn syrup and red food dye.

'Make it look as if they really enjoyed beating me,' Decker insisted.

'They mashed your lips. They messed up your jaw.' Esperanza had applied the mixture.

'Hurry. We've only got fifteen minutes to get to the drop-off site.'

Esperanza quickly tied the bag around Decker's neck and then murmured a Spanish prayer as Decker inhaled and forced the bag to collapse around his head, the plastic clinging to his face, sticking to his skin, stuffing Decker's nostrils and his mouth. Immediately Esperanza poked a tiny hole in the plastic that filled Decker's mouth and hurriedly inserted a cutoff piece of a drinking straw, which Decker gripped between his teeth, allowing him to breathe without breaking the vacuum that made the plastic bag stick to his face.

'My God, Decker, does it work? Can you get enough air?'

Decker had managed to nod slightly.

'The way that bag sticks to your face, you look like a corpse.'

Good, Decker thought as he lay in the muddy puddle, in the dark, behind the refreshment building, listening to the rain pelt the plastic bag. Provided that he breathed shallowly, slowly, and calmly, the small amount of air he got through the straw was enough to allow him to remain alive. But with each slight inhalation, panic tried to force itself through his fierce resolve. With each imperceptible exhalation, his heart wanted to beat faster, demanding more oxygen. The cord that secured the bag around his neck was tight enough to dig into the skin – Decker had insisted on that, also. Everything absolutely had to look convincing. And *feel* so – the cold rain would lower Decker's exterior temperature, making his skin feel like that of a corpse losing body heat. If McKittrick for one moment doubted that Decker was a corpse, he would put a bullet through Decker's head and settle the matter.

The danger was that McKittrick would shoot him no matter what, but Decker was counting on the grotesque appearance of his face to make McKittrick decide that further violence wasn't necessary. If McKittrick felt for a pulse on Decker's wrists, he wouldn't find one, the tight ropes having sharply reduced the flow of blood. He could try to feel for a pulse along Decker's neck, but to do so, McKittrick would have to untie the cord that secured the plastic bag – time-consuming and disgusting. That left pressing a palm against the ribs over Decker's heart, but he wasn't likely to do that, either, because Decker had landed on his left side – to feel the ribs over Decker's heart, McKittrick would have to turn the body over and press his hand against the repulsive mud that adhered to Decker's clothes.

It was still a great risk. 'Insane,' as Esperanza had kept telling him. 'You're going to get yourself killed.' But what was the alternative? If the dropoff didn't occur exactly as McKittrick expected, if Decker's body wasn't there as promised, McKittrick might become suspicious enough not to take the money, fearing that the briefcase was boobytrapped. But the money was what Decker's plan was all about, the money and the homing device that Decker had hidden with the money. If McKittrick didn't take the money, Decker would have no way to follow him to where Beth was being held captive. No matter how Decker analyzed it, there wasn't an alternative. McKittrick *had* to find Decker's corpse.

'Do you love Beth that much?' Esperanza had asked before he tied the plastic bag over Decker's head. 'To risk your life for her so completely?'

'I'd go to hell for her.'

'To learn the truth about her feelings toward you?' Esperanza had looked strangely at him. 'This isn't about love. It's about pride.'

'It's about hope. If I can't trust love, nothing matters. Put that straw in my mouth. Tie the bag.'

'Decker, you're the most remarkable man I ever met.'

'No, I'm a fool.'

Lying in the puddle, breathing slightly, fighting panic, mustering all the discipline of which he was capable, Decker struggled against the temptation to second-guess himself. As his lungs demanded more air, he thought perhaps there *had* been another way. Was it possible that all he wanted was to show Beth the lengths he would go to demonstrate how much he loved her?

Desperately needing to distract himself, he recalled the first time he had seen her, two months ago . . . Could it have been only that recently? It seemed forever . . . in the lobby of the real-estate office – how she had turned toward him, how his heart rhythm had changed. Never before in his life had he felt such instant attraction. In his imagination, he saw her again vividly, her lush auburn hair reflecting the light, her tanned skin glowing with health, her athletic figure making him selfconscious about the contour of her breasts and hips. He was spellbound by her elegant chin, her high cheekbones, her model's forehead. He imagined stepping close to her, and suddenly his imagination shifted to the evening they had first made love, her blue-gray eyes and sensual lips so close they were a blur. He kissed her neck, drawing his tongue along her skin, tasting salt, sun, and something primal. He smelled her musk. When he entered her, it was as if all his life he had been only half of a person, but now he was complete, not only physically but emotionally, spiritually, filled with wellbeing, at last blessed with a purpose – to build a life with her, to share, to be one.

2

In a rush, his senses returned to the present – because, amid the distant drone of traffic and the pelting of the rain, he heard sounds from the bluff behind him. Although the plastic bag muffled his hearing, apprehension heightened his awareness. The sounds he heard were labored breathing, footsteps slipping on wet rocks, branches being snapped.

Dear God, Decker thought. He had been waiting to hear a car pull off the Interstate and approach this section of the scenic lookout. But McKittrick had been here all along, below the guardrail, hiding on the slope. He must have seen Esperanza drag me behind the building, Decker told himself. He must have seen Esperanza dump me into the puddle, leave the briefcase, and drive away. If Esperanza had said just one word to me, if he had made any attempt to cushion me, McKittrick would have realized instantly that this was a trap. He would have shot us.

Decker shivered from the understanding of how close he had come to dying. The cold rain made him shiver, also, and at once he strained to subdue the reflex. He didn't dare move. He had to achieve the appearance of lifelessness. In the past, when he had been about to embark on a dangerous assignment, he had relied on meditation to calm himself. Now he did so again. Concentrating deeply, he fought to purge himself of emotion, of fear, of longing, of apprehension, of need.

But his imagination could not be denied. He envisioned McKittrick peering over the rainswept bluff and scowling at the darkness. McKittrick would be nervous, wet, cold, impatient to finish this and escape. He would be holding a weapon and prepared to shoot at the slightest provocation. He might have a flashlight. He might risk exposing himself by turning it on and aiming the light at the ropes around Decker's arms and legs. If so, he would definitely let the light linger on the plastic bag that covered Decker's head.

Footsteps touched down on wet gravel, as if McKittrick had stepped over the guardrail. This was the moment, Decker knew, when McKittrick might shoot to make sure that Decker was in fact dead. Simultaneously, to prevent his chest from moving even slightly, Decker stopped breathing. His lungs immediately demanded more air. The suffocating pressure in his chest began to build. His oxygen-starved muscles ached with intensifying need.

The footsteps paused near him. Decker had prepared himself and showed no reaction when a shoe pushed at his upright shoulder flipping him onto his back. Through closed eyelids, Decker was able to see the filtered glare from a flashlight as McKittrick studied the plastic bag's seal against Decker's face. Decker had shifted the cutoff section of straw toward a corner of his mouth and inhaled imperceptibly so that the bag was deeper past his lips. He felt light-headed. Desperate to breathe, he concentrated on kissing Beth; his mind filled only with her. Swirling, he felt swallowed by her.

McKittrick grunted, perhaps with satisfaction. At once the flashlight was extinguished. His lungs threatening to burst, Decker heard quick footsteps through water as McKittrick presumably hurried toward the briefcase. But now other sounds confused Decker, clicks, scrapes, aggravating his apprehension. *What were those sounds? What was McKittrick doing?*

Understanding came in a rush. McKittrick was transferring the money to another container, suspicious that Giordano might have put a homing device in the briefcase. Good instincts, but Decker had anticipated. The homing device wasn't secured to the briefcase. Decker had used a knife to cut out the interior of one of the packets of cash. He had inserted the homing device and then had resecured the rubber bands around the packet so it appeared no different from any of the others.

Decker heard McKittrick grunt again, this time with effort. Something flipped through the air, then clattered down the bluff. The briefcase, Decker realized. McKittrick had thrown it away. He didn't want to leave any indication that this area behind the restrooms had been used as a drop site. But if he had thrown away the briefcase—

Jesus, he's going to do the same with me. Decker barely kept his oxygen-deprived body from showing his panic as McKittrick grabbed his shoulders, dragged him violently backward, roughly hefted him up, and doubled him over the guardrail. No! Decker mentally screamed. The next instant, he felt weightless. His body struck something. He flipped off it and again felt weightless. His bound arms hit something beneath him. Unable to restrain the impulse, he moaned in pain. *Had McKittrick heard him?* He toppled, rolled, hit something else, imagined that he was about to begin the long, deadly fall all the way from the Palisades bluff to the Hudson River, and suddenly jolted to an agonizing halt, his head banging against something.

Dazed, he felt something liquid inside the plastic bag. I'm

bleeding! The hot sticky fluid streamed from a cut on his forehead and began to fill the plastic bag. No! He didn't care if McKittrick now saw him move. There wasn't a choice. *He had to breathe.* The plan had been for McKittrick to take the money, leave Decker, and hurry away. At that point, Decker would have reinserted the piece of straw in the hole in the bag and breathed as best he could until Esperanza – alerted by the moving needle on the receiver that the money had been taken – returned to free him. But Decker had never once considered that McKittrick might try to dispose of the body. Decker would never have attempted the plan if the terrifying thought had occurred to him. I'm going to die. The cord that was tied around his neck, securing the plastic bag to his face, dug into his skin, making him feel strangled.

Frantic for air, he worked the piece of straw from the corner of his mouth and poked it through the hole in the bag . . . or tried to – he couldn't find the opening. Unable to control his body, he exhaled forcefully, expanding the bag, and with equal force, totally unwilled, he inhaled. This time, the bag filled his nose and mouth. Like a living thing, it gripped tightly to his skin. The makeup and blood beneath it caused it to stick fast. Esperanza will never find me in time!

Thrashing, he turned in the rain toward whatever he had landed on and rubbed his face along whatever it was that supported him, searching for anything that was sharp, a branch, a jagged outcrop of rock, *anything* that would snag the plastic bag and tear it open. The surface was wet and slick. He banged his head against something – a rock – ignored the pain, and continued squirming. But he felt in slow motion. The blood that continued to slick his face and fill the plastic bag gave him the sensation of drowning. For all he knew, his movements were about to topple him over a precipice. What difference did it make? He was doomed if he didn't . . .

A stakelike object snagged the plastic bag. His consciousness graying, he feebly jerked his head to the left, felt the bag tear, and used a final burst of strength to twist his head even farther to the left. The tear increased. He felt a chill wind against his forehead, the cold rain on his brow. But the plastic still stuck to his nose and mouth. He tried to breathe through the tiny hole at his mouth, but his efforts had twisted the plastic and sealed the hole. He thought he was going to choke on the piece of drinking straw in his mouth. I have to get the bag off my head! Feeling as if something inside him were going to burst, as if he were about to sink into a deep black pit, he made one last attempt to snag the bag on the sharp object, scraped his right cheek, and tore the bag totally open.

When he spat out the piece of drinking straw and breathed, wind seemed to shriek down his throat. The rush of cold air into his lungs was unbelievably sweet. His chest pumped convulsively. He lay on his back, trembling, gulping air, and tried to adjust to the realization that he was alive.

3

Alive, but for how long? Decker asked himself in dismay. Esperanza might not find me. If I stay out in the cold rain much longer, I'll get hypothermia. I'll die from exposure. Turning so that his face was toward the black sky, he tasted sweet rain, breathing hungrily, trying not to be alarmed by the force with which he shuddered and the pressure it put on his bound arms and legs. How long have I been down here? Has McKittrick gone? Did he hear me groan when I landed?

He waited in dread that a dark shape would clamber down the bluff toward him, that McKittrick would turn on his flashlight, grin, and aim his pistol. Indeed, all of a sudden, Decker did see a flashlight glaring at the top of the bluff, the beam moving toward the refreshment building, toward the guardrail, toward the refreshment building again, and responding to the faith that he had felt growing in him, Decker shouted, or tried to shout, 'Esperanza.' The word came out hoarsely, as if he had been swallowing gravel. He tried again, harder. 'Esperanza!' This time, the flashlight beam froze toward the guardrail. A moment later, it blazed down the bluff, and Decker was able to see that the drop here was on an incline, a series of bush-and-tree-studded levels that angled down toward the eventual sheer fall to the river.

'Over here!' Decker shouted. The flashlight beam streaked along the ledge toward him. Not far enough. 'Here!' At last, the flashlight found him. But did it belong to Esperanza? Faith, Decker thought. I've got to have faith.

'Decker?'

Esperanza! Thanking God, Decker felt his heart pound less furiously as the familiar tall lanky figure climbed over the guardrail and began a hurried descent.

'Be careful,' Decker said.

Esperanza's cowboy boots slipped off a rock. 'Holy—' He steadied himself, scurried lower, and crouched, using his flashlight to study Decker's face. 'There's blood all over you. Are you all right?'

'I have to be.'

Esperanza swiftly cut the rope that held Decker's arms behind him. With equal speed, he cut the rope that bound Decker's legs. Although Decker's muscles were cramped, he luxuriated in his ability to move.

'Hold still while I work on these knots,' Esperanza said. 'Damn, the rain soaked into the rope and swelled it. I can't get—'

'We don't have time,' Decker said. 'We have to get to the car.

329

The homing signal is good for only a mile. *Help me up.*'

With effort, struggling not to lose his own balance, Esperanza helped him to stand.

'The circulation's almost gone from my hands and feet. You'll have to pull me up,' Decker said.

Grunting, straining, they worked up the slope.

'I parked about a hundred yards north on the shoulder of the Interstate,' Esperanza said. 'No headlights turned in to the lookout. It was after midnight. I was beginning to think he wasn't going to show up. But all of a sudden the needle on the receiver moved – the homing device was in motion. I backed along the Interstate's shoulder to get to you as fast as I could.'

'McKittrick was hiding on a ledge.' Decker reached the guardrail, gasping with effort, climbing over. 'He must have escaped through the trees. His car must be parked south of here or farther north than where *you* were. Hurry.'

Splashing through puddles, Esperanza reached the shadowy Oldsmobile before Decker did. He grabbed the receiver off the front seat. 'I'm still getting a signal,' he said excitedly. 'The needle says he's driving north.'

Decker slumped into the front seat, managed to slam the door, and felt his body lurch against the seat as Esperanza tromped the accelerator. The Oldsmobile tore up gravel and fishtailed across the soaked parking area, speeding toward the rain-streaked headlights on the Interstate.

4

'The signal's weak!' Decker stared at the illuminated dial on the receiver. His wet clothes clung to him.

Esperanza drove even faster. Barely taking the time to turn on the windshield wipers, he spotted a break in traffic, roared onto the Interstate, and began passing cars.

'Jesus, I'm freezing.' Decker pawed at the switch for the car's heater. With the awkward, almost senseless fingers of his right hand, he fumbled to saw Esperanza's knife across the knot that secured the rope to his left wrist. He studied the dial on the receiver. 'The signal's stronger.' The needle shifted. 'Watch! He's off the Interstate. He's to the left of us up ahead!'

Quicker than expected, the Oldsmobile's headlights revealed a rain-obscured offramp, a sign for Route 9.

'It parallels the Interstate,' Decker said. 'The needle says he's reversed direction! He's heading south.' Decker barely avoided nicking himself as the knife sliced all the way through the rope on his wrist. Blood tingled into the veins of his left hand. He massaged the painful groove that the rope had made on his wrists.

'You told me to make it look real,' Esperanza said.

'Hey, I'm still alive. I'm not complaining.'

At the end of the offramp, Esperanza veered left across the bridge over the Interstate and sped left again, accessing Route 9, hurrying south, approaching a string of taillights.

'The signal's even stronger!' Decker said. 'Slow down. He could be in any of these cars ahead of us.' He severed the rope around his other wrist. Blood flowing into his hand made his fingers less awkward, allowing him to cut harder and faster at the coils around his ankles.

Despite the hot air from the car's heater, he continued to shudder. Troubled thoughts tortured him. What if McKittrick had already killed Beth? Or what if McKittrick guessed that he was being followed and discovered where the homing device was, throwing it away? No! I can't have gone through this for nothing! Beth *has* to be alive.

'The needle says he's turning again. To the right. Heading west.'

Esperanza nodded. 'Four cars in front, I see headlights turning. I'll slow down, so he doesn't see us turn after him.'

Anticipation bolstered Decker's strength. He wiped his forehead and looked at his hand, disturbed by the crimson on his palm. Not corn syrup mixed with red food dye. Coppery-smelling, this was unmistakably the real thing.

'I don't know how much help it will be, but here's a clean handkerchief I found in the glove compartment,' Esperanza said. 'Try to stop the bleeding.' As he followed McKittrick, steering to the right off Route 9, passing a sign that read ROCKMAN ROAD, Esperanza flicked off his headlights. 'No point in advertising. I can barely see his taillights in the rain, so I'm sure he can't see *us* at all.'

'But you're driving blind.'

'Not for long.' Esperanza turned left into a lane, re-illuminated his headlights, made a U-turn, and drove back onto Rockman Road, steering left, again following McKittrick. 'In case he's watching his rearview mirror, which I'd certainly be doing in *his* place, he'll see headlights pull onto the road from his left, which is the wrong direction for anyone to be following him from the Interstate. He won't be suspicious.'

'You're very good at this,' Decker said.

'I'd better be. When I was a kid, I ran with gangs. I had a lot of practice in following and *being* followed.'

'What straightened you out?'

'I met a police officer who got through to me.'

'He must be proud of the way you turned out.'

'He died last year. A drunk with an attitude shot him.'

A blinding flash was followed by a rumble that shook the car.

'Now we're getting lightning and thunder. The storm's worse,' Decker said.

'Shit.' But it wasn't clear if Esperanza referred to the storm or his memories.

The next time lightning flashed, he pointed. 'I see a car.'

'The signal on the receiver is strong. The needle's straight ahead,' Decker said. 'That must be McKittrick.'

'Time to pull off the road. I don't want him getting suspicious.' Past a sign for the town of Closter, Esperanza let McKittrick proceed straight ahead while he himself turned to the right, went around a block, and came back onto Rockman Road. By then, the headlights of other cars had gone by and filled the space between the Oldsmobile and McKittrick's vehicle.

'The receiver indicates he's still ahead of us.' Decker's cold wet clothes continued to make him shiver. Tension made his muscles ache. The places on his back and chest where he had landed falling down the bluff were swollen, throbbing. It didn't matter. Pain didn't matter. Only Beth did. 'No, wait. The needle's moving. He's turning to the right.'

'Yes, I see his lights going off the road,' Esperanza said. 'I don't want to spook him by following him right away. Let's pass where he turned and see where he's going. He might be trying an evasion tactic.'

Having gone through the quiet heart of town, they reached the even quieter outskirts, and now, as lightning flashed, they saw where McKittrick had turned: a modest one-story motel. A red neon sign announced PALISADES INN. Attached plain units – about twenty of them, Decker judged – stretched back toward a murky area away from the street. As the Oldsmobile went by, Decker scrunched down out of sight, in case McKittrick was glancing toward the sparse traffic that had followed him.

Then the motel was behind the Oldsmobile, and Decker slowly straightened. 'The needle on the receiver indicates that McKittrick isn't moving.'

'How do you want to handle this?'

'Park off the street some place. Let's go back and see what he's doing.'

Thunder shook the car as Decker picked up the pistol that he had taken from one of the guards at Giordano's estate. He watched Esperanza pocket the Walther. 'We'd better take the receiver with us. In case this is a trick and he starts to move again.'

'And then?' Esperanza asked.

'A damned good question.' Decker got out of the car and was instantly reassaulted by rain. For an angry moment, he remembered the cold rain that had been falling the night he had followed McKittrick into the trap in the courtyard in Rome. Then Esperanza was next to him, his baseball cap dripping water, his drenched long hair sticking to his neck. In the glare from passing headlights, Esperanza's face looked leaner than usual, his nose and jaw more pronounced, reminding Decker of a raptor.

5

Rather than show themselves at the front of the building, they moved cautiously along an alley that led to the back. Decker noted that the units were made of cinderblock and that there weren't any rear exits. The only windows on the alley side were small and made of thick opaque glass bricks that would be extremely difficult to break.

Skirting the back of the motel, Decker and Esperanza concealed themselves behind a Dumpster bin and studied the front of the units. The needle on the receiver continued to indicate that the homing device was in one of them. Although eight of the twenty units had a vehicle in front, only four of them had lights glowing beyond closed draperies. Two of those units were next to each other, near the Dumpster bin that Decker hid behind. Decker didn't need the receiver to tell him that the signal came from one of those latter units. A car in front of them, a blue Pontiac, made sporadic ticking sounds as its engine cooled. Rain pelting on the Pontiac's warm hood vaporized into mist.

Hurry, Decker thought. If Beth's in one of those rooms, McKittrick might be tempted to kill her as soon as he's back with the money. Or if he checks the money and finds the homing device, he might panic and kill Beth before he tries to escape.

'Wait here,' Decker whispered to Esperanza. 'Back me up.' He moved as silently as he could through puddles and paused next to the softly lit window of the last unit in the row. An intense flash of lightning made him feel naked. A deep burst of thunder shook him. The night again concealed him. Uneasy, he noted that the draperies didn't meet fully, and he was able to see through a narrow gap into a room – a double bed, a cheap dresser, a television bolted to the wall. Except for a suitcase on the bed, it seemed unoccupied. In the middle of the wall to the left, a door was open, appearing to allow access to the room next to it.

Decker stiffened at more lightning and thunder, then shifted toward the next window. Despite the noise of the storm, he was able to hear voices, although he couldn't distinguish what they said. A man was talking, then a woman. The male voice might have been McKittrick's, the female voice Beth's. Hard to tell. Maybe what Decker heard was only a conversation on the television. Unexpectedly, someone else spoke, a man with a severely distorted, deep, hoarse voice, and Decker was briefly confused until he realized that if Beth was in there, someone would have had to guard her while McKittrick went for the money. He imagined Beth tied to a chair, a loosened gag dangling from her mouth. He imagined the gag being reapplied and Beth struggling, her eyes bulging as McKittrick strangled her.

Do something! he told himself. After noting the room number on the door, he hurried back to Esperanza and explained what he intended to do. Then, staying among shadows, he rushed to the street, where he remembered having seen a payphone at a closed gas station across from the motel. Quickly, he inserted coins and pressed numbers.

'Information,' a woman said. 'For what city, please?'

'Closter, New Jersey. I need the number for the Palisades Inn.'

In a moment, a computerized monotonous voice said, 'The number is . . .'

Decker memorized the number, hung up, put in more coins, and pressed buttons.

After three rings, a weary male voice answered, almost sighing, 'Palisades Inn.'

'Give me room nineteen.'

The clerk didn't acknowledge the request. Instead, Decker heard a click, then a ring and another ring as the call was put through. He imagined McKittrick swinging toward the phone, his burly features expressing a mixture of surprise and puzzlement. After all, who would be calling him? Who would know that he was at that motel? McKittrick would be debating whether it was smart to answer.

The phone kept ringing. Ten times. Eleven times.

The clerk finally interrupted. 'Sir, they're not answering. Maybe they're not in.'

'Keep trying.'

'But maybe they're trying to sleep.'

'This is an emergency.'

The clerk sighed wearily. Again Decker heard a click. The phone on the other end rang, then rang again.

'Hello.' McKittrick's voice was hesitant, at half-volume, as if by speaking softly he hoped that his voice would not be recognizable.

'If you use your common sense,' Decker said, 'there's still a chance you'll get out of this alive.'

The line became silent. The only sound Decker heard was the rain against the phone booth.

'Decker?' McKittrick sounded as if he doubted his sanity.

'It's been a long time since we talked, Brian.'

'But it can't be. You're *dead*. How—'

'It's not *my* death I called to talk about, Brian.'

'Jesus.'

'Prayer's a good idea, but I'm in a better position to help you than Jesus is.'

'Where are you?'

'Come on, Brian. I'm the guy who wrote the book on tradecraft. I don't volunteer information. The next thing, you'll be asking how I found out where you are and how many people are with me. But all you need to concern yourself about is you've got the money and I want Beth Dwyer.'

The line became silent again.

'If she's dead, Brian, you don't have any way to bargain with me.'

'No.' Brian made a tense swallowing sound. 'She isn't dead.'

Decker felt a sinking sensation, one of relief. 'Let me talk to her.'

'This is very complicated, Decker.'

'It used to be. But tonight, things got simpler. Nick and Frank Giordano are dead.'

'How the hell—'

'Trust me, Brian. They're not in the equation any longer. No one's hunting Beth Dwyer. You can keep the money and let her go. How you got the money will be our secret.'

McKittrick hesitated, his tense breathing audible. 'Why should I believe you?'

'Think about it, Brian. If the Giordanos were still alive, I wouldn't be talking to you. That would really have been my corpse at the drop site.'

McKittrick breathed harder.

'And it wouldn't be *me* on the phone,' Decker said. 'It would be *them* breaking through your motel-room door.'

Decker heard what sounded like McKittrick's hand being put over the phone's mouthpiece. He heard muffled voices. He waited, shivering from his wet clothes and his bone-deep dread that McKittrick would do something to Beth.

On the other end, something brushed against the phone's mouthpiece, and McKittrick was talking again. 'I need convincing.'

'You're *stalling*, Brian. You're going to try to leave while I'm talking to you. I'm not alone. The moment you show yourself at the door, there'll be shooting, and I guarantee if Beth gets hurt, you'll find out the hard way you can't spend a million dollars in hell.'

Pause. Another round of muffled voices. McKittrick's voice was strained when he came back on the line. 'How can I be sure you'll let me go if I give you Diana Scolari?'

'*Beth Dwyer*,' Decker said. 'This might be a new idea to you, Brian. Integrity. I never go back on my word. When I worked for Langley, that's how I was able to make deals. People knew they could count on me. And this is the most important deal I ever wanted to make.'

From Decker's vantage point in the phone booth, he could see across the street toward the motel units stretching back toward the Dumpster bin. He could see Esperanza hiding behind that bin, watching the two motel units. He could see both windows go dark.

'Why did you turn off the lights, Brian?'

'Jesus, you're that close?'

'Don't try something stupid. You're planning to use Beth as a

338

shield and bet that I won't risk shooting. Think. Even if I did let you escape with her, are you prepared to use her as a shield for the rest of your life? That plastic bag over my head back at the drop site proves I'm ready to take any risk for her. I would never stop hunting you.'

No response.

'Just keep focused on the million dollars, Brian. No one can prove how you got it. No one will want it back. It's yours to spend once you drive away from here.'

'Provided you let me leave.'

'Provided *you* leave *Beth*. This conversation is pointless if you don't prove to me she's alive. *Let me talk to her.*'

Decker listened to the phone so hard that he didn't hear the pelting of the rain. Then he couldn't help hearing the thunder that rattled the glass of the phone booth and the greater thunder of his heart.

The phone made a sound as if it was being moved.

'Steve?'

Decker's knees felt weak. Despite all his determination, he now realized that he had not totally believed he would ever hear Beth's voice again.

'Thank God,' Decker blurted.

'I can't believe it's you. How did—'

'I don't have time to explain. Are you all right?'

'Scared to death. But they haven't hurt me.' The voice was faint and weak, trembling with nervousness, but he couldn't fail to recognize it. He recalled the first time Beth had spoken to him and how he had been reminded of wind chimes and champagne.

'I love you,' Decker said. 'I'm going to get you out of there. How many people are with you?'

Abruptly the phone made a bumping sound, and McKittrick was talking. 'So now you know she's still alive. How am *I* going to get out of here alive?'

'Turn on the lights. Open the draperies.'

'*What?*'

'Put Beth in plain sight at the window. Come out with the money. Get in the car. All the while, keep your pistol aimed at her. That way, you know I won't try a move against you.'

'Until I'm on the street and I can't see to shoot her anymore. Then you'll try to kill me.'

'You've got to have faith,' Decker said.

'Bullshit.'

'Because *I* have faith. I'll show you how much faith I really have. You know you'll be safe after you leave Beth in the room because *I'll* be with you in the car. *I'll* be your hostage. Down the road, when you're sure no one's following, you can let me out, and we'll be even.'

Silence again. Thunder.

'You're joking,' McKittrick said.

'I've never been more serious.'

'How do you know I won't kill you?'

'I don't,' Decker said. 'But if you do, I have friends who will hunt you down. I'm willing to gamble you want this to end here and now. I mean it, Brian. Give me Beth. Keep the money. You'll never hear from me again.'

McKittrick didn't speak for a while. Decker imagined him calculating.

With a muffled voice, McKittrick spoke to someone else in the motel room. 'All right,' he said to Decker. 'Give us five minutes. Then we're coming out. I expect you to be waiting with your hands up at my car.'

'You've got a deal, Brian. But in case you're tempted to go back on the bargain, just remember – someone else will be aiming at you.'

6

Mouth parched with fear, Decker hung up the phone and stepped out into the rain. His chill increased as he hurried across the street and into the motel's dark parking lot, staying within shadows, concealing himself. At the back, he came up behind the Dumpster bin, and using a whisper that was muffled by the rain, he explained to Esperanza the deal he had made.

'You're taking a hell of a risk,' Esperanza said.

'So what else is new?'

'*Cojones*, man.'

'He won't kill me. He doesn't want to spend the rest of his life running.'

'From your imaginary friends.'

'Well, I sort of thought *you'd* go after him if he killed me.'

'Yes.' Esperanza thought about it. 'Yes, I would.'

The lights came on beyond the closed draperies in unit nineteen.

'I can't let him find a weapon on me. Here's my pistol,' Decker said. 'Don't hesitate to shoot him if things go bad.'

'It would be my pleasure,' Esperanza said.

'When I tell you to, pick up that empty bottle by your feet and throw it toward the front of the motel. Throw it high so he doesn't know where you are.'

Trying to avoid revealing where Esperanza was hiding, Decker crept back into the darkness and emerged from the shadows of a different area of the parking lot. With his hands up, he stepped through puddles toward the Pontiac in front of unit nineteen.

The draperies parted, like curtains in a theater. Decker's body felt disturbingly out of rhythm when he saw what was revealed. Beth was tied to a chair, her mouth stuffed with a gag. Her blue-gray eyes looked wild with fright. Her hair was disheveled. Her oval face was tight, her high cheekbones pressing against skin made pale by fear. But then she saw him through the window, and Decker was moved by the affection that replaced the fear in her eyes, by the trusting way she looked at him. The relief she felt, her confidence in him, were obvious. She had faith that he was the hero she had dreamed about when she was a child, *her* hero, that he would save her.

From the left, concealed by the cinderblock column between the window and the door, a person stretched out an arm, pointing a hand toward Beth's temple. The hand held a cocked revolver.

Tensing, Decker heard a noise at the door, the lock being freed, the handle being turned. Light spilled from a narrow gap.

'Decker?' McKittrick didn't show himself.

'I'm at your car – where I said I would be.'

The door came fully open. McKittrick stepped into view, the beefy shoulders of his thirtyish football-player's body silhouetted by the light. He looked a little more heavy in the chest than when Decker had last seen him. His blond hair was cut even shorter than Decker remembered, emphasizing his squared-off rugged features. His eyes reminded Decker of a pig's.

Aiming a pistol, McKittrick smiled. For a dismaying moment, Decker feared that McKittrick would shoot. But McKittrick stepped from the open door, grabbed Decker, and thrust him across the still warm hood of the Pontiac.

'You'd better not be armed, old buddy.' McKittrick searched him roughly, all the while pressing the barrel of his pistol against the back of Decker's neck.

'No weapon,' Decker said. 'I made a deal. I'll stick to it.' With his cheek pressed against the Pontiac's wet hood, Decker was able to see sideways toward the illuminated window and the revolver aimed at Beth. He blinked repeatedly to clear his vision as cold rain pelted his face.

Beth squirmed in terror.

McKittrick stopped his rough search and stepped back. 'My, my, my, you really did it. You gave yourself up to me. So sure of yourself. What makes you think I won't shoot you in the head?'

'I told you – I've got backup.'

'Yeah, sure, right. From who? The FBI? This isn't their style. From Langley? This doesn't involve national security. Why would *they* care?'

'I have friends.'

'Hey, I've been *watching* you, remember? In Santa Fe, you don't have *any* friends, none you would trust to back you up.'

'From the old days.'

'Like hell.'

'*Make a noise*,' Decker called to Esperanza in the darkness.

McKittrick flinched as the empty bottle plummeted onto the pavement near the entrance to the motel. Glass shattered.

McKittrick scowled and continued to aim at Decker. 'For all I know, that's a wino you paid to throw that bottle.'

'The point is, you *don't* know,' Decker said. 'Why take the risk?'

'I'm going to be so damned happy to have you out of my life.'

For a panicked moment, Decker feared that McKittrick was going to pull the trigger.

Instead, McKittrick shouted toward the open door, 'Let's go!'

A figure appeared – of medium height, wearing a black oversized raincoat and a rubber rainhat, the wide brim of which drooped down and concealed the person's features. Whoever it was had a suitcase in his left hand while he continued to aim the revolver at Beth in the window.

McKittrick opened the Pontiac's back door so the man in the raincoat could throw the suitcase into the car. Only when the man got into the back did McKittrick open the Pontiac's driver's door and tell Decker to slide across. The man in back sat behind

Decker and aimed at his head while McKittrick got behind the steering wheel, all the while aiming at Beth.

'Slick.' McKittrick chuckled. 'No muss, no fuss. And now, old buddy, you get what you wanted.' His tone became sober. 'We take you for a ride.'

McKittrick started the Pontiac, switched on its headlights, and went into reverse. The headlights blazed at Beth. Through the distortion of rain streaming down the windshield, Decker watched her trying to struggle against her ropes and turn her head to shield her eyes from the glare of the headlights. As the Pontiac continued backing up, she seemed to get smaller. McKittrick put the car into forward, steered, and pulled away from the motel unit. Grateful that Beth was safe but simultaneously feeling alone and hollow, Decker turned to catch his last glimpse of her struggling against the ropes that bound her to the chair. She stared with heartbreaking melancholy in his direction, afraid now for him.

'Who would have guessed?' McKittrick drove onto the gloomy street outside the motel and headed to the right. 'A romantic.'

Decker didn't say anything.

'She must really have gotten to you,' McKittrick said.

Decker still didn't respond.

'Hey.' McKittrick took his eyes off the road and aimed his pistol at Decker's face. 'This is a goddamned conversation.'

'Yes,' Decker said. 'She got to me.'

McKittrick muttered with contempt, then glanced back at the road. He studied his rearview mirror. 'No headlights. Nobody's following.'

'Did she know who I was when I first met her?' Decker asked.

'What?'

'Was she only using me for extra protection?'

344

'You're something. All that pose about being a professional, about keeping control, and you ruin your life over a woman.'

'That's not the way I look at it.'

'How the hell *do* you look at it?'

'I didn't ruin my life,' Decker said. 'I found it.'

'Not for long. You want to talk about ruined lives?' McKittrick snapped. 'You ruined *mine*. If it hadn't been for you, I'd still be working for the Agency. I would have been promoted. My father would have been proud of me. I wouldn't have had to take this shit job with the Marshals Service, protecting gangsters.' McKittrick raised his voice. 'I could still be in Rome!'

The man in the back seat said something – a gravelly, guttural statement that was too distorted for Decker to understand it. Decker had heard the puzzlingly grotesque voice before – when he listened outside McKittrick's room. But there was something about it that made it naggingly familiar, as if he had heard it even earlier. McKittrick was obviously familiar with it and knew immediately what was being said.

'I *won't* shut up!' McKittrick said. 'I'm not giving anything away! He knows as well as I do, he couldn't stand for me to be successful! He shouldn't have interfered! If he'd let me do things *my* way, I would have been a hero!'

'Heroes don't let themselves get mixed up with scum like Giordano.'

'Hey, since the good guys decided to kick me out, I thought I'd see how the *bad* guys treated me. A hell of a lot better, thank you very much. I'm beginning to think there's not a whole lot of difference.' McKittrick laughed. 'And the money is definitely an improvement.'

'But you turned against Giordano.'

'I finally realized there's only one side in any of this – mine. And you're on the *wrong* side. Now it's payback time.' McKittrick held up an object. For a moment, Decker thought it was a weapon. Then he recognized the homing device. 'I'm not as sloppy as you think. After you phoned, I kept asking myself, how did you find me? Back at the drop site, I threw the briefcase away, just in case it was bugged. But I never thought of the money itself. So I went through every bundle, and guess what I found in a hollow you cut out.'

McKittrick pressed a button that lowered the driver's window. Furious, he hurled the homing device into a ditch that he sped past. 'So who's the smart guy now? Whoever's with you won't be able to follow. You're mine.'

McKittrick turned onto a side road, pulled onto the tree-lined shoulder, stopped, and shut off the Pontiac's headlights. In the darkness, rain drummed on the roof. The rapid flapping of the windshield wipers was matched by the beat of Decker's heart as lightning flashed and he saw McKittrick aiming a pistol at him.

'I can hide for quite a while on a million dollars,' McKittrick said. 'But I don't have to hide at all if you're not chasing me.'

McKittrick steadied his finger on the trigger.

'We had a bargain,' Decker said.

'Yeah, and I bet you meant to keep your end of it. Get out of the car.'

Decker's tension increased.

'*Get out of the car*,' McKittrick repeated. 'Do it. Open the door.'

Decker eased away from McKittrick, putting his hand on the passenger door. The moment he opened the latch and stepped out, McKittrick would shoot him, he knew. Frantic, he tried to think of a way to escape. He could attempt to distract McKittrick and get his hands on the pistol, but that still left the man in the back seat, who would fire the moment Decker made an aggressive move. I can dive for the ditch, he thought. In the night and the rain, they might not be able to get a good shot at me.

Muscles cramping, he eased the door open, praying, ready to scramble out.

'Does she really love you?' McKittrick asked. 'Was she aware of who you were? Was she using you?'

'Yes, that's what I want to know,' Decker said.

'Ask her.'

'What?'

'Go back and ask her.'

'What are you talking about?'

The smugness had returned to McKittrick's voice. He was playing a game, but Decker couldn't tell what the game was. 'I'm keeping my part of the bargain. You're free. Go back to Diana Scolari. Find out if she's worth the price you were willing to pay.'

'For *Beth Dwyer*.'

'You really are a goddamned romantic.'

The instant Decker's shoes touched the rainsoaked side of the road, McKittrick stomped the gas pedal, and the Pontiac roared away from Decker, barely missing his feet. As the door slammed shut from the force of the Pontiac's acceleration, McKittrick laughed. Then the car's taillights receded rapidly. Decker was alone in the dark and the rain.

ELEVEN

1

The realization of what had just happened didn't immediately take possession of Decker. He seemed to exist in a dream. Shuddering from the numbness of the shock that he had not been killed, he doubted the reality that McKittrick had let him go. McKittrick's disturbing laughter echoed in his mind. Something was wrong.

But Decker didn't have time to think about it. He was too busy turning, racing back toward the dim lights of Closter. Despite his exhaustion from too little sleep and not enough food, despite the pain from his numerous injuries and the chill of his wet clothes further draining his strength, it seemed to him that he had never run faster or with a fiercer resolve. The storm gusted at him, but he ignored it, charging through the darkness. He stretched his legs to their maximum. His lungs heaved. Nothing could stop him from getting to Beth. In his frenzy, he neared the town's limits. He had a wavering glimpse of the Oldsmobile, where Esperanza had parked it off the street near the motel. Then the motel loomed, its red neon sign shimmering. Almost delirious, he charged around the corner, mustered a last burst of speed, and surged past darkened units toward the light gleaming from room nineteen's open door.

Inside, Beth was slumped on the side of the bed. Esperanza held a glass of water to her lips. The gag and the ropes were on the floor. Aside from those details, every object in the room

351

might as well have been invisible. Decker's attention was riveted on Beth. Her long auburn hair was tangled, her eyes sunken, her cheeks gaunt. He hurried to her, fell to his knees, and tenderly raised his hands to her face. Only vaguely did he have an idea of his unrecognizable appearance, of his drenched hair stuck flat to his skull, of the scrapes on his face oozing blood, of his soaked torn clothes smeared with mud. Nothing mattered except that Beth was safe.

'Are . . . ?' His voice was so hoarse, so strained by emotion, that it startled him. 'Are you all right? Did they hurt you?'

'No.' Beth quivered. She seemed to be doubting her sanity. 'You're bleeding. Your face is . . .'

Decker felt pain in his eyes and throat and realized that he was sobbing.

'Lie down, Decker,' Esperanza said. 'You're in worse shape than Beth is.'

Decker tasted the salt from his tears as he put his arms around Beth and held her as gently as his powerful emotions would allow. This was the moment he had been waiting for. All of his determination and suffering had been directed toward this instant.

'You're hurt,' Beth said.

'It doesn't matter.' He kissed her, never wanting to let her go. 'I can't tell you how worried I was. Are you sure you're all right?'

'Yes. They didn't hit me. The ropes and the gag were the hardest part. And the thirst. I couldn't get enough water.'

'I mean it, Decker,' Esperanza said. 'You look awful. You better lie down.'

But instead of obeying, Decker took the glass of water and urged Beth to sip more of it. He kept repeating in amazement, 'You're alive,' as if in the darkest portion of his soul he had questioned whether he would in fact be able to save her.

'I was so scared.'

'Don't think about it.' Decker lovingly stroked her tangled hair. 'It's over now. McKittrick's gone.'

'And the woman.'

'Woman?'

'She terrified me.'

Decker leaned back, studying Beth in confusion. '*What* woman?'

'With McKittrick.'

Decker felt his stomach turn cold. 'But all I saw was a man.'

'In the raincoat. With the rainhat.'

A chill spread through his already chilled body. 'That was a *woman*?'

Beth shuddered. 'She was beautiful. But her voice was grotesque. She had something wrong with her throat. A puckered hole. A scar, as if she'd been struck with something there.'

Decker now understood why the guttural repugnant voice had been familiar. However distorted, there had been something about it that suggested an accent. An *Italian* accent. 'Listen carefully. Was she tall? Trim hips? Short dark hair? Did she look Italian?'

'Yes. How did—'

'My God, did McKittrick ever call her by name? Did he use the name—'

'Renata.'

'We have to get out of here.' Decker stood, drawing Beth to her feet, looking frantically around the room.

'What's wrong?'

'Did she leave anything? A suitcase? A package?'

'When they were getting ready to go, she took a shopping bag into the other room but she never brought it back.'

'*We have to get out of here*,' Decker shouted, urging Beth and

353

Esperanza toward the open door. 'She's an expert in explosives. I'm afraid it's a bomb!'

He pushed them outside into the rain, fearfully recalling another rainstorm fifteen months ago when he had crouched behind a crate in a courtyard in Rome.

Renata had detonated a bomb in an upper apartment. As wreckage cascaded from the fourth balcony, the ferocity of the flames illuminated the courtyard. Decker's peripheral vision detected motion in the far left corner of the courtyard, near the door that he and McKittrick had come through. But the motion wasn't from McKittrick. The figure that emerged from the shadows of a stairway was Renata. Holding a pistol equipped with a sound-suppressor, she shot repeatedly toward the courtyard, all the while running toward the open doorway. Behind the crate, Decker sprawled on wet cobblestones and squirmed forward on his elbows and knees. He reached the side of the crate, caught a glimpse of Renata nearing the exit, aimed through the rain, and shot twice. His first bullet struck the wall behind her. His second hit her in the throat. She clutched her windpipe, blood spewing. As her brothers dragged her out of sight into the dark street, Decker knew that their efforts to save her were worthless. The wound would cause her throat to squeeze shut. Death from asphyxiation would occur in just a few minutes.

B*ut she hadn't died*, Decker realized in horror. In the weeks and months to come, McKittrick must have gone looking for her. Had she and McKittrick gotten together? Had she convinced him that she wasn't his enemy, that the Agency had used him worse than *she* had? Had *she* been directing this?

'Run!' Decker screamed. 'Get behind the Dumpster bin!' Hearing Esperanza racing next to him, he urged Beth ahead of him and suddenly felt himself being lifted off his feet by a force of air that had the impact of a giant fist. The burst of light and the roar that enveloped him were as if the heart of the electrical storm had condensed and struck him. He was weightless, couldn't see, couldn't hear, couldn't feel until with shocking immediacy he slammed onto the wet pavement behind the Dumpster bin. He rolled onto Beth to shield her from the wreckage falling around them. Something glanced off his shoulder, making him wince. Something banged near his head. Glass shattered all around him.

Then the shockwave had passed, and he was conscious of the painful ringing in his ears, of the rain, of people shouting from nearby buildings, of Beth moving under him. She coughed, and he feared that he might be smothering her. Dazed, he gathered the strength to roll off her, hardly aware of the chunks of cinderblock that lay around them.

'Are you hurt?'

'My leg.'

Hands shaking, he checked it. The light from a fire in the remnants of the motel rooms showed him a thick shard of wood projecting from her right thigh. He pulled it out, alarmed by how much blood pulsed from the wound. 'A tourniquet. You need a—' He tugged off his belt and cinched it around the flesh above the jagged hole in her leg.

Someone groaned. A shadow moved behind the Dumpster bin. Slowly, a figure sat up, and Decker shook with relief, knowing that Esperanza was still alive.

'Decker!'

The voice didn't come from Esperanza. The ringing in Decker's ears was so great that he had trouble identifying the direction from which the voice shouted.

'*Decker!*'

Then Decker understood, and he stared past the reflection of flames on the pools of water in the parking lot. In the street out front, McKittrick's Pontiac idled. Prevented by wreckage from entering the lot, the car was positioned so the driver's window faced the motel. McKittrick must have followed Decker back to town. His features contorted with rage, he leaned out the open window, holding up a detonator, screaming, 'I could have set it off when you were inside! But that would have been too easy! I'm just getting started! Keep looking behind you! One night, when you least expect it, we'll blow you and your bitch apart!'

In the distance, a siren wailed. McKittrick raised something else, and Decker had just enough strength to roll with Beth toward the protection of the Dumpster bin before McKittrick fired an automatic weapon, bullets slamming against the metal container. Behind the bin, Esperanza pulled out a pistol and shot back. The next thing, Decker heard tires squealing on wet pavement, and McKittrick's Pontiac roared away.

2

A second siren joined the first.

'We have to get out of here,' Esperanza said.

'Help me with Beth.'

Each man took an arm, lifting her, struggling to hurry with her into the darkness at the back of the motel. A crowd had begun to gather. Decker brushed past two men who ran from an apartment building behind the motel.

'What happened?' one of them shouted.

'A propane tank blew up!' Decker told him.

'Do you need help?'

'No! We're taking this woman to a hospital! Look for other survivors!' Holding Beth, Decker couldn't help feeling her wince with each hurried step he took.

In the murky alley on the opposite side of the motel, he and Esperanza paused just before they reached the street, waiting while several people raced past toward the fire. Immediately they carried Beth unseen along the street toward where the Oldsmobile was parked.

'Drive!' Decker said. 'I'll stay in the back with her!'

Slamming his door, Esperanza turned the ignition key. On the rear seat, Decker steadied Beth to keep her from rolling onto the floor. The Oldsmobile sped away.

'How *is* she?' Esperanza asked.

'The tourniquet has the bleeding stopped, but I've got to release it. She'll get gangrene if blood doesn't circulate through her leg.' Alarmed by a spurt of blood when he loosened the belt, Decker quickly reached into his travel bag on the floor in the back, and grabbed a shirt, shoving it against the wound, creating a pressure bandage. He leaned close to Beth where she lay on the back seat. 'Are you sick to your stomach? Are you seeing double?'

'Dizzy.'

'Hang on. We'll get you to a doctor.'

'*Where?*' Esperanza asked.

'Back in Manhattan. We were headed west when we came into Closter. Take the next left turn and the next left turn after that.'

'To go east. Back to the Interstate,' Esperanza said.

'Yes. And then south.' Decker stroked Beth's cheek. 'Don't be afraid. I'm here. I'll take care of you. You're going to be all right.'

Beth squeezed his hand. 'McKittrick's insane.'

'Worse than in Rome,' Decker said.

'Rome?' Esperanza frowned back at him. 'What are you talking about?'

Decker hesitated. He had been determined to stay quiet about

Rome. But Beth and Esperanza had nearly been killed because of what had happened there. They had a right to know the truth. Their lives might depend on it. So he told them . . . about the twenty-three dead Americans . . . about Renata, McKittrick, and that rainy courtyard where Renata had been shot.

'She's a *terrorist*?' Esperanza said.

'McKittrick fell in love with her,' Decker explained. 'After the operation in Rome went to hell, he refused to believe she had tricked him. I think he went after her to make her tell him the truth, but she convinced him she really did love him, and now she's using him again. To get at me. To get her hands on the money Giordano gave him.'

'She hates you.' Beth hardly managed the strength to speak. 'All she could talk about was getting even. She's obsessed with making you suffer.'

'Take it easy. Don't try to talk.'

'No. This is important. Listen. She kept ranting to McKittrick about something you did to her brothers. What did you do?'

'*Brothers?*' Decker jerked his head back. Again he suffered the nightmarish memory of what had happened in that courtyard in Rome.

As wreckage from Renata's bomb had cascaded, a movement to Decker's right had made him turn. A thin, dark-haired man in his early twenties, one of Renata's brothers, rose from behind garbage cans. The man hadn't been prepared for Renata to detonate the bomb so soon. Although he had a pistol, he didn't aim at Decker – his attention was totally distracted by a scream on the other side of the courtyard. With gaping dismay, the young man saw one of his brothers swatting at flames on his clothes and in his hair that had been ignited by the falling, burning wreckage.

Decker shot them both.

* * *

'It's a blood feud,' Decker said, appalled. A wave of nausea swept through him as he understood that Renata hated him even more than McKittrick did. Decker imagined them reinforcing each other's malice, feeding off it, becoming more obsessed with paying him back. But how to get even? They must have debated it endlessly. What revenge would be the most satisfying? They could have just gunned me down in a drive-by shooting, Decker thought. The trouble is, merely killing me wouldn't have been good enough. They wanted to make me afraid. They wanted to make me suffer.

But Decker wasn't only thinking this. Beth's shocked expression made him realize that he was saying it out loud. He couldn't stop himself. His anguished thoughts kept pouring out. 'Nothing would have happened in Santa Fe if McKittrick and Renata hadn't been fixated on me. McKittrick had been forced out of the CIA, but the official story was, he quit. On paper, he looked impressive enough for the US Marshals Service to accept him. He'd been keeping track of where I was living. When you were assigned to him and when he found out the house next to mine was for sale, the plan came together.'

Decker braced himself. His ordeal of saving Beth had been aimed toward this moment, and now the moment had come. He couldn't put off the question any longer. He had to know. 'Were you aware of my background when you first met me?'

Her eyes still shut, Beth didn't answer. Her chest heaved, agitated.

'Before you came to my office, did McKittrick tell you I'd worked for the CIA? Did he instruct you to play up to me, to do your best to make me feel close to you so I'd want to spend all my spare time with you and, in effect, be your next-door-neighbor bodyguard?'

Beth remained silent, breathing with difficulty.

'That would have been their revenge,' Decker said. 'To manipulate me into falling in love with you, then to betray you to the mob. By destroying your life, they hoped to destroy mine. And the mob would pay them for their pleasure.'

'I see lights,' Esperanza interrupted, steering swiftly around a corner. 'That's the Interstate ahead.'

'I have to know, Beth. *Did McKittrick tell you to try to make me fall in love with you?*'

She still didn't answer. How could he make her tell him the truth? Abruptly, as they reached the Interstate, the glare of passing headlights spilled into the backseat, showing Decker that Beth hadn't closed her eyes because she was trying to avoid his gaze. Her body was limp, her breathing now shallow. She had passed out.

3

It was three a.m. when Esperanza, following Decker's directions, sped to a stop at the brownstone on Manhattan's West 82nd Street. That late at night, the affluent neighborhood was quiet, the rainy street deserted. No one was around to see Decker and Esperanza carry Beth from the car and into the brownstone's vestibule. Worried by her increasing weakness, Decker pressed the intercom button for apartment eight. As he anticipated, instead of having to push the button several times and wait for a sleepy voice to ask what he wanted, he received an immediate response. The person upstairs had been alerted by an emergency phone call Decker had made from a service station along the Interstate. A buzzer sounded, the signal that the lock on the vestibule's inner door had been electronically released.

Decker and Esperanza hurried through, found the elevator waiting for them, and went up to the fourth floor, frustrated by the elevator's slow rise. The moment the elevator's door opened, a man wearing rumpled clothes that made him look as if he had dressed quickly hurried from an apartment and helped to carry Beth inside. The man was tall and exceedingly thin with a high forehead and a salt-and-pepper mustache. Decker heard a noise behind him and turned to see a heavy set woman with gray hair and a worried look shut and lock the door behind them.

The man directed Decker and Esperanza to the left into a brightly lit kitchen, where a plastic sheet had been spread across the table, other sheets on the floor. Surgical instruments were laid out on a protected counter. Water boiled on the stove. The woman, who wore hospital greens, blurted to Decker, 'Wash your hands.'

Decker obeyed, crowding with the man and the woman at the sink, using a bottle of bitter-smelling liquid to disinfect his hands. The woman helped the man put on a surgical mask, a Plexiglas face shield, and latex gloves, then gestured for Decker to help *her* put on a mask, shield, and gloves. Without pausing, the woman used scissors to cut Beth's blood stained slacks, exposing her right leg all the way up to her underwear. Now that the pressure bandage was removed, the jagged hole spurted blood.

'When did this happen?' The doctor pressed a gloved finger against the flesh next to the wound. The bleeding stopped.

'Forty minutes ago,' Decker said. Rainwater dripped from him onto the plastic sheet on the floor.

'How soon did you restrict the flow of blood?'

'Almost immediately.'

'You saved her life.'

While the woman used surgical sponges to wipe blood from the wound, the doctor swabbed alcohol onto Beth's injured leg, then gave her an injection. But despite what the doctor explained was a painkiller, Beth moaned when the doctor used surgical tweezers to examine the interior of the wound and determine if there was any debris inside.

'I can't be certain. This will have to be quick and crude, just to get the bleeding stopped. She needs an X-ray. Intravenous fluids. Possibly microsurgery if the femoral artery was nicked.' The doctor gave Beth another injection, this time of what he explained was an antibiotic. 'But she'll need more antibiotics on a regular schedule after she leaves here.'

The woman swabbed the wound with a brownish disinfectant while the doctor peered close to the wound, studying it with spectacles, one lens of which had a small additional lens that he swiveled into place. As soon as the woman finished disinfecting the area around the wound, she put a finger where the doctor had been applying pressure, allowing him to begin suturing.

'You shouldn't have called me,' the doctor complained to Decker as he worked.

'I didn't have a choice.' Decker studied Beth, whose face, moist with rain and sweat, was the gray of porridge.

'But you're not with the organization any longer,' the doctor said.

'I didn't know you had heard.'

'Evidently. Otherwise, you wouldn't have presumed to contact me.'

'I meant what I said. I didn't have a choice. Besides, if you knew I wasn't sanctioned, you didn't have to agree to help me.' Decker held Beth's hand. Her fingers clutched his as if she was drowning.

'In that respect, *I'm* the one who didn't have a choice.' The doctor continued suturing. 'As you so vividly told me on the phone, you intended to cause trouble in this building if I didn't help.'

'I doubt the neighbors would have approved of your sideline.'

The woman peered up angrily from where she assisted. 'You contaminated our *home*. You know where the clinic is. You could have—'

'There wasn't time,' Decker said. 'You once treated *me* here.'

'That was an *exception*.'

'I know of *other* exceptions you made. For a generous fee. I assume that's another reason you agreed to help.'

The doctor frowned up from the sutures he applied. 'What generous fee did you have in mind?'

'In my travel bag, I have an eighteen-carat gold chain, a gold bracelet, a jade ring, and a dozen gold coins.'

'Not money?' The doctor frowned harder.

'They're worth around twelve thousand dollars. Put them in a sock for when times get tough. Believe me, they come in handy if you have to leave the country in a hurry and you can't trust going to a bank.'

'That hasn't been a problem of ours.'

'To date,' Decker said. 'I suggest you do the best job you can on this woman.'

'Are you threatening me?'

'You must have misunderstood. I was cheering you on.'

The doctor frowned even more severely, then concentrated on applying more sutures. 'Under the circumstances, my fee for this procedure is twenty thousand dollars.'

'What?'

'I consider the items you mentioned only a down payment.' The doctor straightened, no longer working. 'Is my fee a problem?'

Decker stared at the half-closed hole in Beth's leg. 'No.'

'I thought not.' The doctor resumed working. 'Where are the items?'

'Over here. In my travel bag.' Decker turned toward where he had dropped it when he helped carry Beth into the kitchen.

'And what about the remaining amount?'

'You'll get it.'

'How can I be certain?'

'You have my word. If that isn't good enough—'

Esperanza interrupted the tension. 'Look, I feel useless just standing here. There must be something I can do to help.'

'The blood in the hallway and the elevator,' the woman said. 'The neighbors will call the police if they see it. Clean it up.'

Her peremptory tone suggested that she thought she was speaking to an Hispanic servant, but although Esperanza's dark eyes flashed, he only responded, 'What can I use?'

'Under the sink, there's a bucket, rags, and disinfectant. Make sure you wear rubber gloves.'

As Esperanza gathered the materials and left, the woman applied a blood-pressure cuff to Beth's left arm. She studied the gauge. Air stopped hissing from the cuff.

'What are the numbers?' Decker asked.

'A hundred over sixty.'

Normal was one-hundred-and-twenty over eighty. 'Low, but not in the danger zone.'

The woman nodded. 'She's very lucky.'

'Yeah, you can see how lucky she looks.'

'You don't look so good yourself.'

The phone rang, its jangle so intrusive that Decker, the doctor, and his wife tensed, staring at it. It was mounted to the wall, next to the Sub-Zero refrigerator. It rang again.

'Who'd be calling at this hour?'

'I have a patient in intensive care.' The doctor continued working. 'I left instructions for the hospital to phone me if the patient's condition worsened. When *you* called, that's what I thought it would be about.' He held up his blood-smeared gloves and gestured toward those on his wife. 'But I can't answer the phone with these.'

It rang again.

'And I don't want you to stop what you're doing.' Decker picked up the phone. 'Hello.'

'Awfully predictable, Decker.'

Hearing McKittrick's smug voice, Decker stopped breathing. He clutched the phone with knuckle-whitening force.

'What's the matter?' McKittrick asked on the other end. 'Not feeling sociable? Don't want to talk. No problem. I'll carry the conversation for both of us.'

'Who is it?' the doctor asked.

Decker held up his free hand, warning the man to be quiet.

'Maybe I'm not the idiot you thought I was, huh?' McKittrick asked. 'When I saw you cinching your belt around the woman's leg, I said to myself, where's the logical place he'll take her? And by God, I was right. I was watching from a doorway down the street when you arrived. You must have forgotten *I* was taught about this place, too. All of a sudden, you're as predictable as hell. You know what I think?'

Decker didn't answer.

'I asked you a question,' McKittrick demanded. 'You'd better talk to me, or I'm going to make this much worse than I planned.'

'All right. What are you thinking?'

'I think you're losing your touch.'

'I'm tired of this,' Decker said. 'Pay attention. Our deal still holds. Leave us alone. I won't give you another thought.'

'Is that a fact?'

'I won't come after you.'

'It seems to me, old buddy, that you're missing the point. *I'm* coming after *you*.'

'You mean you and *Renata*.'

'So you figured out who that was in the car?'

'Your tradecraft didn't use to be this good. She's been teaching you.'

'Yeah? Well, she also wants to teach *you* something, Decker – what it's like to lose somebody you love. Look out the window. Toward the front of the building.'

Click. The connection was broken.

4

Slowly, Decker lowered the phone.

'Who *was* that?' the doctor insisted.

Look out the window? Decker asked himself in dismay. Why? So I'll show myself? So I'll make myself a target? Sickeningly, he remembered that Esperanza wasn't in the room. He had left the apartment to clean the blood from the hallway and the elevator. Had he started in the lobby? Had McKittrick—?

'Esperanza!' Decker raced from the kitchen. He yanked the front door open and hurried out into the corridor, hoping to see Esperanza but finding the area deserted. The needle above the closed elevator door indicated that the compartment was at the ground floor. About to push the UP button, Decker recalled how slow the elevator had been. He charged down the stairs.

'*Esperanza!*' Decker took the steps three at a time, the impact of his shoes echoing in the stairwell. He reached the third floor and then the second. 'ESPERANZA!' He thought he heard a muffled voice shout a reply. Yelling, 'Get out of the lobby! Take cover!' Decker jumped down a half-dozen steps toward the final floor. He heard a heavy clatter, as if a pail was being dropped. 'McKittrick and Renata are outside! Get up the stairs!' He swung toward the final continuation of the stairwell, reached the midway landing, swung again, and was shocked to see Esperanza staring up at him, not moving.

Decker leapt, diving down the remainder of the stairs, colliding against Esperanza's chest, knocking him past the open door of the elevator toward an alcove in the lobby.

Immediately the lobby was filled with blazing thunder. A deafening blast from the street disintegrated the lobby's glass door. Striking the floor with Esperanza, Decker was aware of shrapnel zipping through the air, chunks of wood, metal, and glass hurtling past him, objects slamming against the walls. Then the lobby became unnaturally still, as if the air had been sucked out of it. Certainly that was how Decker felt, out of breath. Lying next to Esperanza in the alcove, he tried to get his chest to work, to take in air. Slowly, painfully, he managed.

Through smoke, he peered up, seeing shards of glass embedded in the walls. He risked a glance beyond the lobby's gaping entrance toward where they had parked the Oldsmobile hurriedly in a no-parking space in front of the building. The car, the source of the explosion, was now a twisted, gutted, flaming wreck.

'Jesus,' Esperanza said.

'Hurry. Up the stairs.'

They struggled to stand. As Decker lurched toward the stairs, he looked to the side and saw a figure – silhouetted by the flames, obscured by the smoke – rush past the entrance. The figure threw something. Hearing it strike the floor, Decker charged up the stairwell with Esperanza. The object made a bouncing sound. Decker reached the midway landing and swung with Esperanza toward the continuation of the stairs. Below, the object whacked against something, metal against wood. The elevator? The doors had been open. Had the grenade landed in—

The explosion sent a shockwave through the stairwell,

slamming Decker and Esperanza to their hands and knees. The shockwave was amplified by the confines of the elevator shaft, blowing up and down as well as to the side, making the stairwell shudder, cracking the exterior wall of the shaft. Plaster collapsed. Flames filled the lobby, smoke drifting upward.

With greater effort, Decker and Esperanza straightened, climbing. At the next landing, the door to the elevator had been blown apart. Hurrying past the gaping shaft, Decker saw flames and smoke in there. He whirled as an apartment door was yanked open. An elderly man in pajamas rushed out to see what had happened, his eyes wide with shock when he saw the flames and smoke. An alarm started blaring.

'There's been an explosion!' Decker yelled. 'The lobby's on fire! Is there another way out of the building?'

The man's lips moved three times before he managed to make a sound. 'The fire escape in back.'

'Use it!'

Decker climbed higher, following Esperanza who hadn't paused. At the next floor, other occupants of the building hurried out, dismayed by the smoke that was rising.

'Phone the fire department!' Decker yelled as he passed them. 'The elevator's been gutted! The stairway's in flames! Use the fire escape!'

He lost count of the floors. Expecting *3*, he reached *4*. The door to the doctor's apartment was open. Rushing into the kitchen, he found Esperanza arguing with the doctor.

'She can't be moved!' the doctor protested. 'Her stitches will pull open!'

'To hell with the stitches! If she stays here, she'll burn to death! We'll *all* burn to death!'

'There's supposed to be a fire escape!' Decker said. '*Where is it?*'

The doctor pointed along the corridor. 'Through the window in the spare bedroom.'

Decker leaned close to Beth. 'We have to lift you. I'm afraid this is going to hurt.'

'McKittrick's out there?'

'He meant what he said at the motel. He and Renata are hunting me. Sooner than I expected.'

'Do what you have to.' Beth licked her dry lips. 'I can handle the pain.'

'I'll get the window open,' Esperanza said.

'Help us,' Decker told the doctor and his wife.

Startling him, the phone rang again.

This time, Decker had no doubt who was calling. He grabbed it, shouting, 'You've had your fun! For Christ's sake, stop!'

'But we've only just started,' McKittrick said. 'Try to make this more interesting, will you? So far you've done everything we anticipated. Who's an idiot now?' McKittrick broke out into bellowing laughter.

Decker slammed down the phone and spun toward Beth, noting the thick plastic sheet she lay upon. 'Is that strong enough to hold her?'

'There's one way to find out.' Esperanza came back from opening the window in the guest room. 'You take the head. I'll take the feet.' Using the plastic sheet, they lifted Beth off the table and carried her from the kitchen.

The doctor went out to the hallway and hurried back, appalled. 'There are flames in the stairwell and the elevator shaft.'

'I told you we need help!' Esperanza looked angrily over his shoulder as he carried the section of the sheet that supported Beth's legs.

'Get the jewelry,' the doctor told his wife, and rushed from the room.

'And don't forget the gold coins, you bastard!' Decker shouted. Bent over, moving backward, holding the portion of the sheet that supported Beth's shoulders, he worked into the bedroom. After bumping painfully against the back wall, he turned and stared out through the open window, its curtains blowing inward from the force of the rain. A night-shrouded fire escape led down the back of the building to what may have been an interior garden. He heard panicked residents of the building rushing awkwardly down the metal fire escape.

'Predictable,' Decker said. 'That's where Renata and McKittrick expect us to go.'

'What are you talking about?' Esperanza asked.

'It's a trap. McKittrick knows about this place. He's had time to check the layout. He and Renata will be waiting down there for us.'

'But we can't stay here! We'll be trapped in the fire!'

'There's another way.'

'Up,' Beth said.

Decker nodded. 'Exactly.'

Esperanza looked incredulous.

'To the roof,' Decker said. 'We'll move across several buildings, reach another fire escape near the end of the block, and use *it*. McKittrick won't know where we've gone.'

'But what if the flames spread through other buildings and cut us off?' Esperanza asked.

'No choice,' Decker said. 'We'll be easy targets if we try to carry Beth down this fire escape.' He eased Beth headfirst through the window until her back was supported by the window sill. Then he squirmed out past her, feeling cold rain pelt him again as he guided her farther through the window. In a moment, Beth was lying on the wet slick metal platform, rain striking her face.

Decker touched her forehead. 'How are you doing?'

'Never better.'

'Right.'

'I don't deserve you.'

'Wrong.' Decker kissed her cheek.

Esperanza scrambled out to join them. 'Whatever was in that bomb, it must have been powerful. The flames are spreading fast. The front of the apartment's on fire.'

Decker peered through the rain toward the top of the building not far above them. 'We'd better get up there before the flames reach the roof.' As they lifted Beth, Decker heard approaching sirens.

'There'll be police cars as well as fire trucks.' Esperanza followed Decker up the fire escape. 'McKittrick and Renata won't try anything against us in front of the police.'

'Or they'll count on the confusion.' Decker carried Beth higher. 'The police won't have time to realize what's happening.'

Flames burst from a lower window, illuminating them on the metal stairs.

'Jesus, now they've seen us.' Decker tensed, anticipating the impact of a bullet into his chest.

'Maybe not.' Esperanza hurried to work higher. 'Or if they did, it might not be obvious we're going up instead of down.'

They came to a landing. Beth groaned as Decker was forced to turn her awkwardly to start up the final section toward the roof. His shoes slipped on the slick wet metal, making him stumble, almost dropping her.

'We're close.'

The fire roared.

'Just a little farther.'

The sirens reached a crescendo on the opposite side of the building. Backing up, Decker felt his hips bump against the roof's waist-high parapet. At the limit of his energy, he stretched one leg and then the other over the parapet, hefted Beth over, waited for Esperanza to follow, and finally set Beth down. Breathing fast, he slumped.

'Are you okay?' Esperanza stooped next to him.

'Need a little rest is all.'

'I can't guess why.' Esperanza squinted through the rain. 'At least this parapet keeps us from being targets.'

Decker's arms and legs were numb with fatigue. 'McKittrick and Renata will wonder why we're not coming down. We have to get away from here before they figure out what we're doing.'

'Take another minute to catch your breath,' Beth murmured.

'No time.'

Beth tried to raise herself. 'Maybe I can walk.'

'No. You'd rip out your stitches. You'd bleed to death.' Decker calculated: to the left, there were only a few buildings before the end of the block. The fire escapes there would be too close to where McKittrick and Renata waited below. To the right, though, there were more than enough roofs to get them away from the area.

Decker crouched and lifted Beth. He waited for Esperanza to do the same, then backed away from the parapet, guided by lights in other buildings and the reflection of flames bursting from the windows of the brownstone.

'Behind you,' Esperanza said. 'A ventilation duct.'

Decker veered around the waist-high obstacle, turning his head to avoid inhaling the thick smoke spewing out.

'The housing for the elevator pulleys,' Esperanza warned.

Decker veered around that as well, alarmed that he could see flames through cracks in the housing.

'It's spreading faster.'

More sirens wailed at the front of the building.

Decker glanced behind him and saw that the next building was one story taller. '*How are we going to—*'

372

'On my right,' Esperanza said. 'A metal ladder bolted to the wall.'

Decker backed against the ladder. 'The only way I can think to do this is—' He struggled to breathe. 'Beth, I don't have the strength to carry you over my shoulder. Do you think you can stand on your uninjured leg?'

'Anything.'

'I'll climb up while Esperanza steadies you. When I lean down, you reach up. I'll lift you by your hands.' Decker mentally corrected himself – by her *left* arm, the one that hadn't been wounded in Santa Fe.

After he and Esperanza helped her to stand, propping her against the brick wall, Decker gripped the ladder and mustered the effort to climb to the next roof. At the top, his back pelted by rain, he leaned over the edge. 'Ready?'

Decker strained to lift her. He almost panicked when he discovered that his strength was failing, that he was able to raise her only a few feet.

Amazingly, the effort became easier.

'I'm resting my good leg on a rung in the ladder,' Beth said. 'Just pull me up a little at a time.'

Decker grimaced, lifting harder. Slowly, rung after rung, Beth came up. Decker moved his grip from her hand to her upper arm and shoulder, pulling higher. Then he saw the murky outline of her drenched head, put his arms under hers, and hoisted her onto the roof. He set her down and sprawled beside her.

Esperanza's shoes thrummed on the metal ladder. In a rush, he was at the top, the plastic sheet tucked under his arm. Behind him, flames spewed from ventilator ducts and the housing for the elevator pulleys. The fire escape was engulfed by smoke.

'Even if we wanted to, we can't go back that way,' Decker said.

They spread out the plastic sheet, set Beth onto it, and lifted her, making their way through another maze of ducts and housings. Decker stumbled over a pipe. He bumped past a TV antenna.

The reflection of flames revealed the edge of the building and the drop down to the next one.

'It won't be long now,' Decker said.

A thunderous shockwave hit him, jolting him off his feet. Unable to keep a grip on Beth, he landed next to her, hearing her scream. Only then did he have time to realize—

It hadn't been thunder.

It had been another bomb.

The detonation echoed through the night. Trembling, Decker lay on his chest, drew his pistol, and stared ahead toward where a shed-like protrusion from the roof had disintegrated.

A voice yelled, 'You're being predictable again!'

Jesus, Decker thought. *McKittrick's on the roof!*

'Walked right into it again, didn't you?' McKittrick yelled. 'I gave you fair warning, and you still did what I expected! You're not as goddamned smart as you think you are!'

'Let it go!' Decker shouted. 'Our business with each other is over!'

'Not until you're dead!'

The voice came from somewhere to the left. It sounded as if McKittrick was hiding behind the elevator housing. Fingers tight on his pistol, Decker rose to a crouch, preparing to charge. 'The police heard that explosion, McKittrick! Now they know this is more than a fire! They'll seal off the area and check everybody who tries to leave! You won't get away!'

'They'll think it was combustibles blowing up in the building!'

Combustibles? Decker frowned. It wasn't the kind of word McKittrick would normally use, but it definitely was a word he would learn from a bomb expert. There wasn't any doubt – Renata was teaching him.

And she was somewhere close.

'Paint cans! Turpentine! Cleaning fluid!' McKittrick yelled. 'At a fire, the police worry about that stuff a lot! Now they'll be afraid something else will blow up! They'll keep their distance!'

Behind Decker, flames burst from the lower roof. We can't go back, and the fires will soon reach us if we stay here, he thought. 'Esperanza?' he whispered.

'Ready when you are. Which side do you want?'

'Left.'

'I'll flank you.'

'Now.' Decker sprinted through puddles toward a large ventilation duct, then toward another. But as he prepared to charge toward the elevator housing, it ceased to exist. A brilliant roar blasted it into pieces. Decker was thrown flat, chunks of wreckage flying over him, clattering around him.

'You guessed *wrong*, Decker! That's not where I am! And I'm not to your right, either! Where your friend's trying to sneak up on me!'

A moment later, in that direction, a blast tore a huge chunk out of the roof. Decker thought he heard a scream, but whether it was from Esperanza or occupants of the building, he couldn't tell.

He felt paralyzed, uncertain where to move. McKittrick must have set charges all over this roof and the next ones, he thought. But how would McKittrick have had time if he was calling from a payphone?

The appalling answer was immediate and obvious. McKittrick *hadn't* been using a payphone. He had been calling from a *cellular* phone. From the roof. While he was placing the charges. That must have been Renata who blew up the Oldsmobile in front of the building and then threw the fire bomb into the lobby. *She's* down in the courtyard. That way, whichever direction we chose, up or down, we were trapped.

Are trapped, Decker thought. The fire's behind us. McKittrick's ahead of us.

What about the fire escape on *this* building? Decker wondered desperately as the flames roared louder. If we can get onto it . . . Too obvious. I have to assume McKittrick rigged explosives on *it*, as well. Even if he didn't, we'd still be trapped between Renata in the courtyard and McKittrick on the roof.

With no apparent alternative, Decker rose to attempt another frantic charge toward McKittrick's voice. But the moment he did, a blast heaved the roof in front of him, knocking him back down, tearing another huge chunk from the building.

'Naughty, naughty, asshole! You didn't ask, "May I?" '

Where *is* he? Decker thought in dismay. If McKittrick was on this roof, he wouldn't be setting off bombs that he'd hidden here. He couldn't guarantee that he wouldn't blow himself up along with me. Then *where*?

Again the answer was immediate. On the *next* roof. The reflection of flames revealed that the next roof was lower. McKittrick must be on a ladder bolted to the wall or on a crate or some kind of maintenance structure. Hidden, he can peer over the top of the wall, then duck down when he sets off a bomb.

Decker aimed, saw what might have been a head inching up from the darkness beyond the building, started to pull the trigger, and stopped when he realized that what he had seen was only a wavering shadow caused by the flames.

Behind him, the blaze surged closer, its progress barely impeded by the storm.

'So what's it going to be?' McKittrick yelled. 'Are you going to wait to get barbecued? Or do you have the guts to try to come for me?'

Yeah, I'm coming for you, Decker thought fiercely. The way to do it was directly in front of him, courtesy of McKittrick – the hole that the last bomb had blown in the roof.

Responding to a sickening flow of heat from the roof behind him, Decker squirmed through puddles, reached the dark hole, gripped its sides, lowered his legs, dangled, and dropped.

5

He imagined jagged planks from the roof, pointing upright, about to impale him. What he struck instead was a table that collapsed from the force of his landing and threw him to the side where he struck a padded chair that tilted, tumbling him to the wreckage-strewn floor. At least, those were the objects he *thought* he struck – the room's draperies were closed; the darkness was almost absolute.

From above, through the hole in the roof, he heard McKittrick yell, '*Don't think you can hide from me, Decker!*'

In pain, Decker struggled to his feet and pawed his way through the darkness of the room, trying to find an exit. Fire alarms blared. He touched a light switch, but he didn't dare turn it on – the abrupt illumination through the hole in the roof would make it obvious where he had gone. Heart speeding, he touched a doorknob, twisted it, and pulled the door open, but when he groped beyond it, he bumped into pungent-smelling clothes and discovered that he had opened a closet.

'*Decker?*' McKittrick yelled from above. '*If you're behind that ventilator duct—*'

An explosion shook the apartment, plaster falling. Urgent, Decker found another door, opened it, and felt a rush of excitement when he saw dim lights through windows. He was at the end of a corridor. Peering down from a rain-beaded window, he saw the chaos of fire trucks, police cars, and emergency workers at the front of the building. Lights flashed; motors rumbled; sirens wailed. Pajama-clad occupants of other buildings were hurrying out, the entrances not yet filled with flames.

Smoke swirled around him. Unable to pause to rest, he turned and hurried along the corridor to reach the back of the apartment. He passed an open door that led to murky stairs and assumed that the people who lived in this apartment had hurried out.

That possible escape route was useless to him. It didn't matter if he saved himself. He had to save Beth and Esperanza. Before the smell of fresh paint warned him, he banged against paint cans, a rolled-up dropcloth, and a ladder. Stumbling on, he reached the rear of the building and discovered that the window to the fire escape wasn't in a guest bedroom but instead at the end of the corridor.

He thrust the window upward and crawled out onto a slippery metal platform. Flames spewing from the windows in the building to his right reflected off the fire escape. He prayed that Renata would not see him from below as he squinted through the rain toward the fire escape on the undamaged brownstone to his *left*. He had hoped that the two fire escapes would be close enough that he could leap from one to the other, but now, in despair, he was forced to accept the reality that his plan was hopeless. The other fire escape was at least twenty feet away. Even under the best of circumstances, in daylight, in peak condition, he couldn't possibly reach it.

Beth's going to die up there, he told himself.

Screaming silently that there had to be a way, he squirmed back into the apartment. The smoke was thicker, making him bend over, coughing. He entered a bedroom off the corridor and opened its window, leaning out. He was now closer to the other

378

building's fire escape. It looked to be no more than ten feet away, but he still couldn't hope to leap from this window and reach the landing.

There has to be a way!

With a chill, he knew what it was. He ran back to the corridor. Flames had started to eat through the wall. Avoiding the paint cans, he picked up the ladder that he had almost tripped over, and guided it into the bedroom. Please, God, let it be long enough. Fighting for strength, he pushed it through the open window and aimed it toward the next building's fire escape.

Please!

The scrape of wood against metal made him flinch. The tip of the ladder grated as it passed over the railing on the fire-escape platform. Had McKittrick heard?

Something roared. Another explosion? Were Beth and Esperanza already dead?

No time! Decker crawled from the window and pulled himself flat across the rungs of the ladder. Rain had already slicked it. The ladder bent under his weight. It began to waver. He imagined it giving way. He shut out the nightmare of his splattering impact against the concrete of the courtyard and focused his complete attention on the fire escape he was nearing. His hands shook. Rain made him blink. Wind twisted the ladder. *No*. He stretched his left arm to its limit, strained to reach the railing, and at once, a stronger gust of wind shifted the ladder completely.

The ladder's tip scraped free of the railing. As Decker felt the vertiginous suck of gravity and began to drop with the ladder, he leapt through the darkness. His left hand grabbed the railing. But he almost lost his hold on the wet slippery metal. He flung up his other arm, snagged the fingers of his right hand around the railing, and hung breathlessly.

The ladder crashed below him. Someone down there shouted. Had McKittrick heard? Would he understand what the sounds meant? Would he come to investigate?

Dangling, straining his arms, Decker slowly pulled himself up. Rain lashed against his face. Wincing, he pulled himself higher. The railing scraped against his chest. He bent over and toppled onto the platform.

The metal-vibrating sound he caused made him flinch. Trembling, he came to his feet and drew his pistol from where he had shoved it into his pants pocket. Staring toward the roof, prepared to shoot, he crept up the last section of steps. He had never felt this exhausted. But his determination refused to surrender.

He reached the top and scanned the roof. McKittrick was to the left, three quarters of the way along a wall that led up to the roof upon which Beth and Esperanza were trapped. Halfway up a ladder bolted to the wall, McKittrick peered over the top, able to use a remote-control detonator to set off bombs without fear of injuring himself.

Decker stalked through the rain toward him.

'*Where the hell are you?*' McKittrick screamed toward the other roof. 'Answer me, or I'll blow your bitch all across Manhattan! She's lying right next to a packet of C-4! All I have to do is press this button!'

More than anything, Decker wanted to shoot, to pull the trigger again and again, but he didn't dare, for fear that McKittrick would retain the strength to press the detonator and kill Beth seconds before Decker could save her.

The clatter of heavy footsteps on the fire escape made him drop toward the cover of a ventilation duct. Indifferent to the noise they made, murky figures charged into view at the top of the metal steps. McKittrick whirled toward what now obviously were three firemen, their protective hats dripping water, their heavy rubber coats and boots slick with rain, reflecting the flames. With his left arm hooked around a rung in the ladder, McKittrick used his right to draw a pistol from his belt. He shot all three. Two of them fell where they were. The third stumbled back, toppling off the edge of the roof. The roar of the flames obscured the crack of the shots and the fireman's plummeting scream.

With his left arm still hooked around the ladder, McKittrick fumbled to put his pistol back under his belt. His left hand held the detonator. Taking advantage of McKittrick's distraction, Decker scrambled from behind the ventilation duct, reached the bottom of the ladder, and jumped, clawing his fingers toward the detonator. He hooked it, and as he dropped, he wrenched it from McKittrick's grasp, nearly yanking McKittrick off the ladder. McKittrick cursed and tried to raise his pistol again but found that it had snagged on his belt. When Decker fired, it was too late – McKittrick had given up trying to take out his pistol and instead had jumped from the ladder. As Decker's bullet slammed against the wall, McKittrick collided with Decker, sprawling with him onto the roof, rolling through puddles.

Decker's hands were full, his left with the detonator, his right with his pistol, his position too awkward for him to aim the weapon. Tumbling onto Decker, McKittrick punched and grabbed for the detonator. Decker kneed him and rolled to gain the distance to aim, but the blow to McKittrick's groin had not been solid, and McKittrick's pain was not great enough to prevent him from scuttling after Decker, striking him again, chopping at his right wrist, knocking the pistol from his hand. The weapon splashed into a puddle, and as McKittrick dove for it, Decker managed a glancing kick that knocked McKittrick away from the weapon.

Decker staggered backward. He bumped against the parapet and nearly toppled over. McKittrick groped again for the pistol under his belt. Decker had no idea where his own pistol had fallen. With a firm grip on the detonator, he pivoted to take cover on the fire escape, felt his shoe slip off something that one of the firemen had dropped, understood what it was, picked up the fire ax with his free hand, and hurled it toward McKittrick as McKittrick freed his pistol from his belt.

Decker heard McKittrick laugh. The next thing, Decker heard the whack of the ax against McKittrick's face. At first, Decker thought it was the blunt top that had struck McKittrick. But the ax didn't drop. It stayed in place, projecting from McKittrick's forehead. McKittrick wavered as if drunk, then fell.

But that was not certain enough. Decker lurched forward, picked up McKittrick's handgun, hoped that the roar of the fire would conceal the noise, and shot him three times in the head.

6

'Decker!'

He was so unnerved he didn't at first realize that Esperanza was shouting to him.

'Decker!'

Turning, he saw Esperanza on the roof where McKittrick had set off the explosives. Behind Esperanza, flames rose, hissing in the rain.

Decker took a step but faltered. Shock and fatigue had finally caught up to him. But he couldn't stop. Not when he was so close to saving Beth. Delirious, he reached the ladder. He didn't know how he got to the top. He and Esperanza made their way around gaping holes in the roof and found Beth crawling in a desperate effort to get away from the fire. Behind her, the plastic sheet she had been lying on burst into flames.

As Decker helped to lift her, flames revealed the further damage that had been done to him. 'McKittrick's dead.'

Beth murmured, 'Thank God.'

'But we still have to worry about Renata.' Supporting Beth on each side, he and Esperanza stumbled away from the heat of the blaze toward the ladder.

Again, Decker's consciousness faded. He didn't recall getting Beth to the bottom of the ladder, but he retained sufficient presence of mind to stop and lean Beth against Esperanza when he came abreast of McKittrick's body.

'What's the matter?' Esperanza asked. 'Why are you stopping?'

Too weary to explain, Decker searched through McKittrick's wet clothing and found what he needed: McKittrick's car key. On the phone, McKittrick had bragged about watching from down the street when Decker arrived at the brownstone. They had a good chance of finding the Pontiac McKittrick had used.

But that wasn't all he had to find. McKittrick had knocked Decker's pistol from his grasp. It couldn't be left behind. He tried to recreate the pattern of the fight and stumbled over where it had fallen into a puddle. But after putting it beneath his belt, he grudgingly understood that he still had something to do. Dizzy, he wavered. 'It's never over.'

'What are you talking about?'

'McKittrick. We can't leave him like this. I don't want him to be identified.'

McKittrick's dead weight was awkward as they carried the body toward the ladder. Esperanza climbed up onto the roof. With effort, Decker hefted the body to him, then climbed up after it. They grabbed McKittrick's arms and legs, moved as close to the flames as they dared, and heaved. The body disappeared into the fire. Decker threw the ax after him.

All the while, he was fearful of Renata. Wary, he and

Esperanza returned to where they had set Beth down. They continued with her across the roof, determined to use the farthest fire escape, one that wouldn't take them down toward where they thought Renata was waiting for them.

'Maybe there's another way,' Esperanza said. He guided them toward a shed-like structure on the next roof, but when he tried to open its door, he found it locked. 'Turn your faces.' Standing on an angle so his bullets wouldn't ricochet toward him, Esperanza fired repeatedly toward the wood around the lock. That section of the door disintegrated, the door jolting open when Esperanza kicked it.

Inside, away from the rain, the dimly lit stairwell was empty. There was no sound of occupants rushing down the stairs.

'They couldn't have helped but hear the sirens. The building must have been evacuated,' Decker said.

'But the fire hasn't reached this far. It's safe to use the elevator,' Esperanza said.

The elevator took them down to the ground floor. When they emerged onto the cluttered chaos of the street, overpowered by the din of engines and water being sprayed and people shouting, they struggled to make their way through the crowd. Flashing lights made them squint.

'We've got an injured woman here,' Esperanza said. 'Let us through.'

They squeezed to the right along the sidewalk, passed a fire truck, and avoided paramedics who rushed toward someone on the opposite side of the truck. Decker felt Beth wince each time he moved with her.

'There's the Pontiac,' Esperanza said.

It was near the corner, a recent model, blue, apparently the one McKittrick had been driving. When Decker tried to insert the key in the passenger door, it fit.

Thirty seconds later, Beth was lying on the back seat, Decker was kneeling on the floor next to her, and Esperanza was behind the steering wheel. An ambulance blocked the way. 'Hold Beth steady,' Esperanza said.

'What are you going to do?'

'Take a detour.' Esperanza started the engine, put the Pontiac in gear, and swung the steering wheel severely to the right. Pressing the accelerator, he jolted up onto the sidewalk.

Beth moaned from the impact. Decker leaned against her, working to keep her from sliding off the seat. Pedestrians scattered as Esperanza aimed the Pontiac along the sidewalk, reached the corner, and jounced down off the curb.

Beth groaned, her pain more severe.

'That'll do it.' Esperanza glanced in his rearview mirror, sped to the next corner, and turned. 'No one's following us. All you have to do now is relax, folks. Enjoy the ride.'

Decker didn't need encouragement. He was so exhausted that breathing was an effort Worse, he couldn't control his shivering, partly because of the aftermath of adrenaline but mostly, he knew, because of his bone-deep chill from having been in the rain for so long.

'Esperanza?'

'What?'

'Find us a place to stay. Fast.'

'Is something—'

'I'm think I'm starting to get –' Decker's voice was unsteady. ' – hypothermia.'

'Jesus.'

'I have to get out of these wet clothes.'

'Put your hands under your armpits. Don't go to sleep. Is there a blanket or anything back there?'

'No.' Decker's teeth chattered.

'All I can do for now is put on the heater,' Esperanza said. 'I'll find a take-out place and get hot coffee. Hang on, Decker.'

'Hang on? Sure. To myself. I'm hugging myself so hard I—'

'Hug *me*,' Beth said. 'Closer. Try to use my body heat.'

But no matter how tightly he pressed himself against her, her voice seemed to come from far away.

TWELVE

1

Decker dreamed of Renata, of a tall thin dark-haired woman with a grotesque voice and a gaping hole in her throat. He thought that the figure looming over him was Renata about to crush his head with a rock, but just before he prepared to strike at her, his mind became lucid enough for him to realize that it wasn't Renata but Beth who leaned over him, and that the object wasn't a rock but a washcloth.

Someone else was with her – Esperanza – holding him down. 'Take it easy. You're safe. We're trying to help you.'

Decker blinked repeatedly, groggy, as if hungover, trying to understand what was happening. His body ached. His arms and face stung. His muscles throbbed. He had the worst headache of his life. In the background, pale sunlight struggled past the edges of closed draperies.

'Where—'

'A motel outside Jersey City.'

As Decker scanned the gloomy interior, he was reminded disturbingly of the motel where McKittrick had held Beth prisoner.

'How long— What time is—'

'Almost seven in the evening.' Beth, who sat next to him, her weight on her good leg, put the washcloth on his forehead. It had been soaked in steaming hot water. Decker instantly absorbed the heat.

'This is the kind of place that doesn't ask questions about people checking in,' Esperanza said. 'The units are behind the office. The clerk can't see who goes into the rooms.'

Like the motel where McKittrick had held Beth prisoner, Decker thought again, uneasy.

'We got here about six in the morning,' Beth said. 'Counting time in the car, you've been sleeping almost thirteen hours. You had me scared that you wouldn't wake up.'

Esperanza pointed toward the bathroom. 'I had a lot of trouble getting your clothes off and putting you into the tub. With hypothermia, the water has to be tepid to start with. I increased the temperature slowly. When your color was better, I pulled you out, dried you off, and put you in bed with all three blankets I found on the shelf. Beth managed to get out of her wet clothes, dried off, and got in bed next to you, helping to keep you warm. I poured hot coffee into you. Man, I've never seen anybody so exhausted.'

Beth kept wiping Decker's face. 'Or so bruised and cut up. Your face won't stop bleeding.'

'I've had easier nights.' Decker's mouth felt dry. 'I could use . . . a drink of water.'

'It'll have to be *hot* water,' Esperanza said. 'Sorry, but I want to make sure you've got your body heat back.' He poured steaming water from a thermos into a Styrofoam cup and brought it to Decker's lips. 'Careful.'

It tasted worse than Decker had expected. 'Put a tea bag in it. Where'd you get . . . ?' Decker pointed toward the thermos.

'I've been busy. While you rested, I did some shopping. I've got food and clothes, crutches for Beth and—'

'You left us alone?' Decker asked in alarm.

'Beth had your handgun. She's in pain, but she was able to sit in that chair and watch the door. There didn't seem a reason not to get what we needed.'

Decker tried to sit up. '*Renata*. That's your reason.'

'She couldn't possibly have followed us,' Esperanza said. 'I was extra careful. Whenever I had the slightest doubt, I went around the block or down an alley. I would have noticed any headlights following us.'

'*We* were able to follow McKittrick,' Decker said.

'Because we had a homing device. Does it seem likely to you that McKittrick and Renata would have put a homing device in their own car? She didn't even have a car to follow us.'

'She could have stolen one.'

'Assuming she knew that we weren't on the roof any longer, that we'd stolen *her* car. Even then, by the time she hot-wired a vehicle, we'd have been long gone. She couldn't have known which way we went. Relax, Decker. She's not a threat.'

'For the moment.'

It wasn't Decker but Beth who made the comment.

'She *will* be, though,' Beth added, somber.

'Yes,' Decker said. 'If Renata went to all this trouble to get even with me for killing two of her brothers, she won't stop now. She'll be all the more determined.'

'Especially since we have the money,' Beth said.

Decker was too confused to speak. He looked at Esperanza.

'After we got to this motel,' Esperanza said, 'while you and Beth were resting, I checked the Pontiac's trunk. Along with enough explosives to blow up the Statue of Liberty, I found *that*.' Esperanza pointed toward a bulging flight bag on the floor by the bed. 'The million dollars.'

'Holy—' Decker's weariness made him dizzy again.

'Stop trying to sit up,' Beth said. 'You're turning pale. Stay down.'

'Renata *will* come looking for us.' As Decker closed his eyes, giving way to exhaustion, he reached to touch Beth, but his consciousness dimmed, and he didn't feel his hand fall.

2

The next time he wakened, the room was totally dark. He continued to feel groggy. His body still ached. But he had to move – he needed to use the bathroom. Unfamiliar with the motel room, he bumped into a wall, banging his shoulder, before he oriented himself, entered the bathroom, shut the door, and only then turned on the light, not wanting to wake Beth. His image in the mirror was shocking, not just the bruises and scratches but the deep blue circles around his eyes and the gauntness of his beard-stubbled cheeks.

After relieving himself, he hoped that the flushing of the toilet wouldn't disturb Beth. But when he turned off the light and opened the door, he discovered that the main room's lights were on. Beth was sitting up in the bed where she had been sleeping next to him. Esperanza was propped up against a pillow in another bed.

'Sorry,' Decker said.

'You didn't wake us,' Esperanza said.

'We've been waiting for you to get up,' Beth said. 'How do you feel?'

'The way I look.' Decker limped toward Beth. 'How about *you*? How do *you* feel?'

Beth shifted her position and winced. 'My leg is swollen. It throbs. But the wound doesn't look infected.'

'At least that's one thing in our favor.' Decker slumped on the bed and wrapped a blanket around him. He rubbed his temples. 'What time is it?'

'Two a.m.' Esperanza put on trousers and got out of bed. 'Do you feel alert enough to discuss some things?'

'My throat's awfully dry.' Decker managed to hold up his hands as if defending himself. 'But I don't want any of that damned hot water.'

'I bought some Gatorade. How about that? Get some electrolytes back in your system.'

'Perfect.'

It was orange-flavored, and Decker drank a quarter of the bottle before he stopped himself.

'How about something to eat?' Esperanza asked.

'My stomach's not working, but I'd better try to get something down.'

Esperanza opened a small portable cooler. 'I've got packaged sandwiches – tuna, chicken, salami.'

'Chicken.'

'Catch.'

Decker surprised himself by managing to do so. He peeled the plastic wrap off the sandwich and bit into tasteless white bread and cardboard-like chicken. 'Delicious.'

'Nothing but the best for you.'

'We have to decide what to do.' Beth's solemn tone contrasted with Esperanza's attempt at humor.

Decker looked at her and tenderly grasped her hand. 'Yes. The Justice Department won't be happy that you didn't show up to testify. They'll be looking for you.'

'I took care of it,' Beth said.

'Took care of—' Decker felt troubled. 'I don't understand.'

'Esperanza drove me to a payphone. I called my contact at the Justice Department and found out I don't have to testify. The Grand Jury was meeting to indict Nick Giordano, but since he's dead, the Justice Department says there's no point in going further.' Beth hesitated. 'You killed *Frank* Giordano, also?'

Decker didn't say anything.

'For me?'

'Keep reminding yourself that you're in the presence of a police officer,' Decker said.

Esperanza glanced at his hands. 'Maybe this would be a good time for me to take a walk.'

'I didn't mean to—'

'No offense taken. You two have a lot to talk about. You could use some time alone.' Esperanza put on his boots, grabbed a shirt, nodded, and went outside.

Beth waited until the door was closed. 'Esperanza gave me an idea of what you went through last night.' She reached for his hand. 'I'll never be able to thank you enough.'

'All you have to do is love me.'

Beth cocked her head in surprise. 'You make it sound as if that's something I have to talk myself into. I *do* love you.'

She had never told him that before. The longed-for words thrilled him, flooding him with warmth. With emotion-pained eyes, he studied her. There was little resemblance between the enticing woman he had known in Santa Fe and the pale, gaunt-cheeked, hollow-eyed, straggly-haired woman before him. This was the woman he had suffered for. Risked his life for. Several times. Been prepared to go *anywhere* and do *anything* to save.

His throat felt cramped. 'You're beautiful.'

Welcome color came into her cheeks.

'I couldn't have gone on living without you,' Decker said.

Beth inhaled sharply, audibly. She looked at him as if she had never truly seen him before, then hugged him, their embrace painful because of their injuries but intense and forceful all the same. 'I don't deserve you.'

Beth had told him that earlier, when Decker had helped her onto the fire escape at the doctor's apartment. Was 'don't deserve you' another way of expressing affection, or did she literally mean that she felt undeserving – because she had used him and now felt ashamed?

'What's wrong?' Beth asked.

'Nothing.'

'But—'

'We have a lot of details to take care of,' Decker said quickly. 'Did your contact in the Justice Department ask about McKittrick?'

'Did he ever.' Beth looked puzzled by the sudden change of topic, by the way intimacy had given way to practicality. 'I told him I thought McKittrick was the man who let the Giordanos know I was hiding in Santa Fe. I said that I'd been suspicious about McKittrick from the start and when we got to New York I slipped away from him. I told them I had no idea where he was.'

'Keep telling them that,' Decker said. 'When McKittrick's body is found in the wreckage from the fire, the authorities will have trouble identifying it. Because they don't know whose dental records to compare it to, they might not *ever* be able to identify it. His disappearance will be a mystery. It'll look as if he ran away to avoid going to prison. The main thing is, don't show any hesitation. Never vary from your story that you don't know anything about what happened to him.'

'I'll need to account for where I've been since Saturday afternoon when I left Santa Fe,' Beth said.

'I'll make a phone call. A former associate of mine lives in Manhattan and owes me a favor. If the Justice Department wants an alibi, he'll give you one. They'll want to know your relationship with him. Tell them I mentioned him to you in Santa Fe, that he was an old friend and I wanted you to look him up when you got to New York. It was natural for you to run to him after you got away from McKittrick.'

'That still leaves another problem . . . you.'

'I don't understand.'

'Esperanza and I don't have to worry about our fingerprints being identified. The Oldsmobile was destroyed by fire. So were the motel room in Closter and the doctor's apartment in Manhattan. But what about *your* fingerprints? While you were asleep, we switched on the television so we could find out how the authorities were reacting to what happened last night. The FBI has stepped into the investigation of the Giordano deaths. There are reports that they've isolated fingerprints on a murder weapon left at Nick Giordano's house. A log pick.' Beth seemed disturbed by the brutal implications of the weapon.

'And?'

'The authorities think it was a mob slaying, a war between rival gangs. But when they identify your prints—'

'They'll find the prints are registered to a man who died fifteen years ago.'

Beth stared.

'Where would you like to live?' Decker asked.

'Live?' Beth seemed puzzled by another sudden change of topic. 'Back in Santa Fe, of course.'

'With me?'

'Yes.'

'I don't think that's a good idea,' Decker said.

'But the mob isn't looking for me anymore.'

'Renata is.' Decker paused, letting silence emphasize what he had said. 'As long as I'm alive, Renata might use you to get at me. You'll be in danger.'

Beth became paler than she already was.

'Nothing's changed,' Decker said. 'So I'll ask you again, Where would you like to live?'

Something in Beth's eyes seemed to die.

'If we split up,' Decker said.

'Split up?' Beth looked bewildered. 'But why on earth would—'

'If we had a very public argument back in Santa Fe, at noon in Escalera or some other popular restaurant, if word got around that we weren't an item any longer, Renata might decide there's no point in doing something to you, because she wouldn't be torturing me if she killed someone I didn't care about.'

Beth's bewilderment intensified.

'In fact,' Decker said, giving her a way out, wanting to learn the truth, 'the more I think about it, the more I'm convinced Renata would leave you alone if we broke up.'

'But—' Beth's voice didn't want to work. No sound came out.

'It would have to be convincing,' Decker said. 'I could accuse you of knowing who I was from the start of our relationship. I could make a scene about how you only pretended to love me, how you bribed me with sex, how all you wanted was a bodyguard living next door to you and sometimes in your house. In your bed.'

Beth started weeping.

'I could tell everybody that I'd been a fool, that I'd risked my life for nothing. If Renata was keeping tabs on me, she'd hear about the argument. She'd believe it. Especially if I left Santa Fe but you stayed.'

Beth wept harder.

'Who killed your husband?' Decker asked.

Beth didn't answer.

'I suppose we could make up a theory,' Decker said, 'about someone in the organization, maybe one of his guards, shooting him, taking the money, and blaming it on you. Another theory would be that Nick Giordano's son, Frank, was so jealous of the attention his father gave to your husband that he decided to set matters straight and blame it on you.' Decker waited. 'Which theory do *you* like?'

Beth wiped at her eyes. 'Neither.'

'Then—'

'*I* did it,' Beth said.

Decker straightened.

'*I* shot my husband,' Beth said. 'The son of a bitch won't ever beat me again.'

'You took the money?'

'Yes.'

'That's how you could afford the house in Santa Fe?'

'Yes. The money's in a numbered bank account in the Bahamas. The Justice Department couldn't get their hands on it, so they let me support myself with it – especially since they wanted my testimony.'

'Did you know who I was before you met me?'

'Yes.'

'Then you *did* use me.'

'For about forty-eight hours. I didn't know I'd be so attracted to you. I certainly didn't expect to fall in love with you.'

Blood trickled from one of the open gashes on Decker's face. 'I wish I could believe you.'

'I've always had an inclination to live in the South of France,' Beth said unexpectedly.

Now it was Decker who wasn't prepared. 'Excuse me?'

'Not the Riviera. Inland,' Beth said. 'Southwestern France. The Pyrenees. I once read an article about them in a travel magazine. The photographs of the valleys, with pastures and forests and streams running down from the mountains, were incredibly beautiful. I think I could do some good painting there . . . Provided you're with me.'

'Knowing that you'd be putting your life in danger, that Renata would want to use you to get at me?'

'Yes.'

'For the rest of your days, always looking over your shoulder?'

'Without you –' Beth touched the blood trickling from the gash on his face. ' – I'd have nothing to look *ahead* to.'

'In that case,' Decker said, 'we're going back to Santa Fe.'

3

'Are you sure this is a good idea?' Esperanza asked.

'No. But it makes more sense to me than the alternatives,' Decker said. They were in the clamorous crowded expanse of Newark International Airport. Decker had just come back from the United Airlines counter, rejoining Esperanza and Beth, where they waited for him in an alcove near restrooms and schedule-of-flights monitors. He handed out tickets. 'I've got us on an 8:30 flight. We switch planes in Denver and arrive in Albuquerque at 12:48 this afternoon.'

'These seats aren't together,' Beth said.

'Two of them are. One of us will have to sit farther back.'

'I will,' Esperanza said. 'I'll check to see if any passengers show unusual interest in you.'

'With my crutches, I'm afraid I can't help being noticed,' Beth said.

'And the scratches on my face definitely attracted attention from the woman at the United counter.' Decker looked around to make sure they weren't being overheard. 'But I don't see how Renata could anticipate which airport we would use. I'm not worried that she's in the area. When we get back to Santa Fe, that's when we start worrying.'

'You're sure she'll be waiting for us there?' Beth asked.

'What other choice does she have? She needs to start somewhere to find us, and Santa Fe is her best bet. She knows if I'm not coming back, I'll need to sell my house and transfer my bank account. She'll want to be around to persuade the realtor or the bank manager to tell her where the money is being sent.'

Beth frowned toward passengers hurrying past, as if afraid that Renata would suddenly lunge from among them. 'But that information is confidential. She can't just walk into the real-estate agency or the bank and expect someone to tell her your new address.'

'I was thinking more along the lines of a gun to the head when the realtor or the bank manager came home from work,' Decker said. 'Renata's an expert at terrorizing. In addition to hating me because I killed her brothers, she has the incentive of the million dollars of her money that I've got in this carry-on bag. She'll do everything possible to get even. In her place, I'd be waiting in Santa Fe until I knew in which direction to start hunting.'

Esperanza glanced at his watch. 'We'd better head to the gate.'

Uneasy about showing themselves, they left the alcove and started through the crowd, each man flanking Beth to make sure no one jostled against her as she used her crutches. Not that she looked unsteady. Although she hadn't been given much opportunity to practice with the crutches, her natural physical abilities had made it possible for her to develop a confident stride.

Decker felt a surge of admiration for her. She looked determined, oblivious to her pain, ready to do whatever was necessary.

And what about *you*? Decker asked himself. You've been through a hell of a lot. Are *you* ready?

For anything.

But he wasn't being entirely truthful with himself. Now that the immediate practical details had been taken care of, he didn't have anything to distract him from his emotions. He couldn't adjust to the reality that Beth was next to him. He had a squirming sensation of incompleteness if he wasn't with her. Even the brief time he had been away to buy the plane tickets had been exceedingly uncomfortable for him.

Ready for anything? he repeated to himself as he walked with

Beth and Esperanza toward the line at the security checkpoint. Not quite everything. I'm not ready for Beth to be hurt again. I'm not ready to learn that she still might be lying to me about her feelings for me. I'm not ready to discover that I've been a fool.

At the security checkpoint, he hung back, letting Esperanza and Beth go through a minute before he did in case the ten thousand one-hundred-dollar bills in his carry-on looked suspicious to the guard checking the X-ray monitor. If Decker was asked to open the bag, he would have a hard time explaining to the authorities how he had acquired a million dollars. The security officers would immediately assume that the money had something to do with drugs, and he didn't want Beth or Esperanza to appear to be associated with him. The X-ray monitor showed the outlines of non-metallic objects as well as metal ones, so, to make the bills look less obvious, Decker had removed the rubber bands around the stacks and jumbled them in the large bag, adding a dirty shirt, a note pad and pen, a toilet kit, a deck of cards, a newspaper, and a paperback novel. With luck, the X-ray guard wouldn't pay any attention to the visual chaos once he satisfied himself that the bag did not contain a weapon.

A woman ahead of Decker set her purse on the monitor's conveyor belt, then stepped through the metal detector with no trouble. His pulse rate increasing, Decker took her place, setting the heavy bag onto the belt. The X-ray guard looked strangely at him. Ignoring the attention he received, Decker put his diver's watch and his car keys into a basket that a uniformed woman in charge of the metal detector took from him. Decker wasn't worried that the metal detector would find a weapon on him – he and Esperanza had taken care to disassemble their handguns and drop them into a sewer before they set out toward the airport. Nonetheless, he didn't want to take the chance of any metal object, no matter how innocent, setting off the detector and drawing further attention to him.

'What happened to your face?' the female guard asked.

'Car accident.' Decker stepped through the metal detector. The machine remained silent.

'Looks painful,' the guard said.

'It could have been worse.' Decker took his watch and car keys. 'The drunk who ran the red light and hit me went to the morgue.'

'Lucky. You'd better take care.'

'Believe me, I'm trying.' Decker walked toward the conveyor belt that led from the X-ray monitor. But his chest tightened when he saw that the belt wasn't moving. The guard in charge of the monitor had stopped the conveyor while he took a solemn look at the fuzzy image of what was in Decker's carry-on.

Decker waited, a traveler who had a plane to catch but who was trying to be reasonable about security, even though there obviously couldn't possibly be anything wrong with that carry-on.

The guard scowled, looking closer at the monitor.

Decker heard pounding behind his ears.

With a shrug, the guard pressed a button that re-engaged the conveyor belt. The carry-on emerged from the machine.

'Your face makes me sore just to look at it,' the guard said.

'It feels even worse than it looks.' Decker picked up the million dollars and walked with other passengers along the concourse.

He stopped at a payphone, asked the information operator for the airport's number, then pressed buttons for the number he was given. 'Airport security, please.'

Pause. Click. 'Security,' a smooth-voiced man said.

'Check your parking area for a Pontiac, this year's make, dark blue.' Decker gave the license number. 'Have you got all that? Did you write it down?'

'Yes, but—'

'You'll find explosives in the trunk.'

'*What?*'

'Not connected to a detonator. The car is safe, but you'd better be careful, all the same.'

'*Who*—'

'This isn't a threat to the airport. It's just that I find myself with a lot of C-4 on my hands, and I can't think of a safer way to surrender it.'

'But—'

'Have a nice day.' Decker broke the connection. Before leaving the Pontiac in the parking area, he had rubbed a soapy washcloth over any sections where they might have left fingerprints. Normally, he would have left the car where street kids would soon steal it, but he didn't want them screwing around with the explosives. By the time the Pontiac and the C-4 were found, he would be on his way to Denver.

He walked swiftly toward the gate, where Beth and Esperanza waited anxiously for him.

'You took so long I got worried,' Beth said.

Decker noticed the glance she directed toward his carry-on. Is the money what she really cares about? he wondered. 'I was beginning to feel a little tense myself.'

'They've already started boarding,' Esperanza said. 'My seat number was called. I'd better get moving.'

Decker nodded. He had spent so much time with Esperanza the past few days that he felt odd being separated from him. 'See you in Denver.'

'Right.'

As Esperanza followed passengers down the jetway, Beth gave Decker an affectionate smile. 'We've never traveled together. This will be the start of a whole lot of new experiences for us.'

'As long as they're better than what happened since Friday night.' Decker tried to make it sound like a joke.

'*Anything* would be better.'

'Let's hope.' But what if it gets even worse? Decker wondered.

Beth glanced toward the check-in counter. 'They're calling our seat numbers.'

'Let's go. I'm sure you can use a rest from those crutches.' Heading back to Santa Fe, am I doing the right thing? Decker brooded. Am I absolutely sure this is going to work?

At the jetway, a United agent took Beth's ticket. 'Do you need assistance boarding the aircraft?'

'My friend will help me.' Beth looked fondly toward Decker.

'We'll be fine,' Decker told the agent, and surrendered his boarding pass. He followed Beth into the confinement of the jetway. It's not too late to change the plan, he warned himself.

But he felt carried along by the line of passengers. Two minutes later, they were in their seats midway along the aircraft. A flight attendant took Beth's crutches and stored them in the plane's garment-bag compartment. Decker and Beth fastened their seatbelts. The million dollars was stowed at his feet.

I can *still* change my mind, he thought. Maybe Beth was right. Maybe the South of France *is* where we ought to be going.

But something he and Beth had talked about at the motel kept coming back to him. He had asked Beth if she was willing to stay with him, knowing that she would be putting her life in danger, that Renata would try to use her to get at him. For the rest of Beth's time with Decker, she would always be looking over her shoulder. Beth's answer had been, 'Without you, I'd have nothing to look *ahead* to.'

Let's find out if she means it, Decker thought. I want to settle this *now*.

The 737 pulled away from the terminal, taxiing toward the runway. Beth clasped his hand.

'I've missed you,' she whispered.

Decker gently squeezed her fingers. 'More than you can ever know, I missed you.'

'Wrong,' Beth said. Engines whined outside their window. 'What you did these last few days – I have a very definite idea of what you feel for me.' Beth snuggled against him as the 737 took off.

4

By the time the jet leveled off at thirty-two thousand feet, Decker was surprised to find that he was having trouble making small talk with her, the first time this had happened in their relationship. Their chitchat sounded hollow compared to the substantive matters he wanted to discuss with her but couldn't because of the risk that passengers around them would overhear. He was grateful when the flight attendant brought breakfast, a cheese-and-mushroom omelette that he devoured. In part, he was ravenous, his appetite having kicked in. But in part, also, he wanted to use the food as a distraction from the need to keep up conversation. After the meal, refusing coffee, he apologized for being exhausted.

'Don't feel you have to entertain me,' Beth said. 'You earned a rest. Take a nap. In fact, I think I'll join you.'

She tilted her seat back just as he did, then leaned her head against his shoulder.

Decker crossed his arms and closed his eyes. But sleep did not come readily. His emotions continued to divide him. The intensity of the long ordeal he had been through left him restless, his body exhausted but his nerves on edge, as if he was having withdrawal symptoms from a physical dependence on the rush of adrenaline. These sensations reminded him of the way he had once felt after his missions for the military and the Agency. Action could be addictive. In his youth, he had craved it. The 'high' of surviving a mission had made ordinary life unacceptable, producing an eagerness to go on other missions, to overcome fear in order to replicate the euphoria of coming back alive. Eventually, he had recognized the self-destructiveness of this dependency. When he had settled in Santa Fe, he had been convinced that peace was all he wanted.

As a consequence, he was puzzled by his eagerness to pursue his conflict with Renata. Granted, from one point of view, it didn't make sense to prolong the tension of waiting for her to attack him. If he could control the circumstances under which Renata came after him, he would be hunting her as much as she would be hunting him. The sooner he confronted her, the better. But from another point of view, his eagerness troubled him, making him worry that he was becoming what he had used to be.

5

'We're not exactly sneaking back into New Mexico. How do we know Renata won't be in the concourse, watching whoever gets off this flight?' Esperanza asked. He had joined Decker and Beth where they remained in their seats, waiting for the other passengers to disembark at the Albuquerque airport. No one was near them. They could speak without fear of being overheard.

'That's not the way she would handle it,' Decker said. 'In an airport as small as this, someone hanging around day after day, doing nothing but watch incoming flights, would attract the attention of a security officer.'

'But Renata wouldn't have to do it by herself. She could hire someone to watch with her. They could take shifts,' Esperanza said.

'That part I agree with. She probably does have help by now. When she was using McKittrick –' Decker glanced toward Beth, wondering if *she* had used *him* just as Renata had used McKittrick. ' – Renata would have kept her friends at a distance, to prevent McKittrick from getting jealous. But once McKittrick was out of the picture, she would have brought in the rest of her terrorist group from Rome.' Decker lifted his carry-on from the compartment at his feet. 'A million dollars is worth the effort. Oh, they're here all right, and they're taking turns, but they're not watching the incoming flights.'

'Then what *are* they doing?'

A flight attendant interrupted, bringing Beth her crutches.

Beth thanked the woman, and the three of them started forward.

'I'll explain when we're by ourselves.' Decker turned to Beth. 'Those stitches will have to be looked at. The first thing we'll do is get you to a doctor.' He shook his head. 'No, I'm wrong. The first thing we have to do is rent a car.'

'Rent?' Esperanza asked. 'But you left your Jeep Cherokee in the airport's parking garage.'

'Where it's going to stay for a while,' Decker said. He waited until there was no one around them on the jetway before he told Esperanza, 'Your badge and your service pistol are locked in my car. Can you do without them for another day?'

'The sooner I get them back, the better. Why can't we use your car?' Immediately Esperanza answered his own question. 'Renata knows your Jeep. You think she might have rigged it with explosives?'

'And risk blowing up the million dollars in this bag? I don't think so. As much as she wants revenge, it has to be sweet. It's no good if it costs her – certainly not *this* much. My car will be perfectly safe . . . Except for the homing device she'll have planted on it.'

6

Midday sunlight blazed as Decker drove the rented gray Buick Skylark from the Avis lot next to the Albuquerque airport. He steered along the curved road past the four-story parking garage, then glanced at the two large metal silhouettes of race horses on the lawn in front of the airport, remembering the misgivings with which he had first seen those horses more than a year ago when he had begun his pilgrimage to Santa Fe. Now, after his longest time away from Santa Fe since then, he was returning, and his emotions were much more complex.

He steered around another curve, reached a wide grass-divided thoroughfare that led to and from the airport, and pointed toward a fourteen-story glass-and-stucco Best Western hotel on the right side of the road, silhouetted against the Sandia mountains. 'Somewhere in that hotel, Renata or one of her friends is watching a homing-device receiver, waiting for a needle to move and warn them my car is leaving the parking garage. Whoever it is will hurry down to a car that's positioned for an easy exit from the hotel's parking area. My car will be followed as it passes the hotel. The person in the car will have a cellular phone and pass the word to the rest of the group, some of whom will have no doubt set up shop in Santa Fe. The person following me will take for granted that cellular-phone conversations can be overheard by the wrong people, so the conversation will be in code, at regular intervals, all the way behind me to Santa Fe. Once I get to where I'm going, they'll move quickly to get their hands on me. There's no reason for them to wait. After all, I won't have had time to set up any defenses. Immediate action will be their best tactic. If I'm carrying the money, they won't have to torture me for information about where I put the million. But they'll torture me, anyhow. For the pleasure of it. Or rather Renata will do the torturing. I don't know where she'll want to start first – my balls or my throat. Probably the former, because if she goes for my throat, which I'm sure is what she would really like to do, to get even for what I did to *her*, I won't be able to give her the satisfaction of hearing me scream.'

Beth was in the back seat, her injured leg stretched out. Esperanza sat in front in the passenger seat. They looked at Decker as if the strain of what he had been through was affecting his behavior.

'You make it sound too vivid,' Beth said.

'And what makes you so sure about the homing device and the Best Western hotel?' Esperanza asked.

'Because that's the way *I* would do it,' Decker said.

'Why not the Airport Inn or the Village Inn or one of these other motels farther down?'

'Too small. Too hard for someone not to attract attention. Whoever's watching the homing-device receiver will want to be inconspicuous.'

'If you're that certain, I can ask the Albuquerque police to check the rooms in the Best Western.'

'Without a search warrant? And without the police tipping their hand? Whoever's watching the receiver will have a lookout, someone outside the hotel checking to see if police arrive. Renata and her friends would disappear. I'd lose my best chance of anticipating them.'

'You're worrying me,' Beth said.

'Why?' Decker steered from the airport thoroughfare and headed down Gibson, approaching the ramp onto Interstate 25.

'You're different. You sound as if you welcome the challenge, as if you're enjoying this.'

'Maybe I'm reverting.'

'What?'

'If you and I are going to survive this, I *have* to revert. I don't have another choice. I have to become what I used to be – before I arrived in Santa Fe. That's why McKittrick picked me to be your next-door neighbor, isn't it?' Decker asked. 'That's why you moved in next to me. Because of what I used to be.'

7

As the rented Buick crested La Bajada hill and Santa Fe was suddenly spread out before him, the Sangre de Cristo mountains hulking in the background, Decker felt no surge of excitement, no delight in having returned. Instead, what he felt was an unexpected emptiness. So much had happened to him since he had left. The clay-colored, flat-roofed, Hispanic-pueblo structures of Santa Fe seemed as exotic as ever. The round-edged adobe-style homes seemed to glow warmly, the September afternoon amazingly clear and brilliant, no smog, visibility for hundreds of miles, the land of the dancing sun.

But Decker felt apart from it all, remote. He didn't have a sense of coming home. He was merely revisiting a place where he happened to live. The detachment reminded him of when he had worked for the Agency and returned from assignments to his apartment in Virginia. It was the same detachment that he had felt so many times before, in London, Paris, and Athens, in Brussels, Berlin, and Cairo, the last time in Rome – because on all his missions, wherever he had traveled, he had not dared to identify with his surroundings for fear that he would let down his guard. If he was going to survive, he couldn't permit distractions. From that point of view, he *had* come home.

8

'The stitches are nicely done,' the stoop-shouldered red-haired doctor said.

'I'm relieved to hear it,' Decker said. The doctor was a former client with whom he occasionally socialized. 'Thanks for agreeing to see us without an appointment.'

The doctor shrugged. 'I had two no-shows this afternoon.' He continued to examine the wound in Beth's thigh. 'I don't like this area of redness around the stitches. What caused the injury?'

'A car accident,' Decker said before Beth could answer.

'You were with her? Is that how you hurt your face?'

'It was a lousy end to a vacation.'

'At least *you* didn't need stitches.' The doctor returned his attention to Beth. 'The redness suggests that the wound is developing an infection. Were you given an anti-tetanus injection?'

'I wasn't alert enough to remember.'

'It must have slipped the other doctor's mind,' Decker said bitterly.

'Then it's due.' After giving Beth the shot, the doctor rebandaged the wound. 'I'll write a prescription for some antibiotics. Do you want something for the pain?'

'Please.'

'Here. This ought to take care of it.' The doctor finished writing and handed her two pieces of paper. 'You can shower, but I don't want you soaking the wound in a tub. If the tissue

411

becomes too soft, the stitches might pull out. Call me in three days. I want to make sure the infection doesn't spread.'

'Thanks.' Wincing, Beth eased off the examination table and pulled up her loose-fitting slacks, buckling them. In order to avoid attracting suspicion, Friday night's bullet wound to the fleshy part of her shoulder had not been mentioned. That wound had no redness around it, but if an infection was brewing there, the antibiotics for the wound in her thigh would handle it.

'Glad to help. Steve, I'm in the market for more rental properties. Got any that might interest me? I'm free Saturday afternoon.'

'I could be tied up. I'll get back to you.' Decker opened the door to the examination room and let Beth use her crutches to go ahead of him to where Esperanza waited in the lobby. Decker told them, 'I'll be out in a minute,' then shut the door and turned to the doctor. 'Uh, Jeff?'

'What is it? You want me to check those contusions on your face?'

'They're not what's on my mind.'

'Then—'

'I'm afraid this will sound a little melodramatic, but I wonder if you can make sure our visit to you stays a secret.'

'Why would—'

'It's delicate. Embarrassing, in fact. My friend's in the middle of getting a divorce. It could get nasty if the husband knew that she and I were seeing each other. Someone might call or come around, identifying himself as her husband or a private investigator or whatever, wanting to know about medical treatment you gave her. I'd hate for him to find out that she and I had been here together.'

'My office isn't in the habit of handing out that kind of information,' Jeff said stiffly.

'I didn't think it was. But my friend's husband can be

awfully persuasive.' Decker picked up the bag containing the money.

'He certainly won't get any information from me.'

'Thanks, Jeff. I appreciate this.' As he left the examination room, he had the sense that the doctor disapproved of the circumstances Decker claimed to be in. He stopped at the receptionist's counter. 'I'll pay cash.'

'The patient's name?'

'Brenda Scott.'

It was highly unlikely that Renata would try to check every doctor in Santa Fe to see if Beth received the medical treatment Renata would suspect she might require. But thoroughness had always been Decker's trademark. He had deliberately avoided taking Beth to his personal physician or to the emergency ward at St Vincent's Hospital or to the Lovelace Health System offices. Those were obvious places that Renata could easily have someone watch to see if Beth and, by extension, Decker were back in town. Decker's precautions were possibly excessive, but old habits now controlled him.

9

The trailer with its yucca-studded gravel area in front looked oddly different from the way it had when Decker had seen it a few days earlier. Correction, Decker told himself. Nights. You saw it in the middle of the night. It's bound to look different. As he parked the rented Buick at the curb, he glanced at the stunted marigolds in the narrow flower garden that hugged the front wall.

'Do you think it's safe for you to show up here?' Esperanza asked. 'Renata or one of her friends might be watching where I live.'

'Not a chance,' Decker said. 'Renata didn't get a good look at you the other night.'

Esperanza, too, was studying the trailer as if there was something oddly different about it. What's making him nervous? Decker wondered. Does he truly think Renata is in the area? Or is it because— Decker remembered Esperanza's references to the arguments he was having with his wife. Maybe Esperanza was uneasy about being reunited with her.

'You took all kinds of risks by coming with me. I owe you big time.' Decker extended his hand.

'Yes.' Beth squirmed to lean forward. 'You saved my life. I can never repay you. To say "thanks" doesn't come close to expressing my gratitude.'

Esperanza continued to stare at the trailer. '*I'm* the one who should be saying "thanks".'

Decker furrowed his brow. 'I don't get your point.'

'You asked me why I wanted to come along.' Esperanza turned, directing a steady gaze at him. 'I told you I needed some time away from my wife. I told you I was a sucker for wanting to get people out of trouble.'

'I remember,' Decker said.

'I also told you I'd never met anybody like you before. Hanging around with you was an education.'

'I remember that, too.'

'People get set in their ways.' Esperanza hesitated. 'For quite a while now, I've been feeling dead inside.'

Decker was caught by surprise.

'When I ran with gangs, I knew there had to be something more than just going nowhere in a hurry, raising hell, but I couldn't figure out what it was. Then the policeman I told you about changed my way of seeing things. I joined the force, to be like him, so I could make a difference, so I could do some good.' Esperanza's voice was taut with emotion. 'But sometimes, no matter how much good you try to do, all the shit you see in this world can get you down, especially the needless pain people put each other through.'

'I still don't—'

'I didn't think I'd ever get excited about anything again. But trying to keep pace with you these past few days . . . Well, something happened. . . . I felt alive. Oh, I was scared out of my mind by what we did. Some of it was plain damned insane and suicidal. But at the time—'

'It seemed like the thing to do.'

'Yeah.' Esperanza grinned. 'It seemed like the thing to do. Maybe I'm like you. Maybe I'm reverting.' He stared at the trailer again and sobered. 'I guess it's time.' He opened the passenger door and swung his cowboy boots out onto the gravel.

As Decker watched the lanky long-haired detective walk pensively toward the trailer's three front steps, he realized part of the reason the trailer seemed different. There had been a motorcycle and a pickup truck in the driveway a couple of nights ago. Now only the motorcycle remained.

When Esperanza disappeared inside, Decker turned to Beth. 'Tonight's going to be rough. We'll have to put you in a hotel somewhere out of town.'

Despite her discomfort, Beth straightened in alarm. 'No. I won't be separated from you.'

'Why?'

Uneasy, Beth didn't answer.

'Are you saying you don't feel safe away from me?' Decker shook his head. 'That might have been what you felt when you were living next door to me, but you're going to have to break yourself of that attitude. Right now, it's a lot smarter for you to stay as far away from me as possible.'

'That's not what I'm thinking,' Beth said.

'What *are* you thinking?'

'You wouldn't be in this mess if it wasn't for me. I'm not going to let you try to get out of it alone.'

'There'll be shooting.'

'I *know* how to shoot.'

'So you explained.' Remembering that Beth had killed her husband and emptied his wall safe, Decker glanced beside him toward the bag containing the million dollars. Is the money what she wants? Is that her motive for staying close?

'Why are you angry at me?' Beth asked.

Decker wasn't prepared for the question. 'Angry? What makes you think I'm—'

'If you were any colder to me, I'd have frostbite.'

Decker stared toward Esperanza's trailer. Stared toward his hands. Stared toward Beth. 'You shouldn't have lied to me.'

'About being in the Witness Protection Program? I was under strict orders not to tell you.'

'Orders from McKittrick?'

'Look, after I was shot, after I got out of the hospital, when you and I talked in my courtyard, I tried to tell you as much as I could. I begged you to go away and hide with me. But you insisted I go without you.'

'I figured that would be the safest thing for you in case another hit team came after me,' Decker said. 'If I'd known you were in the Witness Protection Program, I would have handled it a different way.'

'Different? How?'

'Then I *would* have gone with you,' Decker said. 'To help protect you. In *that* case, I'd have run into McKittrick, realized what was happening, and saved you and me from the nightmare we went through.'

'So it's still my fault? Is that what you're saying?'

'I don't think I used the word "fault". I—'

'What about all the lies *you* told *me* about what you did

before you came to Santa Fe, about how you got those bullet scars? It seems to me there was plenty of lying on both sides.'

'I can't just go around telling people I used to work for the CIA.'

'I'm not just anybody,' Beth said. 'Didn't you trust me?'

'Well . . .'

'Didn't you *love* me enough to trust me?'

'It was a reflex from the old days. I was never good at trusting people. Trust can get you killed. But that argument cuts both ways. Evidently you didn't love *me* enough to trust *me* with the truth about your background.'

Beth sounded discouraged. 'Maybe you're right. Maybe there wasn't enough love to go around.' She leaned back, exhausted. 'What was I expecting? We spent two months together. Of that, we were lovers for only eight days before—' She shuddered. 'People's lives don't change in eight days.'

'They can. Mine changed in a couple of minutes when I decided to move to Santa Fe.'

'But it *didn't* change.'

'What are you talking about?'

'You said it yourself. You're back to where you started. To what you once were.' Tears trickled down Beth's cheeks. 'Because of me.'

Decker couldn't help himself. He wanted to lean over the seat and clasp Beth's hand, to lean farther and hug her.

But before he could act on the impulse, she said, 'If you want to end our relationship, tell me.'

'End it?' Now that the ultimate topic had been raised, Decker wasn't ready. 'I'm not sure . . . I wasn't—'

'Because I won't tolerate having you accuse me of taking advantage of you. I lied to you about my background because I was under strict orders to keep it a secret. Even then, I was tempted to tell you, but I was worried that you'd run from me if you knew the truth.'

'I would never have run.'

'That remains to be seen. But that's all the explanation you're going to get from me. Accept it or not. One thing's for sure – I don't intend to stay in any hotel room while you face Renata by yourself. *You* risked your life for *me*. If I have to do the same to prove myself, that's what I'm willing to do.'

Decker felt overwhelmed.

'So what's it going to be?' Beth asked. 'Are you going to forgive me for lying to you? *I'm* prepared to forgive *you*. Do you want to make a fresh start?'

'If it's possible.' Emotion was tearing Decker apart.

'Anything's possible if you try.'

'If we both try.' Decker's voice broke. 'Yes.'

At once Decker's attention was distracted by the sound of Esperanza's front door being opened. Esperanza came out. The lean detective had put on fresh jeans, a denim shirt, and a stetson. A semiautomatic pistol was holstered on his right hip. But something in his expression indicated that more than his outward appearance had changed since he went in the house.

Esperanza's boots crunched on gravel as he approached the Buick.

'Are you all right?' Decker asked. 'Your eyes look—'

'She isn't here.'

'Your wife? You mean she's at work or—'

'Gone.'

'What?'

'She left. The trailer's empty. The furniture. The pots and pans. Her clothes. All gone, even a cactus I had on the kitchen counter. She took everything, except for my jeans and a few of my shirts.'

'Jesus,' Decker said.

'I was a while coming out because I had to phone around to find out where she went. She's staying with her sister in Albuquerque.'

'I am really sorry.'

It seemed that Esperanza didn't hear him. 'She doesn't want to see me. She doesn't want to talk to me.'

'All because you wouldn't quit your job as a police officer?'

'She kept saying I was married to my job. Sure, we were having problems, but she didn't have to leave. We could have worked things out.'

For the first time, Esperanza seemed fully aware of Decker and Beth. He glanced toward the back and noticed the strained expression on Beth's face. 'Looks like I'm not the only one with some things to work out.'

'We've been playing catch-up,' Beth said. 'Truth or consequences.'

'Yeah, that's the name of a good New Mexican town, all right.' Esperanza got into the car. 'Let's do it.'

'Do . . . ?' Decker asked in confusion.

'Finish what we started with Renata.'

'But this isn't your fight any longer. Stay here and try to settle things with your wife.'

'I don't walk away from my friends.'

Friends? Decker suffered a pang of grief as he remembered the price that Hal and Ben had paid for being his friends. Again he tried to dissuade Esperanza. 'No. Where you work? Where you're known? That's crazy. If there's trouble, we won't be able to cover it up the way we did in New York and New Jersey. Word will get around. At the very least, you'll lose your job.'

'Maybe that's what I finally want. Come on, Decker, start the car. Renata's waiting.'

10

A buzzer sounded as Decker entered the store. The sickly sweet smell of gun oil hung in the air. Racks of rifles, shotguns, and other hunting equipment stretched before him.

The shop was called The Frontiersman, and it had been the first store Decker went to when he had arrived in Santa Fe fifteen months earlier. To Decker's left, a clerk came to attention behind a glass counter of handguns, assessing him. The clerk appeared to be the same stocky sunburned man, wearing the same red plaid work shirt and the same Colt .45 semiautomatic pistol, who had waited on him before. Decker felt a vortex sucking him backward and downward.

'Yes, sir?'

Decker walked over. 'Some friends and I are making plans to go hunting. I need to pick up some things.'

'Whatever you need, we've either got it or we can order it.'

Decker didn't have time to wait five days for the mandatory background check on anyone who applied to purchase a handgun. A rifle could be obtained on the spot. Before Congress passed the assault-weapon ban, Decker would merely have chosen several AR-15s, the civilian version of the US military's M-16, commonly available in most gunshops until the ban. Now his choices weren't as easy. 'A Remington bolt-action .270.'

'Got it.'

'A Winchester lever-action .30-30. Short barrel – twenty-four inches.'

'No problem.'

'Two double-barrel shotguns, ten gauge.'

'No can do. The heaviest double barrels I've got are twelve gauge. Made by Stoeger.'

'Fine. I need a modified choke on the shotguns.'

'No problem there.' The clerk was writing a list.

'Short barrels on them.'

'Yep. Anything else?'

'A .22 semiautomatic rifle.'

'Ruger all right? Comes with a ten-round magazine.'

'Got any thirty-round magazines?'

'Three. Get them while they last. The government's threatening to outlaw them.'

'Give me all three. Two boxes of ammunition for each weapon. Buckshot for the shotguns. Three good hunting knives. Three camouflage suits, two large, one medium. Three sets of polypropylene long underwear. Three sets of dark cotton gloves. A tube of face camouflage. Two collapsible camp shovels. A dozen canteens – those Army-surplus metal ones. Your best first-aid kit.'

'A dozen canteens? You must have a lot of friends. Sounds like you're going to have yourself quite a time. You've covered almost everything – distance, midrange, up close.' The clerk joked, 'Why, the only thing you haven't included is a bow and arrows.'

'Good idea,' Decker said.

11

The total came to just under seventeen hundred dollars. Decker was concerned that Renata had contacts who could provide her with information from the computers of credit-card companies, so he didn't dare use his Visa card and warn her he was in town buying weapons. Instead, he invented a story about having had a big win at the blackjack tables in Las Vegas and paid cash. He needn't have worried that the seventeen one-hundred dollar bills would attract attention. This was New Mexico. When it came to weapons, how you paid for them and what you did with them was nobody else's business. The clerk hadn't even made a comment about the scrapes on Decker's face. Guns and personal remarks didn't mix.

It took Decker several trips to take all the equipment to the Buick. He would have asked Esperanza to come in and help him, but Esperanza had said he was known in the gun shop. In case of trouble, Decker didn't want Esperanza to be linked with him and a large purchase of weapons.

'Jesus, Decker, it looks like you're going to start a war. What's *this*? A bow and arrows?'

'And if that doesn't work against Renata and her gang, I'll piss on them.'

Esperanza started laughing.

'That's the stuff. Keep loose,' Decker said.

They closed the trunk and got in the car.

Beth waited in the back seat, her eyes still red from her conversation with Decker outside Esperanza's trailer. She made an obvious effort to rouse her spirits and be part of the group. 'What were you laughing about?'

'A bad joke.' Decker repeated it.

Beth shook her head and chuckled slightly. 'Sounds like a guy thing.'

'How come you bought so many canteens?' Esperanza asked. 'One for each of us. But what about the other nine?'

'Actually we're going to fill all twelve with plant fertilizer and fuel oil.'

'What the hell does that do?'

'Makes a damned good bomb.' Decker checked his watch and started the car. 'We'd better move it. It's almost four-thirty. We're running out of daylight.'

12

An hour later, after several other purchases, Decker steered off Cerrillos Road onto Interstate 25, but this time, he took the northbound route, heading in the opposite direction from Albuquerque.

'Why are we leaving town?' Agitated, Beth leaned forward. 'I told you I won't let you put me in an out-of-the-way motel. I won't be left out.'

'That's not why we're leaving town. Have you ever heard the expression, "There's no law west of the Pecos"?'

Beth looked mystified by the relevance of the comment. 'I seem to . . . In old westerns, or maybe in a history about the Southwest.'

'Well, the Pecos the expression refers to is the Pecos River, and that's where we're headed.'

Twenty minutes later, he turned to the left onto State Road 50 and shortly afterward reached the town of Pecos, whose architecture was dominated by traditional wood-sided peaked structures in sharp contrast with the stuccoed flat-roofed Hispanic-pueblo buildings in Santa Fe. He turned to the left again. Past Monastery Lake where he had gone fishing for trout his first summer in the area, then past the monastery for which the lake was named, he drove up an increasingly steep winding road that was bordered by tall pine trees. The sun had descended behind the looming western bluffs, casting the rugged scenery into shadow.

'We're going up into the Pecos Wilderness Area,' Decker said. 'That's the Pecos River on our right. In spots, it's only about twenty feet wide. You can't always see it because of the trees and rocks, but you can definitely hear it. What it lacks in size, it gains in speed.'

'This road is almost deserted,' Beth said. 'Why did we come up here?'

423

'This is a fishing area. Back among the trees, you might have seen a few cabins. After Labor Day, they're mostly unoccupied.' Decker pointed ahead. 'And once in a while, someone decides to sell.'

On the right, past a curve, a sign attached to a post read, EDNA FREED REALTY, then in smaller letters, *Contact Stephen Decker*, followed by a phone number.

Directly beyond the sign, Decker turned off the road, entered an opening among the fir trees, rumbled over a narrow wooden bridge above the river, and drove up a dirt lane to a clearing in front of a gray log cabin, whose sloped roof was rusted metal. The small building, surrounded by dense trees and bushes, was perched on a shadowy ridge not far above the clearing; it faced the turnoff from the country road; log steps were cut into the slope, leading up to the weathered front door.

'Just your basic home away from home,' Beth said.

'I've been trying to sell this place for the past six months,' Decker said. 'The key's in a lock box attached to the front door.'

Beth got out of the car, braced herself on her crutches, and shivered. 'I was warm in town, but it certainly gets chilly up here once the sun is low.'

'And damp from the river,' Decker said. 'That's why I bought thermal underwear for each of us. Before we get started, we'd better put them on.'

'Thermal underwear? But we won't be outside that long, will we?'

'Maybe all night.'

Beth looked surprised.

'There's a lot to do.' Decker opened the Buick's trunk. 'Put on these cotton gloves and help us load these weapons. Make sure you don't leave fingerprints on anything, including the ammunition. Do you know how to use a shotgun?'

'I do.'

'Someday you'll have to tell me how you learned. Your injured shoulder won't stand the shock of the recoil, of course. It would also make you awkward if you had to work a lever or a pump action to chamber a new round. That's why I bought double-barreled shotguns. The side-by-sides are wide and flat enough, they won't roll around if you set them on a log. You can lie down behind the log and shoot without raising the guns to aim them. You'll be able to get two shots per weapon. Opening the breach to reload isn't hard.'

'And what log did you have in mind?' Beth gamely asked, surprising him.

'I'm not sure. Esperanza and I are going to walk around and get a feel for the layout. Ask yourself what Renata and her friends will do when they get here tonight. How they'll approach. What cover they'll find most inviting. Then try to think of a position that gives you an advantage over them. It'll be dark in an hour. After that, after we've got our equipment assembled, we'll start rehearsing.'

13

And then, too frustratingly soon, it was time to go. Just before nine o'clock, in thickening darkness, Decker told Esperanza, 'The last flights of the evening will soon be arriving at the Albuquerque airport. We can't wait any longer. Do you think you can finish the rest of the preparations on your own?'

The cool night air chilled Esperanza's breath so that vapor could be seen coming from his mouth. 'How long will you be?'

'Expect us around midnight.'

'I'll be ready. You'd better not forget this.' Esperanza handed him the carry-on bag that had contained the million dollars but that now contained old newspapers they had found in the cabin.

The money was in a duffel bag at Esperanza's feet.

'Right,' Decker said. 'The plan won't work if Renata doesn't think I have the money.'

'And without me beside you,' Beth said.

'That's right, too,' Decker said. 'If Renata doesn't see us together, she'll wonder why we split up. She'll begin to suspect I'm keeping you out of danger while I lead her into a trap.'

'Imagine,' Beth said. 'And here, all the time, I thought you decided to bring me along because of the pleasure of my company.'

The remark made Decker feel as if he'd been stuck by a needle. Was her joke good-natured or— Not knowing what to say, he helped her into the front of the car, pushed back the passenger seat so that she had more room for her injured leg, then put her crutches in the back. Finally, when he got in beside her and shut his door, he thought of what to say. 'If we can get through this . . . If we can get to know each other . . .'

'I thought we already *did* know each other.'

'But who did I get to know? Are you Beth Dwyer or Diana Scolari?'

'Didn't *you* ever use fake names?'

Decker didn't know what to say to that, either. He started the Buick, nodded tensely to Esperanza, and made a U-turn in the clearing. His headlights flashing past dense pine trees, he drove down the lane, over the bridge, and onto the deserted road to Pecos. They were on their way.

But neither of them spoke until they were back on Interstate 25, passing Santa Fe, heading toward Albuquerque.

'Ask me,' Beth said.

'Ask . . . ?'

'Anything. Everything.' Her voice was heavy with emotion.

'That's a big order.'

'Damn it, try. By the time we get to the airport, I want to

know where we stand with each other.'

Decker increased speed, passing a pickup truck, trying to keep his speed under seventy-five.

'A relationship doesn't survive on its own,' Beth said. 'You have to work at it.'

'All right.' Decker hesitated, concentrating on the dark highway he sped along, feeling in a tunnel. 'You once told me something about your childhood. You said your parents had such violent arguments that you were afraid your father would burst into your bedroom and kill you while you slept. You said you arranged your pillows to make them look as if you were under the covers and then you slept under the bed, so he'd attack the pillows but not be able to get at you . . . Is that story true?'

'Yes. Did you suspect I lied to make you feel protective toward me?'

Decker didn't respond.

Beth frowned with growing concern. 'Is that the way you think – that people are constantly trying to manipulate you?'

'It's the way I *used* to think – before I came to Santa Fe.'

'And now you're back to your old habits.'

'Suspicion kept me alive. The fact is, if I had *kept* my old habits, if I hadn't let my guard down . . .' He didn't like where his logic was taking him and let the sentence dangle.

'You wouldn't have fallen in love with me. Is that what you wish?'

'I didn't say that. I'm not sure *what* I wanted to say. If I *hadn't* fallen in love with you, Renata would still be after me. *That* wouldn't have changed. I . . .' Decker's confusion tortured him. 'But I *did* fall in love with you, and if I could go back and do it all over again, if I *could* change the past . . .'

'Yes?' Beth sounded afraid.

'I'd do everything the same.'

Beth exhaled audibly. 'Then you believe me.'

427

'Everything comes down to trust.'

'And faith,' Beth said.

Decker's hands ached on the steering wheel. 'A *lot* of faith.'

14

Apprehensive, Decker left the Buick in the brightly lit rental-car lot next to the Albuquerque airport and walked with Beth into the terminal. On the second level, near the incoming baggage area, he surrendered the car keys to the Avis clerk, provided information about mileage and how much fuel was in the car, paid cash, and folded his receipt in his pocket.

'Catching a late plane out?' the clerk asked.

'Yes. We tried to make our vacation last as long as possible.'

'Come back to the Land of Enchantment.'

'We certainly will.'

Out of sight from the Avis counter, Decker guided Beth into a crowd that was descending from the terminal's upper levels, where the evening's final flights were arriving. Trying to make it seem as if he and Beth had just flown in, they went with the crowd down the escalator to the terminal's bottom level and out into the parking garage.

'And now it begins,' Decker murmured.

The sodium arc lights in the garage cast an eerie yellow glow. Although Decker was certain that none of Renata's group would have risked attracting the attention of security guards by hanging around the airport's arrival gates, he couldn't be as confident that a surveillance team was not in the garage, watching his Cherokee. The garage wasn't as carefully guarded as the airport was. Once in a while, a patrol car went through, but the team would see it coming and pretend to be loading luggage into a vehicle, then go back to watching as soon as the patrol car was gone. But if a surveillance team *was* in the garage, it was doubtful they would try to abduct Decker and Beth in so public a place, with only one exit from the airport. Travelers getting into nearby vehicles would see the attack and get a license number, then alert a security officer, who would phone ahead and arrange to have the road from the airport blocked. No, with too many opportunities for the attempted abduction to go wrong, the surveillance team would want to wait for privacy. In the meantime, they would use a cellular telephone to report to Renata that they had seen Decker carrying a bag that matched the description of the one containing the million dollars. Renata would be lulled into thinking that Decker didn't suspect she was in the area. After all, if he thought he was in immediate danger, he wouldn't be carrying the bagful of money, would he? He would have hidden it.

The Cherokee was to the left at the top of the stairs on the garage's second level. Decker unlocked the car, helped Beth into the front seat, threw the bag and her crutches into the back, and hurriedly got in, locking the doors, inserting his ignition key.

He hesitated.

'What are you waiting for?' Beth asked.

Decker stared at his right hand where it was about to turn the key. Sweat beaded his brow. 'Now is when we find out whether I'm right or wrong that Renata didn't rig this car with explosives.'

'Well, if you're wrong, we'll never know,' Beth said. 'To hell with it. We were talking about faith. Do it. Turn the key.'

Decker actually smiled as he obeyed. Waiting for the explosion that would blow the car apart, he heard the roar of the engine. 'Yes!' He backed out of the parking space and drove as quickly as safety allowed past travelers putting luggage into their cars, any of whom might be his enemy. A half-minute later, he was leaving the garage, stopping at one of the collection booths, paying the attendant, and joining the stream of cars speeding from the airport. Headlights glared.

His heart pounded furiously as he rounded a curve and pointed toward the lights gleaming in almost every window of the fourteen-story Best Western hotel. 'Right now, there's a lot of activity in one of those rooms. The needle on their homing-device monitor is telling them this car is in motion.' He wanted to increase speed but stopped the impulse when he saw the roof lights of a police car in front of him.

'I'm so nervous, I can't stop my knees from shaking,' Beth said.

'Concentrate on controlling your fear.'

'I can't.'

'You *have* to.'

Ahead, the police car turned a corner.

Decker lifted the hatch on the storage compartment that separated the two front seats. He took Esperanza's service pistol from where Esperanza had left it in the car when they had flown to New York. 'They'll be out of their room now, hurrying toward the hotel's parking lot.'

'How do *you* stop from being afraid?'

'I don't.'

'But you just said—'

'To control it, not stop it. Fear's a survival mechanism. It gives you strength. It makes you alert. It can save your life, but only if you keep it under control. If *it* controls *you*, it'll get you killed.'

Beth studied him hard. 'Obviously I've got a lot to learn about you.'

'The same here. It's like everything that happened with us before the attack on my house last Friday night was our honeymoon. Now the marriage has begun.' Decker sped onto the

Interstate, merging with a chaos of headlights. 'They've had time to reach the hotel's parking lot. They're getting in their vehicles.'

'Honeymoon? Marriage? ... Was what you just said a proposal?'

' ... Would that be such a bad idea?'

'I'd always disappoint you. I could never be the ideal woman you risked your life for.'

'That makes us even. I'm definitely not the ideal man.'

'You're giving a good imitation of that hero I told you I dreamed about as a little girl.'

'Heroes are fools. Heroes get themselves killed.' Decker increased speed to keep pace with traffic, which was doing sixty-five in a fifty-five-mile-an-hour zone. 'Renata and her friends will be rushing toward the Interstate now. The homing-device monitor will tell them which direction I've taken. I have to keep ahead of them. I can't let them pull abreast of me and force me off a deserted section of the highway.'

'Do you mind talking?'

'Now?'

'Will it distract you? If it doesn't, talking would help me not to be so afraid.'

'In that case, talk.'

'What's your worst fault?'

'Excuse me?'

'You were courting me all summer, showing me your best side. What's your worst?'

'You tell me *yours*.' Decker squinted toward the confusion of headlights in his rearview mirrow, watching for any vehicle that approached more rapidly than the others.

'I asked first.'

'You're serious?'

'Very.'

As the speed limit changed to sixty-five, Decker reluctantly began.

15

He told her that his father had been a career officer in the military and that the family had lived on bases all over the United States, moving frequently. 'I grew up learning not to get attached to people or places.' He told her that his father had not been demonstrative with affection and in fact had seemed to be embarrassed about showing any emotion, whether it was anger, sadness, or joy. 'I learned to hide what I felt.' He told her that when he entered the military, a logical choice for the son of a career officer, the special-operations training he received gave him further reinforcement in controlling his emotions.

'I had an instructor who took a liking to me and spent time talking with me on our off-hours. We used to get into philosophical discussions, a lot of which had to do with how to survive inhuman situations and yet not become inhuman. How to react to killing someone, for example. Or how to try to handle seeing a buddy get killed. He showed me something in a book about the mind and emotions that I've never forgotten.'

Decker kept glancing apprehensively toward the headlights in his rearview mirror. Traffic was becoming sparse. Nonetheless, he stayed in the passing lane, not wanting to be impeded by the occasional cars on his right.

'What was it he showed you?' Beth asked.

' "When we make fateful decisions, fate will inevitably occur. We all have emotions. Emotions themselves don't compromise us. But our thoughts about our emotions *will* compromise us if those thoughts aren't disciplined. Training controls our thoughts. Thoughts control our emotions." '

'It sounds like he was trying to put so many buffers over your emotions that you barely felt them.'

'Filters. The idea was to interpret my emotions so that they were always in my best interest. For instance –' Decker tasted something bitter. ' – Saturday night two friends of mine were killed.'

'Helping you try to find me?' Beth looked sickened.

'My grief for them threatened to overwhelm me, but I told myself I didn't have time. I had to postpone my grief until I could mourn for them properly. I couldn't mourn for them in the future if I didn't concentrate right then on staying alive. I *still* haven't found time to mourn for them.'

Beth repeated a statement from the quote he had given her. ' "Thoughts control our emotions." '

'That's how I lived.' Again, Decker checked the rearview mirror. Headlights approached with alarming speed. He rolled down his driver's window. Then he veered into the no-passing lane, held the steering wheel with his left hand, gripped Esperanza's pistol with his right, and prepared to fire if the vehicle coming up on his left attempted to ram him sideways off this barren section of the Interstate.

The vehicle's headlights were on their brightest setting, their intense reflection in Decker's rearview mirror almost blinding. Decker reduced speed abruptly so that the vehicle would surge past him before the driver had a chance to put on the brakes. But the vehicle not only rushed past; it continued speeding into the distance, its outline that of a huge pickup truck. Its red taillights receded into the darkness.

'He must be doing ninety,' Decker said. 'If I give him a little distance and then match his speed, that truck will run interference for me with any state trooper parked at the side of the Interstate. The trooper will see the truck first and go after *it*. I'll have time to reduce speed and slip past.'

The interior of the car became quiet.

'So,' Beth said at last, 'emotions make you uncomfortable? You certainly fooled me this summer.'

'Because I was making a conscious effort to change. To open up and allow myself to feel. When you walked into my office that first day, I was ready, for the first time in my life, to fall in love.'

'And now you feel betrayed because the woman you fell in love with wasn't the woman she said she was.'

Decker didn't respond.

Beth continued, 'You're thinking it might be safer to go back to what you were, to distance yourself and not allow any emotions that might make you vulnerable.'

'The notion occurred to me.'

'And?'

'To hell with my pride.' Decker squeezed her hand. 'You asked me if I wanted to make a fresh start. Yes. Because the alternative scares me to death. I don't want to lose you. I'd go crazy if I couldn't spend the rest of my life with you . . . I guess I'm *not* reverting, after all.'

You'd *better* revert, he told himself. You have to get both of us through this night alive.

16

Tension produced the familiar aching pressure in his stomach that he had suffered when he worked for the Agency. The omelette he had eaten that morning on the plane remained in his stomach and burned like acid, as did the quick take-out burgers and fries that he had grabbed for everyone while picking up equipment during the afternoon. Just like old times, he thought.

He wondered how close his pursuers were to him and what

they were deciding. Did they have members of their group waiting ahead of them in Santa Fe? Maybe only a few of Renata's friends had been stationed at the Best Western hotel, not enough to attempt an interception. Maybe they had used a cellular telephone to call ahead and arrange for reinforcements. Or maybe Decker was wrong and his car didn't have a homing device hidden in it. Maybe his plan was useless. No, he told himself emphatically. I've been doing this for a lot of years. I know how this is done. Given the circumstances, I *know* how Renata would behave.

Well, he thought dismally, isn't it nice to be certain?

When he passed the three exits to Santa Fe, continuing to speed along Interstate 25, it amused him to imagine the confusion his pursuers would be feeling, their frantic discussions as they tried to figure out why he hadn't stopped and where he was going. They would all be after him now, though, the ones in Santa Fe as well as those who had followed him from Albuquerque. Of that, he was sure, just as he was sure that he had not yet faced his biggest risks of the night – the isolation of State Road 50, for example.

It was two-lane, dark, narrow, and winding, with sporadic tiny communities along it but mostly shadowy scrub brush and trees. It offered perfect opportunities for his pursuers to force him off the road, with no one to see what happened. He couldn't possibly keep driving as fast as he did on the Interstate. At the first sharp curve, he would overturn his car. In places, even forty-five miles an hour was extreme. He hunched forward, peering at the darkness beyond his headlights, trying to gain every second he could on the straight, reducing speed, steering tensely around turns, once again accelerating.

'I can't risk taking my eyes off the road to check the rearview mirror,' he told Beth. 'Look behind us. Do you see any headlights?'

'No. Wait, now I do.'

'What?'

'Coming around the last curve. One— I'm wrong – it looks like *two* cars. The second just came around the curve.'

'Jesus.'

'They don't seem to be gaining on us. Why would they hold back? Maybe it's not them,' Beth said.

'Or maybe they want to know what they're getting into before they make their move. Ahead of us.'

'Lights.'

'Yes. We've reached Pecos.'

Near midnight on a Tuesday night, there was almost no activity. Decker reduced his speed as much as he dared, turned left onto the quiet main street, and proceeded north toward the mountains.

'I don't see the headlights anymore,' Beth said. 'The cars must belong to people who live in town.'

'Maybe.' As soon as the glow of the sleepy town was behind him, Decker again picked up speed, climbing the dark narrow road into the wilderness area. 'Or maybe the cars do belong to Renata and her gang, and they're holding back, not wanting to make it obvious they're following us. They must be curious what we're doing up here.'

In the darkness, the dense pine trees formed what seemed to be an impenetrable wall.

'It doesn't look very welcoming,' Beth said.

'Good. Renata will conclude the only reason anybody would come up here is to hide. We're getting closer. Almost there. Just a few more—'

17

He nearly shot past the *Contact Stephen Decker* realty sign before he reduced speed enough to turn into the barely visible break between fir trees. Terribly aware that he could be trapping Beth and himself as much as he was attempting to trap Renata, he crossed the wooden bridge above the roar of the swift, narrow Pecos River, entered the gloomy clearing, parked in front of the steps up to the house, and turned off the engine. Only then did he push in the knob for his headlights – the sequence activated a feature that kept his lights on for an additional two minutes.

With the aid of those lights, he got Beth's crutches and the carry-on bag from the back seat. He felt a desperate compulsion to hurry, but he didn't dare give in to it. If Renata and her gang drove past and saw him rushing up to the cabin, they would immediately suspect that he knew he was being followed, that he anticipated their arrival, that they were being set up. Tensely repressing his impatience, he allowed himself to look as weary as he felt. Following Beth up the log steps, he reached a metal box attached to the cabin's doorknob. The lights from his car provided just enough illumination for him to use his key to unlock the box. He opened the lid, took out the key to the cabin, unlocked the door, and helped Beth inside.

The moment the door was closed and locked, the lights turned on, Decker responded to the urgency swelling inside him. The blinds were already drawn on the cabin, so no one outside could see him support Beth while she dropped her crutches and picked up camouflage coveralls that Decker had bought at the gun shop. She pulled them on over her slacks and blouse. As soon as she tugged up the zipper and took back her crutches, Decker hurriedly put on his own camouflage coveralls. Before leaving the cabin to go to the airport, they had already put on the polypropylene long underwear he had bought. Now Decker smeared Beth's face and then his own with dark grease from a tube of camouflage coloring. When they had rehearsed these movements early in the evening, they had gotten ready in just under two minutes, but now it seemed tensely to Decker that they were taking much longer. Hurry, he thought. To avoid leaving fingerprints, they put on dark cotton gloves, thin enough to be able to shoot with, thick enough to provide some warmth. When Decker switched on a small radio, a Country and Western singer started wailing about 'livin' and lovin' and leavin' and . . .' Decker kept the lights on, helped Beth out the back door, shut it behind him, and risked pausing in the chill darkness long enough to stroke her arm with encouragement and affection.

She trembled, but she did what had to be done, what they had rehearsed, disappearing to the left of the cabin.

Impressed by her courage, Decker went to the right. At the front of the cabin, his headlights had gone off. Away from the glow of the cabin's windows, the darkness thickened. Then Decker's eyes adjusted, the moon and the unimaginable amount of stars, typically brilliant in the high country, giving the night a paradoxical gentle glow.

When Decker and Esperanza had walked around the property, assessing it from a tactical point of view, they had decided to make use of a game trail concealed by dense bushes at the back of the cabin. Unseen from the road, Beth was now moving along that trail and would soon reach a thick tree that the trail went around. There, Beth would lower herself to the forest floor, squirm down a slope through bushes, and reach a shallow pit that Esperanza had dug, where the two double-barrel shotguns lay on a log, ready for her to use.

Meanwhile, Decker crept through the darkness to a similar shallow pit that he himself had dug, using one of the camp shovels he had bought at the gunshop. Even wearing three layers of clothing, he felt the dampness of the ground. Lying behind a log, concealed by bushes, he groped around but couldn't find what he was looking for. His pulse skipped nervously until he finally touched the lever-action Winchester .30-30. The powerful weapon was designed for mid-range use in brush country such as this. It held six rounds in its magazine and one in the firing chamber, and could be shot as rapidly as the well-oiled lever behind the trigger could be worked up and down.

Next to the rifle was a car battery, one of the other items he had purchased before leaving Santa Fe. And next to the battery were twelve pairs of electrical wires, the ends of which were exposed. These wires led to canteens that were filled with fuel oil and a type of plant fertilizer, the main component of which was ammonium nitrate. Mixed in the proper ratio, the ingredients produced an explosive. To add bite, Decker had cut open several shotgun shells and poured in buckshot and gunpowder from them. To make a detonator for each bomb, he had broken the outer glass from twelve one-hundred-watt light bulbs, taking care not to use too much force and destroy the filament on the inside. He had gripped the metal stem of each bulb and inserted a filament into each canteen. Two wires were then taped to the stem of each bulb. The canteens were buried at strategic spots and covered with leaves. The pairs of wires, concealed in a like manner, led to the car battery next to Decker. The wires were arranged left to right in a pattern that matched where the canteens were located. If Decker chose a pair and pressed one end to the battery's positive pole while pressing the other end to the negative pole, he would complete a circuit that caused the light-bulb filament to burn and detonate the bomb.

He was ready. Down the lane and across the narrow Pecos River, on the other side of the road, Esperanza was hiding in the forest. He would have seen Decker drive onto the property and would be waiting for Renata and her friends to arrive. Common sense dictated that, when their homing-device receiver warned them that Decker had turned off the road, they wouldn't just follow him into the lane without first taking care to find out what trouble they might be getting into. Rather, they would pass the entrance to the lane, drive a prudent distance up the road, and park, proceeding cautiously back to the lane. They would want to avoid the bottleneck of the lane, but they wouldn't be able to, because the only other way to get onto the property was by crossing the swift river, and in the darkness, that maneuver was too risky.

The moment Renata and her group were off the road and moving into the lane, Esperanza would emerge from cover and disable their vehicles so that, if the group had a premonition and hurried back to the cars, they wouldn't be able to escape. There would probably be two vehicles – one for the surveillance team at the airport, the other for the team in Santa Fe. As soon as Esperanza had made them inoperable by cramming a twig into the stem valve of several tires, the slight hiss of escaping air muffled by the roar of the river, he would stalk the group, using the .22 semiautomatic rifle with its thirty-round magazine and two other magazines secured beneath his belt, attacking from the rear when the shooting started. Although light, the .22 had several advantages – it was relatively silent, it had a large ammunition capacity, and it could fire with extreme rapidity. These qualities would be useful in a short-range, hit-and-run action. The canteens would be exploding; Beth would be using the shotgun; Decker would be firing the Winchester, with the Remington bolt-action as a backup. If everything went as planned, Renata and her group would be dead within thirty seconds.

The trouble is, Decker thought, Murphy's Law had a way of interfering with plans. Whatever *can* go wrong, *will* go wrong.

And there were a lot of question marks in this plan. Would Renata and all of her group go up the lane at the same time? Would they sense a trap and check to make sure that no one was sneaking up behind them? Would Beth be able to control her reactions and fire at the right time as they had rehearsed it? For that matter, would fear paralyze her, preventing her from firing at all? Or would—

18

Decker heard a noise that sounded like a branch being snapped. He nervously held his breath, not wanting even that slight sound to interfere with his hearing. Pressed hard against the dank ground, he listened, trying to filter out the faint Country and Western music from the radio in the cabin, ignoring the muffled rush of the river, waiting for the sound to be repeated. It seemed to have come from near the lane, but he couldn't assume that a human being had made it. This close to the wilderness area, there were plenty of nocturnal animals. The noise might not indicate a threat.

He couldn't help wondering how Beth had reacted to it. Would she be able to control her fear? He kept straining to assure himself that her presence was necessary. If she hadn't come along, Renata might have suspected that Decker was planning a trap and didn't want to put Beth in danger. At the same time, Decker kept arguing with himself that maybe Beth's presence wasn't absolutely necessary. Maybe he shouldn't have involved her. Maybe he had demanded too much from her.

She doesn't have to prove anything to me.

You sure made it seem that way.

Stop, he told himself. There is only one thing you should be concentrating on, and that is getting through this night alive.

Getting *Beth* through this night alive.

When he failed to hear a repetition of the sound, he exhaled slowly. The cabin was to his right, the glow of lights through its windows. But he took care not to compromise his night vision by glancing in that direction. Instead, he focused his gaze straight ahead toward the road, the bridge, the lane, and the clearing. The lights in the cabin would provide a beacon for anyone sneaking up and make it hard for a stalker to adjust his or her night vision to check the darkness around the cabin. Conversely, the spill from those lights, adding to the illumination from the brilliant moonglow and starlight, were to Decker's advantage, easy on his eyes, at the periphery of his vision. He had the sense that he was peering through a gigantic light-enhancing lens.

Crickets screeched. A new mournful song about open doors and empty hearts played faintly on the cabin's radio. At once Decker stiffened, again hearing the sound of a branch being snapped. This time, he had no doubt that the sound had come from near the lane, from the trees and bushes to the right of it. Had Renata and her gang managed to cross the bridge without his having seen their silhouettes? That didn't seem likely — unless they had crossed the bridge before he reached this shallow pit. But the bridge had been out of his sight for only a few minutes. Did it make sense that Renata would have had time to drive by (he hadn't seen any passing headlights), conclude that he was parked up the lane, stop, reconnoiter the area, and cross the bridge before he came out of the cabin? She and her group would have had to rush to the point of recklessness. That wasn't Renata's style.

But when Decker heard the noise a third time, he picked up the Winchester. It suddenly occurred to him that Beth would be doing the same thing, gripping one of the shotguns, but would she have the discipline not to pull the trigger until it was absolutely necessary? If she panicked and fired too soon, before her targets were in range, she would ruin the trap and probably get herself killed. During the ride up from Albuquerque, Decker had emphasized this danger, urging her to remember that a shotgun was a short-range weapon, that she mustn't shoot until Decker did and she had obvious targets in the clearing. The devastating spray of buckshot would make up for any problem that her injured shoulder gave her in aiming, especially if she discharged all four barrels in rapid succession.

Remember what I told you, Beth. Hold your fire.

Decker waited. Nothing. No further sound of a branch being snapped. What he judged to be five minutes passed, and still the sound was not repeated. He couldn't look at his watch. It was in his pocket. Before arriving at the cabin, he had made certain that he and Beth took off their watches and put them away, lest the luminous dials reveal their position in the darkness.

What he judged to be *ten* minutes passed. He had talked to Beth about how it felt to lie motionless possibly for hours, about subduing impatience, about ignoring the past and the future. Get in the moment and *stay* in the moment. Tell yourself that you're in a contest, that the other side is going to move before *you* do. At the Albuquerque airport, Decker had insisted that they both use a restroom, even though neither of them felt an urge, pointing out that at night when they were lying in the forest, a full bladder could make them uncomfortable enough that they might lose their concentration. Getting up to a squat to relieve oneself was out of the question – the movement would attract attention. The only option was to relieve oneself in one's clothes, and that definitely resulted in loss of concentration.

Fifteen minutes. Twenty. No more suspicious sounds. No signs of activity on the moonbathed lane or in the murky bushes next to it. Patience, Decker told himself. But a part of him began to wonder if his logic had been valid. Perhaps Renata had not hidden a homing device on his car. Perhaps Renata wasn't anywhere in the area.

19

The night's chill enveloped Decker, but he felt an even greater chill when the forest moved. A section of it, something low, about the size of someone crouching, shifted warily from bush to bush. But the movement wasn't near the lane, not where Decker had expected it to be. Instead, dismayingly, the figure was already halfway around the tree-rimmed edge of the clearing, creeping toward the cabin. How did he get so far without my seeing him? Decker thought in alarm.

Where are the others?

His chill intensified as he saw another figure near the first one. *This* figure seemed not to be skirting the edge of the clearing but, instead, to be emerging from deep within the forest, as if coming from the north rather than from the west, from the bridge. The only explanation would have to be that they had found another way across the river.

But how? I checked the river for a hundred yards up the road, as far as the group was likely to drive before stopping. There weren't any logs across the river, any footbridges, any boulders that might serve as stepping stones.

As a third figure emerged from the forest halfway around the clearing, Decker fought to subdue a wave of nausea, understanding what must have happened. After parking, the group had separated. Some had come southward down the road to guard the exit from the lane, to make sure Decker stayed put. But the others had hiked *northward*, a direction Decker had not anticipated. Higher up the road, they had come to another property and used its bridge to cross the river. The properties in this area tended to be a quarter mile apart. Decker had never imagined that in the night, feeling pressure, Renata and her group would hike so far out of their way. They had taken so long to get to the clearing because they had crept south through dense forest, moving with laborious slowness to make as little noise as possible. Members of the group would be emerging from the forest behind the house, also, doing their best to encircle it.

Behind Decker.

Behind *Beth*.

He imagined an enemy creeping onto her, both of them caught by surprise but the killer reacting more quickly, shooting Beth before she had a chance to defend herself. Decker came close to shifting instantly out of his hiding place and crawling hurriedly through the dark underbrush to get to her and defend her. But he couldn't allow himself to give in to the impulse. He would be endangering Beth as well as himself if he acted prematurely, without sufficient information. The trouble was, when he did have that information, it might be too late.

His hesitation saved his life as, behind him, sickeningly close, a twig snapped. He felt his heart seem to swell and rise toward his throat, choking him, as a shoe made a crunching sound on fallen pine needles. Slowly, a painstaking quarter-inch at a time, he turned his head. Carefully. With agonizing deliberateness. For all he knew, a weapon was being aimed at him, but he couldn't risk making a sudden move to look. If he hadn't been noticed, a backward jerk of his head would give him away, *would* make him a target.

Sweat broke out on his forehead. Little by little, the shadowy woods behind him came into view. Another footstep easing down on crunchy pine needles made him inwardly flinch. The speed of his pulse made him feel lightheaded as he saw a figure ten feet away. Renata? No. Too heavy. Shoulders too broad. The figure was male, holding a rifle, his back to Decker. Facing the cabin, the man sank down, eerily vanishing among bushes. Decker imagined the scene from the man's point of view. Music in the cabin. Lights beyond closed blinds. Part of Decker's preparations had been to set up timers for the lamps and the radio, so that one by one they would go off within the next hour. That realistic touch would make Renata and her friends confident that they had trapped their quarry.

On the other side of the clearing, the three figures were no longer visible. Presumably they had spread out, flanking the cabin, preparing to attack it simultaneously. *Will they wait until the lights are out and they think we're asleep, or will they hurl stun grenades through the windows and break in right now?*

When they rush through the trees, will they stumble onto Beth?

Decker's original plan had depended on the group being caught together after they crossed the bridge and tried to sneak up the lane, devastated by explosions, simultaneously coming under gunfire from three positions. Now, the only way he could think of to retain the element of surprise was—

Slowly, he squirmed from the pit. Feeling before him, he checked for anything that might cause him to make a noise. His movements were almost as gradual as when he had turned his head. He eased through a narrow space between two bushes, approaching the spot where the figure had sank down. The figure's attention would be centered on the cabin. The others would be staring at it as well, not looking in this direction. It had been twelve years since Decker had used a blade to kill a man. Gripping one of the hunting knives that he had bought at the gun shop and that he had earlier placed next to the Winchester at the side of the pit, he shifted through more bushes.

There. Five feet ahead. Braced on one knee. Holding a rifle. Watching the house.

When we make fateful decisions, fate will inevitably occur.

446

Without hesitation, Decker lunged. His left hand whipped in front of the gunman to seize his nostrils and mouth, the cotton glove helping to muffle any sound the figure made as Decker jerked him backward and slashed his throat, severing his jugular vein and his voice box.

Emotions themselves don't compromise us. But our thoughts about our emotions will compromise us if those thoughts aren't disciplined.

Blood gushed, hot, viscous. The man stiffened... trembled... became dead weight. Decker eased the corpse silently to the ground. Moonlight revealed a wisp of what resembled steam at the dead man's gaping throat.

Training controls our thoughts. Thoughts control our emotions.

20

Hearing his hammer-like pulse behind his ears, Decker knelt behind bushes, straining to detect a sign of where the other figures prepared to make their move. Were there more he didn't know about? Someone would be at the road, guarding the exit from the lane. And what about the property a quarter mile south of here? Decker's hunters would have seen it as they passed it, pursuing Decker's Jeep Cherokee. Had some of Renata's group returned to it, crossing the bridge *down there*, approaching the cabin from *that* direction? Maybe that was how the dead man at Decker's feet had reached this side of the clearing.

What *can* go wrong, *will* go wrong. The group must have had a plan before they approached the cabin. But how would they have communicated to synchronize their movements? Lapel microphones and earplug receivers were a possibility, although it was doubtful that the group would want to risk making even a whisper of a noise. Decker checked the corpse's ears and jacket and verified his doubt, not finding any miniature two-way radio equipment.

What other way could they synchronize their attack? Feeling along the corpse's left wrist, Decker found a watch, but one that had no luminous hands that might give away his position. Instead of a glass face, it had a metal hatch, and when Decker raised it, the only way he could tell the time in the darkness was to remove a glove, then touch the long minute hand, the short hour hand, and the palpable numbers along the notched rim. Familiar with this type of watch, Decker felt the minute hand jerk forward and quickly determined that the time was five minutes to one.

Would the attack on the cabin occur at one o'clock? Decker didn't have much time to get ready. He put on his glove, wiped his fingerprint off the watch, and crawled back through bushes with as much speed as silence permitted, returning to the dank shallow pit, which more and more reminded him of a grave. There, he felt along the row of wires and selected two pairs that were on the extreme right. He separated the pairs, holding one pair in his left hand, the other in his right, ready to touch one exposed tip from each pair to the positive pole of the car battery, the other exposed tips to the negative pole.

Despite the night's cold air, sweat oozed from the camouflage grease on his forehead. He concentrated on the cabin, grudgingly aware that the lights in the windows ruined his night vision. Since touching the watch on the corpse's wrist, he had been counting, estimating that four minutes and thirty seconds had passed, that the attack on the cabin would begin in just about—

He was fifteen seconds off. Windows shattered. Eye-searing flashes and ear-torturing roars from stun grenades erupted within the cabin. Dark figures holding rifles scrambled from the cover of bushes, two crashing through the front door, one through the back. Presumably the man whom Decker had killed would have joined the solitary figure barging through the back door, but that solitary figure (perhaps it was Renata) was so intent on the attack that he (she) didn't seem to notice that the partner hadn't shown up to help.

From the pit, Decker saw urgent shadows that the cabin's lights cast on the window blinds. Angry motions. Shouts. A curse. Not finding anyone in the cabin, the attackers knew that they had been tricked, that they were in a trap. They would be desperate to get out of the cabin before the trap was sprung. Another curse. The shadows frantically retreated. Decker flicked his gaze back and forth to the front and back doors of the cabin. Would they all rush out one entrance, or would they split up as they had going in?

The latter. Seeing a lone figure rush from the back, Decker instantly pressed wires to the poles on the battery. Night became day. The ground beneath the figure heaved in a thunderous blaze, spewing earth, buckshot, and fragments of metal from the canteen. The figure arched through the air. Immediately the two killers rushing from the front door faltered at the sound of the blast. Decker pressed the other pair of wires to the battery's poles, and the resultant explosion was even more powerful than the first, a fiery roar that tore a crater in the earth and catapulted the screaming figures down the steps toward Decker's car. The cabin's windows were shattered. Flames seethed up the outside walls.

Squinting from the ferocity of the blaze, Decker dropped the wires and picked up the Winchester. As rapidly as he could work the lever, he shot toward the back of the cabin, strafing the area where the lone figure had fallen. The unmistakable blast from a shotgun told him that Beth was shooting at the figures who had landed in the clearing near her. Another blast. Another. Another.

If there were more attackers in the area, the noise from the shotguns, not to mention the muzzle flashes, would reveal Beth's position. She had been instructed to grab both shotguns and roll fifteen feet to her right, where another pit had been dug. There, a box of shotgun shells waited for her. Hurrying, she would reload and fire again, continuing to switch locations.

But Decker didn't have time to think about that. He had to have faith that Beth was following the plan. For his part, he fired the seventh and final round that the Winchester held, dropped the rifle, pulled out Esperanza's 9mm Beretta, and tried to stay among shadows as he stalked through bushes toward where the lone figure had fallen. The closer he came to the burning cabin, the more impossible it was for him to be concealed by darkness. But the illumination from the flames had the benefit of revealing a figure on the ground. Decker shot, the figure jerking when the bullet struck his (her) head.

Hearing more roars from Beth's shotgun, Decker rushed forward, aimed down while he shoved the corpse over with his shoe, and failed to see what he had been hoping for. The face below him was not a woman's, not Renata's, instead that of one of her brothers whom Decker had spoken to in the Rome cafe fifteen months ago, when McKittrick had introduced Decker to Renata.

Decker pivoted, feeling exposed, eager to retreat from the burning cabin to the darkness of the woods. At the same time, he was seized by a compulsion to get to Beth, to help her, to discover if either of the two figures she was shooting at (and perhaps had killed) was Renata. He wondered anxiously what was happening with Esperanza. Had Esperanza eliminated the guards whom Decker assumed had been stationed on the road, on the other side of the bridge, at the exit from the lane? But Decker had to believe that Esperanza could take care of himself whereas Beth, as superbly as she had behaved, might now be close to panic.

Even though his choice put him at risk, Decker ran along the side of the burning cabin, planning to find cover at the front and shoot toward the figures who had landed in the clearing, near Decker's car. If they were still alive, they would be concentrating on where Beth was shooting from. Decker could take them by surprise.

But a bullet whizzing past, walloping into the cabin, took *Decker* by surprise. It came from his left, from the section of woods where he had been hiding. The man Decker had killed must have had a companion, who hadn't been as efficient in making his way through the woods from the property to the south. Decker sprawled to the ground and rolled toward a wide sheltering pine tree. A bullet tore up dirt behind him, the muzzle flash coming from the left of the tree. Decker scrambled to the right, circling the tree, shooting toward where he had seen the muzzle flash. Immediately he dove farther to the right, saw another flash, and aimed toward it, but before he could pull the trigger, he heard someone scream.

21

The scream belonged to Beth. Despite the rumble of flames from the burning cabin, Decker heard a disturbance behind him, at the edge of the clearing, bushes rustling, branches being snapped, the sounds of a struggle.

Beth screamed again. Then someone yelled what might have been Decker's name. Not Beth. The voice was grotesque, deep, gravelly, and distorted. Again it yelled what might have been Decker's name, and Decker now was absolutely certain that the guttural voice belonged to Renata. Wary of the gunman in the murky trees ahead of him, risking a glance behind him, Decker confirmed his grave fear. A black-jumpsuited woman, with hair cut short like a boy's, with a tall slim sensuous figure, held Beth captive in the clearing, the left arm around Beth's throat, the right arm holding the barrel of a pistol to Beth's right temple.

Renata.

Even at a distance of thirty yards, the rage in her dark eyes was obvious. Her left arm encircled Beth's throat so tightly that Beth's features were twisted, her mouth forced open, grimacing, gasping for air. Beth clawed at Renata's arm, struggling to get free, but the injuries to her right leg and shoulder robbed her of strength and stability. Indeed her right leg had collapsed beneath her. She almost dangled from Renata's stranglehold, in danger of being choked to death.

'Decker!' Renata yelled, the voice so guttural that Decker had trouble deciphering the words. 'Throw down your gun! Get down here! Now! Or I'll kill her!'

Desperation paralyzed him.

'Do it!' Renata screamed hoarsely. 'Now!'

Decker's hesitation was broken when Renata cocked the pistol. Even with the noise of the fire, he thought he heard only one thing – the snick of the hammer being pulled back. Hearing it wasn't possible, of course. Renata was too far away. But in Decker's imagination, it sounded dismayingly vivid, as if the gun was at his own head.

'No! Wait!' Decker yelled.

'Do what I say if you want her to live!'

Beth managed to squeeze out a few strangled words. 'Steve, save yourself!'

'Shut the hell up!' Renata increased the pressure of her arm around Beth's throat. Beth's face became more distorted, her eyes bulging, her color darkening. Renata yelled to Decker, 'Do it, or I won't bother shooting her! I'll break her neck! I'll leave her paralyzed for the rest of her life!'

Unnervingly aware of the gunman somewhere in the forest behind him, Decker calculated his chances of shooting Renata. With a handgun? In firelight? At thirty yards? With his chest heaving and his hands shaking as much they were? Impossible. Even if Decker tried it, the moment he raised his gun to aim, Renata would have sufficient warning to pull the trigger and blow Beth's brains out.

'You have three seconds!' Renata yelled. 'One! Two!'

Decker saw Renata's right arm move. He imagined her finger tightening on the trigger. 'Wait!' he screamed again.

'Now!'

'*I'm coming out!*'

Although the blaze from the cabin warmed Decker's right side, the area between his shoulder blades felt ominously cold as he thought of the gunman in the forest training a weapon on him while he emerged from the shadows of the pine tree.

He raised his hands.

'Drop your pistol!' Renata shouted, her voice grotesque as if something had been wedged in her throat.

Decker obeyed, the pistol thunking onto the forest floor. He walked closer, feeling wobbly in his legs, dreading the impact that would topple him when the gunman behind him shot him in the back. But dying was better than seeing Beth die. He didn't want to remain alive without her.

Arms high, he reached the slope to the clearing, eased down it sideways, passed his car, and saw the bodies of the two men who had been caught in the explosion at the front of the cabin. He stopped in front of Renata.

'Look, you bastard,' Renata growled, pointing at the corpses. 'See what she did. See *this*.' Her formerly alluring face was made repulsive by the hate that distorted it. 'See what *you* did!' She raised her chin so that, in the light from the burning cabin, Decker was able to see the ugly puckered bullet-wound scar at the front of Renata's throat, near her voice box. 'There's a bigger scar in the back!'

Decker could barely understand her. His mind worked urgently to keep translating.

'You killed my brothers! *What do you think I should do to you?*'

Decker didn't have an answer.

'Should I blow a hole in *your* throat? Should I blow a hole in *her* throat? Where's my money?'

'In the carry-on bag I found in your car in New York.'

'Where's the damned carry-on bag? When I drove past the lane, I saw you taking it into the cabin.'

Decker nodded. 'That's where I left it.' He glanced toward the blazing cabin.

'You didn't bring it out with you?'

'No.'

'You *left* it in there?'

'That's what I said.'

'*My million dollars?*'

'Minus a couple of thousand I spent on equipment.'

'You're *lying*.'

Decker glanced again toward the flames, trying to prolong the conversation. 'Afraid not.'

'Then prove it,' Renata snapped.

'What are you talking about? How could I possibly prove it?'

'Bring me the money.'

'What?'

'Go in there and get my money.'

'In the fire? I wouldn't have a chance.'

'You want to talk about taking a chance? This is the only chance you're going to get. Go in the cabin and ... get ... my ... money.'

The flames roared.

'No,' Decker said.

'Then I'll make *her* go in for it.' Renata dragged Beth across the clearing toward the stairs up to the cabin. At the same time, she yelled toward the dark forest behind the burning cabin, 'Pietro! Get down here! Guard him!'

Beth's eyelids fluttered. Her hands stopped fighting to pull away Renata's arm. Her face an alarming color, she went limp, the pressure around her neck so severe that she lost consciousness.

'Pietro!' Renata yanked Beth up several log steps. 'Where are you? I said come down here!'

The flames roared higher, covering the exterior of the cabin, filling the interior with churning smoke and a fierce crimson glow.

Renata jerked Beth to the top of the steps and halted, repulsed by the savagery of the heat. She released Beth's throat and straightened her to shove her into the flames.

Decker could no longer restrain himself. Even though he knew he'd be shot, he charged wildly toward the steps, desperate to help Beth.

'Pietro!'

Decker reached the first step.

'Shoot him, Pietro!'

Decker was halfway up.

Shoving Beth toward the flames, Renata simultaneously turned to aim at Decker.

The barrel of her pistol was leveled at Decker's face as a hand from behind her came crashing down on the pistol. The hand belonged to Beth, who had only pretended to lose consciousness. After Renata had pushed her, she had lurched toward the flames, staggered back, pivoted, and flung her weight onto Renata. She wedged her thumb between the pistol's hammer and its firing pin an instant before Renata pulled the trigger, the hammer's powerful spring driving the hammer into Beth's flesh. Beth's unexpected weight caused Renata to lose her balance. The two women tumbled down the steps, rolling, twisting, bumping, striking Decker, carrying him with them.

They jolted to a stop at the bottom, the three of them tangled on the ground. Beth's thumb was still wedged beneath the pistol's hammer. She tried to yank the pistol out of Renata's grasp but didn't have the strength. For her part, Renata gave a mighty jerk to the weapon and wrenched it free, ripping Beth's thumb open. Flat on the ground, his arms caught beneath the two women, Decker couldn't move as Renata swung the pistol at him. Wincing, in agony, Beth rolled over Decker, clutched the pistol, and struggled to deflect the gun.

The ground heaved, the explosive in one of the canteens detonating, a blazing roar erupting from the far side of the clearing. A second explosion, a little closer, tore up a crater. A third explosion, halfway across the clearing, threw Beth and Renata back from the shockwave. A fourth explosion, nearer than halfway, deafened Decker. Someone was setting off the canteens in sequence, marching the explosions across the area.

Smoke drifted over Decker. Stunned, he took a moment to recover from the surprise and force of the detonations. In a frenzy, he rolled through the smoke to find and help Beth. But he wasn't quick enough. Amid the smoke, he heard a shot, a second, a third. He screamed and lurched forward, hearing a fourth shot, a fifth, a sixth. The shots were directly in front of him. A seventh. An eighth. A breeze caused the smoke to clear, and as Decker heard a ninth shot, he gaped down at Renata and Beth locked in what might have been an embrace.

'Beth!'

A tenth shot.

In a rage, Decker stormed toward Renata and yanked her away, ready to snap her arm so she'd drop her pistol, to crack her ribs, to smash her nose and gouge out her eyes, to punish her for killing Beth. But the dead weight he held, the blood oozing from numerous holes in Renata's body, dribbling from her lips, showed him how much he had been mistaken. It wasn't Renata who had been shooting but, rather, Beth.

22

Beth's eyes communicated an emotion close to hysteria. She was about to shoot an eleventh time but then realized that Decker was in the way and slowly lowered the weapon, then sank to the ground.

Surrounded by smoke, Decker dropped Renata and hurried to her.

'There wasn't anything wrong with my *left* arm,' Beth murmured in what sounded almost like triumph.

'How bad are you hurt?' Decker quickly wrapped a handkerchief around her gashed bleeding thumb.

'Sore all over. God, I hope there aren't any more of them.'

'There was one in the forest. He should have moved against us by now.'

'He's dead,' a voice said from the other side of the drifting smoke.

Decker looked up.

'They're *all* dead.' Silhouetted by the flames from the cabin, Esperanza stepped specter-like from the smoke. A rifle was slung over his shoulder. In his right hand, he held the bow Decker had bought. In his left, he held a quiver of arrows.

'When the explosions went off at the cabin, I shot two men who were guarding the exit from the lane,' Esperanza said. 'Back that far, the .22 didn't make enough noise to be heard with all the other commotion. But I couldn't use it on the man

Renata called Pietro. He and I were too close to the clearing. She might have heard *those* shots, realized you weren't alone, panicked, and killed both of you before she had planned to.' Esperanza held up the bow. 'So I used this. No noise. Good thing you bought it.'

'Good thing you know how to use it.'

'I meant to tell you. Every fall, during bow season, I head up into the mountains and go hunting. I haven't failed to bring back a deer since I was fourteen.'

'It was you who set off the explosions?' Decker asked.

'Renata was going to shoot you. I couldn't think of anything else to do. I couldn't take a shot at her with you and Beth in the way. I couldn't get to you fast enough to grab her. I needed some kind of diversion, something that would startle everyone and give you a chance to recover sooner than *she* did.'

'It's Beth who recovered first.' Decker looked at her with admiration. 'Help me get her into the car.'

The moment she lay in the back seat, Esperanza anticipated what Decker was going to say next. 'Clean the area?'

'Get everything we can. The authorities in Pecos will be up here to investigate the explosions. That fire will lead them right to this cabin. We don't have much time.'

Decker ran to get Beth's shotguns while Esperanza threw the .22, the bow, and the quiver into the Cherokee's storage compartment. The firearms were important because their serial numbers could be traced to the store where Decker had bought them and eventually traced to him. When Decker returned with the shotguns, Esperanza was disappearing into the forest, presumably getting the Winchester and the car battery. Decker dug up the remaining canteens. He pulled out the light-bulb filaments, gathered the wires, and set everything into the back of the car. Meanwhile, Esperanza had returned with the equipment from Decker's hiding place.

'I'll get the money from where I buried it,' Esperanza said. 'What else?'

'The Remington bolt-action. It's in the pit we dug near the bridge.'

'I'll get that, too,' Esperanza said.

'Beth's crutches. The hunting knives.'

'We'd better make sure we collect all the boxes of ammunition. And the arrow I shot.'

'. . . Esperanza.'

'What?'

'I had to use your handgun. Two shell casings are in the bushes up there.'

'Jesus.' In the firelight, Esperanza seemed to turn pale. 'I loaded it before all this happened. I wasn't wearing gloves. My fingerprints will be on those casings.'

'I'll do everything I can to find them,' Decker said. 'Here are my car keys. Get the money, the knives, the Remington, and the boxes of ammunition. Drive Beth and yourself the hell away from here. I'll keep searching until the last minute, until police cars are pulling into the lane.'

Esperanza didn't respond, only stared at him.

'Go,' Decker said, then raced up the slope toward the trees and bushes on the right of the burning cabin. One of the shots from Esperanza's pistol had been next to a large pine tree, just about—

Here! Decker thought. He tried to re-enact what he had done, how he had dropped to the ground when the gunman shot at him from deeper in the woods, how he had scrambled to the right of the tree, how he had knelt and pulled the trigger and—

The ejected shell casing would have flipped through the air and landed about three or four feet from—

Firelight reflected off something small and metallic. Breathing fiercely, exhaling in triumph, Decker dropped to his knees and found one of the 9mm casings he was searching for. Only one more to go. As he surged to his feet, he discovered Esperanza hurrying toward him.

'Leave,' Decker said.

'Not without you.'

'But—'

'Show me where to look,' Esperanza said.

Skirting the flames from the cabin, they rushed toward the back and ignored the corpse of the man Decker had shot in the head, totally consumed by the hunt for the other casing.

'It could be there or maybe over there.' Decker's chest heaved.

'The undergrowth's too thick.' Esperanza got down, crawling, tracing his hands along the ground. 'Even with the firelight, there are too many shadows.'

'We have to find it!'

'Listen.'

'What?'

'Sirens.'

'Shit.'

'They're faint. Quite a distance away.'

'Not for long.' Decker searched harder beneath bushes, pawing in a frenzy over the murky ground. 'Go. Get in the car. Leave. There's no point in *all* of us being caught.'

'Or *any* of us. Forget the casing,' Esperanza said. 'Come with me to the car.'

'If they find the casing, if they manage to lift prints from it—'

'Partial prints. Probably smudged.'

'You hope. You'd never be able to explain what a casing with your prints was doing up here.' Decker searched among dead leaves.

'I'll claim someone stole my pistol.'

460

'Would *you* believe that story?'

'Not likely.'

'Then—'

'I don't care.' Esperanza crawled beneath bushes. 'Just because I might be implicated, that doesn't mean you and Beth have to be. Let's get out of—'

'Found it! Oh, sweet Christ, I found it.' Decker leapt to his feet and showed Esperanza the precious casing. 'I never believed I'd—'

They charged from the bushes and raced toward the car, scrambling down the slope so fast that they almost tripped and fell. Esperanza still had the car keys. He slid behind the steering wheel while Decker dove into the back seat with Beth. Before Decker could slam the door, Esperanza had the car in gear and was making a rapid turn in the clearing, throwing up dirt. Barely taking the time to flick on the headlights, he sped down the lane, bounced over the bridge, and veered swiftly onto the dark country road.

'Have we got everything? The money? All the weapons?' Decker asked, his voice loud enough to be heard above the walloping din of his heart.

'I can't think of anything we left behind.' Esperanza pressed his foot on the accelerator.

'Then we got away with it,' Decker said.

'Except for—' Esperanza pointed toward the growing wail of sirens in the darkness before him.

He slowed down and turned off the headlights.

'What are you doing?' Decker asked.

'Bringing back memories of when I was a kid.' Esperanza swerved into the lane of the property a quarter-mile below the burning cabin. The flames rose high enough to be seen from a distance. Hiding the car in the undergrowth, Esperanza turned off the engine and peered through shadowy trees toward the road. The headlights and flashing emergency lights of a fire engine and several police cars rushed past, their outlines a blur, their sirens shrieking.

'Just like old times,' Esperanza said. Immediately he restarted the car and backed out onto the road, turning on his headlights only when forced to.

Twice more, they had to veer into a lane to stop from being seen by passing emergency vehicles. The second time, Decker and Esperanza paused long enough to get out of the car and strip off their camouflage suits. Beth winced when Decker took off hers. Using the inside of the suits, they wiped the camouflage grease from their faces, then spread the suits over the weapons in the back and covered everything with a car blanket. When they got to Pecos or when they reached Santa Fe, they wouldn't attract attention now if a police car pulled up next to them.

Decker stroked Beth's head. 'Feeling any better?'

'My mouth's awfully dry.'

'We'll get you some water as soon as we can. Let me check those pulled stitches . . . You're bleeding, but only a little. You don't need to worry. You're going to be all right.'

'The pulled stitches will make the scars worse.'

'I hate to agree with you, but yes.'

'Now we'll have matching sets.'

Decker took a moment before he realized that, despite her pain, Beth was doing her best to grin.

'Like the bullet-wound scars you showed me,' Beth said. 'But mine will be bigger.'

'You are something else,' Decker said.

23

Forty minutes later, Esperanza turned off Interstate 25 onto Old

Pecos Trail and then onto Rodeo Road, heading toward the side street upon which he had his trailer. The time was almost two-thirty. The late-night streets were deserted.

'In the morning, I'll drive into the desert and burn the weapons, our gloves, and our camouflage suits, along with the fuel oil and fertilizer in the canteens,' Decker said. 'I bought the Remington for long-distance shooting, but we never did use it. It's safe to keep. Why don't you take it, Esperanza? Take the bow and the arrows, too.'

'And half the money,' Beth said.

'I can't,' Esperanza said.

'Why not? If you don't spend the money right away, if you dribble it out a little at a time, no one will suspect you have it,' Decker said. 'You won't need to explain how you came to have a half-million dollars.'

'That figure has a wonderful sound to it,' Esperanza admitted.

'I can arrange for you to have a numbered account in a bank in the Bahamas,' Beth said.

'I bet you can.'

'Then you'll take the money?'

'No.'

'Why not?' Decker repeated, puzzled.

'The last few days, I killed several men for what I thought were valid reasons. But if I took the money, if I profited, I don't think I would ever stop feeling dirty.'

The car became silent.

'What about *you*, Decker?' Esperanza asked. 'Will *you* keep the money?'

'I know a good use for it.'

'Such as?'

'If I talk about it, it might not work out.'

'Sounds mysterious,' Beth said.

'You'll soon know.'

'Well, while I'm waiting, I'd like you to ease my worries about something.'

Decker looked concerned. 'What?'

'The gun dealer you went to. If the crime lab establishes that the metal fragments from the bombs came from canteens, if he reads that in the newspaper, won't he remember a man who bought several firearms and *twelve* canteens the day before the attack?'

'Possibly,' Decker said.

'Then why aren't *you* worried?'

'Because I'm going to contact my former employer and report that Renata has finally been taken care of – with extreme denial, as McKittrick liked to call it. Given the catastrophe she caused in Rome, my former employer will want to make sure that it isn't connected to what happened at the cabin, that *I'm* not connected to it. My former employer will use national security as an excuse to discourage local law enforcement from investigating.'

'I'll certainly cooperate,' Esperanza said. 'But just in case they're a little slow, I'm the detective who would normally be assigned to talk to the gun dealer. I can tell you right now that any link between you and what happened in Pecos is purely coincidental.'

'Speaking of local law enforcement . . .' Decker leaned forward from the back to open the storage compartment between the front seats. 'Here's your badge.'

'Finally.'

'And your pistol.'

'Back where it belongs.' But the lightness in Esperanza's tone changed to melancholy as he parked in front of his trailer. 'The question is, where do *I* belong? The place doesn't feel like a home anymore. It sure looks empty.'

'I'm sorry about your wife leaving. I wish there was something we could do to help,' Beth said.

'Phone from time to time. Let me know the two of you are all right.'

'We'll do more than phone,' Decker said. 'You'll be seeing a lot of us.'

'Sure.' But Esperanza sounded preoccupied as he left the key in the ignition and got out of the car.

'Good luck.'

Esperanza didn't reply. He walked slowly across the gravel area in front of the trailer. It wasn't until he disappeared inside that Decker got into the driver's seat and turned the ignition key.

'Let's go home,' Decker said.

24

In contrast with his feelings of detachment when he had returned to Santa Fe from New York, Decker now did feel at home. As he headed into the driveway, he scanned the dark, low, sprawling outline of his adobe compound and said to himself, 'This is mine.'

He must have said it out loud.

'Of course, this is yours,' Beth said, puzzled. 'You've been living here for fifteen months.'

'It's hard to explain,' he said in amazement. 'I was afraid I had made a mistake.'

The driveway curved along the side of the house to the carport in back, where a sensor light came on, guiding the way. Decker helped Beth out of the Cherokee.

She leaned against him. 'What about me? Did you make a mistake about me?'

Coyotes howled on Sun Mountain.

465

'The night after I first met you,' Decker said, 'I stood out here and listened to those coyotes and wished that you were next to me.'

'Now I am.'

'Now you are.' Decker kissed her.

In a while, he unlocked the back door, turned on the kitchen light, and helped Beth inside, holding her crutches. 'We'll use the guest room. The master bedroom still looks like the aftermath of a small war. Can I get you anything?'

'Tea.'

While water boiled, Decker found a bag of chocolate-chip cookies and set them on a saucer. Under the circumstances, the cookies looked pathetic. No one ate.

'There isn't any hot water for a bath, I'm afraid,' Decker said.

Beth nodded wearily. 'I remember the heater was destroyed during Friday night's attack.'

'I'll put fresh bandages on your stitches. I'm sure you could use a pain pill.'

Beth nodded again, exhausted.

'Will you be all right here alone?'

'Why?' Beth straightened, unsettled. 'Where are you going?'

'I want to get rid of that stuff in the back of the car. The sooner, the better.'

'I'll go with you.'

'No. Rest.'

'But when will you be back?'

'Maybe not until after dawn.'

'I won't be separated from you.'

'But—'

'There's nothing to discuss,' Beth said. 'I'm going with you.'

25

In the gray of false dawn, as Decker dropped the camouflage suits and the gloves into a pile in a hollow twenty miles into the desert west of Santa Fe, he glanced at Beth. Arms crossed over a sweater he had given her, she leaned her back against the front passenger door of the Cherokee and watched him. He came back for the canteens filled with plant fertilizer and fuel oil, dumping their contents over the garments, the sharp smell flaring his nostrils. He threw down the arrow that Esperanza had used to kill the man in the forest. He added the .22, the .30-30, and the shotgun, sparing only the .270 because it hadn't been used. A fire wouldn't destroy the serial numbers on the weapons, but it would make them inoperable. If someone by chance found them in the various isolated places where he intended to bury them, they would be discarded as garbage. Decker used the claw end of a hammer to punch holes into the canteens so that no fumes would remain inside and possibly set off an explosion. Because fuel oil burned slowly, he poured gasoline over the pile. Then he struck a match, set fire to the entire book of matches, and threw the book onto the pile. With a whoosh, the gasoline and the fuel oil ignited, engulfing the garments and the weapons, thrusting a pillar of fire and smoke toward the brightening sky.

Decker walked over to Beth, put his arm around her, and watched the blaze.

'What's that story in Greek mythology? About the bird rising from the ashes?' Beth asked. 'The phoenix?'

'It's about rebirth,' Decker said.

'That's what Renata's name means in English, isn't it? Rebirth?'

'The thought occurred to me.'

'But is it really?' Beth asked. 'A rebirth?'

'It is if we want it to be.'

Behind them, the sun eased above the Sangre de Cristo mountains.

'How do you stand it?' Beth asked. 'Last night. What we were forced to do.'

'That's what I was trying to explain earlier. To survive, I was taught to deny any emotions that aren't practical.'

'I can't do that.' Beth trembled. 'When I killed my husband . . . as much as he needed to be killed . . . I threw up for three days afterward.'

'You did what you had to. *We* did what *we* had to. Right now, as bad as I feel, I can't get over the fact that we're here, that I've got my arm around you—'

'That we're alive,' Beth said.

'Yes.'

'You wondered how I learned about firearms.'

'You don't need to tell me anything about your past,' Decker said.

'But I want to. I *have* to. Joey made me learn,' Beth said. 'He had guns all over the house, a shooting range in his basement. He used to make me go down and watch him shoot.'

The flames and smoke stretched higher.

'Joey knew how much I hated it. Even though I wore ear protectors, every gunshot made me flinch. That made him laugh. Then he thought it would be really hilarious to make *me* do the shooting – .357 magnums, .45s. The most powerful handguns. All the way up to .44 magnums. Sometimes, I think he taught me how to shoot because he loved the thrill of knowing all those loaded guns were around me, taunting me, daring me to try to use one against him. He went to great pains to make me understand the hell he would put me through if I was ever foolish enough to try. Then he made me learn to use shotguns. Louder. With a more punishing recoil. That's what I used to kill him,' Beth said. 'A shotgun.'

'Hush.'

'A double barrel. The same type I used tonight.'

'Hush.' Decker kissed a tear from her cheek. 'From now on, the past doesn't exist.'

'Does that mean *your* past doesn't exist, also?'

'What are you getting at?'

'Did you lose the openness you found here? Have you truly reverted? Have you sealed yourself off again and gone back to feeling apart from things?'

'Not apart from you,' Decker said. 'Not apart from *this*.' He gestured toward the sun above the mountains, toward the aspen starting to turn yellow in the ski basin, toward the green of the piñon trees in the foothills and the mustard-colored chamisa in the red and orange of the brilliant high desert. 'But there are things in my life that I do feel apart from, that I don't want you to know about, that I don't want to have to remember.'

'Believe me, I feel the same way.'

'I'll never ask you about those things,' Decker said, 'and you never have to tell me about them, not if you don't want to. I can only imagine the fear and confusion you must have felt, coming to Santa Fe, trying to hide from the mob, knowing I had skills to help you. You saw me as a savior, and you grabbed for me. Was that using me? If it was, I'm glad you did – because I never would have met you otherwise. Even if I had known you were using me, I would have *wanted* you to use me.'

Decker reached into the back of his car and pulled out the travel bag containing the million dollars. 'For a time, after I rescued you, I thought you were staying with me because of this.'

Decker carried the bag toward the fire.

Beth looked startled. 'What are you going to do?'

'I told you I had a good use for this. I'm going to destroy the past.'

'*You're going to burn the money?*'

'Esperanza was right. If we spent it, we'd always feel dirty.'

Decker held the bag over the fire.

'*A million dollars?*' Beth asked.

'Blood money. Would it really matter to you if I burned it?'

'You're testing me?'

The bottom of the bag started smoldering.

'I want to get rid of the past,' Decker said.

Beth hesitated. Flames danced along the bottom of the bag.

'Last chance,' Decker said.

'Do it,' Beth said.

'You're sure?'

'Throw it in the fire.' Beth walked toward him. 'For us, the past stops right now.'

She kissed him. When Decker dropped the bag into the flames, neither of them looked at it. The kiss went on and on. It took Decker's breath away.

A selection of bestsellers from Headline

BODY OF A CRIME	Michael C. Eberhardt	£5.99	☐
TESTIMONY	Craig A. Lewis	£5.99	☐
LIFE PENALTY	Joy Fielding	£5.99	☐
SLAYGROUND	Philip Caveney	£5.99	☐
BURN OUT	Alan Scholefield	£4.99	☐
SPECIAL VICTIMS	Nick Gaitano	£4.99	☐
DESPERATE MEASURES	David Morrell	£5.99	☐
JUDGMENT HOUR	Stephen Smoke	£5.99	☐
DEEP PURSUIT	Geoffrey Norman	£4.99	☐
THE CHIMNEY SWEEPER	John Peyton Cooke	£4.99	☐
TRAP DOOR	Deanie Francis Mills	£5.99	☐
VANISHING ACT	Thomas Perry	£4.99	☐

All Headline books are available at your local bookshop or newsagent, or can be ordered direct from the publisher. Just tick the titles you want and fill in the form below. Prices and availability subject to change without notice.

Headline Book Publishing, Cash Sales Department, Bookpoint, 39 Milton Park, Abingdon, OXON, OX14 4TD, UK. If you have a credit card you may order by telephone – 01235 400400.

Please enclose a cheque or postal order made payable to Bookpoint Ltd to the value of the cover price and allow the following for postage and packing:

UK & BFPO: £1.00 for the first book, 50p for the second book and 30p for each additional book ordered up to a maximum charge of £3.00.

OVERSEAS & EIRE: £2.00 for the first book, £1.00 for the second book and 50p for each additional book.

Name ....

Address ....

....

....

If you would prefer to pay by credit card, please complete:
Please debit my Visa/Access/Diner's Card/American Express (delete as applicable) card no:

Signature .... Expiry Date ....